ONCE UPON A TIME
IN THE

BIG EASY
DOWN ON THE BAYOU

WILSON JACKSON

ONCE UPON A TIME IN THE BIG EASY/ Down on the Bayou
Copyright © 2025 by Wilson Jackson

ISBN: 979-8894791067 (sc)
ISBN: 979-8894791074 (e)

The Reading Glass Books
1-888-420-3050
www. readingglassbooks. com
fulfillment@readingglassbooks. com

CONTENTS

ONE

The large hairy-man wastes no time wrapping his paws around Tara's lean arms, dragging her out of the room.

His ink hair covered everything, including his lips, nose, and eyes. He looks like a walking bush in needing a hedge trim. He didn't talk, instead his actions spoke and crystal clear, taking Tara with him.

Moira felt helpless watching her cousin Tara being man handled through her peep hole by the hairy giant across the hall of the dorm like Tryon House's apartment complex. She wanted Tara to share a room and expenses, but the little cousin wanted independence taking a room across the hall instead. After all, the three story brick building on North Tryon shaped like a college dorm has studio design rooms, and neither wanted to share a bed, so Moira respected her cousin's wish for privacy.

They both worked a modest job working in the mail-room of the Ritz building and Tryon House offered affordable rent; wood floors, brass heaters, a small kitchen, and bathrooms, not confuse for anything fancy, but a fit for young people starting out and old people who lived on a fixed income.

Living in an affordable building uptown also meant not taking the bus getting to work. The Ritz didn't share the same block, but getting up early and walking to work was not a problem since they didn't own a car or needed public transportation. None of that mattered now. Moira cringed seeing her cousin carried away, tucked under the arm of the colossal man like a football. She looked unconscious.

Tears rolled down Moira's cheeks. She recognized the man from the horrific stories Tara told her while trap in a mansion in New Orleans where she and other young girls used for human trafficking.

No one played hero in the cleared hallway. Moira knew the other residents heard the raucous, but like her, knew they didn't stand a chance against the giant. The cousins didn't have a cell phone between them, and no phone in the hallway. Moira wanted to call the MPD, but too late, Tara and her captor gone.

❧ ❧ ❧ ❧ ❧ ❧

The speed bag moved with the rhythm and precision of a well-oiled machine. A boxer's best friend along with the heavy bag to build speed and power. Pone worked the speed bag like a hamster on its exercise wheel. Alternating right and left punches in rapid circular motion. Speed's the key Wisdom used to say. Pone sighed with grief over the death of his mentor, father figure who didn't want him to know he had cancer. Wisdom lost his battle, but now perhaps his life ended with some peace being buried next to his beloved Sheila Green.

"Damn him." murmured Pone. He could still be angry and love the man. Wisdom thought he couldn't handle his illness, but yet he told Birdie and Jade. Hell, even Red knew about his condition.

Pone took his anger from the speed bag to the heavy bag. Damn them too, Birdie and Red.

How could they, his so-called family, keep Wisdom's health from him? The heavy bag took more punishment. The Pin Ball ring tone from his phone save the heavy bag.

T-shirt and shorts drenched in sweat, drops fell off his forehead like rain on the workout bench when he leaned over to pick up his phone.

"What is it, Red?"

"Got a job for you." responded Red.

"On vacation."

"Sorry Pony, time to get back in the saddle again." She hung up.

Pone arrived at Red's office located in the beautiful Ritz building. The building emulated its owner with the same style and grace. He walked into Red's spacious canary yellow themed office and saw the back of the heads of two women seated in front of her grand ebony desk. Even seated, he could tell they were both built with dark hair pulled back in a bun. The back of their necks were tan and Pone noticed some gray strands in the hair of the woman on the left, plus her voice sounded older, along with words of worry.

Red tilted her head forward while stretching her eyes for Pone to stay in the background. The women continued to tell Red their story of sorrow. Red motioned for Pone to step forward, she studied him as he approached them. He still wore his derby, but took it off gentlemen like when meeting the ladies. His attire made Red look at him; gone was the grim reaper black look instead he sported gray slacks, black Doc Martens, cream banded collar shirt and a black bomber jacket.

Red smiled. "Ladies, this is the man I was telling you about."

Both women turned in unison, eye-balling Pone. He smiled and nodded, then took a seat on the sofa.

Red elevated her voice. "We're dealing with an abduction."

Pone gave Red a look. She returned one of her own as if to say wait and hear me out.

"Ladies, meet Chubby Pone." said Red. "This is Cici and her niece, Moira."

"You're sure this man can help us, Miss Brigand?" asked Cici before the flood gates opened and Moira comforted her.

"What's going on here?" asked Pone.

Cici wiped her eyes. "My-- "

"Moira, why don't you take Cici home?" interrupted Red.

"No, Miss Brigand. I need to go back to work," responded Cici.

Red shook her head. "No, you need to go home and rest."

"But I have bills to pay," said Cici.

"Take a pay leave and I will see you when this is over."

Red nodded to Moira to take Cici home. Moira took Cici by the arm and escorted her out of the plush office. Pone strode over, sitting in front of Red.. He sighed, placing his hat on the desk.

"Give me the details," said Pone.

Red snorted. "Almost didn't recognize you."

 Pone pursed his lips. "Get used to it."

"I approve." Red stretched her eyes and took a deep breath. "All three work here, Cici works in the custodian department and the girls work in the mailroom."

"I saw Cici and Moira,"

"Tara wasn't present because of her abduction."

"Who witnessed the shanghai?"

"Moira. She heard and saw everything through her peep hole across the hall. They both live in the Tryon House apartment. A dark, large, hairy man carried Tara off.

Pone rubbed his chin. "I don't want to sound rude, but they talk with an accent?"

"Cajun."

Pone raised an eye-brow. "So you want me to retrieve this young lady?"

"Bring her back home, safe, and sound."

"Sounds like you want me to take a trip."

"New Orleans."

"Don't know a thing about the big easy. How would I know where to look?"

Red pulled open her desk drawer and took a large envelope. "Map out areas, people to contact to get whatever you need and plane tickets."

"Tickets plural?"

Red shrugged. "Might be more than a one-man job."

"Is there something you're not telling me?"

"Not to sound impertinent, but Tara is a beautiful girl. Think she's forced to use her beauty for glee," said Red.

"Prostitution?" remarked Pone.

"Cici didn't say , but it wasn't hard to figure out."

Pone shook his head. "From what I saw of Cici well, she's old, but even if she was young I can't see her making a living by selling her body, and even though Moira is young, well..."

Red frowned. "Shooting from the hip, Pony?

Pone shrugged. "Just saying?"

"Of the three women, Tara's the looker and why she got taken back to New Orleans?" Red inhaled.

"I promised Cici we'd get her back."

"Why do I feel it's not that simple?"

"Her father is the one who is forcing her to do this, which is why Cici paid for both Tara and her," said Red.

Moira to come here away from him. From what I gathered, he's a powerful man," she continued.

"Powerful men means dangerous." Pone glowered at the floor. "If he's forcing his own family into prostitution, then I will do my best to take him down. You got a name?"

"Theiler Lareaux." Red stared at Pone. "Perhaps a change of scenery will do you some good, too?"

"I have a right to be angry."

"Cici's a valued employee. Hope that won't be a problem?"

Pone rose, grabbing his hat. "Sometimes a heart is more than a bank account."

Oh God, thought Tara, awoken from her sleep. She'd hoped to never see the pink walls, white satin sheets, queen-size canopy bed with matching white dresser drawers, rectangle white wood framed mirror laid on a plush white carpet. A room fit for any little girl who was into Cinderella, Snow White, and Alice in wonderland, but Tara's little girl days ended a long time ago. A grown woman thrown back into a tortured childhood. All the beauty in the room couldn't keep tear stains off the flower pattern pillow case.

She came back to hell against her own will, but what choice did she have? Ludwig, the big hairy bear sized gorilla would not harm a follicle on her head, but Cici and Moira … yeah. Tara got into a fetal position on her queen size bed to do the only thing she could do … weep.

Tears came more when she realized she was naked and heard the gravel Cajun voice she thought she'd never hear again.

"Dry up them tears, girl. Your vacation is over. Time to get back to work." crowed Theiler.

Tara kept her focus on the opposite wall. She didn't want to face the portly grizzled man with the dead eye once brown, the live eye, green, and hippie length shaggy ivory mane.

The bed struggled to support his weight. In three months, Tara had gotten used to the articulate words without the back woods accent. She didn't miss the cooking thanks to Cici which wouldn't have been a problem since her new culture had introduced her to a variety of different cuisine. Tara's problem had his raw pitcher mound belly pressed hard against her back. The annoyance kept talking.

"Your best customer, Mister Grant, miss you. Kept on saying, when is my little angel gonna come back." Theiler laughed. His hot stogie breath made the follicles on the back of Tara's neck stands up.

Theiler's stubby fingers snaked its way between Tara's thighs, up to her buttocks.

"Gotta make sure the merchandise is still good. Can't disappoint the customer now, can we?"

❧ ❧ ❧ ❧ ❧ ❧

A knock on the door woke Pone up from a seldom much needed sleep. Pone still in his clothes from Douglas Airport arriving in New Orleans. He and Ben found a suitable motel taking separate rooms. Pone sat on the edge of the bed scratching his chest before he stood in front of the door.

"Yes," sighed Pone.

"It's me, man." said Ben.

Pone opened the door then wobbled back to the bed, falling face first into the pillow.

Ben lumbered in carrying two greased soaked brown paper bags looking like school lunches from hell. He closed the door with the back of his foot.

"Breakfast!" roared Ben.

Pone looked over his shoulder and frowned. "What grease pit did you get those from?"

"A hole in the wall three blocks down."

Pone grunted. "You know I don't deal with hole in wall food."

"Shit'd, your ass too damn prissy."

"Sue me for being accustomed to fine living."

Ben placed the food on the small table near the window. "Got two sausage and egg sandwiches on toast, hash rounds and coffee."

Pone sat up raising an eye brow." The grease comes from the hash browns?" He shook his head. "Coffee for me."

Ben handed Pone the coffee along with some cream. "Sorry I wasn't able to get to the farmers market and get your fruit and veggies."

Pone stirred the cream into his coffee and took a sip. "I appreciate you, but I'm not consuming something with more grease than a auto shop."

"More for me." Ben wasted no time wolfing down the sandwiches.

Pone watched the giant devour the artery clogging sustenance. Red gave him two plane tickets figuring he'd need help, good old Red. He chose Ben who was as clueless about New Orleans, but Pone banked on the fact his enormous presence would come in handy. Sonny could no longer travel far and wide and he couldn't provide any muscle. Pone didn't need to blow up any body or thing so Sonny's talents would sit on the shelf.

Pone smiled thinking of Sonny cursing a storm because two of his poker buddies were out of town. Playing poker, the old man had going for himself in his decaying life. It sure beat the hell out of playing Bingo. Pone sipped his coffee and thought what he could do to make it up to his ancient friend. He left behind creepy ass Stick who he knew would blend in pretty well with Mardi Gra.

His anatomy carried no muscle to speak of, but a presence with his porcupine quill hair, long lean snake like torso, pink pupils and yolk iris. Yeah the man, creepy looking straight out of one those X-men comic books, but his talents weren't needed either. Pone and Ben's set of skills fit the job for this trip.

Red knew he needed to get away after the death of Wisdom and he knew Ben needed to get away after the death of his friend McGee another reason he brought him along.

Mercury had told him about the Medusa ordeal sending chills down his spine just thinking about it. He watched Ben finish off the last of the hash rounds washing it down with coffee.

Pone snorted. "You know just because you're big don't mean you have to fill up."

"Shit'd, ain't wasting my money." He finished his coffee. "That's what wrong with the world today everybody afraid to eat this or that because it's either bad for you or will kill you."

He shook his head. "Shit'd, we all gonna die one day any way."

"So why not eat yourself to death?" remarked Pone.

Ben shrugged. "Ain't wasting no food."

"Bon appetite," Pone finished off his coffee.

Ben belched. "So when do we get this party started?"

Pone grabbed the large envelope off the night stand. He took out some papers with instructions.

He looked them over then cleared his throat. "First place we need to hit is a place called Old Calcutta."

Ben frowned. "What the hell is that?"

"A pawn shop own by one of Red's contacts. Supposed to have everything we need."

"Ben nodded. "Good becauseI don't like feeling naked."

"That's the whole idea of having airport security, Ben."

"I know that… just saying I knew we couldn't do this job empty handed."

Pone nodded and hopped off the bed. "Might as well get going, the faster we do this job the faster we can go home."

THREE

The feminine voice on the GPS gave instructions. Pone and Ben heading down Jefferson Highway to a pawn shop called *Oh Calcutta.* The red and yellow building looked deserted, but according to the website it always closed in the evening at 6:00. It was a little after 3:45 when Pone checked his cell.

Pone and Ben followed the instructions and parked around back, but entered in the front of the building. A pawn shop a front meaning there were other things going on and most of the activity under the radar which meant the law wouldn't approve. In Pone's line of work such facilities serve as contacts, information, or emergency safe houses. If this pawn shop the same, Pone and Ben would soon find out.

Pone and Ben walked through the front door. They spotted a short man leaning on the glass counter reading a blab sheet(newspaper). He had a big watermelon head bald on top with light brown hair on the side and back. He sported a beard with gray strands on the chin.

He straightened up in his dingy white T-shirt and army green pants. A uni-brow sat on his forehead that made him look angry, that's what most uni-brows do any way. His cowboy boots made him taller than he looked as he made his way around the glass counter filled gold bracelets rings,watches, and an assortment of other jewelry. The shop also had an assortment of knives hunting, switch blade, butter fly style, nun chucks, and posters of Bruce Lee. There were also old box TV's that no one use any more and VCR's and boom boxes. Pone raised an eye-brow looking at the DVD VCR combos players on display, he knew a few people who still owned VHS tapes that are as extinct as the dinosaur.

"Gentlemen, how may I be of service?" he asked.

"All I see is red." said Pone.

The man straightened up. "Follow me."

Pone and Ben looked at each other then followed the man to the end of the glass counter through a green door. The man flipped the light switch revealing stairs leading downward.

Ben thought about his encounter with *Black Medusa,* she had stairs leading down to her cryptic basement with an assortment of men she had used her taxidermy skills on including his friend, Al McGee. When they reached the ground floor it was solid gray with a warehouse appeal. The pawn shop not your ordinary hock market. Part man cave: a pool table, a small round table to play cards, a sofabed, a fridge, microwave, small oven, and a 42 inch flat screen TV.

"What do we call you?" asked Pone.

"You can call me, Jock." he said in his Cajun raspy voice.

"French or American version?" asked Pone.

"J-o-c-k." Laughed the man.

"Like a Jock strap?" asked Ben.

"Hilarious, but no. Don't want no man's dick on my face." said Jock. He grabbed a remote and stood facing a wall. "I assume you both played it safe when you took the plane?"

"Came here naked as a jay bird." said Pone.

"We can't have that now can we? Let me see if I got something in your size. Feast your eyes on this," said Jock. He pressed the button and the wall separated into two panels splitting apart.

"It must be Christmas." said Ben.

If you were a killer then you'd be like a kid in a candy store. An assortment of weapons for every occasion. The store up above said pawn shop and some items inside gave it that look, but down below said other wise that this no ordinary hunt mart. Pone and Ben surrounded by guns and accessories galore.

Jock smiled. "Gentlemen, shall we," Pone and Ben followed the portly man inside the wall to wall armory: Guns from the past to the present on display, colts, Smith & Wesson, revolvers, glocks, assault rifles, western rifles and an assortment of shotguns that made Ben stop in his tracks.

"I see the big man likes guns that makes big holes." said Jock.

"You just became his best friend." said Pone.

Ben picked up a shot gun with a cylinder. Jock stood beside Ben beaming.

"What you got there is a MT-255 Russian Cylinder shot gun. It reloads like the the modern day revolver. Check it out." said Jock.

"Way ahead of you." replied Ben. He smiled examining how the cylinder flipped out loading like a revolver hand gun. Ben had heard of the Russian style shot gun, but never tried to get one. He was fond of his pump action shot gun and pistols. He looked at the table and a smaller version caught his eye.

"Whoa boy, you do love shot guns." said Jock using two hands to hold up the smaller shot gun.

"What you have here is a .410 revolving pistol and like it's big brother there, it holds five shells."

Jock placed it back on the table and picked up what looked like a regular revolver. "This baby looks more like a handgun, but also uses shot gun shells."

Ben shook his head. "Too small, I'll take… "

"We're not here to blow up the city. We'll be going small so that will have to do," said Pone.

"Shit'd, what the hell you talking about? We got to be prepared either way," remarked Ben.

"We're under the radar. We can't go any where carrying heavy artillery like we invading Beirut. Take the hand gun." snorted Pone.

He spotted another piece for his large friend.

"And give him a FNX-45."

"You know that ain't my style," growled Ben

Pone smiled. "Jock, give my friend the MT and 410."

Ben smiled and nodded. "Now we talkin'."

"But they will come in play only when necessary and I'm hoping it won't come to that," said Pone.

"Shit'd, you know what business we in, but I'll follow your lead."

Jock went behind the table and loaded up the black duffle bag along with ammo.

Jock looked at Pone. "How about you kind sir?"

"I'll take the Magnum Long Rifle, not the narrow barrel, but … "

Jock gave a look as to say I know my guns. He pick up the piece with the same but enhanced dimension and place two boxes of.22 caliber bullets.

Pone nodded his approval. "Two Smith and Wesson eight shot.357, one Smith and Wesson.327 and that one shot money clip 45 ACP hollow point round holder."

"Damn boy, scarred of you." said Ben.

Jock gave Pone everything he asked for. "I agree with the big man, you sure know your guns. I'm still surprised though,"

"About what?" asked Pone.

"Been holdin' on to your favorite, but you ain't asked for it."

Pone beamed with pride. "The only Tommy-Gun for me is my lady Sally and she's back home. If I touched another she'd know I was unfaithful."

Jock and Ben gave each other a weird look.

"Okay, moving on," said Jock.

Pone took out a thick tan envelope, but Jock stop him before it got half way out of his pocket.

"I'm paying for the guns." said Pone

Jock shook his head. "Your lady friend took care of all of that. She must like you."

"Yeah she does," said Ben.

Pone shot Ben a look and the big man went back admiring his guns.

"You're renting them any way," said Jock.

"Say what?" asked Ben.

Jock held up his hand. "We can negotiate when you finish your job."

Ben smiled and shook his head. That's what I'm talking about."

"Good luck getting them on the plane." said Pone.

"I know a guy who has a delivery truck no questions asked?" asked Jock.

"That's what I'm talking about," said Ben.

Pone rolled his eyes. "Now that we're dressed, we need to talk strategy."

"Have a seat at that table while I get us something to drink." said Jock. He made his way over to the corner grabbing a milk crate and loaded up with some beer, whiskey bottles, shot glasses, and a deck of cards. He placed the items on the table then took his seat.

"I could kiss, you." said Ben.

"Thanks, but I'm good," laughed Jock. He grabbed the remote and the walls came back together sealing off the armory.

"You still open for business?" asked Pone.

Jock held up the remote. "Took care of that a while ago."

Pone wondered how much Red paid the obese proprietor. He pondered if she knew the man rented his weapons like a U-haul truck meaning you don't get your money back. But Jock, willing to sell weapons to Ben when they finished the job. Pone studied the big man who looked like he had the chills.

"You okay, Ben?" asked Pone

"Yeah, man … just a little something crept inside my head." Ben took a shot of whiskey that seemed to settle his nerves. "I'm good, I'm good." The basement brought back that eerie feeling of a basement Ben will have a hard time getting out of his memory. He found his friend Al McGee stuffed like an animal among others who had suffered the same fate as he at the hands of a woman named **Black Medusa.** She got a life sentence, but Ben wanted to end her existence on the spot, a merciful man (*Mercury Slim*) convinced him to let the law do their job and they did. If he ever saw her again he'd pop her head off her shoulders like a bottle cork.

"You sure you all right?" asked Pone.

This get away job is the best thing for me." said Ben.

Pone studied the bottles of beer he saw in the crate. *Slippery Dick*written on the label. A large bottle ofJohnnie Walkersat on the table with a deck of cards.

"Don't you think you might bring some attention for closing up early?" asked Pone

Jock poured himself a shot. "This ain't a cash cow and I'm out in the middle of nowhere.

Most pawn might do pretty good based on their location, but they ain't like me, but if I didn't do business with the likes of you and I mean that in a good way, I'd be out on the city streets saying may I have a quarter please sir?"

All three men roared with laughter.

"How do you know, Red?" asked Pone.

Jock reached in the crate and took out a bowl. He also had a canister of *Pringles* original potato chips he emptied in the bowl, grabbed a couple then washed it down with a shot of whiskey. "Let's just say she knows somebody that knows somebody that knows somebody that knows somebody and that somebody knows me."

"None of your damn business." said Ben.

"He said it, I didn't," said Jock.

"Wasn't trying to pry, but if I wanted to know... " Pone downed the beer and eyed the two men.

"That woman loves this man." said Ben.

Pone gave Ben another look and grabbed the deck of cards. They didn't play poker, but tossed cards on the table to see who would have the highest card. The was just to pass time while they talked.

"You ever heard of a man name Theiler Lereaux?" asked Pone.

Jock rolled his eyes looking like having a seizure and took two shots of whiskey back to back. "Whew, boy… on that question you deserve a straight answer. You know how they say keep mentioning the devil's name and he shall appear, well lets say when his time is up he and devil gonna have a lot to talk about."

"That don't sound good," said Ben.

"If we gonna talk about him," Jock looked at Ben. "Better be glad we got these glasses or I'd be drinking from the bottle."

"Shit'd, he ain't all that," said Ben.

Jock looked at Ben and smiled, but not the kind of smile that said things are good, but the type of smile that said wait till you hear what I got to tell you. "If there's such a thing as a demon escaping from hell, then Theiler Lereaux is that demon. Did I not say he and the devil gonna have a nice conversation when his time is up?"

Ben shook his head. "Shit'd, just another man with some power which means he can go down."

Pone sat in silence allowing his mind to sponge up everything Jock had to say about Theiler Lereaux.

"He's got himself a right hand man named Ludwig. A hairy ass bastard. You can't even see his pupils."

"What is he a fuckin' werewolf?" asked Ben.

"No, but he about your size," said Jock.

"Hairy syndrome." said Pone.

"Say what?" remarked Ben.

"That's this Ludwig's condition, the scientific name is Hypertrichosis. Uncontrollable hair growth."

"Speaking of conditions, Theiler has a dead eye and one green."

"Makes him stand out in a crowd." said Pone.

"Say what?" asked Ben.

"We'll know who he is." explained Pone.

"Yeah, right,?" murmured Ben.

"I hope?" said Pone.

Jock cleared his throat. "That damn Theiler is somethin' else." He shook his head. "He's a business man, but not in the good way. He shakes down small business owners… you know taking a percentage, forcing them to pay for protection if you can believe that, "Jock snorted.

"If you ask me the only protection they need is from him."

"That some low down shit." growled Ben.

"Ha! You would think, my friend, but that's not the tip of the ice burg." said Jock.

"Damn man, you got more on this motherfucker?" asked Ben.

Jock took two quick shot's of *Johnnie Walker* and cleared his throat. "He's a pedophile."

"We've dealt with sick bastards, ain't nothing new about that," retorted Ben.

Jock tossed a card on the table. "Within his own family."

Pone arched an eye-brow.

"Incest… shit'd," roared Ben.

"Daughters are nieces, nieces are daughters, sons… well… he's a father and an uncle rolled into one big ball of shit. Rumor has it all started when he spent a summer with two kinky aunts who lived together. Don't know their story, but I guess they lived together so long and got up in years age wise that the only man they could get was their very own nephew and Theiler took it to the extreme from there. Two sisters and cousins are mother to his offspring. When the girls… the good-looking ones hit their teens he gives them a test drive then offer them out to his customers."

"Motherfucker!" said Ben. "What about his sons?"

Jock shook his head. "He ain't gay. He puts them to work in his other ventures."

"And what are those?" asked Pone.

"Drug and human trafficking." said Jock.

Pone put down his beer. He couldn't take another swallow, he'd prefer his beer replacement,

Malta Goya. He took a trip to retrieve an abducted young woman, but his gut told him a lot of work to do before heading home.

"What's the matter, you don't like the beer?" asked Jock.

"You ever heard of Malta Goya?" asked Ben.

Jock shrugged. "I've seen it on some of the grocery store shelves, but it's a malt beverage, right?"

"It's my beer substitute with out the alcohol." said Pone. "Theiler sounds like a nasty character. Our job is to retrieve a young lady."

"They do have alcohol free beer." said Jock.

"I only drink caffeine coffee and if I do drink beer it's got to have alcohol. Again we're here to retrieve a young woman." remarked Pone.

Jock threw down another shot. "I can tell you now that ain't gonna be easy."

"Now that you've confirmed how nasty he is, how do we get close to him?" asked Pone.

Jock grabbed the deck of cards, shuffled and placed them on the table.

"You about to tell our fortune?" said Ben in his bass voice.

"Pone snorted." Tarot cards does that, Ben."

Ben rolled his eyes.

Jock smiled. "Ain't one of my talents, but you in the right place for some black magic, no?"

He downed another shot. "The man loves Poker." said Jock. "You boys play?"

Pone and Ben looked at each other.

"I take that as a yes." said Jock.

"So he owns casinos, hotels …" said Ben.

"He has a stake in those places." said Jock. "He made a deal with the hotel and casino owners about having the biggest winners of those games come out to his estate to play for a big pot and while they're there they can have some bed warmers and you know what that means."

"Don't tell me those guys go for under age girls?" asked Pone.

"Some of them have integrity, but some of them as low down as Theiler get caught on camera." said Jock.

"So," remarked Ben.

"Some of those men have power. He blackmails them and therefore he becomes untouchable and keeps being a piece of shit." said Pone.

"Son-of-a-bitch!" said Ben.

Jock shook his head. "A lot of people in high places have sick minds and it gets most of them into trouble." He down another shot of whiskey. "Any way if you win big or a lot period, word of mouth gets back to him, then he'll invite you out to his estate for bigger things."

Pone looked at Ben. "Where do we start?"

"You boys ever heard of the Harrahs Hotel Casino and Boom town Casino?"

Ben Shrugged. "The Harrahs a hotel so that speaks for it self. But what's this Boom town casino?"

Jock smiled. "The best attraction about Boom town is it's a riverboat casino."

"Oh hell no!" roared Ben.

"Big man here don't float so well," said Pone.

Ben never told Pone about a childhood tragedy that took place in a fishing pond one summer when he lost his cousin. Both Ben and his cousin were doing what young boys do and that was enjoying a hot summer day in a cool pond. Neither boy could swim and wandered too far into the water. Ben was big for his age while his cousin was an average height twelve year old. Both boys sunk in the deep part of the pool, Ben being taller was surviving on instinct and making his way to safety except his cousin grabbed him by the wrist. The death grip they call it. He had to break his cousin's wrist to escape the fate his cousin suffered once he got away from him. Ben made it to the bank and watched his cousin drown. From that day he avoided swimming pools, rivers, and oceans.

"The only thing water can do for me is quench my thirst and wash my ass." said Ben.

Pone looked at Ben, it was not the first time he saw the big man rattled or the first time he heard him make it clear water not his friend. Pone didn't try to pry out of respect for his friend.

"So," Jock stamped the the shot glass on the table. "No river boat gambling for you, eh?"

"Water is for fishes." murmured Ben.

"There's another way," replied Jock.

Pone snorted. "Shoot,"

"Almost all of the watering holes have an underground game going on." said Jock.

"Like where?" asked Pone.

"The bad side of town, bars connected to dark alley ways, and by the docks." said Jock.

"Right up your alley Ben," remarked Pone.

"Why you say that?" asked Ben.

"You don't like dress up," said Pone.

Ben straightened up and gave Pone a stern look. "What you talking about? I know fashion."

"Buying a new pair of Timberland boots and Wrangler jeans is not dapper." replied Pone.

Jock drank with his eyes moving back and forth like he was watching a tennis match between Pone and Ben.

"You don't think I'd blend around uppity people?" asked Ben.

"You work best in your comfort zone," replied Pone.

"You worse than those three dudes on that wrestling program years back," said Ben.

Pone nodded. "I think I know where you're going with this,"

"Two of them dudes would always go out and eat at the steak house and when the third dude wanted to eat, they just dropped him off at the local seven-eleven." Ben shook his head.

"Well in all fairness, one was a sergeant, one a corporal, and the other guy was a private." smiled Pone.

"That still wasn't fair," said Ben.

Pone frowned. "You do know that was a wrestling story line, right?"

Ben frowned. "Yeah... yeah, I know that shit wasn't real."

Jock and Pone eyed one another and roared with laughter.

"Fine, you go to the Harrahs and I'll explore the bars," said Pone.

"Shit'd, so I can stick out like a sore thumb," said Ben.

"You are six-nine," remarked Pone.

Ben poured himself a shot and toasted Pone. "And that would start the observation."

Pone nodded. He could blend into both environments. He new how to deal with the bar scene thanks to spending time at Nadine and he knew how to rub shoulders with the upper class thanks to attending some of Red's shindigs. Being in both worlds not a problem for him, but for Ben... yeah, but he wanted Ben to admit it to himself.

"It's settled then, you do the bar scenes big man." said Pone.

"Glad we got that straighten out," remarked Jock.

"So we won't travel around together I take it?" asked Ben.

"Two strangers going around town together you know that would bring too much attention. We got to be strangers to each other," said Pone.

"Theiler got plenty of eyes and ears," said Jock.

Ben glared. "I just wanted to confirm what I already suspected. Damn, ask a question and everybody thinks you rode the short bus."

"We good big man?" asked Jock.

Ben snorted and threw down another shot.

"Is this the only way we can get to this scum bag?" asked Pone.

"Unless you want to venture into the swamp and storm his citadel with guns a blazing," Jock didn't throw his shot, instead he nursed it. "You boys might know your stuff where you from, but you ain't in the city. The swamp can be unpleasant if you ain't familiar with her. She can be a real bitch… a regular Pandora's box."

Pone shrugged. "Plans… where would we be without them?"

"So Jock, are you familiar with the estate. ?" asked Ben.

"Only pictures, but from what I saw it's like a walk back in time except no slaves picking cotton and no horse and buggy. It's beautiful, but so was the garden of Eden." uttered Jock.

"Ben grunted. "You just describe a plantation."

"With a moat," remarked Jock.

"You went from a plantation to a castle," said Pone.

"Water surrounds chateau and it's filled with gators and water moccasins," Jock took a swill of whiskey. "He's got men trained to keep them from coming onto the property."

"So you get there by air and water," said Pone. "You still on board with this big man?"

"For the long haul," responded Ben. "So he loves reptiles,"

"He prefers them over dogs and he also have men that are armed." said Jock.

Pone pursed his lips. *He just thought this would be a simple catch and retrieve, now* it seemed to be turning into something more. "Why does he like poker players?"

"Well he plays a lot and he likes the competition and he use it as a recruiting tool. Hired guns and powerful men." said Jock.

"He's that good?" asked Ben.

"From what I hear, he knows his way around a deck of cards. Plus he earns money by making the losers feel better by getting a taste of a nights worth of pleasure."

"When you say pleasure you mean…" confer Pone.

"Yeah, his inbreeding," snorted Jock.

Child prostitution, incest, drug trafficking, and blackmail, thought Pone. "That's all I need to know," He looked at Ben. "I'm in".

FOUR

The sleek black tinted Jaguar sped down the highway away from the city. Two passengers headed to a upper class neighborhood of the wealthy. Red sat in the back in deep thought.

She would have drove herself, but not in the mood for driving and took advantage of being privileged enough to have a chauffeur. Red felt relaxed having someone else driving. Her mother and sisters preferred driven to where they wanted to go; she understood her mother's reason for not driving because of her age, but her sisters Linda and Sue spoiled and will use every bit of royal treatment. Only she and Paul J. enjoyed being their own navigators. Brother Paul J. drove solo to make his rendezvous with his male lovers. Red loved her sister in law Angel who knew about her husbands exploits even before they got married. Angel loved Paul J. , but knew if she wanted to maintain her glamorous lifestyle she would have to put up with his other life. Red took it upon herself to make sure Paul J. practiced safe sex. Red on her way to see mommy dearest and smiled because she and Mary surrounded by servants and security. Her siblings and their kids; the twins and their families lived with her mother.

Angel made sure she and Paul J. had their own place.

Red's turns thoughts about Pone wondering how he was making out in the big easy. She missed him, but knew he needed to get away after Wisdom's sudden death. Red had her own stress dealing with Cici asking if someone had found Tara and on her way back to Metro.

Red had to keep her composure, she understood the woman's concern about her child, but patience and understanding this was a delicate situation. Red frowned, she understood Cici's anguish, from what she told her about this Theiler character. Red cringed thinking about the pedophile and how the disgusting monster treated women in his family. Red almost threw up in the car thinking about it, but took a deep breath calming down because Pone on the job and since he became a troubleshooter he always came through.

Red thought about her mother Mary. Her anxiety about their safety, but the lookalike and their families live under the same roof so she didn't have to agonize them unless they left the house. Mary burden over her youngest, Paul J. and Red since they had their own accommodations. Red and her brother both took precaution keeping their personal lives and personal information nonpublic.

The Jaguar pulled to a stop in front of the gate. The security camera focused on the driver sticking his head out of the window. After recognition, the gate opened The Jaguar made it's way to the grand garage and settled in with a fleet of cars. Red got out and entered the house through the servant entrance connected to the garage. Red saw Mary waiting for her with open arms and a kiss to both of Red's cheeks and a long embrace. Both dressed casual; Red wore a green sweater and Mary pink, both had on blue jeans and white cloth sneakers.

"How did you know to meet me here?" asked Red.

"Of all my children, you're the most humble," admitted Mary.

Red snorted. "So it's just me, you, and the staff?"

Mary nodded with relief in her eyes and a big smile that told Red she relish a break from her house dwellers the clones and their families. Mary locked arms with Red escorting her to the family den. Red fancy having her mother to herself, Linda would always sit in on their conversation, but not today. Red also sensed this visit with her mother had a taste of business.

They sat on a black velvet sofa. The room spacious; a pool table, mini-bar, a shelf full books for a small book store. Red smiled reminiscing about her father having his meeting in the room. A tray of two cups and a white flower pattern tea pot sat on the square tan table Mary poured and both ladies took a sip from their cups.

"Mmm …green tea," approved Red.

"Your favorite," said Mary"So, have you thought about what you might say at the gala?"

"You know I've never done one except attend and don't Linda and Sue handle these things?"

"You own your own firm and I love your sisters, but you have more of a presence."

"Linda and Sue have always handle the fund raising events that dad started, I don't see why you want to buck the tradition."

"They worked nothing political though," stated Mary sipping her tea.

Red took a deep breath and pursed her lips." That little weasel,"

"Now, now Brooke … hear me out," said Mary.

"How dare he drag you into this, when I get my hands on him,"

"Brooke!"

J. Paul gave Red her nickname and brother Paul J. continued what their father started.

The rest of the brood called her Brooke, but when her mother said her name or her siblings name with authority they all knew to be quiet and listen.

"He knows you're angry, but he wants you to help him get his campaign off the ground,"

"Well I got to hand it to him, he is an opportunist,"

"Sorry dear, am I missing something here?" asked Mary.

Mary was like most of Metro City in the dark about the whole Crowe incident. Red didn't tell her mother about the secret coitus with Maxwell out in the middle of nowhere that never took place because of Crowe being a third party. Red wouldn't have told her mother about her sexual encounters any way and she would not reveal Maxwell plotting with Crowe to take out Pone and they succeed she and Maxwell would have ended up dead. Whether Mary would have been like the rest of the family pleased if Crowe had killed Pone she did not know. Mary wore a poker face.

"How is Winslow taking this?" asked Red.

Mary refreshed her cup of tea and pursed her lips. "He committed suicide. Running from a crises."

"Weren't you two close?"

"Your sisters held fund raising events for his previous campaigns." Mary took a sip of tea. "It's good for business."

Red smiled. She knew her mother meant keeping a politician in your pocket can come in handy when you need it. Something they all learned from J. Paul. Yeah, despite Mary's petite stature loomed a nonchalant attitude, Red knew deep down her mother was a true mob wife.

"That's why it's important for you to assist Maxwell on his campaign. I predict he'll be the next mayor." stated Mary.

Red smiled and shook her head. "Winslow must bite it now, he wanted Thomas to be his next deputy mayor. Instead the little twerp is running against him."

"Life is strange," remarked Mary.

"Yes," smirked Red. She had underestimated Maxwell's ambitions, but she had to give him credit. He was gong to take full advantage of the past transgression that took place in the city over the past few months. The way Crowe mortified him and then being rescued by a woman in which Red planned to never let him live it down.

Maxwell knew the cowardice of Mayor Winslow outraged the city running into hiding while the city was at risk of a gang war and even more disgruntled with his administration since it was his deputy mayor Harvey Crowe trying to orchestrate the gang war. That put a black-eye on his regime and he thought by getting Thomas Maxwell to come aboard that it might act as damage control, but instead Winslow got a big surprise when Maxwell ran for mayor himself.

Red thought about what her mother said about having a politician in your pocket and with the diminutive Maxwell that would almost be and besides she could use the incident at the motel over his head to her advantage if she was a devious woman. But she could use it if Maxwell went after Pone. It impressed Red with her when it suit me companion to further his ambition on a lame duck mayor. The noose was around Winslow neck and he knew it. *Well played Thomas, well played,* thought Red. *Even better play trying to get back to me through my mother.*

"When did you speak to Thomas?"

"We've been talking a lot since the two of you took a break,"

"Okay?" smiled Red. "He didn't say we were taking a break?"

"You're adults dear, your lives are your business." Mary took another sip of tea.

Thomas didn't tell and neither would she. It involved the little twerp in a conspiracy against Chubby that almost made him a victim. Only she, and Pone knew Crowe tied Thomas to a chair butt naked. It was a secret Crowe would take to his grave. Red made Pone promise to keep the situation to himself. Pone joked about Red being *Wonder Woman* and Thomas being *Steve Trevor.*

"Though he didn't tell me, he is sorry for what he did," commented Mary.

He didn't tell you the truth after all what would a widow of a late crime lord think a him being a damsel in distress, thought Red. "Fine, I'll do it, but this is more up Linda's alley."

"Your sisters have husbands," remarked Mary.

"They are all about the same height,"

Mary gave her a stern look.

"Thomas and I… " Red frowned.

"You're not getting any younger,"

"Age builds character and sometimes makes you wiser." responded Red who had no intention of walking down the aisle with Thomas

Maxwell. Red has always been the person to play mind games with people who thought they had the right to pass judgment. She liked Thomas, but she didn't like snobs or people who felt they could talk about others and be immune to the same treatment. She dated Thomas because she did liked his company, but to also tell the uppity assholes to mind their damn business. Sure she was tall and he was short, but Red walked among her peers with attitude it would be best for you all to keep your opinion up your ass. Thomas for now in Red's dog house.

Mary turned the cup up to her lips. "Sometimes love starts out that way, but in time it escalates into something more."

"Is that how you and dad started out?"

"Oh heavens no, your father was a tall well built physique man. I'm not ashamed to admit he was out of my league."

Red pondered what her mother said about out of league. Thomas out of her league and no plans of walking down the aisle. "Mother, you were everything dad needed and he knew,"

Red knew what her mother said about her father was the opposite of Maxwell, but Maxwell intelligent and by him trying to be mayor prove he knew to take advantage of an opportunity given to him by Crowe's deception and Winslow cowardice. As for she and he getting married not in the cards. Red left that up to her siblings. The binates despite how she loved her sisters had to settle though her brother-in-laws were both good men. Her brother could however have his pick of female or male and despite his homosexual activities, Red glad he chose a traditional marriage that produced three beautiful children.

"Would it bother you if I didn't marry Thomas?" asked Red.

"What ever makes you happy dear,"

Red kissed her mother on the forehead.

"Where's Mister Pone?" asked Mary.

"New Orleans,"

Mary gave Red a look.

"He's on a job Mother,"

"Everything still professional?"

"There was this time I stared in his one blue crystal eye … "Red withheld when Mary suspend her tea cup in mid-flight to her lips with the look of despair on her face. Just the look Red was looking for. "Oh relax mother," laughed Red.

"It's not me you have to worry about, "

"Sue and PJ have calmed down … it's Linda you're talking about,"

"She is so much like your father."

"Daddy was fond of Pone."

"He killed for your father,"

Red took a deep breath to control her anger. If there was one thing she didn't like about her father was him ordering the death's of others and most of all ordering Pone to carry it out which he did everytime. She also knew if Pone wanted he could take out her family, but knew he would do nothing to hurt her by doing it no matter how much her clan deserve it. Linda however still ordered hits in her own discrete way. The apple didn't fall far from the tree.

"Did he have a choice?"

"Your Mister Pone is a smart man,"

Red stood up to leave.

"You didn't touch your tea dear,"

It was bland and cold, but Red wanted to satisfy her mother. "All gone, I'll see you later mother,"

"Thomas… " Mary smiled. "Overjoyed you agreed to help him with his campaign."

"Oh I can't wait to tell him."

The crying grew louder and louder as Tara approached the mahogany door. One of many inside the impregnable mansion of Theiler Lareaux. She tried the knob and it opened without any resistance. Tara saw a small girl between the ages of ten and thirteen. Swollen watery puffy eyes stared at Tara with knees drawn up to her chest. Tara closed the door and waved her hand for the girl to calm down. A few sniffles and the blubbering stopped. Tara eased herself onto the bed and opened her arms and the girl filled them soaking Tara's blouse.

"There, there… it will be all right," said Tara.

Tara didn't know if the girl her sister, cousin, or both. Anger filled her heart thinking about the monster she would never call her father or anything worth while. Theiler Lareaux the lowest thing this side of the Mississippi. She held the girl like an infant to her breast and could only think she had to get out of here, she was the same size as this girl when Theiler brought her into his sadistic world of incest and child prostitution. She now a grown woman and no longer a child, the only child in the room the one she had in her arms. Plans to escape on her mind, but the problem, nothing change since the last time she held prisoner.

The outside guards with assault rifles and dressed military style fatigues while the inside guards clean cut wearing matching black attire with glocks concealed inside their blazers parading around the mansion. A fenced in moat like pond on the complex except for a stretch of land passage woods for wild game, because Theiler had an appetite for gators. She didn't know how to pilot a helicopter, and there were two type of boats: Theiler owned four air boats, and she knew she couldn't navigate any of them, but the four speed boats he owned, she believe she could learn on the fly.

Tara plans of escape would have to wait because there were too many obstacles and she needed an Allie. So she had to put freedom on hold for now.

"What's your name?" whispered Tara.

"M-Mia," she responded.

"How did you get here?"

Mia looked up with welled up eyes." A hairy monster beat up my mother and brother and brought me here then a fat long white haired man told him to put me in this room."

Gritted teeth and closed eyes kept Tara from screaming. Ludwig was the hairy monster and the fat long white hair was the disgusting Theiler. "Did they touch you in any kind of way?"

Mia shook her head.

Good, she's still pure and innocent, thought Tara. She knew Theiler tested the merchandise before letting his customers have their way with the young girls. Tara knew all too well how blubbery wealthy men old enough to be grandfathers have their pleasure on young flesh while leaving a permanent scar on the girl. Nostrils flared and squinted eyes made Tara clench her fist. The thought *of Mia being another one of his incest daughters for him to violate and pimp out to disgusting men like himself.* Tara felt if she could protect Mia then she could regain what self-respect the pedophile stole from her.

"Don't worry I'll protect you," said Tara.

Mia pulled away from Tara for a moment and sized her up. "How?" Then buried her face in Tara's breast.

Tara laughed. "Size isn't everything and sometimes if you pray, good things can happen." Tara knew Mia was right about the size difference after all she had a wrestling match with the monstrous Ludwig and no contest, but she had to give the frightened girl a glimpse of hope.

"Do we have to pray a lot?" asked Mia.

"There's no limit on praying. It's just that sometimes he takes his time to answer,"

"I hope he doesn't take his time this time,"

A gentle squeeze to comfort Mia and lips pressed on top of her head. "You and me both," Praying didn't pay off for her since she ended up back in the abode of horror.

A missing front tooth on display from a smile and then a long yawn.

Tara raised an eye-brow. "You must have had a long day?"

Mia nodded.

"Why don't you close your eyes and go to sleep?" suggested Tara.

A frantic head shake and wide eyes with fear yanked away from Tara's breast.

"I promise it will be all right,"

"Will you stay with me?" asked Mia.

"Until you fall asleep,"

"You can't stay?"

"I have my room."

"Don't want to be here by myself,"

"Right across the hall from you."

"Can't I stay with you?"

"If you did I'd get into trouble and I know you don't want me to get into trouble do you?"

Mia shook her head. A hand placed to the back of Mia's head escorted her to Tara's lap.

"See, you are, now how about sleep?" Tara eased out of the room closing the door. She was about to enter her room when she saw a young man in his early twenties. He wore a blue shirt, blue jeans, and casual brown shoes. He wasn't a guard which meant he was one of Theiler's runners. He even put his other children to work by putting his sons in the drug business; they pick up payment, distribute, and make deals. They both stared and glared until Tara got inside her room locking the door.

New Orleans, a city with a history of both good and bad. A city of rich tradition, famous for imports, and exports. It remain that way even after the Great Meteor passed the earth causing a future shock. New Orleans luck out and some say the Gods protected the city because of it's past tragedies. In either case it remained the most efficient international ports in the country second to the Big Apple(New New York) in the foreign trade business. It said that New Orleans battled tested against the Great Meteor. It survived hurricanes and flooding in 1965, 1973 and the early 2,000 which presented problems with storms. The city rebounded regaining it's reputation for being big on imports: coffee, sugar, and bananas as well as a classic tourist attraction. The exports it dealt with: oil, petrochemicals, rice, cotton, sulfur, and lumber. The city a major rail, highway, air and river front.

Pone did his research on the city in case he needed to have information if he engage in a conversation with some of the locals. Like himself, half the people tourist. The best part of New Orleans, night time. They say the freaks come out at night and the big easy night life all about weirdos coming out. Every tourist wanted to experience Mardi Gra and the jazz music that made the city famous. *Count Basie* wasn't performing, but good harmony music. All the exotic mask and costumes prove to be as good as advertised, even Pone got back into character with his signature black vest, white banded collar shirt, bowler hat, and black and white pattern wing tips. The only things missing Lucille and Sally.

Pone stepped inside the Harrahs blending in well with all the other high-rollers. He looked every bit like a man with plenty ofloot to spend and lose. He switched up his attire a bit after dealing with Crowe and his cronies, but jumped back into his fancy duds for this occasion. Pone glanced around the hotel casino smiling and making eye contact with some of the cocktail waitresses and female dealers at the black jack tables. Pone spotted a caramel curve who returned his eye contact with a smile.

"Mine if I join in?" asked Pone.

"Welcome handsome," said caramel curve whose smile shined brighter than casino lights.

Pone took his place at the table along side three other participants; a couple and an unkempt man who looked like he became that way because he was about to lose his shirt. The couple at the table, odd; a young leggy brunette sitting next to a silver haired sugar daddy with his arm wrapped around her waist as if someone was going to steal her. Then there was the dark haired unkempt man in a orange shirt and gray suit that was darker thanks to a frustration of sweat.

"This is bull-shit!" Barked the unkempt man who just lost $50,000.

Pone read the name tag on the right shoulder just above caramel curve's breast, Lola.

"Maybe black jack's not your game, sir," said Lola.

The man glared. "Maybe you're bad luck,"

Pone studied the man. A drunk and sore loser. A bad combination, but the dealer kept flashing her pearly whites, the ultimate professional.

The man waved his glass summoning a cocktail waitress. "Hey sweetheart, how about another, chop, chop …" He snorted and looked toward Pone. "I'm bleeding chips here, can you believe it?"

"Like the lady said, black jack may not be your game." said Pone placing a bet.

Lola shuffled the cards like it second nature. Pone's cards slid to him perfectly and Lola motioned for him to reveal them. He displayed aten of diamonds and an eight of hearts, Lola flipped a card and it in Pone's favor.

"We have a winner!" said Lola.

"What the fuck!" remarked the man. "Fucker sits down for a second and wins right away. What the hell you call this, a black thang?"

Pone cleared his throat. "If you play roulette, I suggest you bet on black. I advise you call it a night or watch your mouth."

"My curfew ended a long time ago," remarked the man.

Lola pursed her lips while shuffling the cards. "Sir, you're drunk and lady luck is not on your side. You're loud and rude and pretty soon I have to call security. And I don't want to see you get embarrassed escorted out of the casino."

The man looked at Pone, Lola, the young dame hugging her sugar daddy. He grabbed what chips he had left and Pone handed him few chips of his own.

"For good luck the next time you play," said Pone.

The man took them and wobbled away.

"Mighty kind of you," remarked Lola.

"Why do I feel like I'm in the old west?" asked Pone.

"I always wanted to say that," smiled Lola.

"You look like you been doing this for awhile?"

"Well played," smile Lola. "Now is that better?"

"Maybe tomorrow luck will find him." said Pone. "

"I get off in a few hours," said Lola.

"I'll kill time at the bar," responded Pone.

Pone shared a eye contact with the young brunette whose sugar daddy pulled her even closer. Pone smiled and strolled over to the bar.

Fancy people and wearing dapper clothes were some of the few things that made Ben uncomfortable. Ben at ease not around people moving their eyes up, down under a furrow brow, and a turned up nose telling him he didn't belong among the high society crowd. A black toboggan, a leather jacket of the same color covering a red T-shirt, wrangler blue jeans, and tan Timberland boots. Ben stepped into his element, a dive bar. He scoped out the natives; faded jackets, jeans, scruff faces, scuffled shoes, boots, and Ben knew he belong. Nothing high society about this group. Ben beeline his way to the bar past a few unshaven faces, beer bellies, beer guzzling women that made him feel right at home. The Oyster bar at the docks. Ben perched himself on a stool resting his elbows on the counter. Dried glass rim and spilled beer and alcohol stains along with peanut shells decorated the counter. Ben shoved a few shells out of his way before grabbing a bowl full of nuts and indulge himself. He scanned the bar and saw no smoking policy as ash trays stationed near every pool table; the clacking sound of the cue stick hitting the cue ball sending it to break up the party scattering them to their holes made the bar active with an exchange of money going from loser to winner. Ben's observation broken by the bartender.

Ben look at the man and felt he should have had a carrot. Long rectangular shaped head, donkey ears, a long big nose with wide nostrils, big lips and teeth barely contained in his mouth. The bartender's face resembled a horse. The man made Stick look attractive and made Ben wonder if he had been perhaps affected by radiation from the Great Meteor. The only thing left now if the man's name, Ed. He approached Ben.

"Name your poison?" stated Horse face.

"A beer," responded Ben.

"Comin' right up,"

Ben studied the bartender. Free flowing black T-shirt, saggy blue jeans supported by a belt in it's last notch, and with the help of too much hard liquor, cigarettes gave him bags under eyes, dry crack, enlarge pores, senior citizen skin. Ben peg him at least mid to late forties..

Horse face slid the beer perfect to Ben as some of the beverage spills on the counter. Ben nodded his approval and realized the man not into good house keeping.

Ben took a long sip. "Might want to practice wiping down the counter when things slow down,"

Horse face reached under the counter and pulled out a towel.

"You from the health department?"

Ben took another swallow of brew.

"Any rats and roaches?"

"Cigarette smoke, dirty bar counter, andbad manner customers," remarked Horse face.

"You the owner?"

"He too good to show his face around here," Horse face looked Ben over.

"You a tourist?"

"Out of work. A friend said I might be able to find some work down here around the docks,"

"What can you do? You don't look like no seaman,"

"Fork lift mostly,"

"This is the loading docks, but you might have more luck at the pool tables, but word of advice, the locals sort of feel threatened if a newcomer come nosing around thinking you might take their job." Ben turned and eyed the pool tables.

"These guys any good?"

"Maybe one of two pool sharks, but nothin' to brag about, you a hustler?"

 Ben rose from his stool. "What do you think?"

"You too old to play in the NBA,"

They both laughed.

Ben took another gulp of beer. "Think I'll go try my luck,"

"You big, but don't win too much,"

"They take losing that serious?"

"If you don't win too much money,"

"Only if I'm lucky," remarked Ben. He made his way over to the tables. He saw a man smiling while taking money and chalking his stick. Ben stamped his mug on the outside table. "Next game."

SEVEN

Twelve a.m.

A hard knock aggressive enough to make Tara almost jump off her bed. She knew the knock on her door wasn't from Mia because it was too heavy and strong. She also knew it wasn't from Theiler since he made it a rule of heart for the girls not to lock their doors unless they had company. No this knock came from someone angry.

"Who is it?" asked Tara.

"We shared a moment in the hallway earlier, may I come in?"

The boy in the hallway, well young man to be exact and it wasn't so much as a moment, but an exchange of angry glares, thought Tara.

"What do you want?" asked Tara. *The exchange of looks didn't mean come by later for a good time and if that was what he thought then he had another thing coming.*

"It's important," he replied.

"Go away or Mister Lereaux will here about this,"

"What were you doing with that little girl?" he asked.

Mia… what does he want with Mia? Was he a pervert like Theiler and wanted first dibs on her? Tara had promised to protect her. She took a deep breath and let the young man in. He looked at least twenty-five, average height with a stocky muscular frame and thick jet black hair. *He must be one of Theiler's runners, but how did he get by the guards?*

40

"What's she to you?" asked Tara.

"She's my sister," he said.

"You're the brother living at home with the mother?"

"No, that's our brother Manuel. Mia is the youngest and I have to get her out of here and again what were you doing with her?"

"What do you mean?"

"Were you prepping her, teaching her the trade, getting her ready for that bastard, because if you were… "

"No!"

"Keep your voice down, no one can know I'm here,"

"I was telling Mia… " Tara frowned. "I'd protect her,"

The young man gave her the same look his sister did.

"Okay already, so I'm not a imposing figure, but I had to say something to stop her from crying." replied Tara.

"Why did you lie to her and how the hell are you going to protect her?"

Tara raised an eye-brow. "I could ask you the same,"

"I don't know, but I will,"

"Seems we're both in a bind here," said Tara.

"You more than me. You're a prisoner like Mia."

"And that might not be a bad thing,"

"What are you talking about?" asked the young man.

"I might keep Theiler from doing to her what he did to me and so many others,"

"How?"

"I haven't figure it out yet, okay… "Eye lashes batted to keep back tears. "You'd better go before a guard or someone finds you,"

"He's a cousin."

"You mean?"

"He's hates Theiler too and I promised him some stuff,"

Tara looked at him. "You're one of his runners,"

"Not for long and now that Mia's here I'm more determined to get out of here,"

"I escaped, but here I am,"

"How did he get you back here?"

"Ludwig," Tara said.

He sank against the wall in deep thought shaking his head.

Tara gave a look. "What's wrong?"

"So you're the one." said the young man pointing.

Tara shrugged. "I don't understand."

"Albert is dead because of you." He retorted.

Tara slumped on her bed. Her mother paid a young man to infiltrate Theiler's crew. She didn't ask any questions once he said your mother sent me. How much money Cici spent, Tara didn't know or care.

She wanted to get off the estate.

He dressed as a server in the kitchen and dining room where the girls ate and they talked in the hidden passage way between the kitchen and restrooms. He told her his plan for her to escape. He gave her clothes for a boy told her to hide her hair inside the ball cap. He instructed her to go to the restroom, change then come outside for a smoke. He gave her a cigarette.

Tara met him near a big tree near the water where there no lights. She climbed into the boat with paddles.

"I asked him to come with me."

The young man shook his head. "Well he couldn't or you wouldn't have made it as far as you did. How did you make it?"

"It doesn't matter since I'm back."

The young man nodded. "Well he's dead." He straightened.

"So you can stop telling her lies, You have to keep hope alive." Tara remarked.

"Not if it's false hope."

"What's your name?" asked Tara.

"Beef because I love beef stew,"

Tara gave a look and inhaled.

"Cute, but you better go before you get caught,"

"It's okay I'm always careful,"

"I'm Tara but you need to leave,"

"Okay, maybe we talk again and come up with a plan," said Beef.

"Yeah, maybe,"

"Nice to meet you," Beef cracked the door peeking out and left.

1:00 a.m.

The caramel curve a good description of the woman named Lola who possessed all the tools to satisfy a man. Five-foot-five and about a buck fifty with a luscious booty capped by mouth watering thighs and firm legs that looked fabulous in heels and went great with her black leggings fitting her like a second skin. The white blouse and red vest displayed enough cleavage and enhanced her firm waist line in a respectful none slutty way. Pone marveled her rosy plump cheeks and perky lips painted scarlet, light blue eye shadow was the icing on the cake and she flash a natural smile.

"You're not much a drinker are you?" asked Lola.

"I like having a clear head," remarked Pone.

A finger circled the rim finding it's way into the caramel liquid then inside Pone's mouth. Lola retrieved her finger after pulling down Pone's lower lip. They both smiled.

Lola took a sip of her cocktail. "So … you don't touch the stuff?"

"Except from your finger," Pone grin. "A beer every now and then and Irish cream on holidays,"

"What brand of beer and don't say Dos Equis,"

Pone snorted. "Samuel Adams, but I prefer Malta Goya,"

Lola frowned. "Never heard of it,"

"It's a sweet malt beverage…required taste. He pursed his lips. "So you wanted me to wait around to pick my brain over what swill I like?"

"Well sugah, I like to know something about you before I fuck you."

Pone got moon-eye. "What else do you want to know?'

Manicured nails stroked Pone's hand.

"I tried brandy once," he said. "You could have timed me with an hour glass for how long I took to drink it. Felt like my insides were on fire. I play it safe when it comes to alcohol."

"Ain't nothing wrong with that," Lola took another sip. "You know my name,"

"Excuse me,"

"You read my name tag." said Lola.

"I was looking at your breast," remarked Pone.

"They can be a distraction,"

"So was it a black thang?"

Lola took another drink "That man was an ass the moment he sat down."

"Know of any big games and I mean big games going on?"

"And here I thought you enjoyed my company."

"Did I fuck up?" asked Pone.

Lola leaned in close. "I love your eyes."

"And they like you too,"

"So you a gambler Mister … "

"Pone, Chubby Pone."

"Hmm… even the name is sexy," Lola leaned back.

"So you're a gambler?"

"When it suits me. You know of any games?"

Lola got off the bar stool and walked about ten feet. Looked over her shoulder and caught Pone eye-balling her ass. "You still want my company?"

Lola didn't have to ask him twice.

2:00 a.m.

Ben played the hard luck pool hustler to a T. He lost the first four games giving his opponent the confidence to bet more money believing, another pigeon. He ran a winning streak of his own against lesser pool sharks and knew when to cool his jets when the locals started whispering loud enough for him to hear the word hustler.

Ben worked his way up the self-proclaimed champion of the pool tables. A tall lanky sand complexion man with slick back black hair and decked out in a white suit and black shirt. He had a few bimbo groupies sitting against the wall cheering him on.

Ben took one victory lap before letting his luck run amok again to look like an average hustler against the champion. He got cocky after winning three straight so he let the champ break. A small crowd formed around the table despite Ben getting dominated by the champion. Ben eyed the crowd and took advantage of the gift given to him by the champion. He had solids and they were hitting the corner and side pockets like a mouse to cheese. Ben sat on side lines playing spectator, but when it was his time again the champion put him in a challenging position. Eight ball in the lower left corner pocket. Easy shot accept a striped ball in front blocking Ben's path.

Cue ball across from the eight with nothing blocking it's path, but it takes a solid to hit the eight ball the cue ball must manipulate. Ben had a solid yellow in the middle of the table, but the champion left the cue ball in the lower part of the table across from the eight ball and it's body guard a stripe ball. Ben did enough in high school to graduate and math like so many was not his best subject. Ben loomed over the table studying his situation; he needed to use Geometry.

Ben bent over the table moving the cue stick back and forth between the circle he made with his thumb and index finger. He had to consider his options and it wasn't about how to win the game, but what might happen if he won the game on a trick shot. If he pulled off the feat then he would have to play two games and lose them both to balance the scales to prove he wasn't a pool shark. Time to put math to use; Ben's arithmetic teacher in his senior year of high school asked him if he would use math as a career.

When Ben said no and his teacher saw the sincerity in Ben's eyes he was able sit among his peers on graduation day and marched across the stage when he heard his name called to get his diploma. He wasn't book smart, but book smart doesn't make everyone rich.

Ben wasn't good at geometry, but he would use it to take the smile off his opponents face. The giant called three banks: The dive bar silent not that he needed it to be, but added drama by putting chalk on his thumb and adding blue to the top of his cue before making the cue ball kiss the yellow ball off the left then the right and off the top bank of the table making a diagonal beeline to the eight ball. The yellow ball moving slower and slower making Ben a little nervous, but the yellow ball sneaked past the striped ball kissing the eight ball enough to make it dance in the hole before falling in. A gasp of admiration soon followed by judging sullen eyes.

"Looks like you've done this before," stated the champion.

"How about I give you a chance to win your money back," said Ben.

"Rack 'em up!" said the champion.

Ben lost two games before taking his winnings and headed back to the bar. He got a few looks on his way, but once he stood up straight and gave a look of his own the patrons went back to drinking beer and talking among themselves.

"You're good, I'll give you that," said Horse face.

Ben slapped five twenties on the bar.

"You plan on drinking all night?" asked Horse face.

"Information," said Ben.

Horse face wasted no time pocketing the money." What do you want to know?"

"Do you know of any high-stakes poker games around here?" asked Ben.

Big over bite teeth escaped big lips forming into a smile. "Billiards are not your only game, huh?"

"Make money any way I can," remarked Ben.

3:00 a.m.

Tongue circling hard dark nipples and squeezed by lips made Lola purred like a kitten as the lips pressed against the firm melons skipping the trench that separated them. Pone flipped Lola on her stomach a concentrated on her lower melons. Lips pressed against the plump smooth flesh followed by a tongue moving up the trail of the lower back to the shoulder blades made Lola hum like a humming bird.

Lola turned the tables on Pone flipping him on his back. They were strangers, but all that changed; some men and women when they meet they seem to associate, chemistry between them. No explanation gives them both a sense of touching breast and kissing lips, neck and thigh feeling safe around one another. Pone didn't care for skirt chasing, but he a man and men like women also have needs.

A nipple pinched between fingers of violet painted manicured nails and a tongue to sooth the pain only to set up another nipple tease with gentle bite between teeth brought Pone to a new world. Lola straddled him and the volcano erupt as it entered the black hole. The symphony of purrs and sighs to an ending of two people cuddling.

"I was expecting tongue action," said Lola.

"God gave me food to eat," responded Pone.

"Lola lifted her head from Pone's chest. "Say what?"

"You always practice safe sex?"

"I'm not a slut,"

"I don't know how many men you or any woman been with so I don't believe in oral sex. Is that a problem?"

Lola sat up and studied Pone. "Damn! You ain't lying,"

"Don't get mad at the weather man if you don't like the forecast,"

Lola laughed. "You are too cute," She placed her head back on his chest. "So you don't have anybody special?"

"Sworn to fun and loyal to none," remarked Pone.

"You a player, Mister Pone?" asked Lola.

"Only with women I connect with,"

"How many is that,"

"You can count on one hand."

"What do you do for a living if you don't mind me asking?"

"Told you I'm a gambler,"

"Plenty men done sat at my table hoping to hit the jackpot and turn their life around only dig themselves in deeper hole."

"What makes you think I'm no different?"

"You sat at my table like you had nothing to lose,"

"You take care of your money and it will take care you,"

"Sorry, I didn't mean to strike a nerve."

"What I do isn't very nice," said Pone.

"You a lawyer Mister Pone?"

Pone laughed. "Please call me, Chubby,"

Pearly whites on display. "Chubby, what do you do?"

"I'm a troubleshooter."

Lola sat up in bed and looked Pone up and down. "You don't look like any computer geek I've ever seen,"

"Sorry, but I don't look good in coke bottle glasses and high water pants."

"You work for a big company?"

"I came down here to take care of a little glitch…what's your story?"

Lip pursed and Lola rolled on her back and stared at the ceiling. "School was never my thing and I make good money plus tips and meet people," She smiled at Pone.

"I had a wise grandfather and he said college ain't for everyone, but if you know how to save your money you will be all right and here I am," Pone looked around her bedroom. A mix match pair of dressers black and brown, queen sized bed with out a head board beside a tan nightstand with a cell phone, gray digital clock, and a white lamp sharing space. A 42 inch flat screen across from her bed. A mid-sized closet and a window on the left in a cream colored room. A ranch house built of wood in a modest neighborhood elbow to elbow with wood and chain fences. She drove a blue Nissan Versa. Lola comfortable with her life; she knew how to budget to fit her lifestyle.

"You're at home with yourself, I like that," said Pone.

Pearly whites flashed. "How would you describe yourself, chubby?" asked Lola.

"Like a comic book,"

"My grandfather would've loved you," said Lola.

"I take it he was a collector,"

"More boxes than you could count. Said he needed them to escape the real world."

"My life is a different story every day."

"It's that way for everybody," remarked Lola.

Pone sat up and laid his head against the wall. "You get up in the morning, shower, eat breakfast, go to work, eat lunch and go back to work then go home to a family or by yourself and eat dinner then go to bed and wake up to do it all over again."

"Not the book I'd want to read."

"Where are the boxes now?" asked Pone.

"My brother has three boys as if they need anything to encourage their imagination."

"Who are their favorite characters?" asked Pone.

"Spider-man, Iron man, Captain America, and the Hulk. You?"

Pone snorted. "Wolverine, Daredevil, and Conan."

Lola shook her head and smiled. "You got my interest,"

"Wolverine's small and has a feral appearance, but still get the ladies both young and old, but he only does things when he has to and he is the best he is at what he does and what he does isn't nice. Conan is also a ladies man, but what he does is base on survival. Wolverine has integrity for the young girls having a school girl crush on him, he acts like a big brother to them and for the older women he does what any heterosexual male would do, he fucks them. Conan does the same except not the big brother thing, he has sex with young and old women, he has no morals. Guess you didn't need that in those days, but he mind his own business, but knows what he needs to do if you try to cause him any harm and he don't give second chances."

Lola stared and studied the man and he was a man, but a boy at heart comparing himself to comic book characters. "And Daredevil?"

Pone tilts his head. "Fearless,"

She okay with that because he seemed to know when to be an adult and he reminded her of her grandfather.

Lola natural smile lit up the room. "You a card player, Mister Pone?"

"I said ..."

"I know, I know ... but it makes me feel so sophisticated when I say Mister Pone."

"Yeah, Poker is my game,"

"Well a lot of that around here,"

"So it's big time?"

"Um-hmm, but you don't want none of that,"

"It's high stakes,"

"You like danger Mister Pone?"

"I can take care of myself,"

"I don't doubt that,"

"If you know something then tell me, I think we … "

Lola looked as though she needed a cigarette. She sat on the edge of the bed.. "Had a cousin and I mean had. He much like you playing poker and good at it. I got him in to where I work so he could go through the proper channels to get in on those high stakes games. He couldn't do anything else …I even gave him starter money. He thanked me and agreed to give me a percentage of his winnings."

She turned and looked at Pone. Pearly whites were on display again. Pone studied Lola's smile. A smile hiding pain, but pain she'd share to either steer him away from danger or to unload a heavy burden off her heart.

"He won enough to get that trip to the island of Lereaux, "

Pone sat up straight in bed. He felt a chill from Lola's voice and the conversation got colder.

"Something wrong, Lola?"

"The medical examiner said he was gator bait … body was half eaten and bites on they left what of his arms that looked as though he fell into a nest of vampires.

Body swelled like a balloon. Don't know if he won too much or saw something, but he ended up dead."

"What was his name?" asked Pone. He heard Theiler recruited assassins and politicians he could have something on. Pone pondered if Lola's cousin a killer-for-hire and she didn't know.

"Burdell,"

"Must be a lot of money on the table,"

"Is that all you care about?"

"Anything that makes life comfortable,"

"Ten grand cash gets you in," She looked into Pone's eyes. "I can give you the start up money,"

Pone smiled. "Got it covered. ,"

The automatic smile returned. Smooth velvet hands clasped around a porcelain chiseled face forcing it a collision between two soft lips.

"I don't hook up with just anybody," said Lola.

"That's nice to know," remarked Pone.

Lola straddled Pone and another violent, but passionate lip lock got the engines revved up and they became one.

4:00 a.m.

Ben stuffed the napkin with information from horse face inside his jacket.

He started to climb inside the Suburban when he heard lumbering boots hustling up behind him. Ben pursed his lips, snorted, and turned to face five thick muscular men of different shapes and sizes. All blue collar appeal; work boots, jean jackets,flannel shirts and blue jeans. Leader of the five, the champion pool shark.

Ben scope the five out and nobody packing; no wrenches, lead pipes, or fancy knives.

Just plain old callous knuckles on large hands forming into balled up fist. Ben smiled, he realized he didn't have to kill anybody, but just enjoy a little exercise.

A open hand covering and rubbing a large fist. "Can I help you boys?" asked Ben.

The Champion motioned to his companions. "Me and the boys had a talk."

"I'm flattered," responded Ben.

"Wasn't anything good, you hustled us," stated the Champion.

"I lost my share of games and you pocketed a good bit of money," cited Ben.

"The point is we don't like strangers making a fool of us," stated the Champion.

"What do you suggest I do about it?" questioned Ben.

"Relinquish your winnings and we part as friends," suggested the Champion.

Ben threw up his hands and chuckled. "I got to eat and put clothes on my back,"

Ben took a deep breath and shook his head. He was standing in a circle "So…that's how it's going to be,"

The Champion shrugged. "Tried to be nice,"

They say the eyes have it and in most fights you can look into your adversary's eyes to see rage, fear, and gives you a heads up on what he might do. Ben had ten eyes to worry about, but instead he focused on the Champion. The Champion gave a glance to the man standing behind Ben. Ben did a three-sixty delivering an elbow to the man's face to a sickening sound to a broken nose and sent the man crashing to the pavement.

After that it became a free for all with the other men moving in on Ben with out taking orders from the Champion. It wasn't the first time Ben in a circle taking on all comers.

His high school football days brought back memories of a drill called Oklahoma, one player would be in a circle and the coach pointed at a player to attack him and he had to fend the player off. That drill prepped him for what was about to come and being six-nine didn't hurt either. One man went low grabbing him around the waist. He took a sharp elbow to the spine and he went down with his expression like someone stuck him with a thousand needles.

Another grabbed his thigh and Ben used his free leg to knee the man in his exposed face, but held on and the other man grabbed his thigh thinking the Champion would make his move, but he decided to spectate instead. Their heads close enough for Ben to palm their skulls like basket balls and made them look like two charging rams butting heads.

Both fell to the pavement holding their melons in pain. Four down and one to go.

The Champion looked at Ben, he spread his legs as he got into a fighting stance.

Ben stood tall among the fallen waiting to see what the Champion would do. The Champion made his move, but in the opposite direction hauling ass leaving behind his buddies.

Ben looked at the fallen men realizing that these guys dock workers and not barroom brawlers. Ben shook his head and climb inside the SUV driving off.

A knock on the motel door woke Ben up from his much needed sleep. He checked the time on his cell phone 7:45 a. m. , The bed breathed a sigh of relief once he got up to answer the door. Ben unlock the lock, didn't bother to ask and beeline face first back on the bed, the springs grind supporting his weight. He assumed it Pone doing the knocking.

"Could have been anybody knocking Ben," said Pone.

"Those guys I ran into will think twice about running into me again," remarked Ben.

"In town a short time and already stirring up shit?"

"Nobody dead if that's what you're worried about,"

Boots at the head of the bed, shirt and jacket on the small brown sofa chair. Pone studied the man lying on his belly with only socks and jeans.

"When did you get in?" questioned Pone.

"Been here for two hours before you come a knocking,"

Ben looked over his shoulder. "Looked like you got in and you don't even look sleepy,"

Pone grinned. "Had my little encounter,"

Ben took another glance at Pone. "You got lucky,"

"Wasn't all play, I need ten-thousand to get in,"

"A horse face bartender told me I'd need half of that,"

"My information came from some one prettier."

"Don't want any details,"

"You will not be playing cards at that same bar are you?" asked Pone.

"Wouldn't want to press my luck." remarked Ben.

"We got to be careful Ben. No more altercations,"

"At least I didn't carry a firearm,"

"What caused that fight between you and those guys?" questioned Pone.

"I hustled those barflies over a game of pool. How was I to know they were sore losers?"

"They knew you hustled them,"

"Most fun I had in a long time,"

"Glad you had fun … get back to sleep and if you wake up before I do then come get me,"

Ben snored.

10:00 a.m.

The walls weren't paper thin, but the cries of a child loud enough to wake Tara. She stood at the door listening, The sun blazed through her window and not that she needed it's help, but the rooster crowed. Lereaux raised chickens on his estate and not just for his dinner, but he also had cock fights. Tara wasn't a prisoner, but she knew better than to stray from her room. She wanted to avoid Theiler as much as possible so she stayed in her room unless he came into it uninvited.

Tara headed back to bed hoping Mia would cry herself to sleep until she heard the cold gravel voice of Theiler.

"Come now girl, cut out all that crying. Got to give you a test run to make sure you got what it takes to satisfy my customers needs,"

Tara gasped. She hoped Theiler would at least waited a month or two before trying to put his filthy paws on Mia. The pig already stooped lower; child pornography, a pedophile, and incest. Tara swallowed hard, she promised to protect Mia. A promise she meant to keep. She knew

Theiler would be furious with the intrusion, but a part of Tara didn't mind that one bit. It would be a sacrifice she will take to protect Mia. Tara dressed in her night gown made of silk with shoulder straps. She opened her door and saw Beef creeping closer to Mia's room with a knife in his hand. Tara grabbed him by his arm and yanked Beef in the room. They stood and stared at each other. *That crazy cousin must have gave him a free pass again in exchange for some blow, crazy fool,* thought Tara.

Tara shook her head thinking Beef, Mia, and their cousin could just as well be her siblings and cousins and that thought made her sick.

"What the hell do you think you're doing?" asked Beef.

"Saving your ass," responded Tara.

"Get out of the way," roared Beef.

"Lower your voice before he hears us,"

"He will rape my sister,"

Your sister and his daughter, thought Tara. "He'll kill you,"

"I'll take my chances,"

"No. I'll stop him,"

Beef glared and looked Tara up and down. "I don't have time for jokes,"

The crying got louder.

"Out of my way,"

A pulled up gown released a knee to the groin. The knife fell to floor as the hand holding it joined the other to comfort sensitive private parts. Supported by his knees on the floor, Beef on the floor in a fetal position.

"I will help Mia, but you need to leave," stated Tara.

"I think you crippled me," whimpered Beef.

"You'll live, but not if you keep coming here,"

"What do you mean?" questioned Beef.

Tara shook her head. "Somebody's going to see you and snitch,"

Beef rose to his feet holding himself. "I've been careful,"

"You get caught and no telling what Theiler will do to us or Mia,"

Beef thought for a moment and nodded. He reached for the knife, but Tara placed her foot on it.

"It might tempt you," said Tara.

Beef glowered then peeked outside the door and eased out into the hallway. Tara picked up the knife and sat on the bed. Bad thoughts flooded her head while holding the knife. She thought taking matters into her own hands. She could lure Theiler to her bed and if she failed to slit his throat it could be the end of her.

Daughter, niece or whatever she was to him if she made an attempt on his life and failed he would kill her and bring another one of his incest offspring into the fold. Young Mia. Tara placed the knife on the lower part of her bed board. It would stay hidden there until the human side of her had had enough. Mia's crying got louder and Theiler's gravel voice got more impatient. Tara took a deep breath.

The hallway clear, Beef gone. Tara knocked on the door. A harsh stop that crying girl and she opened the door. Theiler stood shirtless; saggy man boobs, arms so flabby if they were wings he could take flight, and a pitcher mound belly with what looked like a coffee stain on display. Tara understood Mia's crying.

The good thing Theiler did, kept his pants on and wore his silver mop top hair in a pony tail to give him some resemblance of looking human. Theiler put his attention on Tara. He flashed a gold tooth smile.

"My oh my girl.. what do you have in mind?" he asked.

Run like hell and never look back... focus, thought Tara.

The plan of seduction worked. Keep Mia safe and so far it entranced Theiler's eyes on the strapless pink lace mini lingerie. His disgusting wilds came back to concentrating on a woman instead of a child and even if that woman his own daughter created out of sin.

Tara smiled to fight off her disgust. Theiler's presence alive or dead will always make her skin crawl. He touched her body more than she cared to count and not by her choice. This time different and it would be by choice to keep him from forcing himself on Mia. Tara didn't look at Mia. She took Theiler by the hand.

An ear to ear gold tooth smile on Theiler's face made him forget about breaking in a new Philly. He clutched Tara's hand and happy letting her play Pied Piper leading him to her room.

At the end of the hall raging eyes and gritted teeth watched a monster enter Tara's bedroom. Beef clenched his fist and moved on. He wanted to rush in Tara's room and rescue her from that monster. She kept his knife, but Theiler wouldn't be an easy kill. Beef witnessed the pedophile wrestling some alligators. The bastard boasted putting the creatures in a camel clutch.

Tara preached patience and he'd wait because Theiler would get what's coming to him.

NINE

A canvas without paint. Red's face not that she needed any enhancement. She a natural beauty. Today not the time to be fancy sitting on the couch in Thomas Maxwell's condo. She never dressed up except for when they went out on the town and that has not happen since his coup against Pone. Her hair in a bun, white snug fit pull-over, black tight slacks, and black slipper shoes.

Red sat lady-like with her legs crossed with her arm resting on the arm of the couch. She didn't come there for anything romantic what-so-ever. Maxwell knew he in her dog house for trying to help Crowe put Pone behind bars. He thought until he realized he a pawn in the late deputy mayor's failed plans for revenge.

Maxwell took a deep breath. The first time Red came over not wearing a dress or skirt teasing him by showing off her gams. It made for interesting fore-play. Maxwell knew when they had sex it suited Red. The DA okay with that. This visit all business.

"So," Red cleared her throat. "You went to see my mother to convince her to sway me to support your campaign?"

"You didn't return my calls… you had your secretary send me away. So how else was I going to talk to you?"

Red swallowed hard. "Patience. After the stunt you pulled,"

Maxwell shrugged. "I didn't know Harvey had issues"

"That's putting it, mild."

"Pone is still a criminal and you can't erase what he did in the past like it never happened,"

Red straighten up and sat on the edge of the couch. "The current mayor... your opponent has given him a clean slate. I can switch over to his campaign so choose your words."

Red and Maxwell exchanged stares. Red knew she could never get away from her family's criminal activities. She wanted to keep clear of all their doings.

Maxwell knew Red on the straight and narrow for the law. She didn't involve herself in their criminal activities and he knew they still dealt in organize crime, but not into it heavy like J. Paul when he was alive.

"He stopped a gang war and he's my troubleshooter."

Maxwell nodded. "Okay he's a hero and he's doing good things now, but your family has a lot of influence in this town."

"You know Linda rubs shoulders with politicians,"

"She's great and all, but the city's not blind,"

The more Maxwell talked, she realize little chance of her being intimate with him again.

"Did you have anything to drink before I got here?" She asked.

"I didn't mean it that way I..."

"If you're the next mayor of this city I'd need control of your campaign." said Red.

"Your mother made it clear it would be best to have you than Linda."

"The matriarch knows best," Red relaxed back on the couch crossing her legs. *Mother thinks she so smart,* thought Red.

Red knew her mother discrete with the family business even when her father was alive. She wasn't innocent, but she never got involve.

Mary a passive voice behind the scene. She more than willing to let Linda take control of the family affairs and take a little help from Sue and Paul J. Mary ecstatic Red went into law and steer herself away from the family business. She felt Red would take the family name to cleaner pastures and the grandchildren would follow their aunt in the same fashion of success with out the baggage, Mary savvy about Maxwell running for Mayor. Linda dealt with council members speaking on the behalf of those with the best chance to win a seat on the council, but Mary considered that small time politics.

A future Mayor would benefit the family and Red knew her mother's thoughts.

Since she and Maxwell dated she should be the one giving a boost to his campaign.

Mary wouldn't even mind having a Mayor for a son in law. Organize crime and politics make for a strong allies in the city which would lead to a lot of blind eyes and cover ups. Maxwell an excellent chance to become mayor even with out her endorsement since the current mayor went into hiding till the gang war between the Hip-Hoppers and Prohibitions got resolve.

Mayor Winslow lost a lot of city's faith in him to be in charge. A spin doctor made Maxwell look like he went under cover to expose Crowe for intentions of starting a gang strife. Red's testimony gave him strong support. Even though Red and Maxwell knew it anything, but the truth. Red rescued his ass.

She chalked it up as something she could use for a rainy day if Maxwell became Mayor.

"I could use a drink. How about you?" asked Maxwell.

"Wine," said Red.

"Excellent choice," remarked Maxwell and took off to the kitchen.

The day getting close to noon and a drink might loosen things up. Their conversation gone to the egg shell level. Maxwell trying hard not to make ill advised remarks toward Pone pissing her off. He the District Attorney and his job putting away bad guys, Pone under Red's guidance to cleanse his soul.

People called her his guardian angel and Red cool with that since her father the devil made him do the things he did. Red laughed to herself thinking about an old phrase. The devil made me do it. Her dad wasn't a monster, but he was no saint either. He loved and provided for his family.

Maxwell came back with two half filled wine glasses. When Red got hers wasting no time taking a sip.

"I seem to have your mother's full support," said Maxwell.

Red studied the little man many whispered he wasn't in her league when they saw them out on a date. *Is he desperate and don't realize he's dealing with* the widow of a late kingpin of organize crime, thought Red. She knew her mother has her own motives.

"My mother is active in a lot of charities. Having her behind you can help."

"She gave a generous donation."

"Thomas, are you prepared to be a hip pocket politician?" questioned Red.

"Well, Brooke," Maxwell took two sips of wine. "I am short,"

Brooke, Red's birth name she only heard from family and colleagues.

They the organized crime society gave the nickname Red to her and Pone and those in his world recognize her as Red. Maxwell called her Brooke knowing the conversation taking a different turn.

"I'm being serious," said Red. "You know what my family is into and you need to be sure of our association,"

"I'll do whatever you want me to... " said Maxwell.

Red laughed. "Oh Thomas, my mother, brother, and sisters would welcome you with open arms. I run a legitimate law firm and stay away from my family doings that my father left behind. Do you understand me?"

"What politician don't have dirt on their hands?" asked Maxwell.

"The question I have for you is when you're willing to wash your hands of Pone?"

That's the curve ball, thought Red. Maxwell unaware of her family's arrangement she made with them concerning Pone. "Now you're getting nasty,"

"I love you. Brooke."

Another curve ball, thought Red. "You however accepted my mother's donation for your campaign,"

"You need money to run a campaign."

Red nodded. "And that wasn't some Morris code for us to take our relationship up a notch and dump Pone, was it?"

"Neither of us are getting any younger and when I become mayor I will sit down with your mother and get a mutual understanding,"

Red rose and stood above Maxwell which something he got used to.

"You will make a fine mayor. You have all the qualities for a strong leader. It will be an honor to endorse you and when you are sitting firm in your mayor's chair getting use to your surroundings, reality will settle in the Brigand family owns you."

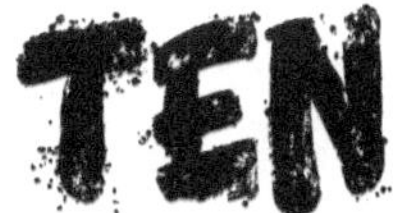

T he woman's voice on the GPS not Siri, but gave directions just the same. Pone and Ben destine to meet up with Jock. Ben drove and his profile like sitting in a recliner. A great view of the road because of his NBA height. Pone wasn't asleep, but rested his eyes during the drive.

"Didn't think we'd be seeing him again," said Ben.

Ben's bass voice better than a alarm clock. Pone eyes were wide like a full moon. He sat up straight.

"He sounded like he had something important to tell us," said Pone.

Ben snorted. "Well he hooked me up so I can't complain,"

Pone relaxed back to rest his eyes form, but not before he cut an open eye at Ben. He closed his eye and hoped Ben would remember they didn't come here to make noise. A simple rescue a young woman from prostitution and her pimp incest father. A catch and retrieve mission.

"Damn man you still tired?" Ben grinned at Pone. "That honey you met must be wearing you out,"

A upside down frown on Pone's lips. Lola would not be a long distance girlfriend and he doubt he'd stay in touch after they did the job. Pone has women in his life; Bird and Jade sisters, Red, well he didn't know what to categorize what between them except call her boss. Then there's Queen and he sabotage that relationship by not staying in touch. But they all knew how to handle themselves, important because of his lifestyle.

Lola lived a simple casual life with a knack for handling stress and she did it well. Whether she could handle his world of dodging bullets he did not know and didn't want to know. Pone didn't want to bring his world to her door.

"She's my contact like horse face is yours," said Pone.

"Anytime you want to trade just let me know,"

We're in too deep," said Pone.

Ben pursed his lips. "Shit'd... I ain't mad you and you know damn well your ass luck out,"

"Gambler's luck and remember you wanted the docks,"

"I'd settle for a Bahama mama," remarked Ben.

"This is business," said Pone. "The sooner we get this show on the road the better,"

Ben nodded. "Yeah I'm homesick too, but at least you got a beauty queen for a contact and I got me a horse-face motherfucker, but he seems cool though,"

Pone rested his head on the window and viewed the country side. Houses not fit to live in , but old people sat on the porch watching the grandchildren play in the mud dirt yard barefoot along with dead trees and shrubs.

The sun out and about the only good thing, but it shone on what looked like endless poverty of folks having a hard time making ends meet.

Some of the houses along the country side; peeling paint, rusted tin roofs, ripped screens kept pesky insects out, windows with card board box lids inserted where a glass window should have been.

The rented SUV made it to just trees and bushes and fields that crops would hope to occupy, but Pone glad for the different view. He made it a point not to judge people because of how he got his wealth, but if a nine to five job gave them their lifestyle then he wouldn't trade his for theirs. Pone mind went back to Ben now done with unpleasant distractions.

Ben never talked about women and sometimes Pone wondered about his large friend companionship. He knew how broken up he was about the death of his friend Al McGee. McGee had a woman and a father, but that didn't mean he a straight arrow. Pone would not question Ben about his sexuality and so far Ben showed no kind of affection towards him. *Maybe I'm not his type,* thought Pone and he smiled. He figured if Ben wanted to tell him about his sex life he would do it on his own time.

"Are we there yet?" asked Pone.

"Turn right and you will be at your destination," instructed the woman's voice on the GPS.

"Here we are," said Ben.

Pone was glad Ben didn't counter his comment with a if you don't settle down back there I will turn this car around.

A small silver aluminum weathered diner was the final destination. Ben parked in one of the available spaces between a late model copper colored Buick and black Ford F-150. Faded lines needing a paint over, but no vehicle parking outside the line. The Mid-night diner displayed a crescent moon logo.

Ben and Pone entered the greasy spoon shaped like a train car. Jock sat near the back around the counter in a what looked like a tight booth built for four.

Jock waved even though he knew the two men had already spotted him.

Pone looked at Ben. He said nothing, but could tell the man who gave them their toys had changed.

Jock still wore his permanent five-o-clock shadow stubble on his plump face. Pone wanted to lighten the mood with a why so glum chum. He and Ben slid inside the booth with Pone being sandwiched in between the two bigger men. Coffee cups were on the table along with cream and sugar.

"Glad you boys could make it," said Jock.

"After what you did for us no problem," said Ben.

Speak for yourself, thought Pone. He still didn't like that Jock gave Ben the heavy artillery of shotguns.

Jock shrugged. "I gave y'all What'cha needed to do your jobs if it called for it,"

Pone had a thing for accents like English, Irish, Australian, and now Cajun on his list. "Something must be going on for you to be out of your element."

A waitress built like a female wrestler wearing a sunflower color dress, white none skid shoes, wore her black gray streak hair in a bun, and had a big bright gap-tooth smile on her full face. Her name tag sitting on top of her left mountain of a boob said Myrtle.

Pone pressed his lips together, he knew this would be a serious conversation when he saw Myrtle carrying a pot of coffee like Jock told her to be ready for their arrival.

"These the two fine looking men you promised I'd be seeing?" said Myrtle.

"Well you sure didn't lie," she poured the coffee,

Pone a early morning coffee man and sometimes in the late mornings.

It early in the afternoon and he would make an exception this time.

"I aim to please," remarked Jock.

"Ain't you a big one," said Myrtle sizing up Ben. "And you so pretty," She smiled at Pone.

Ben blushed and Pone winked.

"Aw now, don't be teasing me and get me all worked up while on the job," She filled their cups. "Mister Jock you got yourself some fine looking friends, yes sir." Myrtle waddled her way back behind the counter. She pointed at their table and giggle with the other waitresses like school girls.

"I was expecting shot glasses and hard liquor. Not cups and coffee to keep me awake," said Pone.

"When you hear what I have to say you'll realize being here and drinking coffee the right choice," replied Jock.

Jock took a sip of his coffee no cream or sugar. He frowned and shook his head like he needed it. By his expression Ben and Pone knew he liked his coffee black and strong.

"You boys decided when you gonna make your move on Theiler?" asked Jock.

"What's your deal, Jock?" asked Pone. "You said so yourself the way to get close to him is to win big at poker."

"We ain't even scratched the surface yet," said Ben.

Jock leaned over his cup of coffee. "There's a little girl he got in his house about twelve... thirteen years old he is about to break in if you know what I mean,"

"Shit'd," growled Ben.

"What's this girl to you?" asked Pone.

Jock took another sip of coffee. "I met her mother at a river I was fishing at and saved her from a gator... "

"And she paid you in kind by having sex," commented Ben.

"No. It wasn't like that," said Jock. "She herself was like a child needing someone comfort her and I took her home, fed her and one thing led to another and then she told she had two sons to get back to," Jock straighten up. "You know how sometimes you meet someone and it feels right, but any way I didn't ask questions I took her home or back to hell,"

Pone added cream to his coffee. "The girl is your daughter?"

"Her mother's name is Amelia and she's Theiler's cousin." said Jock.

Pone bit his lower lip. "And he likes to keep things in the family,"

"Motherfucker," growled Ben.

"Her name is Mia and I don't know if she's mine or his, but she don't deserve what he's about to put her through," said Jock.

Ben gritted his teeth. "When I get my hands on him... "

"Easy big man," said Pone. "The playing field is changing,"

"I can pay you both," said Jock.

Pone sipped his coffee. "I want you to buy Mia as many dolls as She wants,"

"The guns are payment enough for me," said Ben.

Pone shook his head. "Anyway, how did you find out she was at Theiler's place."

Amelia's youngest son made it into town and called me from a phone. Her oldest son is at Theiler's house too working for him. I gave her my number and to use it if she ever needed me." said Jock.

"You said you took her back to hell?" questioned Pone.

Jock nodded." He keeps his family in a ghetto he calls a coral like their his cattle,"

"The more you talk about that snake the more I hate him." said Ben.

"Did you know at the time something related her to Theiler?' asked Pone.

"Look at me," Jock exhaled. "I ain't nobody who can afford to be choosy,"

Ben pursed his lips. "I know a thing or two about caring for somebody you don't know everything about,"

"Don't sell yourself short," said Pone. "Myrtle seems to fancy you,"

Jock smiled. "Yeah well, super models won't ever be on my menu,"

"How we gonna do this Pone?" Ben rubbed his hands. "Give it the bum rush?"

Pone gave a Ben a look. "We hit him where it hurts,"

Ben raised and eye-brow. "Okay that sounds like a plan I can work with,"

"Now Jock," Pone gave a stern look. "Child pornography is not how he build his empire right?"

Jock sipped his coffee. "He's in the drug business, and an arms dealer,"

Pone looked at Ben.

Ben straightened up. "Don't tell me I'm your guinea pig?"

"Too big for that," said Pone. "But horse-face may be the key to that door,"

Ben frowned. "Don't want to hurt the guy,"

"Finesse, Ben. You bait him." said Pone.

"When you say finesse?" questioned Ben.

"I speculate the drug trade comes in at the docks and his connection sit in at one of those dive bars waiting to supervise." said Pone.

"You know they distribute drugs in those fancy joints," said Ben.

Pone leaned on the table. "Focus Ben... I'm talking about the shipment and bartenders are more than just serving drinks,"

"You want me to hit horse-face for information?" asked Ben.

"I need you act like you're in need," said Pone.

"You want me to play an addict?" asked Ben.

"You ever did drugs before?" questioned Pone.

"Shit'd... and mess up my hand and eye ordination," remarked Ben.

"He knows you're a stranger so you have that in your favor. You need to convince him you're in the blow candy business," said Pone.

Ben frowned. "You want me to play an addict?"

Pone snorted. "You got any acting skills?"

Jock laughed.

Ben glared at Jock. 'You know I don't touch the stuff,"

"Either way," Pone cleared his throat. "Pusher or addict if you get to his man you going to sample the goods,"

Ben straightened up." I heard bad things for first timers and some of them ain't around to tell about it,"

"You ever heard of sleight of hand?" asked Pone.

"You a magician now?" questioned Ben.

"Get pass stage one and I will guide you the rest of the way," said Pone.

"We still playing poker?" asked Ben.

Pone stared into Ben's eyes. "I want to meet this Theiler Lereaux character up close and personal,"

Myrtle walked over flashing her gap-tooth smile. "Would you gentlemen care for anything to eat?"

"My usual," said Jock.

"What's his usual?" asked Ben.

Myrtle continued her good customer smile. "A beef patty melt with caramelized onions, fries on the side, and a large Orange soda."

Ben nodded. "I'll have the same,"

Myrtle smiled at Pone. "What about you, sir?"

Pone shook his head.

"What? You trying to watch your girlish figure?" asked Myrtle.

Pone knew in some if not all bars it was mandatory to buy a drink and doubted diners had the same policy. He had a cup a coffee in front of him he he didn't ask for and had yet to touch. But this a place of business and paying customers how they made their money.

Ben and Jock snickered.

Pone cupped his hands and placed them on the table. "Okay I'll have the shredded hash smothered with cheese and bacon and a diet coke."

"Ill have that too," said Ben.

"You will," remarked Myrtle. "And you gonna want desert, right?"

"What's the pie for today?" asked Jock.

Myrtle smiled. "Honey you in luck. We bake an apple pie with cinnamon sprinkled on top of the crust,"

"Bring the whole pie," said Ben.

"Ben?" questioned Pone.

"You and Jock can have a slice," said Ben.

"If we're lucky," replied Pone.

Myrtle smiled. "Coming right up,"

They watched her lumber away. Pone leaned on the table toward Jock.

"You know how he conduct his drug business?" asked Pone.

Jock scratched his head. "Can't say, but he like to have the young boys handle it,"

Pone snorted. "How young?"

"Well, they out of school, but look like they could still be in school. They look somethin' like them boys in your neck of the woods." said Jock.

Pone leaned back. "He got fronts all over the city... to get the answer we need, we will start at the docks,"

"So I am the guinea pig?" Ben nodded.

Pone patted Ben's broad shoulder." You okay with that?"

"As long as I don't play pool I should be okay," said Ben.

"I appreciate this big man," said Jock.

"I can't stand adults who bully kids," said Ben.

Myrtle came back with the food. Jock got his patty melt, fries, and big orange soda. Ben got the same along with the scattered and smothered shredded hash just like Pone. Then she placed the apple pie in the middle of the table. She smiled and served another customer.

All three men dug in. Pone washed his food down, not with the diet coke ,but a glass of water to wash down his food. Jock savored his patty melt and fries while Ben shoveled his food non-stop to his pie hole. He chewed, swallowed, and smiled.

There he stood right where he left him. Horse-face. Ben scanned the bar and saw nothing changed much since the last time. Peanut shells scattered over the bar, glass ring stains, and spilled beer and whiskey part of the dive bar decor.

Barflies and wannabe pool sharks laughing and make bets that some couldn't pay off.

Ben elated he didn't see the ones he left with busted and bloody noses. He relaxed and figured it for the best because now wasn't time for any trouble.

Ben made a beeline to the bar. Horse-face wiping it down.

"Remember me?" asked Ben.

Big lips parted and large strong teeth appeared. "Thought I'd seen the last of you. You gave those boys a real beat down... I knew you a hustler,"

"Man's got to make a living," remarked Ben. "I'm dry, give me somethin' to wet my whistle,"

"What can I do you for?"

Ben grabbed a handful of peanuts. "A cold beer,"

"Good choice to wash down salty peanuts," He slid a tall goblet of golden brew toward Ben.

Ben took a long swallow and nodded." Better make that a boiler maker,"

A bottle of Wild Turkey and a shot glass stamped the bar. Down the hatch and Ben frowned and twisted his neck. He grabbed his nose and pinched it like he smelled something. He pressed the right nostril and blew through the left and then did the same with the right and cleared his throat.

"You okay?"

"Just a habit I got and I'm pissed because I don't know who to talk to being new in town and all," said Ben.

Horse-face frowned. "And you came back here thinking I could be the answer,"

"I know you run a respectable establishment here and I mean you no disrespect."

"Asking for what? You have a sinus problem?"

Ben snorted. "How I know you ain't the law working under cover?"

"Would it be smart to ask me that?"

"Got all this money and it didn't come from hustling pool."

Ben squeezed his nose again.

"You're sure you all right?"

"I get this way when I need a hit… some blow… oh shit," said Ben.

"How do I know you ain't a cop?"

Ben sipped his beer. "Would it be smart to ask me that?"

Horse-face leaned forward and wiped the bar, "Leave me somebody's information,"

"Still interested in the poker game," said Ben.

"Seems like you and me might be real busy,"

Ben grabbed a napkin and took a pen from his pocket. He scribbled down his information. Horse-face put the cloth over the napkin and he and Ben gave each other a nod. Ben wasn't ready to hit the road so he took his beer and strolled over to the pool tables.

ELEVEN

"What if I have to snort the shit?" asked Ben.

Pone shrugged. "You got to be convincing,"

"You know I don't do drugs. That shit will mess your hand and eye coordination,"

Pone reached in his pocket and handed Ben a plastic pouch with a white powder substance.

"Shit'd," growled Ben. "You trying to tell me something?"

"I know baking soda to have many uses according to my Pinterest board. All good in case you're wondering," said Pone.

"You into that social media shit?" questioned Ben.

"It passes the time," shrugged Pone. "Anyway, if you didn't screw up then the supplier should hand you a sample in a small plastic bag and then your sleight of hand comes into play."

"Turning me into a fucking magician," mumbled Ben.

"Whoever sells you the coke might want to know if you have a habit or if you distribute,"

Ben shook his head. "Jock don't have my background intact then you can forget about it,"

"No need to worry about that, you saw how torn up he was about that little girl," said Pone.

"You think this woman playing him?"

"A man like him so down on his looks would care, he'd take having a kid anyway he can get one. One thing for sure, they did have sex. I like Jock and I don't plan on raining on his parade." Pone gave Ben a look.

"Why I got to be the bad guy? The man gave me my guns so you now..." Ben smiled. "You know I don't like impromptu jobs,"

Pone pursed his lips. "Well at least both girls are in the same place."

"And you think messing with his drug business is away to get to his attention?"

"I want to get to him on two fronts and it might keep his mind off those girls,"

"Put that son-of-a-bitch in prison and he wouldn't last a day with his reputation." said Ben.

"Funny how criminals have a credo about things. You can be a cold bloody killer and look down upon criminals who prey on children." Pone shrugged.

"Strange world we live in,"

"Amen to that brother," said Ben.

"You think you convinced horse-face?" asked Pone.

"Damn man," Ben shook his head. "I did what I could to let him know I need the stuff,"

Pone raised an eye-brow." I should have done... "

"I got this," roared Ben.

Pone grabbed his bowler and twirled it around his finger.

"You don't have faith in me, man?" asked Ben.

"Waiting for you to calm down and what you did is what worries me."

"You saying I ain't smart enough to pull this off?"

"I brought you along because of your good looks," said Pone.

A long stare down, a long pause, then loud laughter.

Pone placed his bowler on the small table.

"I will leave it in your hands big man, but you can't over do it,"

Ben nodded. "Yeah, I caught myself over doing it and tone it down. I even mentioned the poker game,"

"Like you said you don't touch the stuff." said Pone.

"Then again when I see him again, I might get a bullet to the head,"

"Jock will come through," said Pone. "He didn't give me any details, but he sound like somebody who has fixed alot of backgrounds,"

"Got to be honest "Ben shrugged. "Till I talked to you,"

"Look at it as a high-stakes poker game. You got your poker face on and..."

Ben cleared his throat. "I see where are you going and again

I got this," Ben studied the bag of baking soda. "Got to work on this slight of hand. I don't want my body asking me what the hell is going on if I have to take the real shit,"

"Trust your instincts," said Pone.

"You'll be outside, right?" asked Ben.

"Blending in with the environment," said Pone.

"Everything goes as it should, you text me describing what the guy looks like and when he leaves, I will tail him."

"You sure you got that taken care of?" questioned Ben.

"Jock will provide me with a jalopy that looks like it belongs unless it's a high class establishment."

Ben smiled." It's a dump and you know I could tail the guy,"

Pone snorted." You'd be like Clark Kent."

"What do you mean?"

Pone got moon-eye. "Please don't tell me you were like the characters in the comic and TV shows and movies unable to see through the disguise. You know how lame for a suit and eye-glasses to prevent you from seeing him as Superman."

Ben's eyes rotated, and he rubbed his chin." Yeah, yeah... I get the point,"

"Let me handle the stealth stuff," said Pone.

Pone relieve Ben saw it his way. He also wonders if the giant a little off his game when told about his nose problem in front of horse-face. Ben mourning over Al McGee and Pone knew amateur night the way he went about trying to convince the bartender he's a coke head. That an amateur move and Ben should have known better.

Pone feared that horse-face might have played along and Ben could be heading for a big set up. He knew about the fight with the locals and thought he'd seen the last of the big man. A bar fight in the parking lot, but in their world if you survive you didn't go back ever again, but a gamble and he and Ben gamblers. They both liked Jock and saw the man in pain.

Pone all about helping people like two innocent girls trapped in a house of horrors and what he and Ben sacrifice for people in need of their help. Pone looked into Ben's eyes and knew he insulted his friend taking a big risk. Pone would do his best to let his large chum know he believe in him.

"You be careful... be yourself and text me,"

Ben nodded. "I'll keep my head on a swivel knowing I'm returning to no-man's-land."

"We good big man?"

"Solid," said Ben.

Pone laughed. He like the sound of Ben's base voice, and knew the big man would rather use the toys Jock gave him. Pone did not want that. They would lose lives and Pone wanted to cut down on the body count. The more he heard about Theiler, he wouldn't mind adding him to the blab sheet's obituary.

TWELVE

The table had a nice spread: fried gator to dip in hot and barbecue sauce, biscuits, dirty rice with all the spices to set your mouth ablaze, saute asparagus tips, crawfish, and an assortment of alcoholic drinks to get your buzz on. Theiler and Ludwig drank bourbon and their guest did the same.

"Senator," crowed Theiler's gravel voice. He washed his gator morsel down with bourbon. "So how was she?"

Senator Robert George Boatman cut from the same cloth like Theiler, he too prefer to pop cherries of under age young virgins. His belly kept him arms length from the table. A pointy bald top, thin gray strand hair around it over lapping ears, and a skin growth on his bird beak nose. The senator resembled a vulture. He frowned at the food while Theiler and the giant Ludwig dug in devouring ever bite. Boatman seemed to enjoy the liquor put before him.

"I'm disappointed Theiler," Boatman sipped his bourbon.

Theiler shoveled more food into his mouth. Food tumbled out when he talked. "How so?"

Boatman frowned. "She cried which killed the mood. Couldn't do a damn thing,"

Theiler shrugged." Well it's her first time,"

"I wanted to take her virginity," said Boatman.

Theiler laughed and more food came out. "You and me both,"

"Say what?" questioned Boatman.

"I test drive the cars before they leave the lot," said Theiler.

Boatman downed his drink and frowned. "Rumor is... "

"Ain't no rumor," howled Theiler. "Blue-bloods,"

Boatman downed another drink and leaned forward. "You mean to tell me... "

"Oh it don't stop or start there: sisters, nieces, cousins, and aunts if they still good-looking and good to go if you know what I mean," grinned Theiler.

Boatman gasped. "You sick Bastard!"

A big massive fist pounded the table. Ludwig straightened.

"Now see what you done do. You upset Ludwig. He don't like it when people disrespect me," said Theiler.

Boatmen looked at the man mountain. He couldn't see his eyes hidden under the thick black bush of hair, but heavy breathing from his nose that looked like a snout and food trapped in his beard from bad table manners along with his heaving body made Boatman realize he better know his place.

Theiler tossed a piece of fried gator in the air and caught it in his plump buccal. "You got nerve passing judgment on me." Theiler pointed an asparagus at Boatman then bit off the tip." You and I cut from the same cloth,"

"I don't do relatives," said Boatman.

Theiler let out a loud belch. "You a pedophile just like me. If they children then it is wrong in the eyes of many whether they related to you or not. The difference between you and me is I like keeping it in the family."

Boatman clenched his fist. After all, he a state senator and despite his perverted ways he didn't like eating in the company of filth. Being around Theiler made him look pale holding his stomach,. He felt like an alcoholic who needed a drink and a smoker in need of nicotine.

"You watch how you talk. I'm a senator." said Boatman.

"Yes you are and I always wanted me one, ain't that right, Ludwig said Theiler."

Ludwig laughed so hard he farted. Boatman covered his mouth and nose.

"Woo-wee, that Ludwig can let it fly can't he," crowed Theiler. "Ludwig, boy we got to work on your manners in front of important people, but I'll excuse it this time," Boatman fanned the air. "What did you mean you always wanted a senator?"

"My hip pocket," smiled Theiler. "People know you are here, but not what you doing here, but they know my reputation and that ain't good for you."

"You can't blackmail me ," said Boatman

"I wouldn't do that to a partner," replied Theiler.

"What are you getting at, Lereaux?" questioned Boatman. "If we were to be partners and that will not happen, I didn't get what I came here for."

The table creaked with the weight of Ludwig's elbows resting on top.

Theiler took another drink and cleared his throat. "The reason you ain't dead is because Ludwig knows how important you are and as for you not getting what you want is your own damn fault." snorted Theiler. "You scared the poor girl. What were you thinkin' letting her see you in the buff? Your body looked like somethin' out of a old black and white science fiction movie. Big saggy sacks and a pecker so small you piss on your balls."

Ludwig's head leaned back and he howled with laughter.

Boatman rose from the table. "How the hell... " He closed his mouth and swallowed hard. "You got me on tape,"

"I know you don't want your wife of thirty years, two boys and that little girl to know your bad habits." said Theiler. "If that little girl of yours was mine... well I better stick to business,"

"What do you want, Theiler?" sighed Boatman.

"I want in on that land development deal you done approve." said Theiler.

"I know there's a lot of money in real estate,"

"Don't you ever mention my daughter again," demanded Boatman.

"Hey, Ludwig," voiced Theiler," Guess the good senator don't think of his little girl when he sniffing other little girls panties,"

Boatman sank back down in his chair and stared at the table.

"Cheer up, senator," taunted Theiler. "I got a girl upstairs just right for you …she's older, but she'll satisfy you as long as you keep your clothes on," He and Ludwig laughed. "I notice you didn't touch the food and that's disrespecting me," Theiler gave a look. "I can see the built, you love to eat."

"Not a crime not to have an appetite," remarkedBoatman.

"I've had my belly full and Ludwig's manners played a hand in that," said Theiler. "You though, go on ahead eat so we can get this partnership off to a good start, Ludwig's presence is still in the air, but consider it more flavor to the food. I don't approve of that thing at the table when it's time to eat and trust me it won't happen again. Oh senator don't be so glum because you are now a member of a special club; I have judges, lawyers, other councilmen, and even athletes on tape so it's all good. Now you eat up if you want to go up stairs and I know you do."

Boatman took a fork full of dirty rice while Ludwig dragged out a long loud fart.

THIRTEEN

There he stood right where he left him, but then again where else would horse-face be if not tending bar. The man works as a bartender and how else would people talk to him if he wasn't in this profession. Horse-face wasn't talking to anybody in particular, but just wiping down the bar. A few patrons at the bar and one of them looked asleep.

The other two shooting the breeze about nothing much. Playing pool good for passing time. Women could have pass for men by their built and they played pool too. The dive wasn't too far off from being a gay bar of homely men.

What was it that Pone said... *oh yeah, be yourself not too anxious and not too cool*, thought Ben. Practice makes perfect.

Ben lumbered up to the bar and nodded to horse-face. Bartender squinted, snorted like a sting taking place rotating his eyes to the right toward a table in a dark corner. Ben nodded and made a beeline over to the table.

Pone stood in a short line at the Circle K two blocks away from the dive bar. He buying; chips, candy bars, and jerky, stake out food. Two small bags of *Lance Star bites* candied coated peanuts and three bags of TGIF'S cheddar and bacon potato skins and a bottle of *Turkey Hill* diet green tea made with Ginseng, Honey, and Mango. This wasn't his usual food, but he decided to splurge.

The snacks cost twenty bucks and some change. Pone gave the clerk, a short stocky scruffy thirty something white male who ask if he wanted a receipt and Pone shook him off and left the store.

❖ ❖ ❖ ❖ ❖ ❖

Ben stood in front of the table. The bar light dim. But where the man with the snow sat made him look like one of those informants whose voice disguise so he couldn't be recognize. All the viewers would see a deep voice talking silhouette.

"Have a seat big man. Hurting my neck," said the silhouette.

Ben sat. The voice not deep, but boyish. Ben got a better look at the figure and instead of a grown man the figure more like a boy.

Pone sat in a 1980 black Ford GT mustang that needed a paint job. The hood look like sweat stains you'd see on a ball cap. It's what Jock gave him and the car blended well in it's environment. Pone got busy working on his munchies. He started with the potato skins, but didn't finish them because the salt made his tongue dry. A swallow of the green tea took care of that and he turned his attention to the candied peanuts.

After a few chews, he took a break to scan the area. The dive bar right at home near the docks. Only low life and people down on their luck would go to or hang out at such a place. He thought the commercials he saw hyping up the vacationers to travel down to New Orleans for a great time. Pone shook his head. What a load of crap, he thought. Just like Hollywood they show the good, not the bad and ugly. The docks ugly and not because of the tragic the big easy had been through, but like any city some parts are forgotten or overlooked. Pone snorted. He had to give the disgusting Theiler Lereaux credit for using the decaying side of the city to bring in his product smart. No doubt his connect foreign.

The Russians? If so they would be easy to spot with their hard facial features; both men and women had that superior serious look about them.

Must be the DNA. It wedged in. The Albanians could be another connect, but easy to point out with their cold-hearten ways dealing with anyone who got in their way. Germans could also be a major player or the Yakuza, but would be hard to go around town being discreet since they wore tattoos like clothing. From the neck down to the feet detailed body art. Pone shook his head. He heard a painful process that lasted for days and he knew a club he wanted no part of The Mexican Cartel could have a hand up Theiler's ass helping him in his drug business. Whoever back the monster, Pone wanted to make them angry as Theiler starting from the bottom working his way up.

❖ ❖ ❖ ❖ ❖ ❖

"You got the stuff?" asked Ben.

"Whoa big man," said the boy silhouette. "How do I know you ain't five-o? This could be a shake down and I ain't down with that,"

Ben chuckled because for a moment the boy silhouette made him feel like he was back in Metro talking to a hip-hopper with street slang.

"Busted. Yo ass under arrest," said Ben.

Silhouette leaned forward and his youthful face matched his voice. He leaned back and relaxed. "Ain't no damn cop. Look dangerous and shit, but ain't no po po. I ain't sayin' they ain't dangerous, but you ain't one,"

"Then you know not to fuck with me," said Ben.

"Hey," Silhouette spread out his arms like a preacher in the pulpit.

"I'm just a business man,"

Ben rose from the table and headed for the restroom. He glanced over his shoulder at silhouette then entered the restroom. Disgusting. No surprise to Ben. The barroom nothing classy so why would the restroom be. Empty except for one stall where someone inside dropping an ass bomb. The odor swarming and toxic which made it unbearable since no air condition and ventilation to take out the odor. A small window above in the back-wall only Ben could reach closed. Ever heard of a courtesy flush, thought Ben. The man who came out of the stall looked like he could shit bricks and he did. Average height with a pitcher mound belly. Thick Brillo beard, balding thin hair and saggy workman jeans that showed his butt crack. The whole restroom populated with the smell and the man looked at Ben like he wanted to say hey it's not meant to smell good.

Ben wanted to tell the man he prove shit smell wasn't supposed to be pleasant. The man stood at the sink and washed his hands and Ben gave him credit for doing that. Silhouette walked in and allowed some of the odor to escape. He wasted no time pulling his shirt over his face just underneath his eyes. The man walked by them both and looked at them as if to say like you two don't take a shit.

Silhouette kept his shirt over his nose. "You sure you want to do this here... now?"

"Time is money," remarked Ben.

"If you gonna test the product you gonna sniff more than coke,"

Ain't that the truth, thought Ben. He reached inside his shirt and took out a thick envelope giving it to Silhouette. "Didn't know how much, but this should do it,"

Silhouette took the envelope and flipped thorough it like a Rolodex His mouth peeked from under his shirt and he smiled. "More than you know," Then he returned his face back under his shirt.

Ben took out a razor blade, small mirror, then rolled up a dollar bill. He looked at Silhouette smiling from ear to ear giving him a tea bag of coke.

Sleight of hand, thought Ben. Thanks to his large hands he held a tea bag of baking soda pressed tight under his thumb and lower part of his forefinger. When Silhouette placed the coke in the palm of his hand, Ben looked toward the door as if someone was coming in and when the youth turned to look he took his other hand grabbing the coke putting it in his pocket. Silhouette turned back to see Ben pouring the white powder on the mirror and cutting rows with a razor blade.

Ben frowned from snorting the baking soda. It burned and he decided one snort should convince the youth. Ben pinched his nose looking up at the lad and nodded.

Silhouette smiled.

"Let's get some fresh air," recommended Ben.

Pone was right, thought Ben. He didn't need Pone to tell him his big hands would come in handy, but practicing the sleight of hand technique hiding the small bag of baking soda inside his big mitts and the dim lighting in the restroom didn't hurt along with the overwhelming odor from the guy blowing up the toilet more than a distraction. Ben squeeze his nose as if to get rid of the stench.

Silhouette gave his contact number and took off while Ben parked himself at the bar nursing a drink. A few bar stools down sat the guy who left the tang in the restroom. He gave Ben an icy glare who in return pinched his nose till the man went back to nursing his own drink.

Pone yawned, stretched, and rubbed his eyes then reacted to zip sound on his cell. (**Average height lanky kid leaving bar now**) read Ben's text. Pone looked toward the bar entrance. He saw what Ben describe, the kid looked to be early twenties getting inside a black Bentley. *The drug trade good,* thought Pone. He text Ben back acknowledging he got the message. Pone counted to ten giving the young drug dealer a head start. Pone put away his phone pursuing the delinquent.

FOURTEEN

Mia wiped her eyes. Tara held her like a mother. She knew her attempts to keep Mia from being violated by Theiler will be futile since he preferred young virgin girls taking pride breaking them in as he saw it. Tara wanted to vomit. Mia continued to whimper burying her face in Tara's bosom. Tara tried rocking her to sleep and felt like crying herself, but knew she needed to keep a brave face for the the both of them.

Tara no longer wanted to use her body to stop Theiler from having sex with Mia. Every time he rode her she puked afterwards, Tara glanced over her shoulders when he gave it to her doggy-style. The pedophile closed his eyes smiling from the pleasure he got from her young tight firm body. Tara gritted her teeth thinking about his callous hands clawing her flesh, pinching, and squeezing her breast and buttocks.

She understood it would be a tall task and she'd have to continue protecting Mia from a non-fictional monster not hiding in the closet or under her bed. Tara pondered how long could she continue to distract him until he figured out what she's doing.

She thought about Beef and letting him go through with his plan to murder Theiler. Tara shook it off calculating Beef would end up getting himself killed. She felt Mia lifting her head from her chest.

"You okay?" asked Tara.

Mia nodded." I'll try to be brave this time,"

Tara observed Mia's eyes reading the floodgates would open again once the child saw the out of shape fleshy pervert in his birthday suit with a body made for a bad science fiction movie approaching her. Tara snapped her fingers looking Mia straight in the eyes.

"You like playing games?"

Mia nodded.

"Okay," Tara inhaled. "I'll be right back,"

Mia clutched Tara's hand. "Promise?"

Tara exhaled. "Cross my heart," To say hope to die would be a poor choice of words, she thought. "You lie down and before you know it I'll be back,"

Tara positioned Mia on her side, lying with her back to the door. She hopped off the bed heading across the hall to her room.

Pone followed Silhouette to a barbershop located in a business park. Vacancy on most of the buildings and the Barbershop a school for future hair-cutters. He drove around back and saw loading docks. It was not the first time he'd seen business park facilities with a loading dock attachment having nothing to do with loading cargo. Before Pone toured the business park he saw Silhouette enter the front glass doors with the help of a tall string-bean youth looking to be the same age as Silhouette. Pone got suspicious when he didn't enter the building with his own key and knew the barbershop offered more than just hair-cuts. His curiosity Pied Piper him to investigate further and he drove and noticed a light house shape sand white shape pillar. No light at the top, and something rotten in Denmark.

Two twenty-somethings sat on the dock sharing a fag. Silhouette open the door chewing out the boys for taking a break. Pone smirked thinking drug dealers on the clock. Guess they too have a deadline to meet for their buyers. He got a good view parking in a small wooded area he shared with a raccoon and a doe. The two slackers shared one last puff and toss the butt away following Silhouette inside the pillar. The pillar tower got Pone's attention.

⋟⋞ ⋟⋞ ⋟⋞ ⋟⋞ ⋟⋞ ⋟⋞

Tara came back to Mia's room. The girl did what she hoped falling asleep. Tara did not want to wake her. She stood over the child, young, innocent, wondering about Mia's mental state. A little girl should be home playing with dolls, pretend tea parties and not forced to entertain disgusting perverted men. Tara sat on the bed caressing Mia's back. She turned over rubbing her eyes then smiled.

"Sorry to disturb your sleep," said Tara.

"You came back,"

"Told you I would,"

"I'm just glad it's you," said Mia.

Tara swallowed hard thinking poor child. She gave Mia a napkin with Alka seltzers.

Mia got moon-eye shaking her head." I'm not sick,"

"I know, but these can help keep the bad men away,"

Mia's eyes welled-up.

"No, no.... don't cry," whispered Tara. "I may not always be around to help you and you'll have to take care of yourself,"

"Where are you going?"

Tara inhaled." I promise to take you with me, but for now we'll have to be brave,"

Mia looked at the seltzers. "I'm not sick,"

"Keep them hidden and use them when needed,"

Mia shrugged. "How will I know?"

Tare held her hand and smiled." We all have something inside that tells us when to do the right thing. You'll know," Mia nodded.

❖❖ ❖❖ ❖❖ ❖❖ ❖❖ ❖❖

The business parked deserted and Pone knew the barbershop wasn't doing any hair-cutting this time of night. He left the car parked on a hidden trail inside the wooded area in walking distance. Pone approached the pillar door, putting on a tech visor with an attached light and magnifying lenses. The door old with a knob not modern day with a bolt type lock and Pone sighed a relief knowing he needed to work fast. He took out a wallet size pouch flipping the flap revealing a set of picking tools: Hooks, Diamonds, Rakes, and Tension. Pone didn't bring a lock picking gun and TV makes it look so easy, you slide it in, click, and wallah the lock is picked. Not so fast, but he didn't bring one.

Pone shook off the thoughts to concentrate on the task at hand. He chose a crooked serpent tip and like a snake the raking pick move in and autonomous in the upper half of the keyway coming in contact with all pins. Pone inserted the tension tool into the bottom of the keyway applying in the direction to unlock the lock. Tension wrenches are not made too solid and too much pressure would break it. Lock picking more delicate, but nothing like diffusing a bomb. The lock picker must develop a light touch with the hand that applies pressure.

Pone knew if the tension too heavy, the top pins will bind below the shear line-line and will not allow the breaking point to meet the shear-line. He applied light tension proceeding with the raking operation slow snapping with upward pressure on the pins with the tip. Pone practiced the technique over and over and he unlocked the door. Pone put away his tools, turned off his light entering pillar. An elevator. Pone shook his head, *what the hell is this Johnny Quest?*, he thought. He took a a five inch carbon hook blade tiger claw knife controlling it with his thumb inside the end circled loop. Pone pressed the button to the elevator.

Two triangular shape lights pointing in opposite directions. The one pointing upward glowed red. Pone got in a low stance waiting for who ever would be inside the elevator. He didn't want to kill another young person like he did the youths in Metro.

"What the hell!"

Tara heard a man screamed across the hall from Mia's room. Her door opened to the sound of heavy feet and a dangling belt buckle racing down the hall. She rushed to the door putting her on the white antique design like the other architecture making the house look civilized from the horror reality. Her ear glued to door and 2 minutes later she heard more heavy feet pounding the hallway to Mia's room.

Tara recognized Theiler's gravel voice cursing in English and Cajun frustrated at Mia for scarring off a perverted man with power who he wanted to place inside his back pocket to blackmail to do his bidding. She also heard another familiar voice. Dr. Theron Brogan, a dented bald head, beak nosed, thick nest of white hair from the ears to his shoulders, pale skin, chiseled face, and bulging eyes. He looked like a walking vulture towering over the average human dressed in black like a undertaker.

The creepy looking doctor carried a kind heart under his white banded collar shirt and his paper thin skin underneath it. He not one of Theiler's loyal subjects and if not for a fabricated malpractice suit he would still be a resident doctor employed at the city hospital. Brogan a victim of human ignorance, His colleagues couldn't get use to his appearance.

They called him the mad scientist behind his back though the whispers were loud enough for him to hear, but building a tough skin since childhood enable him to ignore them. The staff convinced the board that the mad scientist took organs and DNA to do unlawful things and when his patients the ones knocking on death's door, but had a chance to pull through... his mortality rate too high and he was let go.

He didn't argue, fight, or dispute the claim of not being suitable to practice medicine and knew some of his fellow sawbones paid his patients unauthorized visits leading to their deaths.

Brogan felt his god given looks would not change the minds of those holding his fate in their hands. He tired of people not being able to look him in the eyes, acting nervous around him, frowning, glaring at him like a Frankenstein monster without pitchforks and torches.

So with what money he saved up he built his own practice on the low down catering to patients with gunshot wounds they didn't want to have reported to the police which meant not going to the hospital.

Theiler got wind of the mad scientist a nick name Brogan used as a motivator to prove those who wronged him wrong. He knew Theiler to be a snake in the grass, but Brogan no fool knowing he had to make a living agreed to work as a syndicate doctor.

Tara liked the doctor because he kept her and other girls from the house of sin even when they were good and healthy for a length of time. He didn't approve of Theiler, but again the mad scientist no fool knowing he needed to eat and a place to live. Tara hoped Mia would see the kindness inside the man and ignore his creepy outside. Tara listened as the two men voices got loud.

"What's wrong with the girl?" asked Theiler.

"Foaming at the mouth... can be anything," replied Brogan.

"That ain't telling me shit,"

"Rabies could be... "

"Hell no!" roared Theiler." Ain't no dogs in the house,"

"How would you know what your band of perverts do to these girls?" questioned Brogan.

"You just fix her doctor... do your damn job," said Theiler.

"I can't treat her here," said Brogan

94

"How the hell long is it going to take?" asked Theiler.

"You want her in tip top shape?" responded Brogan.

"You keep them so damn long," remarked Theiler.

"I like to make sure my patients are well before I send them back to you," said Brogan.

"Alright already do what you got to do," said Theiler.

Tara cracked the door and smiled seeing the doctor cradle Mia in his arms like a baby.

Mia did what she hoped buying her some time from Theiler and his perverts. The mad scientist will keep Mia for a length of time.

Men and women stripped down to their underwear cooking the product. The workers not as young as their bosses and a good hire considering mature people are more reliable than the young when it comes to labor and less to worry about than compensating drugs for themselves. The workers wore surgical mask covering their mouth and nose keeping them from getting high.

Barbershop is a front, thought Pone. He didn't doubt the boys didn't have hair cutting skills, but today's youth would rather find an easy way to make money rather than get their hands dirty by earning an honest living. You get a kid in the barber chair and the barber starts a conversation like the average coiffeur he or she acts like a concerned bartender, psychiatrist an unlicensed shrink listening to your problems getting you to respond to questions.

Theiler spent a lot of money to have an underground Johnny Quest cocaine lab, thought Pone. He nodded thinking how blowing up this operation would give the incest pedophile crime lord a heart attack losing this source of income. Pone saw all he needed heading back up to the top level. He braced himself in case he ran into trouble. The doors opened and all clear. He eased outside the door locking it shut.

Pone inhale and before he could gather his thoughts on what he witnessed he heard voices coming his way from the barbershop. Pone knew he couldn't make it to the car parked in the woods without being seen so he climb inside a dumpster. The lid open with trash bags inside. Pone buried himself under the trash bags. He coughed from he stench as the door opened. Pone braced himself after hearing Silhouette.

"You hear something?" asked Silhouette.

"Could be a damn raccoon," said a bored voice.

"Dump that shit and closed the lid," ordered Silhouette. "It stinks out here,"

Pone felt two more bags fall on top of him and then lid slammed shut. He listened for the pillar door opened by rattling keys and the pulled shut with force and the humming elevator. Pone eased the lid open peeking enough making sure the coast clear before climbing out of the dumpster. He made a beeline to the car and he sat in thought before turning the ignition.

Pone shook his head. *A coke and arms dealer too,* he thought. Quite a resume` Theiler built for himself. He sat in the car musing putting his trip to the big easy in perspective. Pone concluded Red knew nothing more than Tara getting abducted and taken back to a life of incest and child prostitution. His stomach didn't get queasy, but burned with anger thinking about the disgusting monster Theiler.

Pone felt nauseous from the garbage odor on his clothes and Lereaux though he never met him made him sick too. The sadistic sleazebag built his empire on porn, blackmailing powerful people though they too not so innocent and getting their just deserts for being more than perverts, cocaine distribution, and an arms dealer.

The trip went from catch and retrieve to taking down a monster rearing his ugly head far too long. Pone nodded smiling because now he knew where and how he could hurt the son-of-a-bitch. Cocaine and weapons dealing involve a conglomerate of the cartel and Pone knew enough if you disappoint your buyers who depended on you to deliver because they too catered to their buyers they didn't want to disappoint.

Syndicate food chain nothing to take for granted once you screw up you lose your credibility and your source of income along with a bad reputation for being unreliable.

Refund the money paid to you or end up in the bone yard. What bothered Pone the most, he knew nose candy and firearms led to deaths. Young deaths and he had his fill of young people and planned on avoiding while retrieving Tara. A territory worth crossing if it meant putting a bullet between Theiler Lereaux eyes.

If anybody deserved lead poisoning it would be him. Pone sniff and frown in need of a hot soapy shower.

FIFTEEN

Pawn Shop Basement

Jock sank into depravity since he found out he may have a daughter captive in Theiler Lereaux house of horrors. The thought of Mia molested by the troll and his club of perverts made him morbid.

"If I knew away to tell her everything going to be all right," said Jock.

Pone inhaled pursing his lips. He knew Jock for a short time, but saw a different person than the burly energetic nonchalant business man supplying he and Ben with their tools of the trade paid for by Red. He now looked at a man deflated and helpless about a little girl he may or may not have any connection to.

"The wheels are turning slow," said Pone. "But I feel it's moving in the right direction," Jock shook his head throwing down another shot of hash and stamped the empty glass on the table.

Pone frowned. "You keep hitting the sauce like that and you might not be around to to see your little girl,"

Pone didn't know whether or not Mia was Jock's daughter, but felt it would lift the man's spirit to hear someone else say the girl's his daughter.

"Handling liquor is not a problem for me," said Jock.

Ben toasted." Amen brother,"

Pone gave Ben a look.

"What?" shrugged Ben. "I hate seeing a man drink alone,"

"I told you," pointed Pone." You and I need to keep a clear head,"

Pone knew Ben to get his drink on happy hour or not the giant didn't mind downing alcohol. Ben preferred beer over whiskey unless a drink partner and fortunate for him he didn't mind helping Jock drown in his sorrels.

"When you boys going to make your move?" asked Jock.

"As soon as my man here give the nod," replied Ben.

Pone eyed Jock knowing the liquor taking over his thoughts and

Ben wasn't helping with his drinking and wanting to set off fireworks. Lucky for the both of them Pone wanted to be a fly in the ointment for one of Theiler's operations.

"Pone snorted. "Got any explosives?"

Jock rose grabbing the bottle of rot gut. Pone exhaled wishing he left it behind.

The depressed man took a long swallow of the bourbon leading Pone and Ben to a wall near the back of the basement. Jock walked to what looked like a simple old fashioned light chain. He pulled and the wall open it's mouth. Pone and Ben saw everything from C4 to TNT to blow up a city block. Ben motioned to Jock to hit him with another shot and drew the ire of Pone. The giant returned a glare of his own as if to say I'm a grown ass man.

Pone shook his head." Messes up your hand and eye coordination,"

"I don't plan on killing anybody," Ben sipped." Ought to make you feel better,"

"Poker game," said Pone.

"Yea have so little faith," grumbled Ben.

Pone gave Jock and his bottle a long look as if trying a Jedi mind trick telepathic convincing him not drink anymore around Ben. Jock walked to front putting the rye away for later. Ben stood like a child wanting to play after the game was over.

He put his empty glass inside his pocket. Jock returned.

"Why you need the fireworks?" asked Jock.

Pone didn't want to build up Jock's hope telling him he planned to make a dent in one of Theiler's source of income and even though Ben seemed stoic with not taking the aggressive approach, he knew Ben chomped at the bit to get violent. Pone saw the fire in his eyes telling him about the brawl outside bar.

"I want to make Theiler cry," remarked Pone.

Jock frowned. "You going to blow him up?"

Ben nodded. "Yeah," he growled in his base voice. "A program I'm with,"

"You're Ben the giant... not Sonny the grenadier,"

Ben straighten folding his arms. "Since when you became a bomb expert?"

"I don't mean interrupt a lovers quarrel," said Jock.

"But Theiler enjoys breaking in new Phillies,"

Pone looked at Jock. He respected the man for picking up his vibe about Ben needed to keep a clear head and took away his bottle of sorrow. "We will do everything we can, but he may have already violated her,"

"Son-of-a-bitch!" roared Ben.

"Blowing up his money will take his mind off the girls." said Pone.

"You think I will let you bum rush that fucker alone... "

"Ben!" Pone inhaled." Fire and smoke,"

 Ben shook his head." I ain't following you?"

"He don't know we're here and I plan to keep it that way until we get up close and personal and that's when we do your bum rush thing," replied Pone.

"And in the meantime?" questioned Ben.

"Let me make the noise my way," Pone exhaled." Look at this like a bomb, cut the wrong wire... ,"

"You ain't need to go all college on me," grumbled Ben. "I'll back you all the way,"

Pone felt he weathered the storm. Both Jock and Ben needed patience. He understood Jock having a father instinct of rescuing a child who may not share the same DNA. Ben came from a life of violence leading to a life of taking lives to make a living and relieving stress. Pone understood Jock drowning his anguish in a bottle of rotgut thinking about the monster Theiler Lereaux having his way with innocent girls.

Ben who he brought with him to provide muscle Pone felt that would come in play later on to complete the mission, but Ben had his own demons to face and Pone thought it would be best he did it away from home.

"He owns a ship down at the docks," said Jock." Don't know whether I mentioned it?"

Pone nodded. "Makes sense with the big easy being an import and export and explains where he gets his contraband."

"If you plan on doing your thing you got to know what ship he owns," said Ben.

"That's where you come in," replied Pone.

Ben wore a dubious expression. "What do you want me to do now?"

Pone gave a stern look. "I brought you here for muscle and that's part true... you haven't live this long in what we do by being careless,"

Ben straighten up beyond his six-nine frame beaming with pride taking Pone's words like a plant getting water.

"You know I ain't strategic," said the base voice man. "You want info from barroom talk?"

"Poker games," remarked Pone.

"Okay," frowned Ben." You going to be playing too,"

"You playing in bars not hotel casinos," said Pone looking into the giant's eyes hoping he get the point.

"I'll be playing with guys looking to score if they do or don't win while you'll be in company those with fat pockets," said Ben.

Pone nodded. "Your games played in bars at the docks,"

"I play it by ear?" questioned Ben.

"Let the conversation come to you," Pone snorted." You're unemployed, but they won't know that until they ask and you finesse your answers,"

"Till the right moment," Ben nodded. "I got this,"

Pone smacked the the giant's shoulder.

"You text me what I need to know and I'll do the rest."

"You built like a good strong dock worker," said Jock looking Ben up and down.

Ben exhaled. "This is turning into more than a catch and retreat mission,"

"Too much shit to leave behind," said Pone.

"We got house cleaning to do,"

Jock swallowed hard. "Didn't mean to add more to your plate,"

"There's always uncertainty in this business," replied Pone.

Jock rubbed the back of his head. "Speaking of... you two ain't demolition experts are you?"

Pone readjusted his bowler. "We left him back in Metro."

"Why didn't you bring him along?" questioned Jock.

"He's eighty," murmured Ben.

"Seventy something, but who's counting," remarked Pone.

Jock got moon-eye, "Guess he'd be blowing up more than a boat,"

Ben laughed. "Swears he's sixty,"

Jock shrugged. "Nobody ever said getting old was fun,"

"Lola said the games start tomorrow," said Pone.

"Twenty-thousand to sit,"

"Five-thousand," said Ben.

Pone pursed his lips. "Docks, bars are not high-society, Thugs,"

"Watch it Pone," glared Ben. "You ain't too far remove for earning blood money,"

Pone took off his bowler and twirled it leaning back against the wall. His derby comfort him despite his miracle hair growth. They bullied him as a kid because of Alopecia, but over came it with prayer and painful shots to his head. Before the treatment he gathered mental strength from what doesn't kill you strengthens you.

Ben the giant didn't scare the man who spent most of his life dodging bullets, up and close knife fights, hands and chords constricting his larynx surviving them all. Pone knew how to handle men the size of Ben, you get up close and take away his vision or his testicles. His mammoth friend sensitive and Pone knew he needed chosen words before speaking them to the man with a volcano waiting to erupt.

Pone placed his bowler back on his head. "Ben... there's a reason Theiler's sets up these type of poker games. Meet people with power muscle."

The troubleshooter knew blackmailing a part of the incest pedophile Theiler way to run his businesses. Politicians to vote and grant him privileges, judges to give a slap on the wrist to him and his men if they went to court for a misdemeanor, and men who knew nothing more than earning a buck for enforcing pain and doing harm to others.

"Ben winked." Gotcha,"

"Whew!" exhaled Jock wiping his forehead.

"Talk about intense, you boys had me worried this place would explode."

"We like brothers, we argue disagree sometimes, but love is sill there," said Ben.

"Tell that to Cain and Abel," remarked Jock.

All three men laughed.

Pone observed the explosives.
"The old man schooled me on what to do, but I'm still willing to learn,"
Jock smirked. "On the fly it is,"

SIXTEEN

Twenty long U-shaped red tarp tables with a cut for the dealers fifteen women and five men dressed in red vest, white shirts, blouses, black bow-ties traditional for men, and fancy tied ribbons for the women. The players dressed to impress: women assorted colors of long shoulder strapped dresses showing neck line and for some cleavage hemmed to ankles with slits in the middle and sides waist high revealing gams shape by strap and slip on heels. Women representing united nations wearing their hair short, long, ponytail, bun pointing backwards and toward the ceiling and braided fair maiden style and cornrows.

The men decked out in tuxedos: black slacks, a rainbow color of jackets, and some powder blue as if they were going to the prom. Wingtips and cowboy boots the footwear with the for some stetsons, fedoras and derby. The men wore their hair from no hair, long hair, braided, ponytail, buzz-cut, slick back, Afros, and faces to clean shaven, mustaches, beards, goatee, and close shave stubble. Some men wore bow-ties, no ties and banded collar. Shirt colors went from white, black, green and pink.

Pone sat at a table with three women and a man. He wore his bowler, banded collar white shirt, black vest instead of a jacket, black slacks and white black wingtips. He sat between an Asian woman and a European woman with blonde hair and on next to her a man with a Texas drawl wearing a white ten gallon hat and thick bushy handle bar mustache. A woman the color of night representing Africa sat on the same side as the Asian. All four carried the arrogance of wealth and confidence.

The players introduced themselves; Mai Ling, long and muscled tone thin wore ink hair in a bun staring at the ceiling supported by what looked like two crochet needles pointed on the ends. A silk red body hugging dress with a green and yellow dragon embedded in the fabric. The head at her breast revealing cleavage by the extended V shape neck line and serpent body curving around the hip down her buttocks. The dress slit on both sides and black stiletto pumps.

Her thighs exposed to Pone's eyes, but his maturity told him nothing he hadn't seen before and grinned hearing name because Mai Ling common used in martial arts movies and comic books. Suzanne Downy, blonde hair pass her shoulders parted down the middle showing black roots wore a one shoulder blue single slit satin dress covering her breast and red strap heels. Pone saw her thigh too feeling the same as he did about Mai Ling.

Velma Schism, sitting down and tall as a weed. Face strong and sported a silver close cropped hair cut. Heavy baggy eyes showed her age and her black dress covered her shoulders showing no cleavage though her melons pressed against the fabric. Tex the last player represented the urban legend of being a tall Texan. He look like Yosemite Sam, bushy red eye-brows and mustache on his full face. He wore what Pone would call a powder blue prom tux and rattle snake skin boots.

A bald five-foot nothing man with a hairless mannequin face waddled to the middle of the floor dressed like a Penguin.

"LET THE GAMES BEGIN!"

Poker isn't a just a game of luck-----it's a game of strategy. Whether you're playing Texas Hold 'em, Omaha, or 7-Card Stud. If you can read people you better your chances winning the game.

Fem fatales and the Texan all experts or they wouldn't have entered the tournament. Pone didn't know their reason for taking part in the high-stakes game, to make a alliance with the slime ball Lereaux or the rush of adrenalin to play against the best. He knew the top five would leave the casino games for a trip to his hovel and Pone planned to be on of them.

The game drew on with the quartet having complete perfect control of their faces and body language. They communicate what they want and nothing more, but there's one way to read someone. Tex a true Texan bleeding chips and look more than ready to have dirt thrown on him. Pone saw his weakness in a bottle. The Texan drank bourbon when he held a bad hand and didn't like his balls squeezed by women. Pone observed the ladies enjoying handing him his manhood.

Possum is an animal famous for playing dead and Tex played the animal well, in a miraculous turn of events in which he put all his chips in and ended up with a respectable amount keeping himself from being buried not dead yet. He trailed Pone,Ling, and Downy, but not Schism. The handsome ebony woman advertised her frustration without trying hard; pursing her lips tight, flaring nostrils, rolling eyes.

Pone wondered why she bothered to play. He had already eliminated her from a prospect for Theiler Lereaux. She came across a wealthy lonely old woman hoping to find a spark for her decaying life. Velma had money to burn and the way she played poker and not well at least on this night, became one of many from the other poker tables taking a seat on sidelines. She folded strolling ladylike to the bar becoming a spectator nursing a martini shaken not stirred.

Three of hearts, deuce of spades, five of clubs, Jack of diamonds, and four of hearts gave Pone a shit hand. He interrupted the game flagging down a waiter.

"Ginger-ale," said Pone.

 Then others followed suit.

"Vodka," said Suzanne.

"Gin," ordered Mai.

Tex took off his ten gallon sombrero looking more like Yosemite Sam when his red mane dropped over his face. He brushed back his scarlet rug with his hand then placed his hat back snug on his noggin.

"Everybody thirsty suddenly?"

Gamblers when on a roll hate interruptions. Pone understood

the Texan's anger because he built momentum finding new life while others left him for dead.

"You sound dry," suggested Pone.

"Bullet to the head," requested Tex.

Just like the movie the waiter gave an inquisitive look.

"Add an I between the E and T," said Pone.

"Bulleit bourbon," nodded the waiter who went to the bar to get the drinks.

"Straight," stated Tex. "Good movie,"

Pone knew the cowboy was referring to the *Stallone flick Bullet To The* Head.

"Lucky for you this is New Orleans," said Pone.

He didn't know how accurate the movie was about the rotgut being hard to find or never heard of by bartenders, but Google knew of the Kentucky brand whiskey. Produced by Kirin Brewing company Four Roses Distillery in Lawrenceburg, Kentucky, for the Diageo beverage conglomerate.

The waiter returned with the drinks. Pone and the ladies nursed their cocktails while Tex downed his shot ordering another on the rocks.

"Smart," said Pone." Watered down booze won't cloud your thinking," The ladies giggled.

Hope the break in the action throw you off your game sending the momentum my way, thought Pone.

Tex touch the rim of his hat staring a Pone.

Pone smiled wondering how Ben was doing.

A fog of smoke from cigarette and cigars, burping, whiskey shot glasses and beer mugs staining the table and a large bowl of peanuts.

The way Ben liked his poker games. No glitz and glamour just bad manners and dress attire: jeans, work boots, T-shirts, sweat and flannel shirts, denim jackets, and army surplus clothes.

Ten tables in the back of a dive bar with large round brown tables. Ben pleased each player had their own separate bowl of nuts. Five players at each table. The game monitor, a bartender not Horse-face, but a beer gut hidden under a dingy white T-shirt fighting not in control of the wiggling and jiggling jello swimming around inside the garment. Blue jeans weighed down by the girth waiting to show butt crack.

She walked around to each table making sure the player thought twice cheating their way through the tournament. A crew cut blonde and her noticeable breast hard press against her shirt did not distract the card sharks. The woman built like a female wrestler smiled then settled back behind the bar after making her rounds.

Ben downed his beer and then took a puff from his stogie. The four men sitting at his table as big as himself. Three shared his bald head style while the fourth a Goldilocks tied in a ponytail. Ben grabbed a hand full of nuts from his bowl.

"I'll raise you," said Ben munching.

Two of the bald men folded. The other wearing a black pull-over tossed in his chips as did Goldilocks.

All three leaned back in their chairs expecting the others move.

"I called," said Ben.

Signaling to the other players to show their hands.

Pull-over went first putting down a three of a kind (2H-2D-2S-8C-3D) Goldilocks laid down a straight (KC-QH-JH-9D) Pull-over cursed.

"Damn right," chuckled Goldilocks. He looked at Ben.

Ben took his time. (QS-8S-6S-5S-3S) A flush of spades.

Goldilocks studied Ben's hand long enough for the other observers to wonder if time stood still.

"We have a winner!" exclaimed the bartender.

"Fuck!" Goldilocks slapped the table. "You lucky fuck,"

"I need it," Ben smiled pulling the chips toward him.

"Glad something's working out for me,"

Goldilocks frowned. "What do you mean?"

Ben exhaled. "Out of work... broke... trying to find a job,"

"Big man like you?" Goldilocks pursed his lips. "Construction? Railroad man?"

A waitress came to the table taking Ben's chips touching his shoulder for him to follow her. Goldilocks nodded to Ben to go then motioned he be at the bar to continue their talk. The bartender gave Ben his winnings.

"Set for round two tomorrow night," said Ben.

"What are you still doing here?" questioned Goldilocks.

"Thought you wanted to talk more?" asked Ben

Goldilocks sipped his beer. "Shouldn't you head for bed?"

Ben shrugged. "Still early and ain't ready to call it a night and again you looked like you had more to say,"

Goldilocks looked Ben up and down. "You look like hired muscle,"

Ben shook his head. "Don't know what you mean?"

"Bouncer... body guard? Inquired Goldilocks. "You know if somebody missed a payment I'd hate to be in their shoes,"

Ben motioned to the bartender to bring him a beer, "You need protection?"

"Let's say I know a man who could use someone like you,"

Ben took a long gulp. "I don't make pass the second round I'm yours to hire,"

Goldilocks looked around the room. "Let's not jump the gun,"

 Ben snorted. "Did I read you wrong?"

"Best you win the whole thing,"

Ben frowned. "Playing poker a job rehearsal?"

Goldilocks shrugged." Couldn't hurt your resume',"

"Give me an application," Ben nursed his beer. "I'll give you references,"

Goldilocks finished his beer."Be rooting for you tomorrow," He slapped Ben on the back and left the bar.

"So," said a husky voice.

Ben almost choked on his beer looking around to see who owned it.

His head stop swiveling when the owner of the voice leaned towards him. Ben looked at the bartender whose eyes looked through him.

"You looking for work?" she asked.

Ben frowned swallowing hard. "Say what?"

"Two of the losers were bitching about losing to an out of work big lug,"

"Everybody at that table was big,"

"You didn't lose,"

Ben laughed." They called me a lug, huh?"

"No," she refilled his mug. "I meant it in a good way,"

"Thanks,"

"A compliment," she shrugged. "Compared to what they said about you,"

"Do I look like I give a shit?"

"A big hugable bear," she batted her eyelashes.

"You'd hire me?"

"Can you clean a toilet?'

"That's how you see me?"

"Beggars can't be choosy,"

Ben rolled his eyes. "I ain't begging and I'll pass on being a professional ass wiper."

"Now that's a good one. Never heard that before,"

"Got it from a friend," said Ben.

"There's a Miami cargo down at the docks always looking for help and my name's Mabel,"

Ben studied the thick breasted woman giving her the same look she gave him.

"What do you mean by always?" asked Ben.

Mabel pursed her lips. "They don't seem to stay used long,"

"I don't fancy being in one place long," remarked Ben.

"Then you should fit right in and let's hope that's the case,"

"And who do I need to see for a job?"

"You big lug," said Mabel wiping down the bar. "You'll see him tomorrow night."

One table not ready to conclude the last game of the night. Pone going head to head with Tex. The cowboy made a miraculous recovery dispatching Mai Ling and Suzanne Downy. The ladies wasted no time becoming Pone's cheerleaders. Pot on the table $250, 000. 00 the same for all games and $250,000. 00 for the next round.

"Winner takes all moving on to the second round," said the dealer.

"Down to you and me... a man's game," blurt the Chauvinist cowboy glancing at the fem fatales. "Pokers a man's game,"

Pone saw no wedding ring on Tex finger which meant nothing, but his lack of respect for women loud and clear. He built tension from the harpies no longer involved in the game with his comment. Pone looked at the ladies giving the cowboy dagger stares, and flared nostrils toward him.

Pone smiled." Thanks for putting lady-luck on my side,"

Tex gave a Cheshire Cat grin" Can't be too lucky since they out of the game boy. Takes skill and that's why I'll be moving on,"

Pone didn't know how Tex meant it calling him boy, and if Texans consider themselves to be southerners though they had a similar drawl. He shook his head telling himself not to over think what they said and concentrate on the game. Pone inhaled to keep his body strong. The game hit the tiring stage for him. Win the game you move on and better his chances of meeting Theiler.

Both players owned a mountain of chips, but neither committed to putting it all in. Pone couldn't figure out how Tex weathered the storm to remain in the game, but he did. The cowboy in the worst position in the Texas Hold'em game called under-the-gun. Your biggest decision is deciding to whether play a hand or not.

Before entering a pot you want as much information as possible. When under-the-gun, you have no information about what any of the other players are going to do. Tex at a distinct disadvantage. Pone notice him playing weaker hands feeling out the competition and it worked. Mai and Suzanne had their own purpose, the love of the game or a chance meeting with the proprietor of the games.

They bowed out freelancing their skills making Pone question why they got into the game. He played a part in their departure adjusting the rim of his bowler looking as if he had a bad hand. Tex the Texan a puzzle he didn't care to solve, but speculate the man bled black blood. Oil. Pone figured if Yosemite Sam won, he would give Theiler more options to spread his disease. Lola said a handful would leave for Theiler's estate for big pay off and an alliance. Pone planned to be in that group. He didn't know how they would break it down for the surviving players from the current games, but he remembered five would get the invite.

Pone looked around the room thinking Tex played an entertaining game, he felt like the captive audience... time to end this shit.

"You Texans like to gamble," Pone pushed all his chips to the middle of the table. A gasp ran throughout the room.

"Mister Stratus," said the dealer. "Your call,"

Tex straightens in his chair flipping a chip like coin in a football game. A decision danced inside his head; Call Pone on a bluff, fold taking his loot, but allowing him to move to the next round with the winnings.

"Fuck!" exclaimed Tex. "You only live once," He pushed his chips to middle of the table.

"Your hand, Mister Stratus," said the dealer.

Tex laid out three queens(hearts, spades, clubs,) and a pair of treys (heart and diamond) "These gals bring me all the luck I need."

"Mister McGillicuddy," gestured the dealer.

One by one Pone placed an 8 of spades, 8 of hearts, 8 of clubs, and 8 diamonds and a Jack of hearts.

"Four of a kind beats a Full House," said the dealer." Winner, Mister McGillicuddy,"

"What the hell!" blurted Tex.

Pone smiled." Guess you aren't so lucky with the ladies,"

❧ ❧ ❧ ❧ ❧ ❧

Pone stood outside the grand casino letting the night air clear his head.

He checked his cell wondering why he hadn't heard from Ben. A cloud of smoke covered his face. He frowned turning to the human chimney. He saw a long thin black cigarette holder. Pone thought he was in a 1940's black and white gangster flick. The gasper pressed between Mai Ling's scarlet lips.

"You could've said Hi," said Pone.

"I did," replied Mai.

❧ ❧ ❧ ❧ ❧ ❧

Ben looked out into the harbor. He stood 50 yards from what he believed to be Theiler's contraband ship according to Mabel who gave a tight lip information and he didn't blame her. Ben had a chip on his shoulder; it bothered him knowing Pone saw him as muscle without brains. He knew Pone didn't consider him a dummy, but he still wanted to prove to his college educated friend he possessed savvy.

Mabel said a particular ship always looked intense and more business than the others. Ben liked the bar scene because bartenders to him were psychiatrist and informants. He couldn't figure why the burly dame took a liking to him and if this job went well he'd see if he could pay her back in kind. Ben nodded after observing the ship and agreed with Mabel how the ship carried a serious attitude and the crew men look more like men of action then regular ship mates. He took out his cell and texted.

❖ ❖ ❖ ❖ ❖ ❖

"Second hand smoke is how you greet people?" asked Pone.

"You know your way around a poker table," remarked Mai.

"Semantics,"

"How so?" questioned Mai.

"I couldn't let the jerk win with his attitude towards women,"

Mai nodded." That was quite a streak he had going for himself,"

Pone heard the zip on his phone. He checked the text. *Way to go Ben*, he thought.

"Is that important?" asked Mai.

Pone gave her a look. "Suspicious about Tex winning streak after all he was under-the-gun,"

Mai blew out a stream of smoke. "I consider myself a fair player,"

"Then why bother?" questioned Pone.

"You have one of those days or nights, but it like someone was watching,"

Pone shrugged. "Hotel casinos have cameras... big brother makes sure all is fair in love and war," He noticed a glare from Mai.

"You didn't feel observed?" she asked stretching an eye-brow.

"Maybe I'll wear a low cut thigh high slit body hugging dress tomorrow night?"

Mai winked. "You're pretty enough to pull it off, Mister McGillicuddy,"

Her tone harmonized doubt not believing his real name.

Pone gave a dubious look.

"Your name is McGillicuddy?" she questioned.

"Because I'm black?" remarked Pone.

Mai squinted. "Creole,"

Pone smiled. This is the big easy,"

"You got a quick wit," Mai nodded moving in closer.

"Got a curfew or can you buy a girl a drink?"

"There you are!" shouted a voice from behind.

Pone turned flashing a million dollar smile.

Lola to the rescue latching on to his arm.

"Whose your friend?" asked Lola through her pearly whites.

Pone grinned. "One player at my table. She lost,"

Mai glared sucking on her cigarette holder stick.

Lola pulled Pone away. "Better luck next time,"

SEVENTEEN

Ben woke to pounding on his motel door. He stretched yawned, and sat up scratching his chest. He farted getting up answering the door. Pone blinked falling backwards fanning and pinching his nose.

"Whoa!" frowned Pone." What the hell?"

"Like you don't cut the cheese getting out of bed," said Ben. "Stop being prissy," He turned pulling his underwear out of his ass before falling face down on the bed.

Pone took a moment to get the vision out of his head. He walk in with his bowler covering his nose. He spotted motel matches on the nightstand. He struck two them to kill the odor then closed the door for privacy, but not until he cracked a window.

"Much better," said Pone.

"Fuck you," replied Ben. "Too damn early,"

"Already done that," remarked Pone sitting near the window.. "Did you win?"

"I didn't mention that in my text?"

"Lucky." murmured Pone.

"What's that supposed to mean?" " questioned Ben.

"Hard to play in the clouds,"

Ben sat up. "We going to start this shit again?"

"Think about the girls,"

"Shouldn't you be hitting the sack?"

Pone smirked." Tonight's as good as any to make some noise,"

"Before or after the games?"

"We both need to win."

"Want my help?"

"Suspicion might rise if someone recognize your features loitering around the harbor,"

Ben nodded in agreement. He knew his size had it's advantages and disadvantage, His NBA height didn't give him basketball skills, and it didn't give him skills to kill either he learned that on the fly when a stranger he later on believed the devil himself recruited him for a life destined to hell sin. He killed his first man in a jewel heist.

A middle-age security guard neck snapped in his enormous mitts. For trying to do his job. Guilt weighed on Ben making him think about his life. A father dead before he was ten leaving behind him, his two younger sisters, and a mother a face not capable of getting a glance to attract potential step dads.

The devil stepped in to be his mentor. Ben had to be the man of the house and the money good and easy till the devil thinking of him as a big dumb ox tried to stiff him after a job. Ben argued about his cut being short and ended up making his mentor a stiff. He hired himself out after knowing the devil's contacts supporting his family till the angels took his mother away and his sisters grew up getting married creating their own families. Someone left Ben with the talent to be a career criminal.

"You sure?" questioned Ben knowing Pone would do this job solo.

"This time," Pone got a distant look.

"What's dancing around inside your head?" asked Ben.

"After the game a mysterious exotic woman approached me till Lola came to my rescue,"

Ben inhaled." Were you in trouble?"

"Not yet anyway," remarked Pone." I need to pay close attention to my surroundings."

"Guess I better do the same," replied Ben.

Pone straightened. "What's going on big man?"

Ben shrugged. "Think I'm being recruited thanks to my size,"

Pone observed the giant. He never knew how it felt to be short or Ben's size, but thankful for his height. Ben felt like a misfit and wanted by the wrong kind of people to harm others. Pone hope this trip could put him at ease for something good helping two young girls or more that Theiler held under his clutches.

"You know what to do," encouraged Pone.

 Ben nodded." Finesse,"

"It's okay if you change your mind. I won't hold it against you."

"I ain't going no where, you stuck with me to the end. Let's hope it's a happy one,"

"How are we with names?" asked Pone.

"Buford but I have not been asked,"

Ben squinted and wiggled his head. "A little too close to home,"

Ben snorted. "What about you?"

"McGillicuddy," laughed Pone.

Ben got moon-eye." Man, they bought that shit?"

"Always thought it a cool name,"

"For telling a joke,'

Pone stood and stretched. "Time for me and McGillicuddy to talk to the Sandman,"

Ben laid on his back nodding to Pone.

They shared a glance and Pone left the room.

"You too, brother, you too,"

EIGHTEEN

A king of hearts, Jack of spades, and a of pair deuces diamond and heart. Ben held the hand sitting inside the dive called Bar None. His head cloudy and if he survive the night winning the game moving to the next round he'd heed Pone's advice cutting back on the booze. Ben knew his pairs were low unless he could get four a kind. He'd have to be lucky since he didn't know whether they held by his opponents or buried in the deck He knew time wasn't on his side. One man would soon call and they'd have to show their hand. Ben thought about tossing in his pairs hoping he could get an Ace or two royals to make things interesting. He felt like March Madness, one and done he frowned knowing a mistake for him since his stakes were high.

The two men sitting studied Ben more than they did each other. Whether they knew what he was about he didn't know, but his chips stood taller than theirs and he figured they wanted him to make a move. Ben spotted Goldilocks, he nursed a beer and nodded. Ben checked his hand then looked up and Goldilocks disappeared.

"I'll raise you," said the man on the left. Tossing chips onto the pile. Man on the right pressed his lips then threw two hundred dollar chips on the pile. "Okay,"

Folding not an option and he waited too long to get new cards after man right made his call. He didn't want to show his poker face exposing his hand, but now he knew he'd prove Pone right about him not being smart on their mission and losing this game would be more than fly in the ointment for them.

Ben knew how to call a bluff. He shoved in all his chips. "All in,"

Man right cursed and tossed down his cards deciding to take what money he had but it eliminated him. Man left smiled putting all in chips in. Ben saw Goldilocks standing behind Man left squeezing his shoulder then vanished into the crowd. Man left shook his head looking at his cards then turned them face down on the table. He stood up walking away.

Beer mugs and shot glasses clinked celebrating Ben's victory. The patrons walked by patting his shoulder. Though he won the game, Ben frowned.

The game came to a close holding a Seven, Six, Five, Four, and three all hearts a straight flush gave Pone a ticket to the next round.. He didn't want to waste time not that he did in the first round, but he didn't want to display his talent keeping suspicion of him being a card shark hidden. He had things to do and he would hold back the next game. These players easier to read making him ponder how they won their respective games.

Pone played the gracious winner smiling, shaking hands while nursing a ginger-ale. He checked the time on his cell. Pone pushed away from the bar heading for the exit when a tan hand, long scarlet fingernails gripped him by the elbow.

"The night's still young," said Mai.

Pone exhaled looking at her hand on his elbow. "Gosh, you're strong for a woman."

She giggled then released him. "You're more talented then you led on,"

Pone gave an expressionless poker face though it bothered him the strange thin shapely woman tilting her head looking like the actress Maggie Q.

"Are you flirting with me?" he asked.

She gazed into his eyes. "One blue and one brown... interesting,"

"Nothing sinister," remarked Pone.

"A unique condition," she said stroking her chin." A man of mystery,"

Pone appalled nosy people and now she put herself on his radar and her beautiful exotic look set off a red alert inside his head like the *LOST IN SPACE ROBOT*, **"DANGER, DANGER, WILL ROBINSON."** Mai hanging around observing him made him realize though he was not sure he would call her an enemy, but now he'd might have to keep her close.

"Was that your wife?" she asked with a gaze.

Pone kept his poker face not frowning." Sworn to fun, loyal to none,"

"The way she latched on to your arm,"

Pone raised an eye. "You vice grip my elbow and I still feel claws."

Mai straightened putting her hands on her hips. "Why so serious?"

Pone pivoted toward the exit. "See you tomorrow night,"

Pone blended into the night decked out in stealth attire, backpack, and a Mardi Gra mask. He prepared himself in case he needed evasive action into the city escaping would be pursuers. Pone did his homework noticing the natives celebrating and the tourist doing their best embracing the tradition.

He eased on to the light guarded ship. Theiler must have wanted to be discrete to the naked eye not wanting to reveal he harbored contraband on his boat. They dressed like seamen; blue jeans, cargo shirts, jackets, skull caps, and work boots, but they move like men ready for action keeping their head on a swivel.

Pone didn't want to stray from the assignment Red gave him to retrieve a young woman from her incest father, but like any situation things change. He squatted behind a large faded orange rusted crate, as the unexpected he hid in the shadow of a crew member shone by the moonlight. He then waltzed by a man unaware an intruder on board.

He followed the man to a door he guessed would be the engine room. It had a circle window for looking out.

He twisted an L shape latch knob and not a regular key hole door. The man looked as though walking downward. Pone hoped to the engine room where he'd set the explosives sending a shock to Theiler's putrid world. In the back of his mind he wanted no bloodshed. He realized it might be unavoidable, but part of the business for those involved in his cryptic world.

"Well... well... " said Goldilocks. Like a freight train you keep moving along.

Ben grabbed the java. The drip black, strong, and acrid enough to make him cringe. What he needed to keep a clear head now that he seemed to pick up interest from a man that was becoming less than a stranger. Ben sat near a window staring into the night. Goldilocks noticed his fixation.

"Had a dog who use to do that,"

Ben gave a look.

Goldilocks snorted. "Not calling you a dog just saying he gazed into the night,"

Ben sipped his coffee." Glad you cleaned that up,"

"As if he was waiting to hear from somebody," Goldilocks shrugged." I never understood that since I was his master,"

Ben didn't want to over think Goldilocks words, but he felt insulted being compared to a dog. He made a fist hearing him say master.

"Maybe he was looking for a better suitor," said Ben deep and cold.

Goldilocks threw up his hands." Well he's gone now,"

Ben didn't bother to ask if the dog died or hauled ass. He just want the tongue in cheek comparison to end.

"Buy you a beer?" asked Goldilocks as if he knew he insulted the giant.

Ben held up his chicory. "This is all I need,"

Goldilocks nodded. "Got to keep a clear head for the next game,"

Ben swallowed hard studying the man. He knew skill and luck went hand and hand playing poker. His hand was shit and though he won he felt as if he owed Goldilocks a thank you.

Ben snorted taking a sip of his coffee. "Word is if I need a job you the man to talk to,"

"Keep on winning and you won't need a job," remarked Goldilocks.

Ben cut his eye towards the man. *With your help,* he thought. "Till then a man got to keep busy,"

Goldilocks tighten his ponytail. "Construction?"

Ben shook his head. "You see me doing gymnastics on a balancing beam?" Ben got moon-eye when he saw Silhouette entering the bar. Ben exhaled when the young man sat at the other end. Goldilocks turned to see what got Ben's attention.

"Friend of yours?" he asked.

Ben frowned. "Generation gap," *What the hell is he doing here?* Thought Ben. He realized he wasn't the drug dealer's only client.

"Yeah," Goldilocks drank his beer. "Saw on Facebook an old man marrying a twelve year-old girl,"

"What country?" asked Ben.

"Foreign don't think they do that in states anymore, at least I hope not," replied Goldilocks.

The man has integrity, thought Ben. Elvis and Jerry Lee Lewis just few to jump the broom with girls who should've been playing with dolls or thinking about high school.

The conception by Goldilocks brought an image of Theiler molesting young girls presumed his daughters or nieces made Ben's nostrils flare.

"You okay big man?" asked Goldilocks.

"A bad memory jumped in my head," said Ben.

"Glad we just met,"

Ben smiled toasting his cup of demitasse.

Brogan sat in velvet cushion recliner reading the blab sheet something not done since you can read the newspaper on the internet. In front of the fire place swirling cognac listening to classic *Gregorian chants*. He sniff the cognac then tilt the glass to his lips. The liquid move closer until the door of his European style abode blew open not by the wind, but Theiler Lereaux.

"Where is she?" asked Theiler. "You done had her long enough to make her well,"

Brogan sipped his cognac then placed the glass on the table next to his reading lamp.

He stood towering over the troll who broke into his abode. Brogan folded his paper.

"Good day to you sir," said Brogan.

"Don't shit me," said Theiler pointing." I know you keep these girls when they good and ready to go. I ain't stupid,"

"No." said Brogan giving a superiority look." But you're not a doctor,"

"Don't get smug with me... you ain't the only malpractice asshole," blurted Theiler.

"I found you and I'll find another,"

"They are children," Brogan swallowed hard. "Their wounds are not just physical,but mental,"

"I hired a sawbones not no damn shrink,"

"I have a degree in both,"

"Turned to shit till I came to your rescue,"

"If I had known..."

"Don't you dare get a conscience now... look around you," said Theiler." My money in your pocket the reason you accustom yourself to fine living,"

Brogan pursed his lips and swallowed knowing if not for Theiler he'd be doing something far less glamorous than practicing medicine. The little monster was right and Brogan hated he sold his soul to the devil, but he had enough integrity to bend and not break. Protecting young girls from Thriler's clutches brought comfort to his troubled heart.

"That's right you shut your damn mouth or your ass will be on the street I guarantee,know your role doctor or I'll huff and puff and blow your house down. Now where is she?"

Brogan stood aside without saying a word. Theiler raced past him heading upstairs.

Mia heard Theiler's hideous voice and found a corner she figured as a comfort.

In a short time she'd grown to accept Brogan's creepy appearance realizing underneath his frightening exterior he possessed a kind heart. Mia pulled her knees to her chest burying her head between them when Thriler barged in her room "Time to grow up girl," said Theiler. "Got some acquaintances waiting to enjoy your company,"

Mia cried.

Theiler sat on the edge of the bed leering at her. "Stop that blubbering... you done had plenty of time to get well and you look fine. I understand you nervous and all, you got to take that plunge and you'll be just fine I guarantee,"

Mia refused to look up and cried louder.

Theiler inhaled "Damn girl you hush up that fuss!"

The roar of Theiler's voice opened up the flood gates.

"Now if you come on over here... I promise to be nice and gentle, but if I have to come and get you I'll break you in like a bronco instead of like a Phillie, I guarantee"

Theiler leaned toward Mia holding out his hand. "What's it going to be, girl?"

❊ ❊ ❊ ❊ ❊ ❊

Digital timer set for 3:00 minutes and counting. Pone headed up the metal steps. The man he saw entering left after doing a circle around the engine room. Pone didn't bother looking for crates with guns or drugs, he based everything on Ben's Intel that Theiler owned this tender and the way the crew behave walking around making sure nothing out of the ordinary going on.

Pone stopped half way after a face covered the port hole. *Shit,* he thought. *Always drama when you least expect it.* Pone had enough drama with explosives on a timer and hoped he did it right, but didn't want to be a guinea pig to find out. The man didn't bother to enter for a closer look. Pone slumped down on the stairs saw his shadow in the moonlight on the wall and feared the man saw it too making him think twice before entering.

Pone pondered a worse case scenario the man would think the night playing tricks having him believe the shadow a figure of his imagination or call for and they go up in a blaze of glory. Pone refuse to look back at the timer. A thump and the man's face with his eyes closed pressed against the glass sliding down. Pone didn't care what made the man do what he did, but took it as his cue to get the hell out of dodge.

❊ ❊ ❊ ❊ ❊ ❊

Ben couldn't help glancing at Silhouette and Goldilocks enjoy watching them like a tennis match.

"You sure are interested in that kid," implied Goldilocks.

Ben shrugged. "Looks too young to be in a bar,"

"Whatever floats your boat," remarked Goldilocks.

Ben wanted to snapped Goldilocks neck. The bitterness of his java added fuel to his fire.

"Excuse me, do I know you?" Ben's voice more base with his question.

Goldilocks smiled. "Easy big man... didn't mean to step on your toes,"

"You implying something?" Ben more concerned about Silhouette walking over to him revealing to Goldilocks still a stranger his fake hankering for coke. He knew he made a mistake eyeing the drug dealer, but didn't fancy being judge for liking young boys.

"You could walk over to him and ask how old he is." suggested Goldilocks.

"Look man I don't tip-toe through the tulips,"

"A bull in a china shop,"

"If I have to," said Ben.

"I agree," said Goldilocks looking Ben up and down. "You ain't no Tiny Tim,"

"He been dead a long time, and no I ain't no fairy tale."

"I watch a lot on the retro channel when television was... "

Ben toasted his cup of coffee. "Amen to that brother,"

The storm building between the two men quieted with the agreement how television lost it's integrity.

BOOM! A Shockwave shook the bar and a fluorescent red yellow glow brighten the sky over the harbor.

"What the hell is going on?" questioned Goldilocks looking out the window.

Ben turned smiling from ear to ear looking down at the bar. "The fourth of July,"

❧ ❧ ❧ ❧ ❧ ❧

Pone breathed a sigh of relief knowing the crew made it off the ship whether legit seaman or Theiler's goon-squad he didn't want them soaking in blood. The Mardi Gra came right on time getting fought off by the local authorities to take a different route for their celebration. Pone didn't know if they were drunk,crazy, or accustomed to seeing things blow up, but the music kept playing and Pone wet and all put on his mask blending in the crowd.

The group of party-goers found a street and Pone thought he saw a curvy cat suit dressed woman ducking into one alley. He shook his head realizing it wasn't an illusion thinking about the man falling unconscious. His reluctant partner in crime a woman, but who?

❧ ❧ ❧ ❧ ❧ ❧

Theiler gritted his teeth. "You done had plenty of time to get use to me now girl,"

Mia look towards the door.

"Don't know who you looking for, girl... Frankenstein knows his role and your guardian angel is bearing me," said Theiler.

Mia cried.

Theiler inhaled. "Done had about enough this," He grabbed the frighten and screaming Mia carrying her to the bed. Mia kicked and land a foot to Theiler's groin. He dropped her on the bed and glared. His chest heaved up and down. "I was going to be nice and gentle, but you done, done it now, girl,"

Theiler grabbed his private parts and exhaled. He stood spreading his arms and legs walking toward Mia like a wrestler. Mia closed her eyes pulling her knees up to her chest. She cringed feeling Theiler's weight on the bed.

A loud knock on the door. Theiler clenched his fist grinding his teeth.

"What the fuck do you want doc?"

"It's me sir... very important,"

Theiler recognized the voice of one of his men.

"It damn well better be or it's your ass," roared Theiler. He climbed off the bed and swung open the door." Go ahead and spill it boy," Theiler glared.

"The ship blew up,"

NINETEEN

"You done it now!" Jock fell back roaring with laughter.

"And then some," remarked Pone sipping a Malta Goya.

"The night sky was beautiful," said Ben drinking an O'doul's a non-alcoholic beer.

Pone smiled knowing that Jock paid heed to his words on how important keeping clear head to complete their task.

"Almost didn't make off that boat before it went boom," stated Pone.

"I'm listening," said Ben.

Pone placed his elbows on the table to support his chin. "Making my why back up and a face appeared in the port hole looking down upon me," He took a sip of his Goya. "I wanted none bloodshed not saying they wouldn't deserve, but the guy's face got pressed against the window. So far the news has reported no casualties,"

Jock gulped down his O'doul's then grabbed another. "You didn't get a look at your rescuer?"

"Guess my mission not as secret at I thought," remarked Pone. He didn't want to say he saw a black cat suit figure of a woman.

Ben cleared his throat. "Red had your back from afar,"

"I'm not mad at her for saving my life," said Pone.

"Then again this is New Orleans and maybe the spirits don't like what's going on and gave you some help," said Ben.

Jock grunted. "You talking about Voodoo?"

Ben shrugged. "Just fooling around,"

"We take that stuff serious down here ain't no joke to us," said Jock.

Pone shook his head." Whoever helped me rest assure it wasn't a zombie or nothing like that," He exhaled wanting to squash what he considered nonsense talk between Jock and Ben. "A breathing flesh and blood human came to my rescue, there's more to these poker players than we know,"

Ben nodded thinking about Goldilocks. "You think Lola got skills?"

"Beautiful smile, warm personality… a resume` for our line of work," remarked Pone.

"Somebody knew what you would do beside us," snorted Ben.

"I will keep that beautiful woman far away from my world," said Pone,

"You ain't falling for her are you?" questioned Jock.

"When this done I hope to stay in touch" replied Pone. "Did fireworks help you win the game big man?"

"Over before, but Silhouette dropped in," said Ben.

"Say what?" questioned Pone. "You didn't call him did you?"

Ben shook his head. "You don't think?"

Jock rose from the table." Gentlemen take it easy," He raised his beer to Pone and Ben. "We should celebrate for now we are winning the game. Don't know how Theiler going to react hearing his boat load of money no pun intended got turned into splinters," Jock smiled.

Both Ben and Pone exhaled and nodded to each other. The giant thought about telling Pone about Goldilocks and how he helped him advance, but judging he acted after hearing of Silhouette's arrival he figured it best to keep the strange Goldilocks to himself.

Tara cracked her door looking out into the hall, no sign of anyone. Mia had not returned and that a good thing. She gritted her teeth knowing soon Theiler would do to Mia what he done to her and others

giving what he called a test drive. The monster had no problem incest his bloodline. Tara hoped Mia adapted to Brogan's presence seeing the good doctor cared about the girls and used his cunning to keep them from Theiler's clutches as he did her.

Tara closed her door after hearing footsteps coming her way. She listened hearing the guards talking about Theiler spitting fire getting news about a boat blowing up. Tara didn't know all of Theiler's affairs, but the news of Theiler being upset brought a smile to her face. A knock on her door. *God please don't let it him*, she thought. Tara inhaled opening the door. Beef with a smile on his face.

"Girl, I got something to tell you."

❖ ❖ ❖ ❖ ❖ ❖

"I said I know damn it!" roared Theiler." It's on me and I will compensate you I guarantee, this won't happen again, "Theiler took a deep breath taking the phone from his ear before getting back on." Yeah... I'm still here... what you mean don't yell at you? You raising your voice at me... fuck me... fuck you too... okay, okay... accept my apology and again it's on my ass and I'll make up for it," Theiler slammed down the phone. He checked the caller ID biting his lower lip knowing he'd lost not only money, but respect from his buyers and connects.

He already spent half the day making and answering calls promising to clean up the mess. The relief he got was the blackmailing of people in high places for being perverts on tape and he'd use that to get the money he needed to pay off and back his clientele and get him a new ship for his contraband. Theiler needed something to relieve him of his stress. He glared at the messenger.

The man sat in the sturdy oak tan chair with the help of Ludwig making sure he stayed put.

Theiler leaned in face to face. "You know they say kill the messenger,"

The man frowned and trembled. "Y-y-y-y-yes sir..." He swallowed hard almost vomiting from Theiler's bitter breath he inhaled through his nose landing on his tongue. "In all fairness sir it's not my fault,"

Theiler nodded. "Well today's your lucky day because I ain't no Roman Spartan,"

The man frowned thinking Romans and Spartans are not the same, but smart not to correct Theiler. "Thank you, sir,"

Theiler gave a gruesome grin showing yellow and brown teeth. "Since you delivered me bad news I will give you a chance to bring me good news."

"Whatever you need, sir," said the man

"What I need, huh?" remarked Theiler. "For starters a boat and men capable guarding my cargo when you convince the ones on my ass I'm their man and find me some new contacts," Theiler bobbed his head up and down making sure the man got the point.

"I can do that sir,"

"I have faith in you, boy and send in them boys from the ship because I got something to say,"

The man nodded.

Theiler pointed his finger. "The next time I see your narrow ass you better make me happy or I'll let Ludwig play with you and let me tell you boy whoever he plays with I guarantee they don't get seconds,"

The man nodded looking up at Ludwig and hustled through the door. Theiler stagger back behind his desk plopping down in his chair. Opened his lower desk drawer taking out a long neck bottle with a wide square bottom of brown fluid.

He decided not share twisting off the black cap turning the bottle to his lips and swallowing hard.

"Ludwig, somebody done come in my back yard and took a shit with out covering it up," Theiler took another long drink of his cognac stamping the bottle down on his desk. "Ludwig," Theiler pointed. "I know you ain't much with words, but you make some rounds to the people I pay good money to who ain't doing their jobs using eyes and ears keeping me in the loop about who trespassing in my city,"

Ludwig stood like a palace guard nodding.

"The bars and casinos where your contacts are and bust some heads to get my point across because we got some tourist who doing more than sight seeing,"

The behemoth with hairy condition nodded and grunted.

Theiler leaned back. "Glad you agree with me because if you going to crap on my business you better know how to wipe your ass."

Beef sat in the chair across from Tara's bed smiling ear to ear. *Something to occupy Theiler from thinking about his perverted ways,* she thought. Mia still pure brought a smile to Tara's face.

"I knew that would make you happy." said Beef.

"Yeah." Tara nodded. "Knock before entering, okay." She got a chill thinking about her half brother sneaking and sitting for how long in the room while sound asleep. The word creepy came to mind and she didn't like him getting too comfortable. He acted as if she was the enemy when they first met forcing Tara to prove she Mia's well being at heart. She wondered if he etched in his head now that they share the same dislike for their father that he can enter her room when he pleases unannounced? She saw he got her point about his visit across by the somber look on his face.

Beef looked like a child who got his hand smacked. "I am sorry" He looked to the floor. "I'll never do it again."

Tara wanted to tell him no big deal, but thought better of it. She wanted boundaries living in the house of ominous. Beef meant well, he needed manners which was not taught to him. Theiler if he was his father not qualified and his mother traumatized giving birth to incest children.

"You can make it up to me." said Tara.

He nodded.

Tara inhaled. "I'd like to get back in touch with nature. Haven't been outside in awhile."

Theiler kept the girls locked up like prize possessions. Tara figured with him distracted, she felt it might take his mind off of having them locked up.

"I'll talk to our cousin. He's in good with Theiler." Beef got up and left. Tara jumps out of bed and locks the door.

Jock roared with laughter. The Cajun enjoyed sitting with the duo in his basement pawn shop hearing about their adventures disrupting Theiler's empire. Pone drank his usual Molta Goya and Ben joined Jock throwing down brewsky.

"Word spreading like wildfire about that ship blowing up." said Jock.

"The beginning of his problems." said Pone toasting his comrades.

"Sounds like more to come?" Ben questioned. "What's next?"

"One of his bake shops." Pone replied with a stern look.

"Meths labs?" Ben asked.

Jock nodded. "Now you're talking." He took a swill. "Where you going to start?"

Pone inhaled. "Targeting where I followed your street pharmacist." He looked at Ben.

The giant gave a dubious look. "And where might that be?"

"Camden road." said Pone.

"I know where that is," said Jock. "Where the hell can he hide blow making factory in that neck of the woods.

Pone leaned back stretching his legs crossing his ankles. The area surrounded by a forest with a neighborhood and block away sharing the strip with a BP gas-station across the street and circle K facing it. Then a down and out business park with a barbershop school.

"I tailed your boy to a barbershop school. He went around back entering a door of cone shape tower." Pone sat up straight. "I picked the lock and found a stairwell leading to an underground lab where they cook the product."

Ben frowned. "No security?"

"There are other businesses and some of them take deliveries it might bring suspicious thoughts about why would somebody look like they are protecting the back of a barbershop school at night. Though everything looked closed." said Pone.

"The boy knows how to cut hair." Ben remarked.

Pone exhaled. "Money on the side. He owns a nice ride for someone his age. Don't think his clientele has deep pockets for his hair-cutting talent."

"Damn big man." said Jock. "How much you paying for that nose candy?"

Ben glared. "Shit, I flush it as soon as I got it." He glanced at Pone. "You really want to topple the man?"

"Brick by brick." Pone replied. "Down to his knees."

"Doubt the piece of shit knows how to pray." said Jock.

Pone inhaled." He will when I get through with him."

"You going to do this fast?" Jock asked.

"We have to be careful." said Pone.

Ben nodded. He played the silent partner watching, listening to Jock and Pone babble about what do next. It was all new to him. He'd go out on a job; snap a neck, put a bullet in the melon, or toss a target off building hearing a scream before going splat. Ben a fish out of water when it came to strategy for a job. He didn't want to shoot the bull on a job as important as this so he sat, drank and gave his undivided attention. Pone a friend, no a brother needed him and he didn't want to disappoint. Snake and Sonny cool too. But one too damn weird and the other too damn old to have anything in common except playing poker.

Pone a different breed of killer. Educated, philosophical, and in touch with whats going on in the world. Ben's first assignment not to kill anyone and the big man felt good helping for a good cause, rescuing innocent girls from a monster. He would not let Pone down.

"You okay big man?" Pone asked.

Ben tipped his beer bottle acknowledging Pone. "I'm being a sponge." He straightened in his chair. "You want to keep pissing in his pool."

"No." said Pone. "I am going to."

"You already got your target so I guess it's a matter of when, right?" Ben inquired.

Pone downed his malt beverage. He looked Ben over pondering the giant's inquisition. One, two, three, A, B, C, his motto. See the target, get the target, and annihilate the target then get paid. Pone no longer an assassin since working for Red. His jobs more strategic in the form of troubleshooting. Stop a problem before it got started or don't let it go any further than it already has.

Ben gave Pone the finger.

Pone laughed. "That wasn't necessary."

"I know what you thinking. You ain't the only killer with a degree." said Ben.

"They kill all the time in the corporate world. The difference the victims get another chance to correct their mistakes."

Jock leaned back sipping his beer observing the two men acting like a married couple disagreeing.

"I'm done feeding your ego." said Pone.

"What the hell that's supposed to mean?" Ben requested.

"You got low self-esteem." Pone remarked.

Jock cleared his throat. "Okay you two don't forget why you're here or do I need to call Red?"

"Shit." Ben remarked. "That's his woman."

Pone chuckled looking at Jock. "We cool , right big man?"

Ben nodded. "Solid brother, solid."

"The meths lab. I plan on hitting it." said Pone.

Ben and Jock eyeballed each other.

"They might cut hair in that barbershop, but they cook the product down below." said Pone.

"I got a role in this?" Ben asked.

"You're not here to just take up space." said Pone. "You are a major player."

Ben shook his head. "You ain't figure this out yet have you?"

"Don't want to kill anybody, but I need a distraction. The place needs to be empty when I make my move." Pone replied.

Jock pursed his lips. "Think I got what you need." He rose finishing his grog. "Follow me."

He took out a small rectangle black remote. A red button sat at top of it and he press down. The walls parted like the red sea. Pone never concerned himself about how people looked, but figured more to Jock than his stubby grisly presence. A pawn shop for a front containing enough arsenal to field an assault team. Either deep pockets supported him which was how he knew Red or serious contacts from the military.

"You ever heard of a man name Mercury slim?" Pone inquired.

Jock's body jolted. "A cool name, but no."

Ben gave Pone a look and he waved him off.

Jock waltzed over to two crates grabbing one and gestured to Ben to get the other. They carried them to a table. Jock opened his with care. One crate contained what Pone wanted, he smiled thinking Jock read his mind. The crate contained stun grenades, flash bombs, pineapples, fireballs, other names, but the same results. Pone wanted to stun not kill. He didn't want any casualties. Zero body count on the ship explosion a win and he wanted it to continue. The toys in front of what he needed; the flash grenade renders the mind senseless with blinding light. Marvel comics heroine *The Dazzler* a misused character that should've had her own Netflix series instead of *Jessica Jones*. A combination of blinding light and loud noise turning your brain into scramble eggs.

Jock stood over the fireballs like a hen over her eggs. "How many do you need?"

Pone smirked. "If I'm lucky one." He inhaled giving Ben a look. "In our line it doesn't always go the way we want."

Ben snorted. "So you going to need me?"

"We going stealth in all black and follow my lead." said Pone.

"You really want to piss off the bastard?" Jock remarked.

"Incest and a pedophile." Pone inhaled.. "If up to me, I'd put a bullet between the eyes. I have to keep in mind it's a catch and retrieve, but nothing putting a foot in his ass." Pone eye-ball the other crate.

Jock popped it open and Ben got moon-eye.

"Buck shot." said Ben.

"No." said Jock shaking his head. "They make a big bang though so you better cover your ears."

Pone observed what Ben confused as buck shot. "Cracker Jacks."

"Say what?" Ben questioned.

"Poppers." said Pone. "What you see here lying in sawdust big man is called Poppers. Good for a distraction. Think you can handle that?"

"Tell me what to do and I'll get it done." said Ben.

"Make sure you do it outside." said Jock.

"I'll take all of those," said Pone. "And half of the stun grenades though one might do the job."

"They look like shot-gun shells." said Ben.

Pone gave a dubious look.

"I know," said Ben "No killing."

"We're far from done big man." Pone replied.

Ben nodded. He knew it was Pone's way of saying taking a life might be unavoidable, but tread light and pay heed not shed any blood.

"That's why we doing this at night." said Pone. "The last time there pretty crowded and a lot of youth, but I have a plan for that." He looked at Jock.

"Hold on," Jock got moon-eye. "This is the best you'll get out of me. I ain't much use in field. Just slow y'all down."

"How are using a burner phone?" Pone asked.

Jock shrugged. "What am I an operator?"

"Can you text?" Pone asked.

"Anything to help the cause." said Jock.

"Big man," Pone motioned to Ben. "Give Jock silhouette's number."

Ben did as asked.

"No talking and I'll write down what you need to say when I contact you at the time you need to send the text." said Pone.

Jock nodded. "I'll be ready and waiting."

Pone looked at both men. "No one died on that ship and I want the same for this task." He thought about the impromptu help he got that save him form killing one of the crew men standing in front of the port hole holding up his escape. The athletic figure look like a woman, but he didn't complain who it was that had come to his rescue.

"For the record," said Ben. "I know you want everything done on the down-low, but Theiler ain't dumb."

"If he finds out it us he'll regret it." Pone said in a stern voice.

Ben nodded. "My man."

"Flash bombs." He nodded. "Cracker Jacks on the fly."

Jock rolled his eyes. "Let me give you boys a crash course."

Pone smiled.

ed set the tray on the coffee table and perfect timing to sound of the door bell. Linda stood smiling dressed in a gray dress hemmed at the knee, pearls around her neck and hair in a bun. Her usual look except she looked slender. Linda strolled past her observing baby sister parking herself on the couch in front of the refreshment tray.

Red exhaled and smiled. "The trip to Europe seems to have done you some good."

Linda gave a side view profile batting her eyelashes. "You notice." She pursed her lips. "It was nice to get away."

Red twisted her mouth thinking to her self. You, mother, Sue, the husbands, children, and staff. She and Paul J the two who branch out to their own homes and privacy against their mother's will fearing Red and Paul J made easy pickings for their enemies to divide and conquer. So far she and big brother still alive and well. Linda and her clan living with mother not a curse but growing up with big sister who thirty minutes older than Sue a no brainier to go out and get your own place. Plus no way Angel was going submit herself to Linda's torturous words mocking her modeling career and lucky to be married to Paul J to live a life of luxury.

Mary had a house full and Red could tell in their conversations she wouldn't mind the twins taking their brood and leave the nest and then again with Dad resting in peace, she sometimes welcomed the company of her family. Red tried convincing Sue just because she and Linda twins she didn't need to play follow the leader all the way into adulthood. When they were kids having tea parties, Red stormed off not because she couldn't have her way being the youngest, but Linda controlled everything and Sue did her bidding.

She even married the same type of man, portly, average height with the only difference the hair, and she gave birth to boys instead of girls. Linda kept Sue in the low self-esteem closet putting her down making her feel lost with out her. Red surprised Sue didn't tagged along on the Linda's vacation, but glad she didn't. There may be hope yet.

Red sat down fixing her cup of coffee and grabbing a Belvita blueberry biscuit dunking it into her java." So how's the family?"

"Mine or everyone?" Linda replied.

"Pick one," Red remarked.

"Your brother-in-laws are the same." said Linda.

*Overweight, boring, and hen pecked,*thought Red.

Linda turned her eyes toward the ceiling. "Your nieces and nephews are growing up fast and mother is in good health and as for our brother and his crew... well I haven't heard anything bad so I assume they are fine." She exhaled.

Red shook her head. Angel thought it better to keep her distance and Paul J stuck by his wife's decision to see the family if it meant business, birthdays, and holidays. "What did you do?"

"Why must you assume the worst of me baby sister?" Linda inquired.

"I grew up with you and when you call me baby sister you are eager for me to ask." said Red.

Linda rolled her eyes. "Well... you notice I lost weight and now Sue is trying to do the same." A Cheshire cat smile grace her face. "I just told her it won't be easy."

Red swallowed hard. The golden age of television came to mind thinking about Lucille Ball and Ethel Mertz played by Vivian Vance. Lucy wanted her counterpart to be on the heavy side because she wanted to be the slim one proving what you love about characters on TV can be a bitch in reality." Hope you weren't too hard on her. You know of all of us she has a fragile ego." Red gave a stern look. "Thanks to you." She muttered.

"Did you say something? I didn't quite catch your last words." said Linda.

"We are not kids anymore." Red replied.

Linda nodded. "True and in any case mother always picks up the pieces."

I'll have a one on one with Sue, thought Red. Not the first time she pulled her to the side to convince Linda's better half she needed to blaze her own trail. "Why do you do that?"

"What are you inquiring?" Linda questioned nibbling and sipping.

Red smiled shaking her head. "You know Sue idols you and yet you make her feel obsolete."

Linda pursed her lips. "We shared the same room for nine months. If I had my way I'd ask for a separate room." She studied Red's stare. "You ever heard of tough love?"

"Do you know the difference?" Red questioned.

"I asked her to join me on my crusade but she abort. You know the old saying you can lead a horse to water... you know the rest."

Red nodded. Linda looked good, but Red didn't want to swell her head more than it already was. Red sat back crossing her leg.

"Time to get down to business." said Red

"Thomas Maxwell the next mayor of our fair city." Linda remarked.

"He hasn't won yet." said Red.

"He will and I hope he'll be ready to play ball." Linda replied.

Red swallowed hard. "I warned him."

Linda got moon-eye." Hope you didn't scare him from running?"

"Don't get your panties in a bunch." Red remarked. "He knows with the family backing him we expect something in return as long as it's nothing sinister."

"Is that you or him talking?"

"He's good man Linda." said Red.

Linda smiled. "So you care about him."

"He has integrity." Red replied." Don't ask him to sell his soul."

Linda raised an eye-brow. "That's harsh considering Dad supported a lot of politicians." She sipped her coffee. "Relax. It's business."

"That's what I'm afraid of." Red gave an icy glare.

J Paul was a good husband, father, uncle, brother, and son, but no saint. Red had visions of him bathing in blood and enjoying it. The Brigand band empire financed by blood money. She ponder if that the reason for the color of her hair as a reminder of her family wealth. Blood on her father's hand transferred to her hair. Paul J hair blonde, the twins sandy/brunette and her's scarlet.

"He'll fit in your back pocket." Red winked.

Linda cleared her throat. "Is he still in your dog house?"

"Mother wants me to speak on his behalf instead of you."

Linda leaned forward. "You know him better than I do." \

"You want details?" Red remarked.

"Show some class." Linda snorted. "At least tell me to surf the Internet."

"You're not bothered about not being at his side." Red questioned.

"In case you haven't noticed I have a man and political candidates have a significant other standing next to them."

From childhood to adulthood Linda craved the spotlight; school plays to local theater. She was front and center standing out from the crowd. "I believe he went whining to dear mother anyway." Linda muttered.

"What?" Red asked.

"What?" Linda responded.

"You smart off didn't you?" Red suggested." I know because that look you gave me."

Linda shrugged drinking her coffee. "That's me being me."

"No." Red straighten. "It's me and you. You got something to say spill it."

"He was doing his job." Linda bounced her head around. "Not by the books, but his job."

Red sat back folding her arms and crossing her legs. "He didn't prevent the gang war."

Linda nods rolling her eyes. "Okay Mister Pone came through."

"Winston pardon him." said Red.

"In secret." Linda snapped her finger. "As if that's going to save his political career."

"He has a clean slate working for a respectable prominent attorney."

"Why is it when me or anyone in the family or outside say something about Pone you look like you're about to erupt like a volcano?" Linda questioned. "I hope it's not what I think it is."

"And wouldn't that be the pot calling the kettle black?" Red glared.

Linda pursed her lips. "Caution baby sister, you can hide behind your law degree, but the city knows your family history."

"If I hadn't become a lawyer you and I wouldn't be doing what we're doing now." said Red.

"Is that the real reason you became a lawyer?" Linda questioned. She turned up her nose. "That's better than Sue and PJ."

Red snorted. "One's a follower and the other don't give a damn."

"Well Murray and Stanley serves their purpose." Linda remarked.

Red gave a stern look. "Sue loves her marriage."

Linda exhaled. "We have obese husbands. We gave grandchildren, but since you're a lawyer observe what I'm saying."

J Paul met with his future son-in-laws one on one. A banker and a real estate. You need financing and who better to have on your side, but a banker to give you the money you need by property to set up businesses and a Realtor to know what, where, and how the right spot to lay down the foundation for expanding the family empire.

"I know the standard dad set for you and Sue." Red voiced apologizing for her father.

"He put baby brother to work." said Linda.

Paul J did background checks on both men to see if they were high in their area of expertise in banking and real estate. The son in-laws prove to be a valuable assets to the Brigand band family.

"Did you have another in mind, Linda?"

Linda gave a faint smile." I couldn't disappoint our beloved father."

"You have a right to be happy and so does Sue." said Red.

"They worship us." Linda replied. "How many women you know can boast that?"

Red looked Linda up and down." Is that the reason for the transformation? You plan on stepping out?"

"Bite your tongue." said Linda. "Hubby has lost a few pounds himself and besides I'm too old... oops, I should bite my own tongue calling myself old."

The sisters laughed.

Linda inhaled. "I'm off the market. I'm wealthy, a loyal husband, beautiful children, life is good and plenty of money till the day I die."

Red exhaled. "And if Thomas wins you have your pocket politician."

"It would be better if he became a member of our family."

Red got moon-eye and sat up straight." I knew that was coming."

"And why not?" Linda inquired. "What are you waiting for?"

"I don't want a businesses arrangement."

"You mean like your sisters?" said Linda.

"Sue is love, but you?" Red raised an eye-brow.

"Don't play holier that thou with me." said Linda. "You afraid you wouldn't be faithful?"

"We are supporting, banking his campaign and that should be enough." Red replied.

"It doesn't hurt to put icing on the cake." Linda remarked.

Red frowned." Too much sugar is not good for you."

"What are you afraid of?"

"Caring about someone and in love are two different things." said Red. "He's got banking and any place inside the city to deliver his speeches. No need for me do except be there for show and nothing more."

"He loves you." said Linda.

Love, the word that scares the hell out of most people because it means committing yourself to one person who hopes to have you forever or till death due you apart. Red wouldn't tell Linda, but no man and no children good for her. If she needed to be around kids she'd borrow the nieces and nephews. A companion, Thomas fit the bill. She never the one to host male callers though she could have her pick of the litter. No the single life good to her. She owned a business, money she built on her own not needing the family fortune to enhance her lifestyle and she believe that made Linda jealous trying to convince her time to jump the broom.

Red waited for Linda to play the age card.. Aging never bothered her since it's unavoidable so why worry about gray hair and wrinkles. It happens to all who are fortunate to carry on with life. The ones who stress over it were people who missed out on life while they were young and made life for themselves worse contemplating on what could have been. She on the other hand felt lucky.

"I'm not the marrying type. I'm a spoiled independent woman." said Red." I care about him, respect him, and want the best for him, but I could never take what I can't give back."

"You keep him around for what?" Linda asked.

"Women with the reputation of having a lot of men don't get high-fives and praise. We're frown upon and called sluts. Why the boys get worshiped for being womanizers." Red exhaled. "I'm a solid six-foot in bare feet and he's five-foot what ever inch wearing lifts in his shoes and that helps but so much. Most men his lack of stature wouldn't dream of approaching a woman taller than him and ask for a dance. I admire him and we've had good times. But you are raising the stakes and need to lower your expectations."

"Is there any other reason you wouldn't marry him besides height?" Linda asked.

Red frowned." He hasn't asked… are you twisting his arm forcing him to?"

"I love you too much to dig in your personal life." said Linda.

The sisters inhaled taking the tense conversation down a notch. Linda pressed the right button getting a rise out of Red. They didn't agree on a lot of things. But when push came to shove, blood is thicker than water.

"I'm going to sound like mother telling you are a grown woman and can do as you please, but I hope you're not holding out."

Red squinted." Please indulge me, Linda."

"Pone." Linda snorted. "Taller, educated, handsome, sexy, charming, quick wit, and dangerous gives him an edge."

"Let' not forget he's no longer a hired killer." Red remarked.

"But… "Linda held up a finger.

"But nothing." Red injected." Our business and the people we deal with in my firm… my clientele and associates pay good money for problems that they and the police cannot handle. Pone is a troubleshooter and so far things have worked out well since his transformation. His background comes in handy and let's not forget we don't live in a perfect world and if he has to make a decision to keep himself alive well as you and I both know it comes with the territory."

"Not what I was aiming for, but let's not compare him to the police." said Linda.

Red smiled shaking her head." You're right because our boys in blue dust off a man holding a hammer. More than one of them they filled the poor sap full of holes."

"Okay, "Linda shrugged." I never said the flatfoots were perfect and some should not wear the badge. They do come in handy from time to time."

Red inhaled deep releasing a long exhale. Dirty cops and crime families a dime a dozen and she saw enough coppers in her youth in and out of the family estate talking, drinking, and laughing with her father. The lot of the police paid heed fearing her because of the family name and most of them on the payroll. Red disgusted with the connection with the constables and knew Linda kept the tradition their father left behind going.

"Chubby works outside of the law, but for the right reason. You and I both know the law isn't perfect." Red snorted." Is that your reason for your sudden health craze? I saw the two of you at the family dinner."

"Did you tell him I wanted his head on a silver platter?" said Linda raising her eyebrow.

"You almost jumped out of your skin when I told you he wanted out after daddy's death." said Red.

"We can't take any chances of someone so close to the family running around unsupervised."

Red swallowed hard. "Chubby wanted revenge. He got involve to get close and you know the rest. Daddy saw his talent and used it to his advantage and was wrong for doing so."

"Eternal checkout is the way you leave." said Linda.

"There's a place for us all in the bone yard. We just don't know where, when, and how. What are you afraid of?" Red asked.

"We have to much to lose and you know that."

"The worst that can happen is the government swoop in and crumbled our family empire. You know better than me, God don't like ugly."

"We all fall together." Linda replied.

Red shook her head. "And that's the problem. Sins of the father. Do we know his exact crimes? I don't want to sound naive, but I don't know who or when... "

"He made sure we have enough bread to burn a wet mule (very rich). It's called business." said Linda.

Red cleared her throat. "Despite the smudges on our family, dad kept us in the dark how they got there." She gave Linda a stern look. "Unless you've done something on your own."

Linda laughed which meant she had gotten her hands bloody, but not pulling the trigger. No she has an enforcer for that, but Red knew she gave the go ahead to carry out threats against the family.

"You do know we have relatives and people in the government." Linda remarked.

Red took a sipped of her coffee now cold. She saw it as sign meaning J Paul covered everything up even from the grave. The government wouldn't be bum rushing the Brigand Band anytime soon since it would put the bulk of them in a bad situation. The family safe from any discretion because the man was brilliant when it came to organize crime.

"Here we are talking about dad, what if, and doing it in prohibition dialogue. Is your house bugged?" Linda questioned.

"You better do a Houdini(disappear, leave in a hurry)." Red remarked.

Linda giggled. "What was Pone going to do? Put that degree to work?"

Red gave a look." He's not Wisdom."

J Paul retired Wisdom to a humbling job writing violation tickets keeping an eye on the deteriorating ex-killer. The Brigand Band knew he didn't need the job since he swam in a pool of blood money, but he wanted a peace of mind to sooth his soul from his violent life.

Linda brush back her hair. "The dead tell no tales."

"Not verbal anyway." Red replied.

Linda poured them both of them a fresh cup. "To Wisdom." She waited till Red hoisted her cup. "May he rest in peace."

The sisters toasted.

Linda cleared her throat. "I want to clear the air with Mister Pone putting him at ease."

Red exhaled. "You did the math."

Linda squirmed. "Yeah... okay... I know if he wanted he could erase us. You broke the family rule."

Red pursed her lips. "Not that it's any of your business."

Linda got moon-eye. "Oh contraire. It's the family's business. I felt the chemistry between the two of you."

"We have a connection you wouldn't understand."

"He's hired help and should know his place."

Red smirked. "He's not on my payroll. He has refused pay, but I pay him anyway under the table."

Linda swallowed hard. "If you say he's a partner, I'll throw up."

"Follow your nose to the bathroom." Red remarked. "He doesn't have to do what I tell him."

"He cares about you." said Linda.

"As I about him." Red replied. "Are you here on behalf of the family?"

"Our conversation stays here." said Linda. "If you jump the broom it better be with the politician."

"Is that a threat?"

"A lot of people knows Pone's reputation." said Linda.

"So you know how much damage that do to my career." Red replied.

Linda nodded satisfaction that her sister had enough sense to recognize she and Pone could never be. Red ran a respectable law practice and her competition would jump at the bit to smear her reputation.

"A cute pet name." said Linda.

"What's that?"

"Pony." said Linda. Mind if I use it."

Red shrugged. "You might not get the same results."

Linda inhaled." A word of caution little sister."

Red ran her hands through her hair then rest them on her lap. Giving Linda her uninvited attention.

Linda gave a stern look. "Make sure that bond doesn't break the wrong way."

Red straighten. "What's that supposed to mean?"

Linda held her hands like a justice balance scale. "Pone and Maxwell? Maxwell and Pone?"

She smiles. "Politician and former assassin."

Red gave a stern look. "I'm not the marrying type." She shook her head. "If Maxwell wins he will be a hip pocket politician. What more do you want?"

"When he wins." Linda stated holding up a finger. "Positive thinking dear sister. A married candidate strengthens his position."

Red relaxed her body keeping her composure. Linda had overstayed her welcome and she could tell the way Linda kept moving on the sofa she knew it was time to end her visit.

"You are still part of this family." said Linda.

Red gave a smirk. She wanted to be a lawyer since she was six years old. She didn't know much about the family business until six years later and the law wouldn't help erase her bloody past. Linda wanted Pone because it defined every thing their father put in front of him by voicing his opinion on how to handle situations different than his other gun-men even Wisdom. Red rescued Pone from her clutches by saying he'd work for her firm as a personal troubleshooter keeping the peace. The two sisters didn't hide their animosity toward each other.

Mary trumped whatever grievance they had saying they are sisters and needed to act like it. Red would not become a bend the rules attorney not even for her family. She wanted a clean conscience for the sins committed by her brood. Red demanded a clean lineage telling her clan they needed discretion dealing with her. She knew they would not change the way they did business.

Red smiled. "This city knows who I am and where I come from, but my practice is not dirty."

"I'm not asking you to smudge your immaculate reputation, We are very proud of you. A role model for the next generation of Brigands. Some of your nieces and nephews talk about following auntie Brooke's footsteps."

"And you're okay with that?"

Linda looked at Red sideways. "Myself, Sue, and PJ want our children to earn their way despite knowing they have the family fortune to fall back on. We don't want to leave the empire in careless hands."

"You should take advantage of their youth and scare with bed time stories if they mishandle the wealth their ancestors will rise from the grave to punish them." said Red.

Linda toasted. "Oh dear sister you do have a wicked sense of humor."

Red returned the gesture. "I'm glad to hear they won't be sucking on the silver spoon."

Linda nodded. "Thought that might cut through the tension in the air."

"So everything in the universe is good?" Red asked.

Linda pursed her lips. "Every politician needs a good woman by his side."

"No wedding bells." Red muttered.

"You can't be a trophy without the wife."

Red rose from her seat. "For the family."

Linda stood. "The family."

TWENTY-ONE

Pone sat in his motel room with Ben looking over the crates of flash grenades and popper on top of the saw dust. He then took a moment looking at his accommodation. The place clean, beds made, fresh towels, and no sign of infestations. The flophouse located in a nice area of the big easy surrounded by two greasy spoons that Ben enjoys, but Pone keeps his distance eating the deli sandwiched shops they pass by on their way back to the caravansary. An upscale motel six the owner cared enough to keep immaculate so the tourist might want to come back to and give rave reviews to family and friends.

"What's going on my man?" Ben asked.

"You know I'm accustom to fine living." Pone laughed.

"Wondering when that spoiled pretty boy was going to appear." said Ben.

"I know we couldn't be discrete in a five star hotel."

Ben snorted. "I'll be glad when this shit is over too."

Pone nodded. "Trying to figure out having zero casualties."

Ben swallowed hard. "Unless you bum rush in screaming and yelling you better get the hell out of here or you going to die and they believe you and haul ass."

"If their in there cooking, I can't flash bomb them because I die and that wouldn't be good for me." Pone replied. "Youthful guys making the product."

"I was hoping to hear your favorite catch phrase."

Pone frowned. "What are you talking about?"

"When I die, I'm really going to miss me." Ben smirked.

"What can I say? I love myself better than I love myself."

Ben straighten in his chair." What's bugging you?" He shook his head." You ain't got over that shit yet have you?"

Pone exhales. It was the first time and he hoped the last time he would take lives so young. He wasn't weighed down with guilt like Ben thought. Pone sad, but glad he has a conscience because it meant he is human. The youthful lives he took didn't understand you live by the sword you die by the sword. They left behind love ones that missed, but hated Pone even though he stood on the right side of the scales of justice. He avenge the life of an eight year old boy. Pone felt at peace about that, burning the bodies made him think he went too far, but it felt right at the time sending a message he not one to be toyed with. He didn't attend the funerals though he imagined picture frames hung above the closed caskets.

The Hip-hoppers said he had parlay, but Pone knew those words of crossed fingers hidden behind their backs. The boys tried to kill him influenced by easy cash, cheap women, and a gangster lifestyle. Pone shook his head despite being out of killer-for-hire business, he'd have to watch his back because their would be some old-heads and upstarts waiting to make a name for himself who took down Chubby Pone.

"You got that kid's number?" Pone asked.

Ben frowned." Yeah, so?"

"I got a plan and Jock can help."

Ben shook his head." You do know there's a chance we won't get out of here without a body count?"

Pone swallowed hard. "I don't want a high casualty, Ben. I am aware we're going to leave some scars behind. You don't need to remind me."

"I am because you trying to be too cautious and that might be our asses. That my brother would be a casualty. Whether you want to admit it or not we are in the business of delivering death."

Pone gave Ben a look.

Ben snorted. "Okay I'm in that business. I'll follow your lead... I'm the killer and you a troubleshooter putting you on the other side of law." He nodded. "I'm the scum bag."

Pone raised an eyebrow. "I'm not going to argue with you."

Ben glared. "To hell with you, man."

"Things are going to get hot and heavy. I opened a wound and I'm going to keep pouring the salt." said Pone. "You all in?"

"I got your back." Ben replied. "What if shit happens?"

"We haven't played the game this long being sloppy." Pone remarked." We have extra motivation and I plan to save those girls."

Theiler threw down his second shot of hash. His face soured to the taste of the strong bourbon and poured himself another. He dropped down hard on the chair behind his desk. Theiler couldn't drink enough to drown his sorrows. What fools would invade his house opening his refrigerator without asking his permission. A loud knock door brought the pedophile from the depths of depravity.

"Enter." said Theiler.

Ludwig stepped in taking up the door space before turning sideways allowing the messenger inside taking a seat in front of Theiler's desk. Ludwig shut door standing in front like a palace guard preventing entry and no escape. Theiler threw down another shot then focused on the man he hope brought him good news.

"Make me smile," said Theiler.

Peary, Theiler's PR man who is in charge of wheeling and dealing with making business connections and his man to look into matters when they go bad which didn't happen too often until recent. The average height, gray suit bow-tie wearing slick back black hair clean shaven man except a Hitler style mustache sitting on top of his lip. He look Theiler in the eye.

"Whoever took out your boat is an outsider." said the bookworm man.

Theiler straighten leaning back in his chair." I ain't smiling."

Peary pursed his lips. "Your poker games sir,"

"What about it?" Theiler questioned.

"It's an easy way for your enemies to get close to your operation." Peary replied. "Talk to people and ask discrete questions."

Theiler pondered Peary words. He hated the man's arrogance how he showed no fear addressing him unlike the others in his camp. Ludwig with his hairy condition was hard to know what he thought, but anything Theiler asked of him he did with out any questions. He found Ludwig as a boy left to fend for himself being treated like an outcast because of his hairy features looking like a twenty-four hour werewolf he had no control over. Theiler took him in unaware the youth would grow as tall as an NBA player and becoming his body guard and enforcer. The benefit Theiler enjoyed from Ludwig, his loyalty.

Ludwig's strange condition would not be good for going out into the field for face to face negotiations and that's where Peary came in. The man educated and most of all he loved money which won Theiler's heart. He didn't trust anybody who didn't love money. Whoever said the best things in life are free he would not befriend. Peary not a friend, but a valuable asset taking care of business. Theiler considered them his non-biological sons, brawn and brains. In brawn he trusted, but brain a malaise. A man with a good head on his shoulders working for you... needed to be scrutinize.

"The games have been going on for long time now and I never had my property destroyed so why now?" Theiler questioned.

Peary shrugged." Perhaps you have something whoever did this wants."

"What could I have besides what I have?" Theiler remarked. "My wealth is hard earned and I ain't the only one who broke the rules to get it I guarantee."

"It's personal." said Peary." They target your pocket."

Theiler pour another shot. He didn't drink it right a way, but studied it letting what Peary said sink in. He used the games for money, recruit talent and lure men to his house to see if they shared his perverted desires. He'd catch them on video and blackmailing them to do his bidding. Court judges, and politicians his focus and his plan worked. No way any of them would try to get back at him since if he were to die by their hands what he contained on tape would be all over the Internet. The skeleton in the closet maneuver prove to be very profitable. When he needed money or favors they did not turn him down and he loved that kind of power. Those under his thumb kept his empire afloat and that habit he plan to keep.

"You know the games must go on." said Theiler.

Peary nodded. "Of course, sir. You need the perverts and whatnot in your fold too continue your success."

Peary lowered his eye and swallowed hard knowing his silver tongue went to far. He felt the presence of Ludwig and Theiler's glare weighing him down.

"Why'd you look at me when you said the word pervert?" Theiler asked.

Peary crossed his legs, sat up straight folding his arms to his chest." I was taught to look a man in the eye when talking to him. You hired me because you saw in me what your previous men in my position didn't have... balls to speak open. I was not referring to you, but I know men who prey on the young male or female for pleasure are what you are looking for to expose them if they don't do your bidding. Since I know this, that means I know too much to ever think of leaving your fold unless in a body bag. With that being said I meant no disrespect."

Theiler gave a long stare. His pedophile habit put on hold during the current events; exploding contraband ship, mending fences and some still pending repair. Money took precedence over pleasure.

"How do we weed out my disturbances according to you because boy, I have so many?"

"You own the bars at the docks and your dealers at the casinos."

Peary snorted. They are your eyes and ears."

A gruesome grin came across Theiler's face." Keep talking boy, I'm listening."

Peary smile to hide his displeasure of Theiler calling him boy. He didn't know it a Cajun habit, but Theiler used it a lot when he got frustrated and this frustrating times for the kingdom had been infiltrated.

"Talk to them, ask if they notice any particular characters stand out. I know it's a stretch since New Orleans is a tourist attraction, but it's a start to stop this thing from festering. Whisper a slight reward to motivate them to keep a close eye and if they spot something or someone out of the ordinary then contact as soon as possible."

"I don't have an virtues so you can forget about patience. I want results fast." said Theiler.

"That's what you hired me to do. I'll make some calls to spread the news and I won't mention the amount you'd pay for valuable information, but it needs to be quick and discrete." Peary replied.

"Pay heed, pay heed." said Theiler.

Peary rose from his chair taking that as his cue to leave. The money good but like many employees he loathed his boss, but the money too good to ignore and a nine to five not for him, but if and when Theiler met his demise no tear would be shed. Ludwig played bellman opening the door for him to exit. Theiler drank the rot gut savoring the taste to ease his frustration. He wanted to get back to his hobby, but believe the distraction would interrupt his satisfaction.

Instead his mind turned to what he'd do to the perpetrators once he found them. He'd torture them slow with severe pain. Theiler would have Ludwig soften them up by breaking an arm or a leg and use their noggin for a speed bag with his big mitts. His smile turned to more of a concern wondering if the interlopers were going to be like a mosquito flying around him making that annoying buzzing noise waiting to find a spot on him to suck more blood. He turned the shot glass upside down slamming it on the desk.

TWENTY-TWO

Pone sat beside Ben looking through the infrared binoculars, "Is that him?" Pone asked.

Ben peered through his matching pair. "Yeah." He said in his base voice nodding. "That's my dealer."

Pone wanted confirmation though he followed the youth to the front barber shop,he yet wanted Ben's seal of approval.

"Your dealer, huh?" Pone mocked smirking.

"We playing a role. Right?" Ben replied. "What's so damn funny?"

"You sure you didn't snort?" Pone questioned.

"He thought so, except for the sleight of hand." Ben frowned. "I ain't putting that shit inside my body."

Pone put his attention back on the door. "Okay here they come... three, four... damn."

"Problem?"

"Got to be more." said Pone. "It was the last time I was here."

Ben shrugged. "Somebody called in sick?"

"Doubt that," said Pone. He watched Silhouette lead his skeleton crew to the front of the abandoned business park. "Okay, Jock did his job and now it's showtime."

"What about the guy left behind?" Ben asked.

"Let's hope they do have sick days." Pone remarked.

Ben smirked. "Shit, you don't believe that."

"Nobody said this was going to be easy." Pone checked his black back pack then attached it to his back. "Look sharp and if anything unusual, well I trust you can handle it."

Ben snorted "I'll do my best."

"This is not the time, Ben."

"Then don't insult me." Ben replied.

"You keep that in mind when you see me go inside." Pone took off like a rabbit thinking he better make this quick before Silhouette figure the text a ruse. He got to the door, took his lock pick using the moon-light and like a professional he got inside. Pone crouched down lifting his head quick like a Jack-in-the-box. The coast clear, he made a beeline down the stairs to an empty Meth lab so he thought till he heard a flush. *Damn, the one that got left behind,* he thought.

Mimosa Grill on 300 South Tryon where white collar and blue bloods go to wine and dine. A small square table in romantic lighting with two large wine glasses filled to the rim and water glasses with lemon wedges flanking the dinner plates. A Filet Mignon drenched in A-1 steak sauce, steak fries with a silver saucer of ketchup, and lemon salmon sitting on a bed of wild-rice. The fork sliced the tender pink morsel like a hot knife through butter. Linda sipped her wine to wash it down then dabbed the corners of her mouth ladylike.

"How's your Salmon?" Maxwell asked.

"Oh," Linda smiled." Chef Whales never disappoints." She examines Maxwell's plate. "Your steak?"

"The way I like it." He chewed, swallowed, and drank." Rare enough to see blood."

"Indeed." Linda replied. She saw the little district attorney as a squeamish man. Rumors swirled around the city how Brooke played *Wonder Woman* rescuing him from the clutches of Harvey Crowe who has disappeared from existence. Linda had her ideas about what happened to the lieutenant governor taking the lives of two gangsters children. The Hip-hoppers and Prohibition formed a once in a life time unholy alliance giving Crowe a deserve send off. A spin doctor came in to rescue Winslow making him the master mind preventing the gang war between the two rival gangs "Daddy use to say it's still breathing."

Maxwell nodded and smiled taking another bite then sipped his wine.

"So." Linda placed her fork on the table resting her hands by her side." Are you ready to be the next mayor of Metro city?"

"Well, yeah, sure... "Maxwell shrugged." It's time for a change."

Linda gave a stern look." You don't sound sure of yourself?"

Maxwell twitched carving his meat into small bites." Oh, I'm confidant, never the less underestimate your opponent."

"Bullshit!" Linda remarked.

A few patrons and Maxwell gave Linda a dubious look. Her outburst not very etiquette.

"Excuse me?" Maxwell whispered. He smiled to the concern faces trying to defuse the fire.

He and Linda sat in a romantic area of the eatery not by candle light. The dinner not romantic though business and in the company of socialites; the kind who fine dining with symphony music and peace to aid in digestion.

"Well, that's not very ladylike." said Maxwell.

"I'm a business woman first and a lady when I get what I want." Linda responded.

Maxwell put down his fork sitting up straight. The conversation with Red hit home. He saw himself as a puppet with the strings attached controlling his every movement or worse a dummy sitting on Linda's lap with her hand up his ass being his ventriloquist uttering her words. His own mind asked him a question; was he a man or mouse. Maxwell inhaled. He grabbed his his half filled glass of wine and down the hatch.

Maxwell looked Linda straight in the eye swallowing hard. "What do you want?"

Linda inhaled giving the district attorney a faint smile. She had awaken the sleeper. The bold woman reached across the table grabbing a french fry off his plate dipping it the pool of ketchup. She held up the morsel allowing it to drip. "Blood."

Maxwell frowned. "Excuse me?"

Linda devoured the fry. "You need a killer instinct."

Maxwell straighten his tie. "I will run a clean campaign."

Linda nodded. "No mudslinging, but let me give you some flash cards."

"What do you mean?" Maxwell asked folding his arms."

"Talk about the incumbent regime; Harvey Crowe and Winston fleeing the city when he was needed most."

Maxwell exhaled. "I have a great staff and speech writer."

"Just give them that and run with it."

"You know I am working with Brooke, right?" Maxwell questioned.

Linda winked. "You two have history."

Maxwell snorted. "And I know I..."

"Fucked up." Linda uttered.

Maxwell rubbed the back of his head.

Linda leaned in. "Was that ladylike enough for you?"

"What did she say about me?" He asked.

"Do you care about her?" Linda retorted.

Maxwell got moon-eye. "I love her."

"Strong words that sometimes ruins a relationship." Linda remarked.

Maxwell frowned. "I guess she doesn't feel the same way about me."

"Have you asked her to marry you?"

Maxwell pursed his lips." She'd shoot me down."

"The city respects her for being a good lawyer and not because of the Brigand name. That alone should help your bid for mayor." said Linda.

"Is that why she's taking the bull by the horns instead of you?" Maxwell questioned.

"You have our support,however she'll get you to the finish line." Linda stated.

"What's your stake in my winning?"

Linda batted her eye-lashes." What do you mean?"

Maxwell swallowed hard." I feel you're going to have me on speed dial."

"Absolutely." said Linda." We are banking your campaign. Favors will be expected. Brooke didn't go over this with you?"

Maxwell exhaled. He felt like he sold his soul to the devil. Linda's words sent a chill down his spine. Red mentioned and warned he'd be a pocket politician. He wasn't mayor yet he could feel Linda digging her claws deep into his flesh.

"I appreciate the funding for my campaign, never the less I am hopeful there wouldn't be any strings attached." said Maxwell.

"You will be free to do as you please so relax." said Linda seeing Maxwell hadn't touched his plate since the conversation. "You haven't lost your appetite, have you?"

Maxwell smiled." It's important we have an understanding, right?"

"Such as?" Linda questioned.

"When I become mayor I plan to go after Chubby Pone." Maxwell stated.

Linda cackled." Jealousy doesn't become you."

"He's going down."

"He's off limits."

"He's a criminal." said Maxwell. "Are you protecting him?"

"Where have you been... under a rock?" Linda replied. "Cleared after saving the city from a gang war which the spin doctors made it look like he was working for the DA's office." Linda harpooned her salmon with a bed of rice added to it. She looked at Maxwell teasing him placing her food inside her mouth. "You and I know the truth plus he's been exonerated from all crimes."

"You plan to get in my way?" Maxwell asked.

"You think he's the reason you're not married to my sister?"

"She needs to stay away from him. He going to damage her image." said Maxwell.

Linda saw rage and envy in Maxwell. She hoped Red and Pone not under the radar involved yet they gave no clue they were not and did a good job keeping the family on edge with worry they might have an intimate relationship. Red did nothing to prove they weren't and in her own discrete way telling them none of their damn business. Red told Linda she was furious with Maxwell for planning a coup against Pone with Crowe. If not for her and Pone she and the DA might end up dead and Maxwell owed them both his life. Linda felt that misdeed by Maxwell strengthen the relationship between her sister and the troubleshooter.

"He works for her and they have a bond." Linda retorted.

"I thought you hated him?"

Linda sipped her wine." He's a fantasy."

Maxwell gave her a look.

Linda shook her head." Like you don't surf the internet for porn." She reached across the table touching Maxwell's hand." If you want to get back on my sister's good side, you better leave him alone."

The one who got left behind stood confused wondering why would they leave turning the flames up high. Did they want to cause an explosion and bale leaving him to die to take the blame. Pone move in with cat quickness putting him in a choke hold rendering him unconscious. The street pharmacist a puny tyke and his neck muscles weak. Pone placed the flash bombs in place and carried his small package over his shoulders to safety. He aborted leaving flash bang grenades lying around after turning up the burners. Pone didn't want to blow up the neighborhood.

Pone dumped his package in the woods a safe distance from the business park. He text Ben to go ahead and set off the poppers outside of the neighborhood and he'd rendezvous with him at the end of the woods. He scurry back to the compound where they made the product and dumped one flash bomb to get the party started. Silhouette and his crew still out front and a good thing. Pone made note inside his head to remember and ask Jock what his text to the street pharmacist. He hauled ass back to the forest away from where he left the unconscious small package then settled behind a tree.

Silhouette and his boys waited until he got a bad feeling in his gut something wasn't right. He turned to the others and before he could utter a word, loud deafening blast came from down the street leading to the highway. Then ground under foot rumbled.

"Run!" Silhouette screamed. He realized while racing away from danger it was a set up to lure them out of the lab. How and who danced inside his head or worse there would be hell to pay. The blame would fall on his shoulders since he in charge of the operation to keep things moving in the right direction. He'd have to explain why he left the lab unattended. In the distance he heard sirens from both police and fire departments on their way to deal with the fireworks. He and his boys had to blend in with the crowd to avoid questioning, for now their business shut down.

Pone crawled out of the bushes to meet Ben who arrived on time. He hopped in the car.

"Time to call it a night, big man." said Pone.

Ben nodded and both men smiled.

TWENTY-THREE

Tara inhaled and exhaled enjoying nature at it's best. Sunlight, a cool breeze, plant life a lot better up close and personal than viewing from her window. She closed her eyes embracing the warmth of the apricate. Spring season a few months away, still though it good to sit in beam of the sun. Tara leaned back on the green wooden bench observing the enormous back yard. The trees with there orange, yellow, and brown leaves representing the chilly months. This was the best of times and the worst of times viewing nature from her window. *Thank God,* she thought getting out of the room she considered a prison cell.

The girls some her age, younger, and older acting like children running around chasing one another holding hands dancing in a circle till they got dizzy falling to the ground. They all needed a retrieve or break from Theiler and his disgusting clients. Tara smiled thinking about the current events told to her by Beef. Whoever sticking it to the king pedophile, please keep on doing it. She looked to the heavens praying for it to continue. Somebody came to New Orleans to let the big bad wolf they were not afraid of him.

The pervert frustrated enough to occupy him from knocking on their doors for his perverted pleasures. Theiler cared more about his businesses than violating young girls. Tara happy watching the girls laughing and talking, but good times don't last and how long would chaos keep them from Theiler's crusty body from lying next to them. His fingers felt like talons, the weight of his lard belly, stench of his breath, and when sex was over it left the girls crying in a fetal position. Tara got a good feeling thinking about the tide turning, now his turn to feel the weight of trouble on his mind that a perpetrator has come to town to ruin him. *Let the good times roll,* she thought leaning back closing her eyes enjoying the cool breeze on her face.

❧ ❧ ❧ ❧ ❧ ❧

"What the hell is going on?" Theiler roared." Blew up my boat and this shit!"

Peary took his normal place front and center to explain the current events. Ludwig stood at the door standing like a palace guard.

"The authorities are investigating." said Peary.

Theiler gave a look.

Peary shook his head." This won't get trace to you if that's your concern."

The front barbershop was one of Theiler's venue to produce his product. The scraper serve it's purpose. He made sure if anything did happen, he wouldn't pay the price by keeping his name away from harms way. Peary and his spin doctors worked their magic covering up the contraband and selling an engine problem caused the boat to explode.

"Where's the boy who was in charge of running things?" Theiler asked.

Peary held up his hand." Again sir, nothing will lead back to you."

Theiler lean forward." That's what I pay you for right? When shit starts stinking you make sure to flush it." He swallowed hard." As you can tell I'm stressed because somebody's messing with my money. Money comes first in my life and what's going on here is messing with my past time."

Peary inhaled to keep from throwing up. He got paid well working for Theiler, never the less he despised the man for what he stood for and well aware of his disgusting habit. Peary smart enough to know his place. "The young man is waiting out side the door, sir."

Theiler snorted. "Get his ass in here."

Ludwig opened the door and Silhouette tread in stepping on egg shells.

Theiler snorted. "Sit your ass down." Theiler gave a burning hole glare." Explain yourself."

Silhouette farted. Peary got up holding his nose walking to far side of the room. Ludwig grunted pulling his shirt to his face and Theiler frowned.

Please sir, I beg you." said Silhouette. "Don't kill me." The flood gates opened with tears running down the youth's face.

"Stop that blubbering!" Theiler demanded. "Man-up, but you pass gas again I will kill you," He looked the youth up and down shaking his head. "Thought I had a man running things. No wonder you fucked up."

Silhouette wiped his tears on his sleeve, sat up straight exhaling.

"What's your name boy?" Theiler asked.

"Terry." He said." Terry Moss."

"Tell Mister Lereaux what happened Mister Moss." said Peary.

Moss shrugged. "I got this text telling me to take my guys to the front of the building for a special task."

Theiler inhaled. "And you didn't bother to ask why?

"My text wouldn't go through and I thought it was from the top and did as I was told." Moss replied.

"Just as you should when you hear from the top brass." Peary stated.

Theiler gave Peary a look.

Moss nodded. "Yes sir, I always follow instructions."

"This the first time you ever gotten a text?" Theiler questioned.

"Like I said I believe it's from above, I don't question I just do." said Moss.

Theiler discrete dealing with his operations having Peary and others do the middle man work while he tends to his other business, but now with things going the wrong way he thought about rethinking how he should take a more hands on approach.

Theiler leaned forward. "And who was your contact?"

"We use burner phones." Peary intervened. "We can't afford to be compromise." He looked at Theiler. "Don't you agree?"

Theiler swallowed hard. He didn't need anymore Intel with Peary acting as the boy's guardian angel. The business need to be careful to keep the authorities at bay, still you can't have contraband ships, Methlab going up in smoke. It can derail your business and you lose valuable contacts who now consider you sloppy. Mistakes happen but you have to be consistent dotting your I's and crossing your T's. Theiler studied the boy. He had done a good job running the west-side Methlab. The lad right thinking Theiler wanted to put a bullet inside his head.

Organize crime credo so the next in line know he needed to be careful with no room for error. Theiler would spare the boy's life and not because Peary seems to have an interest him. Killing the youth would serve no purpose with the damage already done besides you need an audience to send a message putting fear inside them. Ludwig, Peary, and those in question present so Theiler would hold off his intimidation.

"So you and your crew didn't notice anything strange before this happened?" Theiler asked.

"Business as usual." Moss shrugged. "A few haircuts during the day and at night we close up the barbershop and started cooking the product till I got that text."

Peary cleared his throat getting the ire of Theiler.

"Another is waiting outside you might want to question sir." said Peary.

Theiler eyed both Moss and Peary. His intuition stirred inside his head there must something between the two and he'd keep it in the back of his head in case Peary cross the line. He motioned for Ludwig to get the other youth. A nerdy string-bean built shallow twenty-something stroll in looking to the floor avoiding eye contact.

"Let's slow down." said Theiler directing his attention back to Moss. "I ain't done with this one yet."

Peary chest heaved. Moss got moon-eye, and the nerd stopped in his tracks.

"I want you to think real hard." Theiler instructed. "You didn't meet anybody strange or unusual in the past few weeks?" Theiler asked giving Peary a look which he took as to butt out of the conversation.

Moss pursed his lips. "I go to the bar hoping to find new clients, but… "

"We instruct them all to do that," said Peary. "That's how we grow our business finding those who wants to venture into a different world with some help."

Moss lips trembled as if wanting to speak.

"What is it boy?" Theiler asked.

Moss turned around looking back at Ludwig." Him."

Ludwig inhaled rotating his shoulders getting loose in his suit.

"Whoa now boy. You better think twice if you got something to say about Ludwig." said Theiler.

"No… I mean a black man the same size as him hit me up for some nose candy." Moss replied.

Theiler nodded." Now we getting some where."

"Sir." said Peary." New Orleans has a lot big black men."

"But he's the only one I've seen that size come to the bar." Moss retorted. "It could be something?" Moss sounded like he was trying to make amends for mistake to save his skin.

Theiler turned to Peary. "Got to start somewhere and with someone."

Peary walked over to Moss." Is he a regular?"

"I've done business with him twice. He should be running low." said Moss.

Peary looked at Theiler. "Have Terry and the bartender to be on the look out and shadow in the bar to follow this stranger and see what happens."

"What's the name of this bar?" Theiler asked.

"The Last Chance." said Moss.

"An appropriate name." Theiler remarked giving Moss a look.

"It's where you hold your front poker games looking for potential muscle, sir." Peary replied.

"Is he a player?" Theiler asked.

"He won't need to buy product to keep tabs on." said Peary. "The bartender, this kid, and a shadow should have things covered."

"Why not you?" Theiler asked.

Peary straighten his bow tie then brush dust off his shoulders." Dive bars not my kind of place, sir."

Theiler smirked. "On the count of you being so prissy and all. Whose the bartender?"

"Some rectangle shape head fucker with a bug eyes and a long nose." said Moss.

Theiler leaned toward Moss. "How you know he ain't family you talking shit about, boy?"

"No, no sir." Moss responded trembling. "No disrespect."

Theiler roared with laughter." Sound like you describing a horse, but I know the guy and some call him horse-face."

Moss turned pale and his his head sunk between his shoulders like a turtle retreating back inside it's shell.

"Phillip Epstein, sir." said Peary motioning for the nerd to come and have a seat next to Moss.

Theiler rubbed his chin looking at the youth." Tell me a story, boy. Don't put me to sleep."

"One of my best cooks, sir." said Moss.

"Well he ain't cooking shit now is he?" Theiler remarked.

Moss looked toward the floor shaking his head.

Theiler pointed to Moss." How about you sit this one out. I'm curious to hear what this one has to say."

Epstein swallowed hard." I woke up in the woods and saw the lab on fire."

Theiler snorted. "Were you taking a shit and took so long you got bored or what?"

"I did use the bathroom inside the building and when I came out I saw the burners turned up and then I was grabbed from behind arms around my neck and I black out."

Theiler realized who ever did this didn't want to murder, but damage his business. The attacks directed at him. Both incidents ended with zero body count. A blown up ship and now a Methlab gone up in smoke putting a dent in his bank account.

"What did you do when you came through?' Theiler asked.

"I stayed put when I saw the police and fire department waiting for the coast to clear." said Epstein.

Theiler inhaled. "You boys have been a big help. Y'all clear on out and Mister Peary will deal with you. We're done in here."

The somber lads left the room.

Peary sat down facing Theiler." I put them at another location and Moss won't be in charge, but he's still valuable to finding if this poker playing stranger is part of what's happening around here."

Theiler grunted." We dealing with some professionals."

"It appears so." said Peary. "A lot of enemies."

"Yeah." Theiler nodded. "But this is a first."

"You want the games to continue?" Peary asked.

"It's the best way to recruit my muscle and investors." Theiler replied.

Peary nodded pursing his lips. He didn't agree with Theiler's answer knowing the investor remark meant luring perverted men such as himself into his web of deceit. Politicians, judges, and corporate 500 CEO's blackmailed getting caught on video molesting young girls and boys inside of Theiler's sinful brothel. The pedophile got his wealth in mysterious ways. Theiler owned contraband ships, Methlabs, and people too.

"Professionals." said Peary.

"Come again," Theiler rebuked.

"Guys who know how to get in and out sounding off the alarm letting you there hiding in the shadows watching your every move. Somebody's targeting you." Peary stated. "If not blood would have been spill.

Theiler's one urine eye got wide, his gray crusty moon crater mug turn an unhealthy pale. He wasn't naive he made enemies getting his riches. Killing family members leaving some alive to tell about or plot their revenge. He took over businesses, territories, ordering men not of his to execute their bosses. That was the young Theiler and he no longer use those methods since he created his empire which he pondered if the people he left alive sat around through the years plotting his demise. He shook his head because he has people keeping tabs and those he spare now work for him.

Theiler swallowed hard. "Don't you worry when I get my hands on this or perpetrators I'll be washing my hands in their blood." He nodded. "I agree with you about them targeting me."

Peary snorted. "No need to worry nothing that has happened so far will lead back to you."

Theiler gave a look." And that's a good thing, but so far, huh?" He questioned. "I want this shit to stop now!"

Peary nodded." I'm on it. I got people in the bars and casino looking at video who look the type to do what they're doing to you."

"And?" Theiler shrugged." It's a who's who."

"I'll have the bartenders and dealers questioned since they are your poor-man's version of shrinks."

Theiler gave a gruesome smile punching the palm of his hand.

TWENTY-FOUR

Pone, Ben, and Jock met in the pawn shop basement. He wondered how Jock made any money considering his topside business more closed than open. Red no doubt paid him a handsome sum of greenbacks since he carried everything a mercenary could ask for. A good front since pawn shops didn't have a revolving door of customers coming and going so what Jock did was common sense smart. Ben and Jock desire a taste of the sturdy stuff, substituting beer for rotgut getting Pone's approval and he had his malt beverage of Molta Goya.

"My compliment sir, getting the crew out so I could go to work. One stray I got out safe and sound so he could live to tell about it." said Pone.

Jock gave a gap tooth grin." I got skills."

Ben clink bottles with Jock.

Pone delivered a nod, though in the back of his mind he consider the victory lucky, never the less that's what gamblers do. They depend on luck and it got them another win against the pervert Theiler Lereaux. Pone reached inside his vest pocket taking out a deck of cards to shuffle. He left his Chinese balls home or he'd be rotating them in his hand.

"What no more bum-rush tactics?" Ben asked.

"Two of his businesses got hit. Don't think he won't have his eyes wide open." Pone replied.

Ben snorted. "Are we going to take it easy?"

"He has more labs and a new ship, but we were fortunate to find the two we did. We made some noise and he'll have sleepless nights, but we have to be careful who we talk to when we go back to the casino and bars." Pone retorted.

"Play dumb." Ben remarked. "I get it, if someone bring up the current events you give the look bewilderment."

"You got it big man." said Pone. "Right he and his brain sources are plotting to see who would dare come his house and piss in his pool. We don't want him to know it's us yet."

Ben nodded." Yeah. He'll be lying in wait for us."

Pone gave Jock a look." You keep digging and see if any thing come up about where his other money sources are."

"Anything to hurt that bastard you can count me in." Jock replied.

"Be careful." Pone stated.

"Like I said I got skills." Jock answered.

Pone pursed his lips." Things are hot we'll keep putting logs on the fire one wood at a time."

"We both moving along in the games." said Ben.

"Got to win to get to Lereaux." Pone remarked." I know it can't seem to easy."

"That's my point." Ben retorted.

Pone took a sip of his drink placing it down on the table giving Ben a look." You want to tell me something?"

Ben swallowed hard." There's always somebody better... you and I both know that."

"Keep doing what you're doing. Don't let on." said Pone.

Ben nodded." See how it plays out. But?"

"Describe him?" Jock inquired.

Ben shrugged." Three inches over six feet, strong stocky built, a goatee, and long gray hair in a ponytail."

"Familiar?" Pone asked.

Jock took two swills of his beer then cleared his throat. "Might be a recruiter for Theiler and taken a liken to you because of your size."

"He got a thing for big men?" Pone asked.

"I ain't gay." Ben stated.

"Muscle, body guard. Somebody hard to handle in case things get out of hand." said Jock.

"The better for you Ben. When or lose it seems you have a ticket to paradise." Pone remarked. "Either way we need to take it easy. We playing tourist, but who knows how many ears and eyes he has on the lookout in the casinos and bars?" He looked at Ben. "Try to be all business and less sociable at that dive bar."

"Wouldn't I draw attention if I act like a stranger?" Ben questioned.

"You already stand out like a sore thumb and you know what I mean." said Pone.

Ben stretched." Don't hate me cause I'm beautiful."

"The cover of Vogue." Pone remarked.

"You two are better than watching TV." said Jock.

"What are you going to do when we're gone?" Ben asked.

Jock shrugged." Go back to watching TV."

They all toasted and laughed.

"Pone." said Ben. "What happens if one or both of us lose?"

Pone inhaled." Shit happens." He looked at Jock." You know Theiler's layout?"

"He has a fortress." said Jock." I don't see y'all losing."

"As the Prohibition would say not the time to crap-out." Pone retorted.

Maxwell stared at his reflection in the mirror; checking his teeth, doing the breath smell to hand test nodding his approval. He touched up his hair, brush lint off his shoulder then he heard the doorbell. Maxwell inhaled nodding to his reflection as if to say showtime then stroll away to answer the door. He made a quick stop at the white cloth table to light two cream color candles highlighting the wine glasses, fine china and silverware. Maxwell cleared his throat then answered the door.

The statuesque beauty waltzed in handing the DA her coat. Maxwell got moon-eye admiring the red headed gorgeous fem fatale wearing a strap pink body hugging dress two inches below the knee, and white pumps. A pearl necklace with matching ear-rings, and he hair a librarian bun. Red's perfume hypnotic like a siren luring his nostrils for a smell. Maxwell put away her coat then escorted to the table seating her in gentleman fashion. He poured wine after displaying the label and she nodded as if to say that was a good year.

Red sipped and smiled. Maxwell headed for the kitchen and returned with two plates placing them down on the table.

"I've prepared Lemon Salmon with Asparagus spears." He said.

Red nodded her approval observing the diminutive man wearing what she knew lifts in his shoes adding an inch to his height, though neglected by the heels of her pumps. Maxwell took his seat.

"Hope you're hungry?" He inquired.

"Famished." Red replied. "Are you okay?"

"Hope you're pleased with the entree."

Red pursed her lips" It's looks edible."

"Thanks a lot," Maxwell muttered.

"You're doubting your skills." said Red.

Maxwell shrugged." I follow the recipe from the Internet."

"Because it knows everything." Red joked. She cut into the salmon impressed the fork penetrated the fish like a hot knife through butter. Maxwell watched Red delicate place her salmon inside her mouth. She allows the flavor of lemon tantalize her taste buds closing her eyes leaving some on her tongue washing it down with wine. She winked making Maxwell blush.

"Who am I kidding." said Maxwell. "I catered it."

"It's the thought that counts." Red remarked grabbing an asparagus between her thumb and index finger taking a nibbling bite tilting her head. Maxwell saw it as flirting squeezing his legs together under the table. He took his turn combining the meat and vegetable.

"I spoke with your sister." Maxwell stated.

Red swallowed hard. Good timing she thought just when walls of romance were about to fall. Poor Thomas. Maxwell recognize the look of why bring my sister at a time like this on Red's face realizing desert now off the menu.

"You mean after dinner?" He inquired.

Red exhaled. "Slow down, Thomas."

Maxwell looking troubled." Don't tell me you're still hung up on that Pone thing?"

" Unbelievable." Red shook her head. Now you're bringing him up."

"Okay." said Maxwell. "Sorry. He's forgotten, but you were right."

Red frowned." About?"

Maxwell pursed his lips." A pocket politician."

Red leaned back folding her arms and batting her eye-lashes." Are you surprised?"

"Well... "Maxwell stated.

"Right." Red interrupted." You shouldn't be. It's not too late to back out."

Maxwell rose from the table." I'm all in unless you don't think I can handle it?"

"You're a grown man." said Red sizing him up with her eyes.

"Now you making jokes about my height?" He questioned.

"Your insecurity not mine." Red retorted." Height doesn't make the man."

Maxwell sat back down. He knew many prominent leaders were

under six-feet tall and he plan to join their company. "I'm the right guy to lead this city."

"And I know you'll do a fine job." Red smiled.

Maxwell inhaled. "So I want be working with you?"

"I'm not blind to my family business." said Red. "We won't be on your staff. They will ask you favors and expect you to deliver."

"Or what?" Maxwell questioned.

Red gave a troubled look. "Thought I made that clear? Did Linda beat around the bush?"

"I won't go into hiding from a threat of a gang war then reappear when the smoke clears."

Red lifted her wine glass taking a sip. "That's why you have my endorsement."

"And you want nothing if... when I win?"

Red twirled the wine in her glass. "I have my practice I built, you're not about to offer me a position on your staff since I told the family is not interested?"

Maxwell smiled. "Speaking of position."

"Caution Thomas." said Red. "This dinner became business a long time ago."

Maxwell retreated like a turtle's head back inside it's shell. "You know how I feel about you?"

"You have concerns and you should." Red replied. "I don't condone my family's lifestyle."

"When you say pocket..." Maxwell swallowed hard. "I won't do anything shady?"

Red straighten. She steered her firm away from the family history. Rivals getting offed by snipers a rumor through the grape vine, but true if you are part of a crime brood. Linda called the shots like their father proving a chip off the old block. J Paul smiled like a preacher never the less ruthless if threatened. Linda a daughter, sister, wife, and mother, but nasty as a rattlesnake if treading the wrong way into Brigand territories. Red positive Sue and Paul J aware of Linda's activities keeping a blind eye and walking on egg shells with the matriarch of the clan Mary doing what she does best leaving the business in the hands of daughter Linda like she did her husband.

The four siblings minus Mary, and brother-in-laws. Linda inherited J Paul's savvy being fair with an iron hand. Red hope to wash the blood off the cognomen giving the patronymic a clean slate running a legit law firm. She and Linda went toe to toe over on how her firm could benefit the Brigand Band. The youngest offspring won out making sure no smut would tarnish her image.

Red cleared her throat then sipped her wine." When you're mayor you will have the power to say no."

"Say no to what?" Maxwell shrugged." Murder... arson? Granting someone an early release from prison?"

Red pursed her lips." Linda wouldn't go that route with you. She'd rather have your signature on city permits to break ground for building." She raised an eye-brow." Nothing sinister."

"One can only hope." Maxwell remarked loosening the top button on his shirt near his neck." But you should know she is your sister."

Red leaned forward. "She intimidates you?"

"She exist." said Maxwell." I already have a shadow."

"I'll be at your side when you announce your candidacy." Red smiled. "If that makes you feel better?"

"What would make me feel better," Maxwell rose from the table reaching inside his pocket taking out a small black box. He got down on one knee removing a sparkling diamond ring. "You be my wife."

Red slumped feeling three inches shorter. Maxwell threw her a curve ball. She knew being his wife would strengthen his campaign and with her being a Brigand they'd get a lot of votes with her family name striking fear to most of the city population.

Thomas wouldn't need to marry her to win the election. The city knowing he has the support of the Brigand family would weigh heavy on the voters. Red pondered if mother and Linda put him up to it. They'd have hell to pay, her private life her business and they crossed the line. Red consider her self a trend setter, she never looked for men taller then her for companionship, if you could stimulate her mind, have confidence in yourself, comfortable in your own skin. Maxwell possessed those qualities unless attending functions with her. He wore lifts which helped little making him walk like a baby taking first steps with her hanging on his arm. Red heard whispers turn into jokes describing them like a mother teaching a child how to walk. Maxwell cute, thinning hair, but intelligent and he worshiped the ground she walk on yet he did not capture her heart. Red didn't want to break his and saying no would distract him from his campaign. She swallowed hard taking a deep breath sitting down on the couch. Red smiled at her Napoleon on bended knee knowing what she needed to do, continue wearing heels at social events because flats for her donning the dresses she wore would get her arrested by the fashion police and keep the mayor in waiting as a companion.

"Thomas." said Red. "Keep that in your holster."

Maxwell stood and smiled.

TWENTY-FIVE

Fine china settled on the coffee table with Mary and Linda sitting in the family den sipping tea and eating Chess Men cookies, "Won't be long now,." said Linda.

Mary used the napkin on the corners of her mouth. "I hope you didn't over indulge yourself."

Linda pursed her lips. "It look better for a politician to be married running for office."

"You know your sister won't stand for you manipulating her life."

Linda gave a stern look. "Don't you mean us?"

Mary shook her head. "No you."

"It's a push in the right direction." Linda replied.

Mary nibbled her Chess Men. "There's a difference in finesse and aggression."

"What would daddy had done." Linda asked.

Mary leaned back sipping her tea. "Let things play out. He always put the pieces in place then sat back and watch where it goes. '

"If you say so," Linda murmured.

"What's that?" Mary questioned.

Mary portrayed a delicate flower. She sat in the back ground because J. Paul took care of business allowing her to be the daunting mother. A lot of bodies populated the bone orchard was the pieces her father saw go if he got crossed. Linda consider Mary a rose. Like the famous flower she had thorns despite beauty and a pleasant smell. She overhead her mother making calls after J. Paul's death snuffing out potential threats. Mary knew when to be as deadly as a silent fart.

"She was his favorite." Linda retorted.

"He respected the way she stood up to him."

"I was not afraid of him." Linda remarked.

"You all showed proper respect despite circumstances." said Mary.

Linda inhaled knowing what Mary meant Paul J's homosexuality. He married, but J. Paul stressed when the Paul J's first born a girl, but daddy dearest settled down when two boys followed easing his conscious about carrying on the family name.

"Brooke displayed her lawyer skills before she became one." said Mary.

Linda sipped her tea swallowing her words of calling baby sister a coward trying to separate herself from the family business.

"Does she know how important this is?" Linda asked.

Mary exhaled. "We both spoke to her and Maxwell. I want Brooke to be happy."

"I want the same." said Linda. "This is business,"

Mary nodded. "Family comes first."

Pone couldn't put his finger on it, something felt different. Pone sat at the playing table with his mind elsewhere instead of on the game at hand. He knew that wasn't good for a poker player. His spidey senses tingle when the casino he noticed every move he made, men and women got into position eyed his every move. He noticed the dealer giving him a eerie look. Pone ponder if the gig was up and a matter of time before the walls closed in. His unwanted escorts spread out getting into place surrounding him as if to cut any chance for a quick exit. It occurred to him Theiler no dummy, but just a disgusting sewer rat preying on children. If the current events of being a fly in Lereau's ointment brought him attention blowing his cover then so be it as long as it distracted the pervert from molesting children. Pone scanned the casino and noticed the siren Mai Ling sitting next the old black woman sticking to her nature wearing her silver mane in a high-top bun. What's their deal and why stick around after losing. Pone glanced at his cards getting moon-eye holding a Royal Flush. A winning hand feeling insecure. He wondered if Ben's night as weird as his.

Goldilocks tour around the tables looking at every hand of cards to cast his eyes upon. Ben didn't survive this long in the game of death relying on intuition, he just needed to pointed in the right direction of the target and he'd take it from there. Things felt different than the last time he sat at table playing poker for a trip to meet the wizard. Ben noticed a lot nodding from players after Goldilocks made his rounds. They set the stage with stale smoke in the air from cigarettes and cigars. Beer and rot gut the drinks and Ben relieved smoking and drinking allowed at the tables as he nursed his beer ordering another. Pone playing his game at a fancy casino hotel atmosphere not around mothering him about his drinking, thank God. Ben looked over his cards and he held a four of a kind known as quads 7's not good enough win unless you know how to bluff and Ben didn't believe in bluffing which made him question how he won in the poker game so long. Before Goldilocks finished his rounds, Ben noticed slight touching on the other players shoulders. Something strange and wicked going on making Ben think about the noise Pone made announcing to Theiler he has haters in his city. The giant knew now he had to stay on his toes.

Pone played his poker player intuition betting a lot of his chips and then folded with out being asked to the chagrin faces around the room and at the table. The dealers face exposed his concern with a frown which prove he dealt Pone a winning hand on purpose during the deal. Pone thought would this continue through the entire game and if so would the other players get wind of the deception. He studied the other players and they didn't wear good poker faces either cutting their eyes at one another and it didn't take long for Pone to put two and two together. The game, for him to win.

❖❖ ❖❖ ❖❖ ❖❖ ❖❖ ❖❖

Ben counted his chips and he possessed plenty, but didn't feel good about it. Goldilocks didn't make anymore rounds around the table as if the other players knew their role and Ben assumption correct, he and Pone no longer a secret and the head man wanted to meet them. The giant didn't know what Pone's night was like, but guessed he wasn't going lose his games either. Ben hands shit. He looked at Horse-face at the bar and showed no concern what-so-ever about the happenings of the games that would pave the way to Theiler's abode. Ben knew he and Pone would have a lot to talk about at the motel.

❖❖ ❖❖ ❖❖ ❖❖ ❖❖ ❖❖

Pone stopped and stare at the faces burning a hole in his back after he won and advanced in the tournament. The game played for him and he didn't need to, Pone kept looking till the last face move out of his sight. You didn't have to be Einstein to know this wasn't right. He'd be a billionaire if all his poker games went the way it did tonight. He didn't break a sweat and the players at table were actors and again he was not sorry for taking Theiler's mind off his perverted activities putting his disgusting mind on his money.

Pone opened the door to his rental.

"Mind giving a girl a lift?" Lola asked. "My car's in the shop."

Pone swallowed hard." Get in." He growled.

Lola got in giving a look." Maybe I should have taken a cab."

"Did anybody see you?" Pone asked.

"The usual. Why?"

"Slump down and don't get up till I tell you." said Pone. He drove far enough making sure the casino no longer in sight." Okay get up."

"Yes sir, but are you sure?" Lola sat up straight. "Don't want bystanders thinking I gave you a blow job."

"That's something beautiful women should never do." Pone replied.

Lola raised an eye-brow." Are you serious?"

"You think I want to taste my sperm or worse?" Pone shook his head.

"Don't know how many women you've been with and it's not my business... "

Pone snorted. "I'm not naive."

"You went down on me." said Lola.

"Followed by the big finish." Pone retorted.

"Right." said Lola. "You've passed my street."

"I've been a bad boy." said Pone.

"And I'm guilty by association."

"It meant the games for me to win." Pone stated. "I pissed in a pool."

"Ouch." said Lola. "You're not the only fresh face in his poker tournament."

"No, but I'm sure he's paying people lots of money to dot his I's and cross T's to single out what newcomer can put him in a world of hurt."

"Am I in danger?"

Pone swallowed hard." They got you on camera and I rely heavy on my gut feeling."

"You saying I can't go back to work?"

"Not leaving from your house." Pone replied.

'What kind of shit did I step in?" Lola asked.

"Not as deep as you think." Pone replied. "I want to make sure you're safe."

"I can go home again?"

"What's that they say, you can never go home again." Pone remarked.

Lola punched his shoulder." No jokes."

"Tell me you got relatives?" Pone questioned.

"A cousin and sister on the other side of town." said Lola.

"Go by your place and pick up some things." Pone nodded. "I need to circle the block."

"You think that's wise?" Lola asked.

"I hope somebody suspicious do drive by." said Pone.

Lola frowned. "Do I need to ask?"

Pone wanted to send a message to whomever was on to him not to give a progress report. He didn't want Lola in his world, but knew casino cameras didn't take the day off. If his cover blown then a dead body would let them know to tread light.

"You know too much already and for that I'm sorry." said Pone.

"What am I, the cat?" Lola questioned." Because I don't recall being curious."

"I didn't volunteer information." Pone retorted.

Lola shrugged. "We hit it off and then you hit it."

Pone laughed. Lola a bright spot on his catch and release trip to the big easy. The caramel curve knew her way around his body. Her magic fingers stimulated his earlobe, lips, nipples, and the love below like no other woman. Lust not love brought them together, Pone felt Lola thought the same once his job done they'd never see each other again. New Orleans her home and Metro his natural habitat. He would not miss the swamp, snakes, and alligators that came with the territory not that he came across any and hope to continue avoiding them. The climate similar to that of Metro, but still not home.

"You check your rear view mirror in case we're being followed?" Lola asked.

Pone took precaution before leaving the parking lot. No tail after five miles down the road, but sure the security camera got the plates. He'd change vehicles after taking care of Lola.

"You sure you haven't done this before?" Pone questioned.

"I watch a lot of TV." Lola remarked.

Pone pulled up parking near Lola's house. Though he'd rather stop and bought whatever she needed. No one followed them after following protocol making four left turns.

"Park around back." said Lola. "Then come inside and help me gather my things."

Pone gave her a look.

Lola leaned toward Pone. Her top button tremble keeping her cleavage at bay.

"Might have enough time for a lasting memory."

Ben sat on his bed playing Solitaire passing time with his thoughts on the poker that should have sent him home. Instead he advanced to the winner take all round. A boat load of money and a trip to see the wizard, Theiler Lereaux. The giant got an uneasy feeling pondering if acted to bold interfering in Theiler's business. He felt like they were in a massive hunt down for a who's who would dare trespass in the perverts domain. He should have been on the outs instead of going to the winners' circle and felt he and Pone might have to shoot their way out of the big easy.

A knock made the big man stand up, gripping the piece wedged between his pants and backside.

"Who is it?" Ben asked.

"You expecting somebody, big man?" Pone questioned.

Ben opened the door, letting him in. He brushed by Pone, parking himself on the bed.

"You homesick?"

Pone pulled up a chair." I think our cover is in jeopardy."

"I'm thinking the same thing."

Pone smirked." Too late to rethink things now. We got to see this through or you can bolt." Pone shrugged. "I won't hold it against you."

Ben straightened and frowned." Man you full of shit. You know damn well we got a better chance getting that girl and freeing them people from that crazy ass tyrant together than you going solo."

Pone snorted." It's our destiny to see him."

Ben laughed. "Your games rigged too, huh?"

"Firsts deal." said Pone." A hand nobody could beat and I folded to test the water."

Ben nodded. "You were Jesus for one night."

"How well did you float?" Pone asked.

"My hands were shit, yet I made it to the final round."

Pone slumped into a deep thought. He and Ben had to keep their heads on a swivel not that they didn't have to before. If the jig is up, then why he and Ben still breathing.

"You think he knows who we are?" Ben questioned.

"When you are a kingpin, you don't get there without smarts." Pone replied.

"I hear a but coming."

"We would have been snatch up by now in fear of doing more damage to his empire." said Pone. "Something else is in the air or better yet someone is manipulating the situation."

Ben exhaled." You telling me a third party is helping us along? He frowned." If that's the case how is he unaware of it?"

Pone shook his head. You know as well as I do there is a Judas in the ranks waiting to let a Trojan horse inside the palace."

Ben swallowed hard. "You saying one of his own trying cut his throat with someone else hands?"

"He or she wants us to do it since our hands are already dirty." said Pone.

"Hell." Ben remarked. "Because we're expendable."

Pone shrugged." Every body in our business is."

"We being played?"

Pone shook his head." No."

"How can you say that?" Ben asked.

"We get inside and that house of cards is coming down." said Pone. "There won't be any empire to take over."

"I got your back brother." said Ben. "It keeps him from hurting innocent people."

"Yeah... " Pone sobered. "About that,"

"What did you do?" Ben asked.

"I might have put Lola in danger."

"What do you mean?"

Pone pursed his lips. "By association. She came to me for a ride home."

Ben gave a dubious look." So?"

"They might target her to get to me." said Pone. "I took Lola to her sister's place, she knows to act normal."

"You think that's wise for her to go back to work?"

Pone inhaled. "What part of acting normal did you not understand?"

"The part that she still could end up dead." Ben retorted.

"I can't be around her 24/7 or that would blow my cover."

Ben shook his head. "You ain't that cold blooded killer no more. You got a conscience."

"Nothing will happen to her as long as she stays within a crowd and leave with friends."

"If you say so." said Ben.

Pone gave his giant friend a poker face of no concern if anything were to happen to Lola. Ben's remark ate at him. They were not an item, but he'd grown quite fond of the caramel curve.

"Thanks a lot, Ben." Pone glowered.

Ben shrugged. "What?"

"I'll ask Jock if he knows someone discrete and he'd get paid well to watch her."

Ben went back to playing solitaire." I was just saying."

Pone headed to his room. "See you in the morning."

❦ ❦ ❦ ❦ ❦ ❦

"So," Jock grimace after throwing his hooch down the hatch. He poured another. "You're compromised?"

"We didn't say that," said Pone.

"That's what it sounded like to me." Jock replied.

"I don't think we'd be sitting here talking to you." Ben stated.

Jock nodded, sipping his drink." Got a point, big man."

"We believe we're being helped along." said Pone.

Jock swallowed hard. "What the hell you say?"

Pone pursed his lips. "I said... "

Jock held up his hand. "Yeah, yeah, I got the message. Somebody's making sure y'all don't lose."

"Our tickets punched." said Ben.

"Is that a good or bad thing?" Jock questioned.

"We are still alive and that's always good." said Pone. "But are we getting set up for an ambush?"

Ben inhaled. "We can't tuck tail and run."

"You know newcomers can't carry weapons on his estate." Jock retorted.

Ben cleared his throat. "I can conceal a weapon... '

"Do what you got to do Ben, but keep the details to yourself." said Pone.

"I second that," Jock retorted.

Ben looked at Jock. "What you talking about? You going to help."

"What say what now?" Jock questioned.

Pone's thoughts wondered to another matter while laughing at Ben and Jock discussing Ben's disgusting gesture of carrying when they arrive at Theiler's. Pone believe Jock could help, but didn't blame him not wanting to get a view of Ben's ass.

"What else is on your mind and yes I am trying to change the subject." said Jock.

"I might have put a woman in danger." Pone replied.

Jock shook his head. "Sorry to hear that, you need anything from me?"

Pone exhaled relief and nodded. "You know anyone who can shadow while being discrete?"

Jock shrugged. "I know a guy qualified to do what you want,"

"How much?' Pone asked.

Jock smiled. "Hell, he'd do it for free, but if you want to pay, then okay. I just need information."

"He'll know trouble when he sees it and how to react?" Pone asked.

Special op his background. Your lady friend will be in excellent hands." Jock gave a stern look. "She's special, I can tell. I got your back."

Pone leans back rubbing his chin. "No distractions if I'm going to hell."

TWENTY-SEVEN

The balcony allowed you to see miles of land space; thick trees, swamp, and predators that dwell in a body of water with more mystery than the sea. Theiler puffed a stogie gazing over his kingdom. The creaking doors to his balcony aroused him.

"Hope you got some good news?" Theiler demanded.

Peary stood behind the man he considered a parasite, but money too good and he knew too much to step away. "The poker games will come to end this weekend."

"Come and be by my side boy." Theiler took a long draw from his cigar. "I ain't going to bite you."

Peary eased up to the oak rail painted white for purity the opposite of the man in his presence. He notice Theiler staring at the young girls who he had or has yet to molest since the distraction took his perverted mind off the girls proving money prevails even over disgusting habits.

"Now since I am the one who shortened the games... what you telling me ain't news." Theiler blew a puff of smoke in Peary's face. "Can you fly, boy?"

Peary eased back from rail. He wanted to use his wit thinking better of it. "No sir, but if you want to get the perpetrators than your plan should bring them to your door."

Theiler snickered. "I know and you are zero for two."

Peary snorted. "It's good you have rules no one sets foot on your property carrying weapons and there are two people in the group who look like they would dare interrupt your business."

"You don't say? Who might that be?" Theiler questioned.

Peary look around feeling a sigh of relief Ludwig no where to be seen. He wasn't sure how sincere Theiler's threat of giving him flying lessons and didn't want to find out. He worked for a perverted psycho.

"Your money well spent and I trust my sources. We'll be able to sort them out once they arrive." said Peary.

"You going to keep me in suspense, boy?" Theiler questioned.

"I'm the messenger and we both knows how the story goes."

"Now boy, I'm just playing." Theiler drew from his stogie. "Wouldn't hurt you for the world."

Peary nodded and smiled. "Knowledge is power."

Red parked her car next to Paul J's Bentley. Another family dinner, but intuition told her it would not be the same as any other. She walk inside the Brigand mansion where her coat and hand-bag taken then led to the study of what look like an intervention.

Red got moon-eye and waited for her escort to exit. "I am not an alcoholic or strung out on drugs."

"Please dear," Mary smiled. "Come and join us."

Red sat next to Paul J. across from the lookalikes, Linda and Sue. The room pure Brigand blood and no in-laws to be found.

"Been awhile since we all gathered for a sit down." said Red. "Makes me feel young again."

"We still do it." Paul J replied. "You never show up."

Red inhaled. "Now you know why,"

"Good one, baby sis," Sue remarked.

Red smiled. Sue spoke which was rare. She'd sit like now with her hands folded on her lap nodding agreeing with what Linda and mother said. Sue spoke when asked by the two elder statesmen. Red ponder is if she now come out of her shell instead of waiting in the shadows. Mary stretched and rose.

"I'm going to take a nap." said Mary. "You children play nice."

"I'll come with you." said Sue.

"No." Mary retorted leaving her offspring to talk.

"A candidate looks more attractive to voters if married." Linda stated.

Red swallowed hard. I will kill that dwarf if he came running to the family trying to force my hand in marriage, she thought.

Paul J placed a gentle hand on Red's shoulder. "Before you blow a gasket." He smiled. "We called him."

Big brother had a special way with his sisters. The binates adored him and Red always felt good in his presence. Little brother to the duplicates and big brother to her and a good one with advice and protector when they were kids growing up.

"You mean Linda." said Red.

"We're in this together." Paul J retorted,

"If I get married, it want be like this and it will be out of love." Red looks at Paul J.

The marriage between Paul J not loveless providing three children with two boys to carry on the family name giving J Paul hope knowing his son preferred to bed the same sex. Paul J played it straight until death of their father. Red made brother dearest promise safe sex to his trophy wife who could have taken half the family fortune in a divorce, but remained in the marriage.

Paul J straighten as if Red hit a nerve. "The decision is yours." He replied. "It looks better on paper."

Red delivered a kiss on his cheek as if to say except my apology. The two youngest of the brood connected better since the two peas in a pod had each other.

196

"We can't force you to do anything against your will," Linda remarked.

"Glad we agree on something," said Red.

"Just give it some thought, Brooke." Sue replied. "Thomas can and will win, but I never heard of a bachelor in office. Maxwell could be the first, but it's okay to play it safe."

"It would be cruel of me to marry Thomas for business." said Red. "I know and he knows what's going to happen once he's in office. We don't need him in our hip pocket. The Brigand name strikes fear throughout the city and the other crime families. Unless there is a hick-up and I mean a big one, then I agree having a mayor to call upon would be an advantage. Hell I could run for mayor, but I am not that ambitious."

"We thought about that and myself with a political science degree." said Paul J.

"Okay," Red nodded.

"With our family reputation, it disqualified the both of you." Linda stated.

"That's why I keep my firm separate," Red remarked.

"Didn't get you too far now did it?" Linda retorted.

Red smirked. "My last name keeps me from hiding and never said I was running."

Paul J cleared his throat. "We are proud you. Your firm has clean up the family image." He patted her knee.

Sue smiled and nodded. Linda pursed her lips inhaling deep. Red knew Linda loved her and carried a heavy envy. She played with words questioning why she didn't get father's height and mother's features. The younger won the DNA lottery while she and Sue got respectable features. Paul J a handsome man, tailored features for women. Linda and Sue not bad on the eyes yet they didn't hold a candle to baby sister. Linda unlike her clone kept her weight down , wore her hair longer, and mastered the art of make-up separating her from the identical association. Red picked up vibes at the last family dinner. Linda convinced Pone while flirting with him she never threaten his mortality. She didn't blame Linda for yearning how it would be to have Chubby hold her in his arms. Red couldn't tell her since she herself never crossed that bridge. The advantage she has over Linda, not married and Pone troubleshoots for her firm. The contact between the two gives her free passage down temptation alley with out the guilt.

Red got a text. She exhaled after reading it.

"Problem?" Sue inquired.

"An employee matter," Red shook her head. "No worries."

"Not Mister Pone… " said Linda.

"He's working out of town." Red retorted.

"On assignment?" Linda questioned.

"He works for me." Red retorted.

"Nothing dangerous, I hope." Linda commented

Red smiles sitting back folding her arms and crossing her legs. Sue and Paul J eyed one another knowing a matter of time a storm waiting to erupt.

"Where is he by the way?" Linda asked.

"The big easy," said Red.

"New Orleans," Linda exclaimed. "Romantic if you know where to go. Mardi Gra being whatever you want to be… business or pleasure?"

"You tell me?" Red asked.

"Excuse me?" Linda blushed.

"Good thing we were there or you would have thrown yourself across the billiard table." Red smirked.

Linda frowned." Watch where you tread baby sister."

"Stanley kept looking at you, Pony, and himself." Red shook her head. "Poor brother-in-law."

"What about your fantasy?" Linda retorted.

"I'm not married." Red remarked.

"So you admit it," Linda stated.

"Nothing to be ashamed of," Red shrugged. "Unlike you I'm not married."

Linda pursed her lips. "Whether you jump over or on it, decide."

Red rose. "You don't tell me who, how, or when," She gave a look. "My life is my business."

"You can sit in your firm, but you can't hide from who you are," Linda said standing up to Red.

Red gazed down. "That sounds like a threat?"

Sue gave Paul J a look and nod.

"Okay," Paul J stepped between his siblings. "Neutral corners ladies,"

Paul J always seem to calm the sisters no matter what crises came upon them. Red and Linda started crossing bridges that neither needed to and Sue knew baby brother could do what she couldn't and that was to stop a storm from brewing.

Paul J inhaled. "Family meeting adjourn."

Linda raised an eyebrow. "I haven't -"

"When conversation go in circles then meeting adjourn." Paul J remarked in a harden voice. "There's business: family business and personal business. You two are putting too much business you need to keep to yourselves,"

"Brooke started it," Linda retorted acting kike a child.

"And I'm finishing it," Paul J stated. "Brooke has her own world and I wish I'd done the same, we are proud and she has never strayed from the family. She knows what to do when the time comes. The elections are around the corner and I trust Thomas will serve this city well and the Brigand family will benefit with him being in office. It's been a long day."

Red gave Paul J a kiss on his cheek strolling tall and graceful out the family lounge.

TWENTY-EIGHT

beautiful day to enjoy the pleasures of nature. A luminous sun surrounded blue sky with a surprise cool breeze making it a wonderful day. Tara enjoyed breathing fresh air having her skin bathed in the apricate rays. The day far from perfect being gazed upon by Theiler. Tara felt fortunate of late has become the norm. Her smile grateful to whomever disrupted Theiler's business and hope it would continue for her sake and the other girls on his estate. Mia has been missing in action and Tara considered it a good thing. Her virginity still intact after a few close calls. She knew Doctor Brogan a good man hanging around protecting them as best he could from Theiler's clutches. Whatever the good doctor was doing worked keeping Mia pure. Tara didn't know what he did to lose his license, but he made up for it as a protector. Tara's luck ran out as the pedophile had his way. She didn't like sacrificing herself protecting Mia from his claws and glad the good doctor gave her a break. Tara took a brief intermission from the fiery star behind a grand Oak tree. She detected Theiler's eyes upon her making her skin crawl. Tara glanced around the tree, the monster went back inside his cave she'd hope. He'd sometimes send his goons to escort a girl to his room and Tara prayed that wouldn't be the case. She inhaled the fresh air knowing enjoy the freedom while it last. Tara didn't know who convinced Theiler to allow the girls to breath since once upon a time they confined to their rooms for weeks and months with out any daylight except form an open curtain. She saw a difference in all the girls delighted to be outside. Yes, she thought these days good times, but how long would it last was another question.

Pone and Ben followed Jock's directions with help from the GPS. The two men on a mission wanted some place out of town that serve good food and drinks. Jock mention a tavern not fancy, but with a grade A 98. 5 inspection certificate. Pone and Ben took a corner table facing the doorway. The eatery dim lighted to Pone's liking since being discrete part of the profession. They sipped water brought to them by a thirty something waitress average height, pony-tail hairstyle, red lipstick, black slacks, white blouse, and no slip shoes. Her face attractive with an expression if she could do her life over. She took their orders strolling back to the kitchen.

"What's the plan?" Ben asked.

Pone squeezed juice from the lemon in his glass of water stirring. He sipped. "We know what the girl looks like... whoever sees her first grabbed her and run."

Ben glared." You going to get us killed."

Pone sipped his water shaking his head. He was out of his zone. His mind on Lola hoping she safe under the watchful eye of a man Jock referred. Tara and Mia who Jock believes to be his daughter. Three dames; one old and two young taking up rent inside his head. Lola wasn't on Theiler's estate, but he felt uneasy she'd be at work. Pone paused trying not to over think if trouble would follow Lola back to her sister's place. "Shit," He muttered. That makes four.

"What's going on with you?' Ben questioned.

"However this turns out, somebody going to get hurt."

"I'm rooting for that pervert." Ben retorted. He looks at Pone knowing Theiler wasn't the one causing him concern. "You better get back in the game."

Pone knew get back in the game meant getting focused. The giant right about having a clear head since they were about to venture inside the belly of the beast. If his mind wondered while on the job then he and Ben would end up dead. Pone inhaled. Time to be a professional, Everybody crowding his mind still alive a good thing. Now to make sure he and Ben come out of this in one piece. The waitress brought them there steaks with a bake potato with butter melting on top and sour cream and chives. She put down two Samuel Adams.

Ben raised an eyebrow.

Pone grabbed his bottle. "Cheers,'

Ben did the same. Then attacked his steak.

"Okay, big man," said Pone. "We're flies caught in the spider's web.

Ben drank his beer washing down his steak. "Don't like the sound of that,"

"It's going to be Helter Skelter since we don't know what we're getting into. Since we both getting help to get to his place," Pone inhaled. "You do what you do best to survive,"

"The last thing you said I like that, that other shit not so much," Ben remarked.

'We can't go in reckless,"

Ben snorted slicing into his steak. "You don't have a plan, no weapons, and I don't plan on dying... "He shrugged. "So anything goes,"

Pone had yet to touch his plate. He was famished, but mind on the job took place over hunger except for his large friend. Pone didn't regret having Ben for a wing-man, but knew him to be a cold hardened killer. He had toned it down a bit since meeting Pone and that made the troubleshooter proud feeling he had influence Ben to think before acting.

"Man when you planning to drop this gig?" Ben asked.

"What do you mean?"

"The worst thing you can do is worry and that makes you second guess yourself and that makes you dead."

"I'm not going anywhere," said Pone.

"Then eat your damn food before it gets cold."

Pone dug in and Ben cleared his throat.

"What?' Pone shrugged holding his knife and fork.

"You're supposed to say, who are you, my mother?"

Pone frowned. "You serious?"

"Just eat,"

Pone swallowed washing his steak and potato down. "Lives are at stake. The priority are those girls."

Ben nodded. If I get to them, they as good as secured."

Pone stopped eating eyeing the entrance. Ben knew the code of not giving away the obvious of letting someone they've made. He gave Pone a one eye-brow nod to give him details.

Pone kept his head low. "Two tall fit men looking like built for action gave us a stare down." Pone whispered.

Ben frowned and not because in a normal world he'd say so, but he and Pone did not live in a utopia meaning a bulls-eye painted on their backs all the time.

"How long you think they been tailing us?" Ben asked.

Pone smirked. "They haven't, "

Ben took a swallow of beer. "You saying- "

"Bug," Pone retorted. Our ride is tagged and that means- "

"They know the flophouse we're staying at,"

The two men played by the rules acting natural eating their dinner while talking. Pone took glimpse of the men when washing his food down. They were amateurs with the man with a crew cut sitting facing them burning a hole through Ben's back and they other slick back hair-do taking anxious glances over his shoulder.

"If there Theiler's men, then what the hell are they trying to do?" Ben questioned. "He trying to keep us safe till he can get his hands on us?"

"They're not Theiler's men." Pone retorted.

Ben frowned. "How would you know that?" He inhaled. "Swamp people can't look fit or cultured? They got to be unkempt, cut off jeans and boots?"

Pone gave a look. "What hell is up with you?"

Ben shrugged shaking his head as if he went to another place coming back to the present. "Sorry, man... I took a step back in time."

"Yeah, well," Pone snorted. "Memories from child hood or whatever not the time,"

Ben nodded. "What's the plan?"

Pone looked at Ben's plate. No surprise the giant his own dishwasher. Pone didn't clean his plate, his appetite turn to finding out who were their trackers.

"You finished big man?' Pone asked waving for the check.

Ben looks dubious. "You?"

Pone took one more bite and drink then tossed his napkin on his plate.

"Guess so," said Ben.

Pone took care of the check, he and Ben exit the eatery. They waited five minutes for the two men to follow. Pone observed them walking by, complimentary water sat on their table. They didn't come to eat, but to survey them. Pone pulled out of the parking lot far enough to tease then sped off watching in his rear-view and saw a mad scramble to their vehicle. Pone drove far enough where hills and trees surrounded the road. He killed the engine. Pone got out lifting the hood then got back inside.

"They will be here soon," said Pone. "Go into the forest and make sure you get behind them."

"What are you going to do?" Ben asked.

"We're gamblers, Ben." Pone retorted. "One gets out to see what the problem is and the other your dance partner." He gave Ben a stern look. "No killing. Now go,"

TWENTY-NINE

A faded mustard color stain cloth recliner parked in front of a 32 inch flat screen on a wobbling TV stand. Lars Lambert sat with remote in hand channel searching. He shook his head frowning and thinking with all these channels, cost of cable, repeated programs shown meaning not a damn thing to watch. Lars kept surfing and nursing rot gut from a bottle half empty. A knock a the door didn't stop him trying to find something to peak his interest.

"It's not locked," said Lambert.

The door creaked open, a slight man entered with a black skull cap, brown jacket, stone colored blue jeans, white smudge sneakers. He closed the door. "Love what you've done to the place."

"Fuck you!" Lambert retorted. "Took you long enough."

The man approached with caution holding glock in hand. He didn't want take any chances with the hood up signaling car trouble. A frown took over his face when he saw empty seats inside the vehicle. A kick from under the SUV to his right side knee caused him to drop low enough for Pone to roll out from underneath the Escalade. Pone straddle the man with cat quickness holding down his gun hand then delivering solid punches to the face forcing the back of his head to bounce off the pavement rendering the man unconscious. A car door opened. Pone busy checking for identification glanced then return back to business. Ben wrap his mammoth arm around the man's neck cutting off his air supply. The giant walked up to Pone with a glock he compensated.

"Found anything?" Ben asked.

Pone held up a wallet. "Feds."

Ben got moon-eye swallowing hard.

"Your man still alive, right?" Pone questioned.

Ben nodded. "What's going on?"

"We will not figure it out here," said Pone placing the wallet and gun back on the man's person. "Let's put these two to bed." Pone searched under the SUV finding the tracking device under the rear bumper. He and Ben put the two agents in the front seat with everything intact. Pone placed the tracking device beneath the back bumper. He joined Ben inside the Escalade.

"Ain't that a bitch?" Ben retorted.

"We ditch this ride, get our things and move in with Jock." Pone stated while sending a text.

Ben shook his head. "Better roll before they wake up."

The SUV sped off.

Maxwell wanted to cover the chair with a newspaper. Lambert's flat made his skin crawl; carpet stains, torn paper, crushed insects, and dried food crumbs littered a rug in need of a vacuum and shampoo.

Maxwell inhaled sitting down on the wooden four legged chair he pulled from the kitchen table. "You'd think now that you're in the cleaning business, you should know how to tidy up."

Lambert belted a loud belch." You know where the door is,"

Maxwell frowned observing the room. "From the looks of things,

I walk out of here and your chance of getting back to fine living since you change careers will be history."

Lambert exhaled. He turn off the tube, slump over putting his shot glass on the stand then held his hands together in deep thought. Wife and kids gone along with a two car garage house in an immaculate neighborhood because of greed. It started out good for Lambert working as a mob lawyer. He got paid well, but wanted more and all good until he hit a snag. Paul J Brigand proved too much of a task for the up and coming attorney to handle. He used trust as a Trojan horse getting inside the Brigand empire. The Brigand band had too many resources and the end results, trading in his law degree for a mop and broom. Lambert thankful to still be alive, but cleaning toilet seats felt like a bullet to the head.

"You surprise how accustomed I've become to living this way?"

"Thought you might say that," Maxwell retorted. "I might have something to motivate you."

Lambert exhaled. "Money makes life more comfortable, but I've shit and stepped in it,"

"I can help scrape it off," said Maxwell.

Lambert looked around his surroundings yearning to return to days of fine dining and drinking good liquor. "I'm listening,"

"Chubby Pone."

"Feds, huh?" Jock questioned rubbing his head.

"Young and raw," Pone remarked

"I didn't sign up for this shit," said Ben looking at Pone. "I know... too late to turn back now,"

The trio sat at their usual round table drinking and trying to figure out what was going on.

"You boys settle in I hope?" Jock asked.

"I'm good," said Pone. "You Ben?"

"No complaints so far," Ben retorted.

Pone exhaled. "Getting a free ride to the house of horrors and Feds on our tails,"

"You think Theiler in with the government?" Ben asked.

Pone shrugged. "I can buy corrupt politicians."

"How the hell we going to touch this guy?" Ben asked.

"They're clean. Not seasoned enough to get frustrated to turn a blind eye at corruption."

"Pone's got a point," said Jock. "Don't look surprised, but retirement money not all it's cracked up to be with some guys and they get their hands dirty."

Ben frowned. "Greed don't have no age,"

"Okay," said Pone. "We need to be cool and keep our heads on a swivel."

Ben gave a look. "You think?"

Ben's comment brought silence among the three men though Jock had his on thoughts on the matter, Pone believe his giant friend concerned about being in the cross hairs associating with him. A lifetime criminal, Ben's resume` long with bodies he put in the bone yard. He took jobs paying well enough to live a comfortable life. Pone didn't know Ben's retirement plan, his jobs under the radar. Ben's zone was shakedowns, loan-shark collecting, and assassin. He had legal jobs as a bouncer making eighty dollars a night and a repo man in which he is a silent partner known to Pone. This gig in the big easy a big pay day, but Pone knew that wasn't the reason Ben tagged along, it was to watch his back and Pone couldn't have ask for better wing-man.

Jock nodded to Pone. "You should be relieved,"

"What do you mean?" Pone asked.

"If it's the FBI, then your Lola is not in danger," Jock retorted.

"Your man still on the job?" Pone inquired.

"That's a good thing, right?" Jock asked.

"I thought you were clean after becoming a good guy?" Ben asked.

"Whatever going on here won't follow us back home," said Pone. "One thing for sure something is going on, but the important thing is it's not trying to stop us from winning the poker games."

"Maybe the feds been watching Theiler and -" Ben paused scathing his head. "Shit, man, I don't know... do they know who we are?"

"We either dead or in handcuffs." Pone retorted.

Ben shook his head." I know I'm on a mission. Got to protect my skin."

"You saying around with me might put you on the FBI most wanted?" Pone suggested.

"Didn't know you left bread crumbs." Ben remarked.

"You want me to call you Gretel?" Pone replied.

Jock snickered.

"This shit ain't funny," Ben growled.

"Relax," said Pone. "We'd be in chains by now,"

Jock cleared his throat. "There's another player with his own rules."

Pone nodded. "To help or hurt us is the question."

Ben frowned. "Either way I don't like it."

"Red is discrete, but she can't help she has connections." Pone retorted.

"See," Ben pointed. "You know my concern,"

"Red inherited those connections, she didn't seek them out," Jock commented.

"I can do this alone," said Pone. "You can go back to Metro like you weren't even here,"

A loud stamp came from Jock's shot glass. He eyed both men giving a stern look. "For you two to be bad ass killers," Jock pursed his lips. "Stop acting like a couple of Mewling Quims."

Ben frowned. "What say, say what now?"

"He's calling us whimpering vaginas." said Pone

"That's right," Jock stated. "I ain't no expert, but you both done this long enough to know to keep your eyes and ears open. You've driven places and this car seems to go the same way you are and you pull over only to notice it might be a plain Jane, ordinary Joe, a teen-age, and they drive by you not giving a glance meaning you don't mean shit to them, they have their own world."

Pone and Ben look like to boys who got sent to the principle's office for disturbing class getting scolded for their behavior. They knew Jock was right and they had better get it together.

Ben exhaled then down his drink. "This is bigger than the both of us. You ain't invincible, Pone." Ben shook his head. "The devil is topside and I want to help send him back where he belongs."

Pone tipped his hat. "I worry too, Ben. I worry too."

❧❧ ❧❧ ❧❧ ❧❧ ❧❧ ❧❧

"They say the enemy of your enemy is your friend," said Lambert.

"Does that mean you're in?" Maxwell asked.

"He gave me a nick name,professional ass wiper," Lambert retorted.

Maxwell smirked. "I have to admit the toilets are clean."

"Fuck you," Lambert replied giving the finger. "I take shit from him, but not from you,"

"How's your bank account?" Maxwell asked.

Lambert's face hardened. "You had me at getting even with Pone."

Maxwell showed the thick envelope to Lambert then pull it back." You know if you take this side hustle it can't lead back to me."

Lambert snorted. "Hey, I have to cover my ass. I'm walking on a sheet of ice."

"I can change that for you." said Maxwell.

Lambert looked at the money envelope pondering it. "What?" He shrugged. You'll give me enough so I can make a clean break?"

Maxwell laughed," You sure they didn't put a GPS up your ass?"

"Fuck you!" Lambert retorted. "You know you can get your own guy to do your bidding."

Maxwell frowned. "Crowe tried that and he got the Jimmy Hoffa treatment."

Maxwell and Lambert stared for a moment. The former deputy mayor was no where to be found. Dead a given, but where was his body. People whispered in bars, and barber-shops that he was under a new built skyscraper or swine bait, translation encased in cement or fed to the pork.

Lambert and Maxwell knew the two suggestions made since considering it the credo of the mob. They give you a death of no respect or where love ones if you had could pay their respects, so was the life of organize crime.

Maxwell shrugged. "You know what, sorry I bothered you." The district attorney whirled toward the door.

Lambert looked around his surroundings. A dump of a flat and the neighbors not fit for a sewer rat. He missed his fine living and though he'd never practice law again, if Maxwell walked out that door, the opportunity to be civilize would never come through it again.

"Stop." said Lambert. "It won't lead back to you.

Maxwell stood facing the door patting the envelope on his thigh. He too ponder what he was about to do. He said it inside his head that this wasn't him. Red came to mind. His love for her blinded his thinking. He hated Pone enough to hire a rat like Lambert to find someone lower than him to kill the troubleshooter. Pone's death wouldn't guarantee Red's hand in marriage. He swallowed hard wondering why she protected the former assassin. Why she kept him close at hand as her right-hand man sending him on assignments that her personal clientele needed a hush, hush job Pone qualified to do. Maxwell realized that made Red not so innocent, but nobody is perfect and he head over heels in love.

"Here," Maxwell tossed the envelope to Lambert. "Use that money to find yourself some digs that won't make me want to take a shower as soon as I enter the room."

THIRTY

Tara gazed into the radiant blue sky outside her window. The fluffy cotton white clouds forming shapes she wished to identify while under the sun. Unfortunate for Tara, the great outdoors a no go trapped inside her room. She sat on her bed staring bumming about a life she didn't ask for. A tear rolled down her cheek plopping on the floor. Tara stopped praying for miracles to end her nightmare. Her face hardened. She realized sometimes you have to make your own luck. Tara needed to escape from Theiler's hell. She felt relief knowing Doctor Brogan found away to keep Mia from the peripheral's clutches. He tried to do the same for her when she was younger, but failed. Mia pure cutting it close escaping Theiler's slimy grubby clutches. Tara didn't know how long Mia would be under Brogan's care, but she would to no longer give homage.

Tara gritted her teeth, shaking her head feeling Theiler clawing her body. His urine stain one good eye, the other dead yearning for an eye patch' and golden grinders too close for comfort. Tara straightens, escape jump into her mind. It had never happen before, but it made history by first timers. Escape and find people who'd listen bringing down this plantation of hell. She'd get caught then Theiler would make an example of her. Death would bring her freedom, not from the pedophile, but from everything else and she didn't want that. Tara, still young enough to know a good life within her grasp. She'd have to take it, frustrated waiting to be rescued or for the old sleaze bag to drop dead. Opportunity knock once they got the privilege to go outside. She felt a revival hearing someone disrupting Theiler's business taking his mind off the girls.

A much needed break from the sadistic world molestation. Tara nodded thinking time to make history. She needed help and the one person cable of assisting her, Beef. Tara hadn't seen him after setting boundaries. She hoped it did not scare Beef off, but coming into her room without an invite standing over the bed while she slept disturbing. Tara pondered if he fantasize gazing at her lying helpless on the mattress and if so she had no desire to have an incest love affair as with their father... uncle. Tara almost vomit thinking how disgusting.

Tara didn't want to hurt Beef's feeling yet appreciated his updates on Theiler's troubles. A wall had to be put up in case he develop feelings for her. He knew Mia his baby sister and though no proof fathered by the monster so he should know they could be half sibs... she shook her head trying to find a better thought. Beef would be all in on her coup and would join her escape from hell. A cousin working as a guard Beef mentioned not too found of Theiler could be an ally and with every thought, Tara felt optimistic.

She and the other girls got to go outside. No perverts at the estate since the disturbance. She inhaled knowing that wouldn't last and before you know it, back to business. Tara made a fist pressing her nails into the palm if her hand, She stared at her mitt glad the pain didn't draw blood. A knock on the door made her stand. Tara wasn't frightened thinking it might be Theiler. He'd barge in violating without guilt. She recognized the voice on the other asking for permission to enter.

Tara smiled. "Come in, Beef.

❧ ❧ ❧ ❧ ❧ ❧

Pone frowned checking his phone. He exhaled putting it face down on the table.

"Problem, brother?" Ben inquired.

Pone stretched his eyes. "Maybe she's mad or something,"

"Your girl?" Ben questioned.

"I told her to stay in touch and she hasn't return my text and she is not my girl." Pone replied.

Ben smirked. "My bad, but your body language says different,"

Pone straightens. "You one to talk,"

Ben nodded. "It's okay to care about someone."

Pone gave a thumbs up. He never saw Ben with anyone yet it devastated the giant losing his friend Al McGee.

"Lola and I connected." said Pone. "Considering the type of world we live in."

"Does she know what you do?" Ben asked.

"I made no secret it involves violence,"

"And she hooked up with you anyway?" Ben remarked.

"What can I say?" Pone shrugged. "I'm cool like that,"

Ben wave him off shaking his head. "She might be busy or pissed not being at her own crib."

"Trying to keep her safe." Pone replied.

Ben snorted. "She might rethink things,"

Pone frowned. "We're not a couple,"

"Yeah, but now her life is upside down." Ben shook his head. "She don't feel right going to work. Staying with a love one till you say it's safe to go home. Lola will feel different."

"That's why we don't get involve,"

"Then you shouldn't be worried," said Ben. "But you are,"

"She's innocent,"

Ben snorted. "Friendly fire,"

"That's what I'm trying to prevent," Pone retorted. "Wonder what's keeping Jock?"

Ben exhaled. "Groceries, remember?" He cleared his throat. "Volunteer to cook for us."

"Planning a feast, gone so long." said Pone.

"You want to know if he checked in with his man."

"It won't hurt to ask," Pone replied.

"Be patient, you have her behind the black jack table when we play our last game before we go off to see the wizard."

"Who said patience was a virtue?" Pone inquired.

"He'll kill us," Beef stated.

Tara got moon-eye. She didn't expect a jump a for joy, but taking the air out of the balloon half way not expected.

"I thought you'd be on board?"

"Others have tried," Beef replied.

Tara shrugged. "Okay, so where are they now? Maybe we can talk to them?"

Beef folded his arms, exhaled, and leaned against the wall. "In the swamp inside some gator's belly if they are lucky."

Tara frowned. "What? You mean they got caught and he fed their remains."

"No!" Beef straightened. "He took them to the swamp. They begged and pleaded not to ever try to escape again."

Tara pursed her lips. "You saw this?"

Beef shook his head. "Word of mouth."

"So," Tara snorted. "It would be a suicide run?"

"Miracles happen." said Beef. "Just not for everybody."

"Don't know why I even thought I could get away," Tara retorted.

"What do you mean?" Beef inquired.

"I made it out of here from a stranger my mom knew. Ludwig

tracked me down, here I am."

Beef swallowed hard. "He left your mother and cousin alive."

Tara gave a dubious look. "What are you talking about?"

"Like I said, there's talk, but in whispers,"

Tara licked her lower lip. "The man who helped escape... "

Beef exhaled. "He won't be helping anyone again,"

"Well at least he tried." Tara retorted.

"And he died."

"He didn't have enough help." said Tara.

Beef stared at the floor." I thought long and hard about seeing you again. If I knew it was going to be this, I'd stayed away."

"I'm glad to see you... I felt-"

"We're family and I get it. I came in unannounced you waking up seeing me in your room creepy." Beef nodded. "I got too comfortable, won't happen again." He opened the door making sure the coast was clear then looked back. "Have faith and be grateful the way things are now."

❧ ❧ ❧ ❧ ❧ ❧

Peary strolled down the hallway sporting a fresh haircut; faded sides, a curly bush on top, custom tailored olive suit, white shirt and crimson tie. He arrive at his destination then knocked on the door.

"Enter!" A booming gravel voice commanded.

Peary did as he was told closing the door behind him. Cigar odor strong filled the room. Theiler clenched stood facing the window puffing and blowing smoke like a chimney. The two of them alone with no sign of the hairy giant.

"Tell me, boy," said Theiler. "What you know good?"

Peary snorted never caring for the term boy figuring it was Theiler's habit making him feel superior.

"We're in the last phase of the poker tournaments and the men behind your stress will arrive soon."

Theiler turned facing his harbinger creating a smog from his pie hole between them. "You don't know them for sure, boy?"

Peary waited for the smoke to clear. It didn't faze him to have the minor diversion from a face that scarred young girls for life.

"I know there are not politicians though you could hire them out." said Peary.

"You do have an idea who they are and it's not just one man?" Theiler questioned.

"Professionals I am certain, once they arrive you can sort them out and do as you please."

Theiler sat down taking another puff from his fag. "Oh I'll make them pay, you can be sure of that, boy." He snorted. "If you know the two culprits then tell me."

"So you can act reckless?" Peary retorted.

"You telling me how to conduct my business, boy?"

Peary sat down clasping his hands. "Sir, we are almost back in the good graces of our clientele. You don't want to go off half cocked since the majority investors prefer to be discrete." Peary gave a look. "The wrong attention could blow up the trust we've rebuild."

Theiler clenched. He'd spent a fortune to keep his empire afloat. The pedophile wanted to crush the perpetrators who put a dent in his financial standing. Theiler knew Peary was right yet he didn't want to boost the nerd's ego by telling him. The business man side of him said to lay low and pounce when the time was right.

"You done good, boy." said Theiler. "But I ain't a patient man."

"A group of men will travel by air and sea."

Theiler frowned. "Meaning what, Paul Revere?"

"My queries have given me descriptions of the men causing you anxiety." Peary snorted. "The best way to get rid of stress is exercise."

Theiler nodded.

THIRTY-ONE

"Keep the money, I don't have the stomach for it." said Maxwell. Lambert pulled up his jacket collar to take the chill off his neck and ears. Maxwell dressed humble; wearing a skull hat, denim jacket, jeans, and work boots. The diminutive men stood side by side using the railing of the bridge to support them. They stood between their parked cars facing in opposite directions.

"When I told the guy about the job," Lambert gazed into the river's abyss. "The look in his eyes told me he'd do it for free."

Maxwell smirks knowing Pone has enemies on both sides of the law. How he survive this long a mystery or he's that good.

"Fine, I just want out," retorted Maxwell.

Lambert's laugh echoes through the forest across the river. Maxwell shivers not because of the night air, but Lambert's cackle sounded creepy.

"Look at you," Lambert looks straight ahead. "Trying to wash your hands before they get dirty."

"Damn!" Maxwell sounded off." I knew I couldn't trust you."

"What are you talking about?" Lambert questioned.

Maxwell looks around. "Where is he?"

"Who?"

"You didn't come out here alone. You got a man taking pictures, recording our conversation?"

"No." Lambert replied. "I'm keeping the money I got left for me."

Maxwell wanted to breath a sigh of relief. Instead he tried shrugging off what felt like a blade of ice penetrating his spine.

"I can't trust you?"

"What goes down won't trace back to you." said Lambert. "You have my word."

Maxwell swallowed hard. "I didn't tell you when Pone will be arriving because I don't know his flight or when he'll return."

"My man assured me he'd stake out the air port. He knows what Pone looks like."

Maxwell pursed his lips. "Okay, what do you want?"

"Keep the money coming,"

"Shit!" blurted Maxwell.

"Happens,"

"Blackmailing me?" Maxwell shook his head.

"I'm not greedy, the same amount or close to it," Lambert replied.

"And if I don't,"

Lambert exhaled." Your conscience is your weakness."

"Excuse me?" Maxwell questioned.

"To err is human," Lambert replied. "Love makes you do stupid things. You won't kill me." He placed his hand on Maxwell's shoulder. "Don't worry the payments stop when Pone is in the ground. It's getting late and it's best we don't get in touch again till the job is done."

Lambert got in his car, driving off leaving Maxwell with his thoughts.

A bottle of rot gut half empty sharing a table with a shot glass. Maxwell paced back and forth inhaling and exhaling. He shook his head regretting his choices. Running for mayor not one of them. He beamed with confidence making that decision, and not because the Brigands backed him. Maxwell raised to do things the right way, parents both educators and strict teaching him and his siblings no matter what you follow the straight and narrow of life avoiding making the wrong turn. He bypassed the glass grabbing the bottle instead taking a long hard drink.

Maxwell thought of his parents, what would they say now that he crossed the line getting help from a disgraced attorney to kill a man standing between the love of his life Brooke Cassidy Brigand. A goddess in the eyes of Maxwell. What would she think of her self if she found out what he did. Red respected him because he stood for justice. She never let their height difference get in the way of their get together. His bravado asking her out and to his surprise she agreed without hesitation. Maxwell hit the bottle hard hoping the rot gut might burn some sense to his situation.

His love for Red blinded him She never led him to believe other men are in her life. A strong woman, successful with brains and beauty to match. Maxwell knew he was not in her league, but she was with him. He laughed thinking why was he jealous of Pone. A killer working for her father order the hits and Pone carried them out. Red born in to a crime family yet she ran a clean law firm. Maxwell thought about the annual family dinner watching the two of them shooting pool. Pone and she cleaned his clock humbling him in front of the family.

Whether she was showing whose boss, Maxwell didn't know smiling, thinking foreplay? Either way, it's no excuse for him to cross the line paying someone to give him the long good-bye. He did and now too late to wash his hands. Maxwell felt dirty realizing a part of him died when he heard Lambert say the deal was done and the shooter relishing to take out Pone. Maxwell felt like a true politician, a corrupt politician. He wanted to clear his conscience confessing to Red what he had done. He finish the hash frowning tossing it across the room. She'd slap him silly and to get out of her life. Red loves Pone, but not enough to make it public. Maxwell knew she cares for him too, beating Pone at billiards when he on purpose shot the cue ball at him.

The DA smiles knowing the one thing Pone hasn't done and he has, sleeping with Red. Lambert would approach Red revealing his alliance, instead he is blackmailing until the task is done. Pone returning to Metro? The DA had no clue when his venture would conclude which meant he'd be paying out his pocket for being stupid. Love does strange things to the mind. Maxwell slumps down on the couch burying his face in his hands, He should have settled with knowing what it felt like to bed Red instead of going to the dark side.

Pone looks around the casino, Lola not at the Black Jack table where she made some happy and others curse themselves for bad luck. Don't panic he thought, Lola entitled for days off or calling in sick. She never missed tournament nights. Lola loves her job and getting to know him put her career in jeopardy. Jock hasn't given him any updates and no news is sometimes good news. Pone didn't bother to ask believing Jock would tell him if something awful happened. He exhaled, ask someone, coworkers would know.

Pone sat at the bar where if anyone knew anything it would be the barkeep.

"Name your poison?" said the Bartender.

Pone smirked. He knew whether upper or lower tier watering holes, the person behind the counter had an ear for retrieving gossip.

"Lola?" Pone questioned. "She working tonight?"

A rub on the chin, wondering eyes highlighted by a smile. The actions told Pone Lola has an admiring coworker.

"Hadn't seen her of late," Bartender shook his head.

Pone pursed his lips. "Nothing bad, I hope,"

Bartender shrugged. "Management knows and they don't kiss and tell at least not with me."

"I hear you," Pone nodded.

"You dry?" Bartender inquired.

Pone smiled. "Got to keep a clear head, poker tournament."

"Right," Bartender retorted. "For all the marbles."

"More than you know," Pone remarked.

The gaze from horse-face didn't give Ben chills, but made him vex. The giant didn't believe in intuition yet he had a hunch something wasn't right. If this was any other bar he'd march up to the man demanding to know what his deal before inflicting pain. Ben didn't use his size to bully though he didn't regret having what his mother called a gift. Horse-face kept staring with a purpose. A rage in the pit of Ben's stomach began to rise. That strawny ass thinks he can take me, Ben thought. Pone said to lay low letting things play out. He's not here now acting as my conscience, thought Ben. Horse-Face kept throwing dagger eyes and the giant had enough, making a bee-line to the bar. A hand grabbed him by the elbow.

"Whoa, big man," said Pony-tail. "The game is this way,"

Jock hasn't said anything good or bad and again no news good news till it wasn't. Pone shook off the last part thinking positive thoughts. It would be on him if something bad happened to Lola. The feds following he and Ben no doubt got reassigned since they got burned. Pone trusted his intuition that something sinister loomed not from Theiler's estate, but around the big easy, too. His spine tingles from a caressing rake of finger-nails interrupted Pone's pondering. He smiles hoping it might be Lola, whirling around to find the seductive touch belong to Mai Ling. Pone's delight turns dubious.

Ling steps back holding up her hands. "Not good for a girl's ego."

"What are you doing here?" Pone asked. He couldn't help how

fetching she looked in a one shoulder strap black dress slit displaying waist high thigh and pumps. Her hair in a bun held together by knitting needles.

"I want to see how this ends." She replied.

"You're not a sore loser, I give you that," Pone remarked.

"I'm on the other end." said Ling. "I want to see if your luck runs out."

"Wow?" Pone snorted. "We'll have to play one on one,"

"Sounds fun." Ling winked.

"For now you can continue to be a groupie,"

Ling got moon-eye. "Speaking of egos,"

"It's called confidence, you should try it sometimes," said Pone.

"You looking for someone?" Ling asked.

Pone smirked. "Checking out the competition,"

"Why?" Ling gestured. "This is a strange tournament,"

Pone raise an eye-brow. "The other four players go the mansion win or lose." She frowned. "Don't you think that's strange?"

Pone pursed his lips. "The other players will fill a void if something happens to the winner."

Ling tilted her head. "You believe that?"

"Best answer for your concern,"

"An observation," Ling replied.

Pone inhaled. He didn't smoke, but got a craving to do it. That drink would come in handy now talking to this inquisitive woman. Pone saw Ling's observation as a nosy. She asked him if he was looking for someone. Yeah, but not any business yours, he thought. Pone couldn't help pondering if Mai Ling appearing at the utmost time shadowing him. The players who lost on the first day tournament no where to be found yet Ling kept lingering around.

The woman eye catching though no chemistry not that they couldn't mix it up with each other, but Pone's mind on Lola hoping nothing awful happened to her. He thought of Ben at his poker where the final five would also go on to see the wizard win or lose. Pone knew what Ling was talking about how bizarre the game yet wanted to keep her in the dark about being aware of that the game focus on recruitment of killers and politicians.

Red said she took care of his and Ben's background to make sure they qualify for the type of men Theiler looked for to help keep his empire thriving. Mai Ling, what's her deal? Friend? Not a chance, but a foe perhaps. She could be on Theiler's payroll and might know something about Lola and wanting confirmation he knew the caramel beauty using her for possible leverage. He played his poker face waiting for the game to start.

Ling checked the time on her cell. "Game's about to start." She allowed Pone to glance at her phone."

"Guess you'll be cheering me on?"

Ling squinted. "I'm a sore loser."

Pone grinned. "Rooting against me, okay."

"I'm Switzerland." Ling replied. "I'm a fan." She twisted her index finger inside Pone's cleft chin then strolled to the bar.

THIRTY-TWO

"Who the hell are you?" Ben asked.

"A fan," Pony-tail replied. "You've come to far to go back now," Win or lose those in the top five get a free pass to see the pervert wizard. Ben didn't understand the concept and it hurt his head trying to figure it out. Pone might be able to shed some light on things. He look to the bar and Horse-face was gone. Ben pondered if he should be concern.

"A piss break," said Pony-tail.

"And you know that how?"

"A guess?" Pony-tail shrugged. "What the shit would I care if he hit the John?"

"You said it not me," Ben remarked.

"Well," Pony-tail threw up his hands. "You want be distracted so you can keep your mind on the game."

Ben frowned. "What's it to you?"

Pony-tail smiled, slapped Ben on his shoulder and head for bar calling for a drink.

Pone sat at the rectangle table holding once again a winning hand. He exhaled getting the attention of the other players who couldn't tell if he happy or frustrated. Pone did an inside grin, he couldn't have ask for a better poker face. The other players gave one of their own. Did they know when to lose knowing they would be tagging along to the big house? Pone scoped them out; they looked like politicians young and old. He decided to put them in categories. Two of the four men were old, one portly with snow white hair making him a politician or judge.

The other older man long and lean with a bald head, but silver grass on the sides giving him a horse shoe. He much like his fat counter part in the same field. Theiler does his research on people with power who have pervert desires same as him using their disgust against them. Pone pondered if Red set him up as a killer for hire? He observed the other two men looking his age, height, and build. Pone classified them as white collar assassins. Men hired to take out important people; corporate, and political types.

They were handsome, tall, and educated presence about them again similar to Pone. The game itself needed a winner, why him, thought Pone. He felt uncomfortable being singled out since the five of them would be going to meet Theiler no matter the outcome of the game. Did the pedophile know he's the one disrupting his business. Would he and Ben be examples of what happens to men trespassing? They'd be at his mercy if he knew they were the men affecting his business. Unarmed, surrounded by his army with no where to run or hide once on his property.

Pone inhaled thinking in order to play poker your mind had to be on the game, but he destined to win again. Lola and her whereabouts should not concern him while playing yet he could have other thoughts knowing the outcome. The mission of rescuing a young woman and not just her, but a group of others younger than Tara from Theiler's clutches. Pone kept a poker face, The younger men at the table could be adversaries once they set foot on the estate to prove their worth. Pone sat at the table among the players and those who watched the game. He knew at Theilers house of sin he'd have to be a Trojan horse bringing the killer inside him.

Ben sat at the table holding a shit hand. His poker game not sophisticated like Pone's since the dealer played among them. Pony-tail supervise walking around the table. All the men about the same size, built, and unkempt. No doctors, lawyers, or Indian chiefs sitting at this table. Hardened criminals who'd take a life if the price was right. Ben knew they put him in the company of hired muscle. Brains not necessary, but the comprehension of doing as you are told. He frowned and the other players notice. Ben got inside their heads by accident. They didn't know he hated his situation; this win or lose shit and you still move on to the palace of horrors. (What the hell am I doing?) he thought. Ben folded and in a blink he a piece of paper dropped in his lap.

❖❖ ❖❖ ❖❖ ❖❖ ❖❖ ❖❖

The dealer made no eye contact with Pone and he got the same. They'd played it straight not letting the others know lady luck had already picked her champion. Pone even folded twice then decided to let things play out declaring him the winner. He watched as beautiful shapely waitresses delivered neat folded notes on silver platter to all the players went their separate ways. One of the younger men hit the black jack table, another met with two female admirers, the two older sat at the bar drinking whiskey on the rocks. Pone observed the men and none showed expressions, but put their message inside their pockets. Pone did the same believing they got instructions where to meet with date and time. The troubleshooter survey the club looking for Lola with no such luck. Pone didn't get the chance to agonize over the whereabouts of his lady friend. Fingers soft, but strong touched his hand and the aroma of perfume scent of flowers teased his nostrils. He turned exchanging pearly whites with Mai Ling.

"To the victor goes the spoils," she said.

❖❖ ❖❖ ❖❖ ❖❖ ❖❖ ❖❖

The Scarlet body hugging dress matched her hair, Red stood with arms folded under firm breast looking down on the seated Maxwell. He sat with hands clasped, looking down at the floor like a scolded child.

"What's going on Thomas?" Red asked with a furrow brow. "It can't be that bad."

She looked down on the man who won her over with his bravado. Now losing respect and pondering what she ever saw in the shrimp sitting like he wanted to cuddle with his mother.

"I am losing my patience." She stated.

Maxwell inhaled. His eyes took a journey from Red's heels up her legs, torso, to her ravishing features. He swallowed realizing admitting what he had done would cast him out of her life.

"Jitters." Maxwell muttered.

Red snorted sitting down next to her diminutive man. "What did you just say?"

Maxwell bobble his head. "I'm nervous about leaving the D. A. Office." A lie he thought, but the best he could do since he shit and stepped in it.

Red pursed her lips. "You have a good track record for putting away the bad guys, but you have my family backing your campaign and the incumbent mayor is on borrowed time." She sat back crossing her legs. "Bull-shit!'

Maxwell straightened. "Excuse me?" He saw a furrowed brow and arms folded under her breast.

"You know how many men your size or a bit taller approach me shuddering to ask me out?"

Maxwell shook his head.

"I'm not buying what you're trying to sell." Red stated.

"OK." He cleared his throat. "I'm at a lost."

"You did something and you're afraid to come clean and even more afraid if I find out with out you telling me how it would affect us." She gave a stern look. "So, What did you do?"

Crap. Maxwell thought aware he's dealing with a fellow lawyer trained to read body language and listening to speech patterns. He wasn't going to come clean with hiring some hit-man through Lambert to take out Pone once he arrives back to Metro. The former attorney now custodian made it clear he's not backing out. The low life salivating on the opportunity to take out Pone. Maxwell too felt deep down erasing the former Brigand trigger-man would have some affect on he and Brooke's relationship. Pone dead, and he alive to give his tall drink of water the comfort she'd need grieving his death.

"The debate." said Maxwell.

Red shrugged. "What about it?" Uncrossing her legs, unfolding her arms leaning forward cupping her hands.

Maxwell stood up strolling around the room. "What if he brings up Pone?"

Red inhaled. "Why would he do that?"

"Politics." Maxwell replied.

Red chuckled. "Winston cleared him of any wrong doings after he prevented the gang war." She gave a look. "A small circle knows about his past and that includes within law enforcement. Winston knows he's keeping the seat warm yet I respect him for not going down with out a fight."

Maxwell knew Pone could buy groceries like the average patron who wouldn't know they stood next to a killer. Brigand crime family a hush, hush among the public and people in high places kept their dirt swept under the rug. Pone handed it to them, but now it was within the law. A handful of people if that had record of his past and legs up to her neck protected him at any cost.

"Why you worrying about Pony?" Red asked.

Maxwell exhaled keeping calm. He hated the pet name Red used for her troubleshooter. If she said it to unnerve him, it worked. His dark-side told him to keep his trap shut and when Pone came back to town a bullet would be waiting to greet him.

Maxwell whirled facing Red. "Just a thought, a guy could change his mind."

"Winston's a coward, but he has some integrity." said Red.

"You're right," He waved her off. "I was concern over nothing. I'll get out of your hair, see you later?"

"I call you." Red replied.

Maxwell smiled closing the door then gazing back at his goddess with puppy dog eyes.

Red exhaled seated raising her dress slipping off panties, parting her legs like the red sea. Maxwell shut the door locking it. He dropped on all four crawling towards the invite.

Pone held his cue with both hands waiting his turn in thought. The woman knew her way around the bedroom. She got up hitting the shower first then after toweling off, stood in front of the mirror pretending not to notice his gaze at her thin feminine muscular body. Ling took her time getting dressed, silk covered her body, black the theme for underwear, her dress, and heels all matching the same hue as her hair. Pone saw the Asian beauty in a different light, her skin bronze and smooth, hair draped pass shoulders eye-brows thick yet trimmed neat with out make-up she didn't need. The dress exposed shoulders, slit in the middle allowing legs to breath. Ling used her reflection to talk, telling him hot pot of coffee on the tray in front of the bed and hurry to get dressed then follow her to the next room. He showered, dressed, drank his coffee then entered the room to a display of legs and a billiard table. Ling sat on the edge holding a pool ball. Pone checked out her gams while entrance by seductive gaze.

"Two games to none," Mai said with a smirk.

Pone shook himself back to reality. It was the second time a ravishing woman handed him his ass in what the English called a gentleman's game. Red gave it to him to defend her elf after he shot a ball off the table at him on purpose. Pone now win less against dames who handled a cue as good as he.

"Want a chance to salvage what's left of your manhood?" She gloated.

"Sure, why not?" Pone shrugged. He already lost two out of three, but wanted a chance to at least get one game and information. It danced in his head how this woman knew he enjoyed pool as much as playing poker. Ling hung around from day one after her defeat in the tournament to hell. The other players gone to from whence they came, but Ling stayed around like a groupie. Pone figured he'd find out why before he left for Theiler's estate. Ling did as she did before, hitting the balls with a perfect crack scattering them to pockets and taking her choice for which balls to play. Pone snorted shaking his head to a third straight defeat. He'd enjoy the show watching the fem fatale bend and twist her body to make her shots.

"So," said Ling. "You looking forward to your trip to riches?"

"Beats the nine to five grind." Pone remarked.

"Isn't that the truth," Ling retorted. "What if you win?"

Pone's intuition about the mystery woman told him to keep her off balance. Ling wouldn't be coming with him so why the interest. He studied his adversary, athletic, no damsel in distress, strong frame, a woman confronts danger and not run from it. Pone knew he'd better tread light.

"You're good." said Pone. "And what is it you said you do for a living?"

Ling gave a Cheshire cat smile. "I didn't, and you?"

"Ditto," Pone retorted.

Ling nods pursing her lips. "A card shark?"

"A pool shark until now." Pone remarked. He tossed his cue on the table interrupting Ling's game winning shot.

"Hey!" She gave a look.

Pone exhaled. "I've seen this before, second time around a beautiful woman deflating my ego."

Ling place her stick on the table. "Popular with the ladies?"

"It's my eyes." Pone smiled.

Ling move in for a closer gaze. She purred like a kitten.

"You mean you didn't notice them before?" He questioned.

"One brown and the other blue." Ling batted her eye-lashes.

"Nothing sinister." Pone remarked.

"Mysterious, intriguing, and sexy." Ling murmured. Her hands gripped his collar twirling him till he landed on the table scattering the balls. Ling climbed on top unzipping his pants playing with his hat. Pone inhaled as their lips met.

THIRTY-THREE

Ben checked his cell waiting for a text.

"You expecting something important?" Jock asked.

Ben glower shaking his head. "That damn Pone got me playing Uber, Lyft, and Taxi for his ass. He should've been ready to go when I left that funky bar."

"Did you win?" Jock inquired."

"I wasn't cool," Ben snorted. "Since regardless of the outcome the final five still move on so what the hell."

Jock studied the troubled giant taking a sip of rot gut. He grabbed another shot glass and the bottle taking a seat at their round meeting table. "Take the load off big man and tell me your troubles."

Ben strolled over planting himself then scooped up his shot downing it.

"This ain't you is it?" Jock asked."

"What gave me away?"

Jock filled up Ben's glass. "Were you forced or did you volunteer?"

"One guy is old as shit and the other don't look human. I know I stick out like a sore thumb, but he needed someone to have his back."

"You both do the same thing," Jock stated.

"He's cleaner than me." Ben retorted. "I walk down a dark path."

Jock sipped and nodded. "So if the person is innocent?"

"If the money's right," Ben slumped. "You can judge me."

Jock frowned. "Not my place and not qualified. We do what we got to do until it ends and then judgment begins."

Ben toasted. "Until then?"

"Never too late to change,"

Ben sat in deep thought, he wanted to laugh not because what Jock said was funny, but turning over a new leaf would not get him through the Pearly gates. He helped his family when his father died and stayed in the lane never straying.

Jock cleared his throat. "You're here for a good cause and that's what counts."

"I will see this through, ain't no turning back now."

"When you see Pone, don't tell him--"

"Way ahead of you," said Ben. "Don't have time hearing his shit."

Jock gave a look. Ben nodded.

"If it hits the fan it will be on me. They won't know me and Pone are together."

Jock straightened. "It's going to take the two of you to pull this off."

Ben frowned." Don't Theiler have an ensemble?"

"Sometimes miracles do happen,"

"You know something?"

Jock threw down his drink. "I pray."

"Think I forgot how." Ben remarked checking his phone. He stood looking at Jock.

"You can practice while you drive."

"One of my hands will be on the wheel."

Pone hopped in feeling Ben's eyes burning a hole through him.

"Shouldn't we get moving?" Pone questioned. "We need to have a plan once we get to Theiler's estate."

"Was it good?" Ben asked.

Pone gave a look. "You want blow by blow?"

Ben put the car in motion. "She did the job." He wanted to ask if it was Lola knowing Pone's concern about her.

Pone smiles. "They all seem to have their talents."

Ben glanced and snorted. "Lola didn't show up for work?"

The mood inside the truck got somber. Pone's brief joy turned to worry. Where was his caramel beauty? Alive or dead he did not know. Was she in trouble and yes he would be at fault. An innocent woman who enjoyed her job not wanting no more then to see the best in people, living a normal life working and paying the bills. Pone inhaled with the thought of the normal life gone since he entered her life. Lola absent and he shuddered if that good or bad.

"Earth to Pone, you still with us?" Ben asked.

"Miles to go before I sleep." Pone shook his head. "Got to stay focus so we close this thing out and go home."

"Amen. Brother," Ben nodded. "Amen."

❧ ❧ ❧ ❧ ❧ ❧

Linda sat lady-like across from Maxwell wearing long length prohibition dress covering heels. Hair fixated looking like a golden-age starlet.

"You comfortable?" Maxwell asked.

Linda exhaled the question with a glare. "Why did you call me here?" Linda growled. "And it better not be about confidence."

Maxwell swallowed shaking his head. "No, I had a talk with Brooke."

Linda frowned. "You didn't propose?"

Maxwell snorted. "Being mayor will be no different than being District Attorney."

"Okay," Linda replied. "I sense something,"

"I visited her to talk about what I did, then realize she wouldn't understand."

Linda shrugged. "I'm finding it hard to comprehend you."

"Would our world be so bad with out Chubby Pone?"

Linda straightened putting done her cup of coffee. She leans forward giving as stern look." You have me intrigued,"

"Fuck it!" Maxwell swallowed hard." Pone's a dead man once he sets foot back in Metro."

Linda got moon-eye. "A corrupt Mayor? You've been busy,"

"I'm telling you because you want the same,"

Linda pursed her lips. "And where did you hear that?"

Maxwell sat back taking a deep breath to relax. He and Red had spoken about how Linda threaten to end Pone's life if he decided to leave the family. The dinner at the Brigand estate,Maxwell remembered Linda getting chummy with Pone. It was anything but a woman out for blood making her own husband envy of his wife.

"If Brooke and I marry, we don't need him lingering around."

"Does she know?" Linda questioned.

"Not a clue." Maxwell replied with a smirk.

Linda observed the diminutive man. She crossed her legs, folded her arms then sat back exhaling. "You called me here to level the playing field."

"When I become mayor, I will help as long as it's within the law." Maxwell stated. "Anything other than that need not cross my desk."

Linda flashed a brilliant smile. "What if I tell my sister?"

"You don't know who, what, or when it will take place." Maxwell retorted. "You've got a soft spot for Pone, but you want to see how this plays out."

"What makes you so sure?"

You're a gangster daughter. You live by the code. The way out is death and though Pone is still in the fold, you worry."

"What you lack in stature, you make up in heart. But don't ever think you know me." Linda retorted.

"How long is your sister's leash will always be a concern."

"If your plan fails?" Linda inquired.

Maxwell shrugged. "Never spend money you can't afford to lose."

Linda sipped her warm coffee. She laughed in secret at Maxwell thinking revealing his sinister plot to off Pone made them equals. Linda was not afraid to rat on Maxwell to Red about murdering her troubleshooter. The soon to be mayor clueless not to know in the mob world threats are a part of life and he'd find out soon enough once he made his seat warm and comfortable till she lit a fire under his ass. Let the little man have his delusional victory. He will learn he can't cut the strings and their puppet as long as they need him. Linda knew Red would have nothing to with Maxwell if she found out what he had done. Pone and Red's bond strong, built since childhood. Linda herself had become fond of him and deep inside she hope whatever Maxwell has planned would fail.

She toasted. "Well played Thomas, well played."

Pone kept his thoughts to himself pondering this could be it. The business of guns and bullets lucrative, but high on mortality. He didn't know what they were walking into and getting out alive no guarantee even with a plan in place and Pone had none.

"Tomorrow we go and meet this, Lereaux." said Ben. Traveling by air and sea... why is that?"

"We'll find out, be patient." Pone replied.

"You boys pray?" Jock asked.

"Forgot how." Ben remarked.

"Ain't no shame," said Jock. "But nothing wrong with asking for help."

Pone snorted lowering his head towards the floor. He read Ben's frown like a book. The big man has killed good and bad, but his conscience giving him the business of taking innocent lives for blood money. Pone agreed a higher calling would beckon on a man with a dark soul. Luck the combine killers called upon when doing a job not heaven above.

"Go ahead," Pone gestured. "But in silence and closed eyes." He nodded to close his eyes. Jock held out his hands for the two assassins to take hold of.

The orison lasted less than a minute and all three men exhaled once it ended.

Jock did the usual throwing down hash and Ben joined him.

"Vino would have been more appropriate." Pone joked getting a hint of smiles around the table.

"No plan?" Jock questioned.

"Act as if we don't know one another." Pone replied.

Ben cleared his throat. "Do I drop you off--?"

"It will be daytime so you go on to the docks and Jock will be my taxi." said Pone.

"Not a problem." Jock acknowledge.

"We won't be packing?" Ben confirmed twirling his shot glass.

Pone inhaled. "At the mercy of our enemies." Pone remarked.

Two small blades no bigger than a pinkie placed on the table. Pone motioned to Ben.

"Take and conceal."

The giant grabbed one, it fit inside the palm of his hand. He nodded to Pone.

"I knew you had something brewing inside that head of yours."

Pone snorted. "Just in case."

"You will be search," said Jock.

"Not in certain areas," Ben stated.

Jock got moon-eye. "Spare me details."

Laughter filled the room.

Pone rose from the table stretching and yawns. "Guess I'll drain the snake and hit the sack."

"Good-night." said Jock

"Don't stay up too late, Ben." Pone retorted.

"Okay, dad." Ben frowns.

Pone disappears to the bath room. Jock gives a look.

"Is he all right?" Jock asked.

"For what we do there is always something on our minds." said Ben.

Pone threw himself on the futon. He was glad Jock didn't give them cots. The futon's weren't mattresses, but more comfortable. Lola occupied his head while he laid on his back with closed eyes. He knew he needed to close her out before getting Theiler's estate in order to take care of the task at hand.

Where are you Lola? Pone didn't bother to ask Jock, if he heard anything from his man whose supposed to guard Lola with out her knowing. It made him more concern something happen and Jock too embarrass to mention his guy failed or worse. No police report or six o'clock news about a homicide though Pone knew that it could mean a professional hit. Bodies get erase like they never existed. Thoughts clouding Pone's head made him open his eyes staring into the darkness. If his eyes could glow they would lit up his room with antimony. If Theiler found out about he and Ben then they better be prepared and if he knew about Lola who was innocent, but harm her anyway then the pedophile would pay by any means. Pone took a deep breath shutting eyes forcing sleep. He'd need to be alert to any surprises the pervert might have in store for them.

Ben threw down a shot motioning for Jock to pour another now that his conscience went to bed.

Jock poured. "You should be in bed, but I hate drinking alone."

"Heard from your man watching Pone's lady friend?" Ben questioned.

Jock pursed his lips then downed his rot gut. "Your friend is a class act."

Ben nods taking the comment as something bad has happened.

Jock inhaled. "He was told to give day by day report. I didn't have the heart to say anything, but I know Pone suspects something not right."

Ben glowered. "Damn."

"Think that going to interfere with what y'all got to do?"

Ben shook his head. "We're professionals. You'd be crazy to think things will turn out perfect." He exhaled. "What or if anything happened, we'll find out once we get to the estate."

Jock swallowed hard. "Don't envy you boys. The stress that comes with what you do."

"Smokes and a strong drink is my recipe." Ben replied.

"He has a family." Jock frowned. "Made him promise not to tell what the job was, but that it's a big pay day and he'd be gone for awhile." He filled his glass. "Break the news to them when this is over."

Ben leaned back. Jock's words hit home. He lost a friend who had a family when he took a solo job making a detour that caused him his life. Ben knew the circumstances were different yet same results. Like his friend, Jock's guy took the long good-bye.

Ben exhaled rising from the table. "Get some shut eye and don't worry too much."

Jock raised his glass. "You do the same big man. You do the same."

THIRTY-FOUR

A thick fog blown from dry cracked lips. The stogie held loose between dry fingers; thumb, index while a glass of cognac sat in the other hand. Theiler inhale smoke puffing it out like a chimney then taking a sip. He sat in his recliner smiling now that he was in good with clientele and most important revenge. He would see the men who pissed in his pool. Peary promised the men would be present and he could make an example of them in front of others who'd think to cross or step out of line. Theiler nodded and stared at the wall as if eyeing an expensive painting.

The pedophile sips, smokes, and smiles. Clientele restored, money flowing like a river, and new recruits on the horizon. The dent in his empire smooth over and all that left was to take out his moment of frustration on the perks who caused him his stress. They will be here soon and he will teach them a lesson. You don't mess with Theiler Lereaux. He'd make them feel right at home then the party begins. Theiler blew a puff of smoke and when it cleared he vision slow torture or instant death shaking that thought off thinking that would be too good for them. They were fresh to the big easy, not given the proper hospitality. One thing Theiler knew was how to be hospitable. He snuffs out his cigar in the ash tray, downs his last drop of rot gut stamping the glass on the desk not using a coaster. Theiler waltz over to a door opening it with a gruesome smile. A young teen-age girl sat on the edge of the bed. He shook his head thinking things were getting back to normal.

Now I know what a can of sardines feel like along with the fishy smell. Ben pondered what the hell did I get myself into. The hired muscle traveled coach the bad way; no elbow room is bad for oversize men. A moldy creaky tug boat if you wanted to call it that would be a compliment.

Ben shrugged thinking the monster didn't want to bring attention to himself, smart for him, but the accommodations shit. He swallowed focusing on the mission putting an end to child or human trafficking. The boat ride wouldn't last forever yet smoother sailing on a yacht... too late now that they the voyage had begun. Ben exhaled pondering what awaited he and Pone if Theiler knew they were the guilty party sabotaging his empire. Head on a swivel and on their toes once they hit land. Pone would get there faster traveling by air. Ben shook off the thought of his friend getting ambush since Theiler knew two perks caused him stress. He'd wait till everyone arrive before playing his hand. Ben got a queasy feeling in his gut thinking about walking into a trap. The giant would think twice agreeing to help a friend in need if it meant putting his own life on the line. Ben leaned forward trying to give himself room in the cramp tug boat. What awaited him and Pone he did not know, but he needed to be focus, He on a mission and had to keep a clear head. Then somebody farted.

"I'm good," Pone said flashing a million dollar smile.

"If you change your mind." Stewardess replied displaying her own pearly whites.

Drinks and women making the flight to Theiler's estate pleasurable. The women serve beverage and park themselves on the men's sweet spot. At least they weren't young girls. The pervert owned a private jet giving the top five poker players royal treatment. Pone pondered if it would be his last taste of the good life and how was Ben doing traveling by boat. He felt eyes on him, not the burning kind, but admiration. Pone looks up, the stewardess. Her brilliant smile shone upon him, she strolls toward him when one of the poker players grab her arm. Pone rose then sat back down rethinking rescuing the damsel in distress. She smiles digging her claws into the man's arm and he got the message releasing his grip. The stewardess sat down across from Pone.

"Change your mind?" She asked.

"I was about to come to your rescue," Pone remarked.

"Do I look helpless?" She retorted still smiling.

Pone tipped his bowler. "Not anymore,"

They both smirked.

"Now," She said. "Change your mind?"

"Is it okay if we talk?" Pone gestured.

She folded her arms, smile now a grin. Her hair reddish brown in a bun,eye glasses gave an intellect look on her bronze complexion. Average height and hour glass build hid behind the miniature rectangle table. She motioned to Pone to start the conversation.

"Is this your fist rodeo?" Pone asked.

"Third,"

Pone saw this an opportunity to pick a brain for information about his host. "So you are aware of the situation?"

She pursed her lips. "What do you mean?"

Pone snorted leaning back in his seat. He pondered whether to try the finesse approach.

"So, you toured the grounds?" Pone questioned.

The stewardess face turned sour. "That troll gave me the creeps."

Pone knew she referred to Theiler. He never saw the man in person yet hearing his name gave a define hideous.

"Just one look and that's all it took?" Pone questioned.

Her glance was that of making sure not to be heard. "The place looked guarded and that told me it might be safer to stay on the plane and the other girls did the same as me."

"Do you want to go somewhere private?" Pone asked.

The stewardess frowned. "Why you so interested?"

"If there's trouble I might not get off the plane." Pone retorted.

"Nothing happened, but I felt safer on the plane and I didn't want him gazing at me. He made my skin crawl."

"Could I have a beer if you don't, mind."

"Sure," she smiled leaving Pone heading to the front of the plane.

The troubleshooter use the speculate the circumstances of Theiler's estate. He figured armed guards though the stewardess didn't call them that, but what else would they be since he recruited mercenaries for hire. He would have one beer, now that what information he gathered told him danger surround him once he step off the plane and Ben complete his boat trip. Pone cringe at the thought going in armed light except for the knife he gave Ben and he hid inside his shoe. The stewardess returned with the bottle of brew.

"Will there be anything else?' she asked.

"A Tommy gun?"

She gave a dubious look. "Excuse, me?"

Pone winked then downs his beer.

He stood on the balcony sipping cognac, smoking a cigar, and a cool breeze has his albino locks floating in the wind. Theiler wasn't sitting on the dock of the bay watching the tide rolling in, but the tug boat on horizon carrying his cargo of muscle. The pedophile smirks thinking about the nick name he gave men with brawn and no brains though that wasn't all true. He knew some of the men had smarts yet hired to do one thing, his bidding.

Assassins and palace guards or all the same, they didn't get paid to think, but just to protect and destroy. Theiler's recruiting of such men worked so far until now, one man came to his manor gave him a black eye and the other would arrive soon by air. A puff of smoke followed by a swill of rot gut then a long exhale allowing himself to stretch.

"Excuse, me sir, don't mean to disturb you." said Peary.

Theiler downed his drink then toss his stogie. He whirls toward Peary standing like an obedient soldier straight as a statue.

"Relax,boy" said Theiler. "The gang's almost here."

"How you going to handle this?"

Peary frowned. He regretted asking the question when he saw Theiler's decaying toothy smile.

"Been a long time, boy." Theiler replied. "You'll be front and center watching what I do to those who wrong me."

Peary snorted. "Do you need the festivities?"

"What's a matter, boy?" Theiler questioned. "Ain't got the stomach?"

"Torture, murder, or whatever you do to people is not my concern and I don't see where you need me to be present." Peary retorted.

The balcony rumbled from Theiler's laughter. "As long as the money's good, huh, boy?"

Peary straightened taking a deep breath.

Theiler nodded. "You're a true asset, I give you that boy. You made Ludwig jealous."

Peary swallowed hard, he tread light around the giant. "Not my attention to get in his way."

"Relax, boy," Theiler exhaled. "Ludwig knows his lane. He's my muscle and you my Intel."

Peary pursed his lips. He mull over how Theiler could tell what the hairy giant thought. Ludwig's condition, excessive hair growth masked his entire visage. Pilosism is the condition of hairiness. The walking hair ball, Peary contemplated if his whole body covered in shrubbery. He shook off the thought glad the condition not his problem. Peary knew making Theiler happy more than enough concern on his plate and so far so good.

"Do you intend to act upon sight or take care of them in close quarters?" Peary asked.

Theiler stroked his stubble chin sounding like sand paper. "Good point, but no, inside where I can play cat to the mice." He glanced at Peary. "Can you point them out to me?"

"Sure," Peary replied. "I didn't see them in person, my sources gave me an excellent description once the set foot here, I can tell you who they are."

"Good to hear." said Theiler staring out into the body of water. "You'll get your chance now that the boat is almost here."

Ben stretched and yawned shaking his head. He looked around for Pone stepping off the decaying molded boat. Fresh air, he thought and no more tug boat rides for him. His friend no where in sight and chalked it up as he hadn't arrive yet. A pear shaped man wearing overalls, scruffy brown work boots, a faded red ball cap, blue denim jacket walked behind Ben and the other men who all stood on the ground like kids on the first day of school waiting for the bell to ring.

The Pear shaped man cleared his throat. "Alright, you boys get in line and keep your trap shut. You will speak when spoken too if that."

Ben thought of his ancestors at a slave auction. He felt like livestock and if anyone grabbed his mouth to check his grill then all bets were off. They'd pull back a nub. Ben didn't know what Theiler look like or if Jock describe him, he didn't remember, but keep your hands to yourself his motto. A short pudgy man wearing a white suit and his hair the same hue. His skin a dull faded tan, dry craters on a face as rough as sandpaper. Ben inhaled pegging the man as Theiler. The feeling building inside the giant made him wanting to end the pedophile where he stood. Theiler made his way to Ben, he stopped sizing up his new recruit.

"Ain't you a big one. Woo o-wee." Theiler roared. "You and

Ludwig should get along real nice. He'll love having someone your size to play with."

Ben staggered after getting a whiff of Theiler's breath. He wanted to spit holding his saliva waiting for a proper time to rid the toxic taste from his mouth.

Theiler mosey on down the short five man line and Ben let out a small waterfall breathing a sigh of relief.

"Okay," said Theiler. "I've seen all I need to see, take them up to the house and treat them to food, drink, and a companion of their choice." You boys get rested and I will give you all a proper introduction."

THIRTY-FIVE

Theiler snapped his fingers. A harem of under-age girls came out on the lawn dressed in white Summer dresses. Pone inhale controlling his composure. The tale of the monster before him started rearing it's ugly head. He pictured Tara's face and though at least twenty girls stood in front with faces painted like dolls, holding each others hands trying to be brave.

"You can have pleasure and food a nice spread you will see once entering my abode." said Theiler.

Pone looked at the other men who hid their appall as he did. Tara stood near the end of the line and Pone made a beeline to her. He took her hand breaking the connection with the girl's hand she held. They waltz inside the mansion, Tara didn't resist and Pone release her hand. The surroundings unlike it's owner, immaculate. Antique furniture laid on wood varnish floors, and spacious rooms from what Pone could see, he heard the other men and girls coming in behind them. Pone pulled Tara close whispering in her ear.

"Take me to your room." He ordered.

Tara swallowed. "Wouldn't like a bite to eat?"

"I've lost my appetite."

Tara gave a look. The man embracing her handsome, Pone's features calmed her; his ice water iris with one brown and blue pupils fetching and his touch comforting unlike the other men she encountered. Tara took his hand then led him upstairs. The others followed inside, but the men decide the feed their faces before taking the girls they chose to bed.

Tara sat on the bed crossing her leg revealing a thigh for Pone to gander.

"Does he like to watch?" Pone asked.

Tara shrugged." I never checked the room, but-"

"Follow me to the bath room." He said offering his hand.

Tara looks into his eyes trusting the beauty she saw in his one brown, and blue orbs. Taking his hand believing he'd take her any place better than here. She sat on the toilet seat he rested on sink's edge after closing the door and turning on the water.

Pone witnessed the curiosity in her eyes. "Hope he's not to perverted and the water drowns out listening."

Tara frowned. "Who are you?"

"I work for Brooke Brigand." Pone replied.

Tara mouth crinkles wanting to smile. Instead she beamed inside optimistic her prayers may get answered, but not to bullish knowing benediction can go unheard.

"Did you come alone?" Tara asked.

"A big... no, immense man should have arrive before me."

Tara got moon-eye. "Two against-"

"A small army." Pone nodded. "Yeah, I know what you're thinking."

"That I should continue to pray." Tara remarked.

"We're professionals," said Pone.

Tara gave a look. "Okay..." She knew the men Theiler recruited came to the estate unarmed and given weapons when they met his approval. Tara decided praying would end up in disappointment. Professionals or not what can two men do against a small army even if armed. Tara exhaled thinking she'd have to die to escape her fate a second time.

"I have two cousins, if that helps." She retorted.

"Are they experience in these type of situations?" Pone questioned.

"One works as a guard and the other not so much." Tara remarked.

Pone snorted. "Then it's best they stay on the sidelines."

"The big man you spoke of earlier, yes I saw him, but he took none of the girls, just food and I haven't seen him since."

Pone used a poker face to hide his concern for Ben. If he didn't know where the giant was then how could they get together plan a strategic. Pone studied Tara demeanor, she went from looking like a bright-eye kid on Christmas day to a face of letdown when the gift she wanted not under the tree. Silent voices took stage with faces of depression. The sound of running water continued to flow and Pone pondered if he should pray.

He opened the door to leave almost getting a fist to his face. "Whoa!"

"Oh... " said Peary. "Checking on all our guest."

"It was satisfying," Pone remarked.

Peary nodded. "Tara is one of our best."

Pone wanted to end the nerdy right-hand man where he stood. "You bed her?"

Peary stepped back studying Pone. He didn't want to let on how sick it made him young girls used for sex to Theiler's pleasure. "Mr. Lareaux awaits your presence"

Pone gestured. "Lead the way,

Peary took the troubleshooter to a double door room. Pone walked feeling at home; dim lighted, pool table, bar featuring a bartender, and a round table that would have made King Arthur proud. The table built for poker and Theiler sat with the men who accompanied Pone to his estate. A seat reserve for him not next to Theiler. Pone glad of it.

"Please have a seat. Mister Abercrombie." said Theiler.

Pone sat down across from the pedophile, he gritted his teeth pondering the horror of such a monstrous sandpaper face rubbing against young innocent virgins that are his daughters or nieces products of incest. Pone thought of medieval times when blue bloods wanted to keep what they believe was pure having family members bed each other and though that too disgusting, Theiler took his keeping it in the family too far and Pone planned to put a stop to it.

"You okay there, boy?" Theiler questioned.

Pone looked around as all eyes on him and realized it was he Theiler addressed.

Pone nodded. "It's all good."

"You had me worried for minute." said Theiler. "If looks could kill."

You got that right, thought Pone. "No, just ready to play cards."

"Our champion," Theiler retorted. "Of course we're all winners here, so don't worry we ain't playing for money. This is a bonding game, sort of welcoming you boys to my family."

Pone held up his hand.

"Yes sir, Mister Abercrombie," said Theiler.

Pone swallowed hard thinking he shouldn't ask, but had to know if he could get information on Ben. Pone knew he'd be putting his head inside the lions mouth, but what the hell since he was in his den.

"I thought crowded." Pone replied.

"If you're talking about the others, they already had their orientation and you'll get acquainted with them soon." said Theiler.

Pone shrugged. "No worries, just thought I'd ask."

Theiler smiled. "Now that's what I like, showing concern for your fellow man."

"It's important to know who I'm working with." said Pone.

"Oh, don't you burden yourself boy. Now let's play some Poker." said Theiler.

Red wipes her face. Her pillow and bed sheets wet from sweat. She had a nightmare. A first since priding herself with meditation and self-discipline handling stress. Pony, was he okay, she thought. They were not lovers though together up close and personal she felt chemistry and believe he felt it too. Their passion for each other forbidden, a working relationship wall stood between them. Yet, she dreamt of the two of them holding each other. Red hops out of bed racing to the bathroom splashing water on her face. She told her reflection to get a hold of yourself. Red knew strength a big part of surviving in a crime family and weakness crumbles an empire. She shook her head. Pony, was he more than a employee... yes, chemistry... yes, and had feelings for him? Red didn't want to answer her self on that question. She hated second guessing the decision sending him to the big easy on a catch and retreat, but knew they thought it was the right thing to do helping those who couldn't help themselves.

"Pony, be safe," Red whispered.

❧ ❧ ❧ ❧ ❧ ❧

The game Texas Hold 'EM, one of the more popular played card games you see on TV. It comprise over nine or ten players, but six was the number at the table and a dealer with a long face and enormous nose. He wore a white long sleeve shirt and black slacks. Pone observed the man pondering Ben mentioned he met with the same features. He dealt everyone two cards.

"This is all in fun, no money." Theiler roared.

"Is this a bonding?" Pone questioned.

Theiler nodded. "Something like that-"

"You sound like you don't know," Pone retorted.

The other players looked at one another and at Pone and Theiler. The pedophile gave the troubleshooter a devious grin. Pone wanted to get down to business erasing Theiler. Lola, Tara, and now what happened or where was Ben on his mind. If Theiler had something to do with Lola's disappearance and if Ben in trouble.

"Mister Abercrombie, right?" Theiler questioned.

Pone snorted. "So much for attention to detail."

Amber teeth and a thick tongue licking cracked lips. "You got a quick wit there, boy." Theiler hinted.

The men present wondering if hey were going to play poker. Instead they held their cards and watch the host and fellow mate feeling out each other.

"I know what I need to know about the people who set foot on my property." Theiler corrected.

"You can never be too careful." Pone retorted.

"No, boy," Theiler stated. "Not in my business."

Pone placed his cards face down. "Speaking of business, I don't do under-age girls."

"Okay, boy," Theiler nodded. "Tara is legal."

"Still too young for my blood." Pone remarked.

"A killer with integrity." Theiler blurted. "But your ass still ain't perfect are you now boy?"

Pone smirked glancing around the room. "Sinners aren't we all?"

"Yeah, boy," Theiler dragged. "You got wit, style," He shook his head. "I like that,"

"Do you like to watch?" Pone questioned.

"Making sure you ain't concealing," Theiler remarked.

A man, tall, his tan suit hugging muscles stood grabbing himself. "I guilty."

Theiler nodded. "Yeah, boy... you keep working on your weapon. It grow one day."

Laughter filled the room.

"Are we going to play or what?" A man demanded. He had no eye-brows, facial hair, sporting bald on his pointy dome.

The room got quiet. Poker playing left the area. Pone and Theiler's conversation took center stage for entertainment.

Pone stretched his shoulders releasing a deep sigh. "I can't do this,"

Theiler ran his fingers through his long thick silver locks. "Do what?"

Pone inhaled tossing his cards on the table.

Theiler frowned. "You folding already?"

"This," He waved his hands in directions. "I am all poker out. Played to get here and here I am so what's the point?"

Theiler nodded. "So much for breaking bread, huh? "Let me give you a moment to exhale and the rest of you gents follow Mister Peary out into the hallway."

Pone watched the men following his lead discarding their cards on the table. His experience as a killer gave him a six sense. It told him when the jig was up. Horse-face, a man Ben described remained since he was the dealer though playing cards an after thought. Theiler poured himself a cognac giving Pone a look. A poker face no, Pone knew that look the pedophile gave meant time to get serious. His mind prepared for whatever Theiler had to dish out. The bottom of his right foot containing his miniature knife felt uncomfortable and doubts of using it for an emergency not going to happen. Theiler knew his identity doing a poor job being discrete. The men following his assistant would return armed and dangerous. Pone inhale to find a comfort zone, you need to relax when sensing discomfort. You never decide out of fear.

"Abercrombie, right?" Theiler gestured.

Pone smiled. "Okay,"

Theiler snapped his finger pointing to Horse-face. "We're not playing cards, but deal Mister Abercrombie a hand."

Horse-face blinked then smirked. He dealt Pone a hand already repaired. Pone picked up the cards laughing out loud. A pair of black Eights, aces, and a red Jack.

"Dead man's hand." said Pone. "The fifth card never proven."

"I threw in the Jack to spruce it up." Theiler remarked.

"Why not a king?" Pone retorted.

"You looking at him." Theiler stated.

"Of shit," said Pone.

Theiler snorted. "You got a mouth on you boy."

"Call me by name since you know who I am." said Pone tossing the cards on the table. "So I'm a dead man?"

Theiler took a hard swallow of his cognac. "Got to make an example. You being a celebrity and all."

Pone pursed his lips. "This is how you treat famous people?"

"You can't come in my house and shit where you please. Boy." said Theiler.

"Sending you a message." Pone remarked.

"Loud and clear, boy, loud and clear." Theiler replied.

"What's next?" Pone asked.

He watched Theiler throw down his hash with authority. Pone smirks watching Theiler frown from the inside burn of his drink.

"You caused me a lot pain, boy." Theiler shook his head. "A freight train is coming your way to hit you hard." Theiler pointed.

Pone straighten, he didn't like the sound of Theiler's words. Lola missing and thoughts of Ben in trouble rush inside his head.

Theiler gave Horse-face a look. The ugly man pulled out a gun. Pone inhale not surprise knowing heat was coming eventually.

"Peary!" Theiler called out.

The nerdy man walk in not packing, but the four men who followed him into the hallway came back into the room aiming their heaters at Pone. The regular guards enter armed doing the same.

"Boy, now that's what you call respect." Theiler roared.

Peary approached Pone with a zip tie. "If you be so kind,"

Pone shrugged extending his arms. "Why not."

He was not new to zip ties. Presenting his hands to his captors with fists clenched and palms facing down. It made his wrist bigger creating room for him to slip out. Experience, the key to getting out of a zip tie was to free his thumb then the rest would take care of itself if the opportunity for escape surface. He smiled at Peary who felt he did a secure job binding his wrist. The troubleshooter played smart knowing too many guns to make a move and he'd have to wait to see how things played out. Theiler mentioned not in so many words, about bringing pain. Pone pondered if Lola or Ben met their fate and the monster standing before him taped their demise. He inhaled thinking how he would meet his maker if Lola and Ben deaths came at the hand of the walking disgust. Pone would take 100 bullets to make him pay.

Theiler motioned his head. Pone got punched on his shoulder. He got up knowing the drill, time to move. His lead, a gun between the shoulder blades, flanked the other poker buddies escorting him to his next destination. They stopped in front of grand bronze double door, two gold handles on both sides. The room they entered resemble a theater. Pone inhaled shuddering the thought of an uneasy feeling something sinister this way comes. One of the gunman broke rank pulling open both doors. A mini movie house. The pedophile put his fortune on entertainment. Pone pondered if it was child pornography, he shook his head. He got shove forward taking a seat on the front row. Theiler lumbered by, then stood front and center with a gruesome grin.

"Hope you're prepared for double feature?" Theiler gloated.

Pone smiled. "Please, don't tell me or you'll ruin the ending."

Theiler laughed leaning forward." Boy, I got to give it to you. Despite your situation you got a sense of humor." He looked at the men in the room. "You got to love it."

Pone exhaled. "You better hurry and start the show. Your banter boring me to sleep."

"Woo o-wee!" Theiler crowed. "Love your wit, boy, but that can only carry you so far."

Pone snorted. "Now's the time you tell me watch my mouth?"

Theiler placed his hand on Pone's shoulder. "Hold on boy, I'll make you speechless yet, I guarantee."

The room dark, the wide screen bright and the sound of snapping fingers got the entertainment rolling.

Pone straighten when he saw what look like live action. A giant hairy man so hairy it covered his eyes making the troubleshooter squint trying figure out what he was looking at. Theiler narrated.

"I see I got your attention, boy." Theiler snickered. "The big hairball is my enforcer, Ludwig."

"Sasquatch?" Pone mocked.

"Ha! Ha!" Theiler shook his head. "I love your wit, boy." He cleared his throat. "Now Ludwig is big and I raised him since he was a teen. Never could find him a susceptible playmate." Theiler glanced at Pone after feeling a bulge in his shoulder. "I think you know where I'm going with this now don't you boy?"

The screen expanded and Pone got moon-eye seeing Ben sitting tied to a chair, one eye swollen shut, bloody nose, bulging lip, and leaning over as if ready to fall flat on his face.

"What the fuck!" Pone roared.

Theiler patted Pone's shoulder. "How's that wit working for you now, boy?"

"You disgusting piece of shit!" said Pone.

Theiler inhaled. Soon, you'll start calling me worse. I can see you're very upset. The best is yet to come, I'll let it sink in.

Pone lowered his head glaring at the floor. He never saw or expected Ben looking helpless as a newborn baby. Pone gritted his teeth taking accountability for his friend's predicament. He should have never brought him along. This should have been a solo job. Pone's exhale slow and deliberate.

"How many?" Pone questioned.

Theiler putting a hand to his ear leaning in. "What's that?"

Pone swallowed hard. "How may assholes?"

"Well now boy," Theiler gloated. "Your boy is one tough son-of-a-bitch I tell you what," He shook his head. "I can't say this in front of Ludwig on account I hurt his feelings, but it's the first time he needed help taking someone like your friend down."

"Fuck!" retorted Pone.

Theiler nodded. "Yes he is and so are you." He grabbed Pone by his chin. "As you can see Ludwig ain't done playing with him yet or at least not until I tell him."

Pone pursed his lips. "How did you know?"

"That he was the one taking a shit in my toilet and not flushing." Theiler motioned to his right.

"Horse-face," Pone muttered.

Theiler frowned. "What you say... Horse-" He took a gander then nodded. "Oh yeah, he is ugly."

"Pot calling the kettle black." Pone remarked.

Theiler cackled. "I haven't quite taken care of that smart ass mouth. On to the next feature."

The screen went black with Pone relieved Ben wasn't dead yet. Showtime again and Pone cringed realizing this feature dated and not live. Grinding teeth, boded clenched fist, tensed legs, and icy stare from Pone after what he witnessed. A woman in bondage, gagged, tear drenched face in a compromising position. What made matters worse, a grinning smiling gold tooth troll strutting towards her. Theiler directed the camera to capture every moment of his pleasure; clawing, backside getting smack, squeezing breast, oral examination, penetration, and a sandpaper tongue licking tears from a blubbering face. Pone closed his eyes leaning back, stretching his neck upward.

"Careful boy," said Theiler. "You going to hurt yourself." He laughed. "Not to mouthy now are you?"

The other men joined in on joviality while Pone pondered. It's his fault what was happening and happened to Ben and Lola. Ben alive, but Lola he didn't know and after what he saw Theiler put her through see might have wished for death. He inhaled knowing the pedophile needed to taste serious damage.

Ooh, wee, boy I know now what you liked about that brown sugar," Theiler boasted. "That was some sweet ass."

"Did she survive the horror?" Pone asked.

Theiler pointed. "See boy, that mouth of yours is why your ass is in trouble now." The pedophile exhaled. "She was still breathing, but I told my man on site he could have the leftovers then dispose when he was done."

"You piece of shit," retorted Pone.

"Again with the mouth." said Theiler. "I'll say this, she convince me I can have as much pleasure fucking outside of my family."

Pone sat up straight clearing his face of anguish. He tilted his head toward Horse-face. "May I have a word with him?"

Theiler shrugged. "Don't see why not,"

Horse-face strolled over to Pone who held his head low. The man stood with his hands on his hips displaying a horse-tooth grin. Horse-face beamed with pride as if he'd done a good deed. "Whats the matter?" He teased. "Thought you could come down here and do what you please?"

Pone kept silent in deep thought. He couldn't grasp seeing how he put Ben and Lola lives in jeopardy. Ben still breathing till Theiler gave the word and Lola who he assumed dead since the monster left her in the hands of one of his predators. Pone waited for Horse-face to get closer and then he'd level the playing field.

Horse-face looked at Theiler. "Gee boss, guess you took care of that wit." He leaned closer breathing heavy on Pone's head. An upward head butt to the nose like a raging Ram made sickening crack. The bystanders grimaced watching Horse-face rising above Pone with a busted nose acting as a geyser and a moon-eye look. He stood like a statue then fell hard like a chopped down tree. His head bounced off the floor when he hit. Peary rushed over checking for a pulse. He looked to Theiler waving his hand sideways pronouncing him dead.

Theiler roared with laughter squatting in front of pone. "I knew it boy, when I first set eyes on you, you were a stone cold killer."

"Fuck you," said Pone exhaling.

Theiler moved in closer gripping Pone by his hair making sure he didn't end up like Horse-face. "Guess you got a headache, huh?" He snorted. "That's what you get for using your head. Theiler move in closer gazing into Pone's eyes. He wet his mouth with his tongue delivering a pressing smooch to Pone. The disgusting kiss left his captive's lips soaking wet. The men frowned while Pone's body deflated.

"If that was your kiss of death then life is unfair since I'm still alive." said Pone.

"So pretty, I couldn't resist." Theiler retorted.

Pone nodded working the mucus from his nostrils mixing it with the saliva in his mouth. He smiled at Theiler hoping to entice him for another lip-lock. The pedophile oblige except he got a loogie in the face. Theiler rose dripping in slim, he delivered a rock solid backhand to Pone's jaw. Theiler pointed looking at his men.

"Soften this boy up, but don't kill him." Theiler ordered wiping the bile off his face with the sleeve of his arm. "Guess I should've listen to my mama, to always keep a handkerchief."

Pone closed his eyes falling to the floor enduring kicks, stomps, and punches on every inch of his body feeling numb then succumbing to silence and darkness.

THIRTY-SIX

"Why the hell do I need to where white, Linda?" Red asked flaring her nostrils.

"When you stand next to Thomas it will give the voters a look of purity when they gaze upon you two." Linda stated.

"You are getting on my last nerve." said Red pointing her finger.

Linda smirked. "But you love me anyway,"

"Are you coaching him?"

Linda frowned. "Pardon?"

"If he drops to a knee, I will storm out of there." Red glared.

Linda inhaled. "We own the city, not you dear sister."

Red relaxed on the edge of her desk. Linda's remark lightened the mood. Marriage not in her plans since she enjoyed her independence, Thomas a side piece to relieve stress. The arrangement worked well so far and as they say if it's not broken then why fix it.

Red folded her arms. "Don't jinx it."

Linda gave a look. "Why are you speaking in riddles?"

Red exhales shaking her head. "Thomas might want to push the envelope, but..."

Linda held up her hand. "He is one lucky little fellow." She sat back crossing her legs. "You just want to be the good auntie, and that's fine all but, one day you might look around you and wish you had that little offspring to talk to or do you have a favorite niece or nephew I don't know about?"

"I have no favorites." replied Red. She smiled to hide her lie. The niece and nephews she gave a gold star belong to Paul J. His daughter had her features, tall, red hair, and his sons young, but she could tell athletic bodies as they continue to grow. Red adored Linda's and Sue's children yet spoiled rotten by over protected parents.

"We won't have this conversation again and I am bored."

Linda pursed her lips. "Just family- "

Red interrupted. "My law firm is separate."

Linda rolled her eyes. "I know, you keep reminding me."

Red chuckled. "You know the reruns?"

Linda shrugged. "Why do you always have to make a point?"

"I'm a lawyer, it's in my blood." remarked Red.

"Brigand runs through your veins as well." retorted Linda.

Red snapped her finger. "That's why I'm going to make this clear, those TV shows from back in the day should stay on the shelf and kept there." She maneuvered back behind her desk taking a seat. "Our conversations are reruns."

Linda sat in silence, for first time she felt like a client instead of a big sister. Linda inhaled to absorb what was about to be delivered to her from Red.

Red leaned forward cupping her hands together supported by her desk. "I will do whatever I can supporting Thomas's campaign, this talk is a rerun and now permanent sitting on the shelf."

A slight breeze cleared cobwebs opening eyes to a blurry sight. Feet ankle deep standing in goo. The moon light painted a not so pretty picture once his vision returned, he gave his view a sullen look. Pone groggy yet his senses told him he was in a predicament. He stood upright with arms extended with rope tight on his wrists. Pone grimace trying to move scraping flesh, opening small wounds on his back. The grand tree they tied him to old, but brittle. A Cajun style torture rack. Murky water miles around and it came up waist high. Theiler wanted to make him pay for disrupting his lifestyle and succeeded placing him in swamp water. Pone fumed realizing the bastard strip him down to his underwear. He cringed pondering what type of bacteria swam around in the deluge. A parasite could find it's way inside his penis if he took a piss. He remember that from watching a movie. Pone look to the sky where the moon hung high. It would be awhile before daylight. He at the moment alive and that a good thing. Pone knew time to work for freedom, his motivation... Theiler.

The mangrove uncomfortable against his flesh and the texture should aid in freeing him from the rope. He moved his arms forward feeling slack after each pull. His thoughts on what danger awaited him in the Miasma once freed trekking back to dry land. Rope breaking, a slight smile replaced by a chilling feeling when Pone saw ripples in the dark water. Something wicked this way comes and his movements summoned one of the marshland's inhabitants... oh shit!

Ben sat in the creaking chair that fought to contain his weight. Dozing off and waking up, he assumed it night time after hearing his equal in size yawning in a chair in the far corner. Ben worked on loosening his bonds. He studied Ludwig checking his phone. A call or text to end him. Ben use the time planning his escape. A zip sound and though hair covered his face like a rain forest, a sinister smirk came from within. Ludwig put his cell away then lumbered toward his captive. Ben gritted his teeth twisting his wrist to break his bonds to no avail and not successful applying more weight on his chair hoping it would break under his density. Ludwig loomed over him, his body shook front smirking. Ben inhale shaking his head hearing the man his equal enjoying his situation. Things got more itchy when the hairball stood behind him and Ben heard a snikt. A sound a knife makes getting flicked out of it's cover. Ben squirmed like a worm on a hook, but relaxed when the blade cut through his bonds freeing his hands.

He got moon-eye realizing his fortune getting a gift of life. Ludwig stood in front of him near the door putting is knife away then gestured for Ben to untie his legs. The ebony giant didn't need to be told twice and stood with his chest heaving approval of freedom. Then Ludwig spread his stance, raised his arms turning his open hands into fist. Ben exhaled, the hairy giant must not have like beating a man held against his will. Ludwig did as he was told to the delight of Theiler his boss. Ben respected his adversary for not taking pride pummeling a defenseless man. Ludwig wanted to prove himself the better man and Ben understood the laws of the jungle. He observed the shaggy colossus conceiving in another lifetime they could have been partners making a hell of a team. Ben realize one would get out the room alive, he inhaled then charged.

Pone felt the ropes succumbing to the rigid bark. A torpedo coming his way with bad intentions, guess whose coming to dinner and he the main course. Pone planned to give whatever creature lurking in the muck a belly ache without him inside it's gut. His arms free in the nick of time. The gator or croc, Pone couldn't tell, all he knew one had a long snout and the other a short rounded nozzle. The long scaly native of the marshland lunged at him, Pone evade the reptile straddling it's back. He saw alligator wrestling on TV yet it didn't impress him to make it a sport to watch like baseball or football. Pro-wrestling he'd prefer though it was better back in the day compared to the cartoon presence it is now. Pone shook away the thoughts since he engaged in a man versus beast. His first encounter with nature's man-eaters and he didn't like it. Pone's rage and a life at stake gave him adrenaline for survival. He used the rope like a garot chord wrapping it around the beast neck. The gator or croc not as big and Pone glad for it, but dangerous and hungry the same. Flesh rubbing against jagged tree bark or sandpaper what the inside of Pone's thighs felt like riding the reptiles back. He closed his eyes gritting his teeth pulling it under the abyss.

Fist size mallets hitting it's target no doubt bouncing the brain around inside the skull. Both giants leaning over and against the wall trying to regain their senses and stamina. Ben in need of a cut man, his swollen left eye shut, right eye a gash running plasma down the side of his face, nose and lip bloody with no referee to stop the fight. Ludwig slumped over, his left arm hanging toward his knee and right arm holding his ribs. Ben gave Sasquatch a severe pounding sacrificing his face for a punching bag. Combatants taking deep breaths straightening, Ben couldn't see Ludwig's eyes yet he knew the fight had to end. They charged like sumo wrestlers, Ludwig grunted wrapping Ben in a bear-hug. His intention, breaking Ben's ribs. The ebony giant remembered Pone telling him as long as you keep your arms free, you have a chance of surviving any dilemma. Ben felt his chest burning and ribs giving way to pressure applied by Ludwig. He butted the hairy behemoth with his head, once, twice, and on third time Ludwig fell back against the wall still holding Ben in his vice grip. Ludwig raised his head shaking it to clear cobwebs giving Ben his opportunity. He grabbed a handful on Ludwig's hair and his chin then a violent twist ending with a sicking crack. Ludwig release Ben slumping down the wall, his head forward and chin deep in his chest. Ben placed a hand on Ludwig's shoulder. "Rest in peace," He whispered checking pants pockets. Ben took Ludwig's knife, and phone then eased out of the room into the hallway.

Pone rose above the crimson stain mixed in with murky water. The reptile topside tough, but soft underneath. Pone used the rope cutting into the creatures skin strangling it. He tensed his muscles, breathing fast and heavy combined with flaring nostrils and a furrow brow. Pone thought of what he would do once he got his hands on Theiler. He was half naked, his testicles soaked in swamp water, Ben and Lola dead, and young girl in child trafficking motivated him to move forward. Pone walked through the shallow muck not knowing where he was headed. He realized other marshland inhabitants lurking by licking their chops. He saw a glimpse of hope of what looked like sun rise and then again the fires of hell provide light. Pone spotted a thick scaly demon hanging from a branch. He shook his head knowing this wasn't the garden of Eden trekking toward the serpent. Cottonmouth or water-moccasin not a constrictor but,venomous. Native of the bog and he the trespasser. Pone walks in the face of danger. He didn't want to deal with consequences if the serpentine dropped into the water. Pone thought it best if the zigzag hung from the branch. The snake reared back ready to strike. Pone with cat quickness grabbed it's head and body extending it then bit the reptile in two. He tossed the head and body in opposite directions. Pone's rage made him fearless giving the strength pulling off the feat. If anyone ask it snake taste like chicken, he'd tell them hell no.

THIRTY-SEVEN

Theiler woke rubbing his eyes looking around bewildered. "What the hell is going on?" He muttered.

Gunshots and what sounded like helicopters got him out of bed. He made a beeline to the window witnessing a nightmare in broad daylight. His empire crumbling before his eyes. Law enforcement dropping out of the sky gunning down his men. Theiler swallowed hard. He grabbed a shirt, pants, slipped on loafers, and reached in his top drawer grabbing a glock. He raced out of his rooms ordering his remaining men to go out to stop the invasion he knew a lost cost. Theiler frowned gritting his teeth. He thought of Pone blaming him for what was happening. The swamp he figured claimed the troubleshooter, he stopped in front of Tara's room kicking in the door. Theiler looked around, "Come on out girl."

He would take his frustration out on her. A sound inside the closet. Theiler opened the door grabbing Tara. He pressed his gun against her skull. "You did this, you did this."

Tara's face drenched, eyes wide, and mouth open. Theiler yanked her out into the hallway. She stumbled getting dragged by the pedophile to his study. A place too familiar for all the wrong reasons.

Tara heard the noise outside her bedroom window though too frighten to look. She found the strength to snatch her arm from Theiler's grip.

Tara rubbed her wrist. "The end is near," She pursed her lips. "You might as well give up, your empire of disgust is over,"

Theiler got moon-eye pointing the gun at Tara. "You shut your

"

mouth girl," He swallowed. "Mind your manners, show some respect."

Tara straighten then snorted. She saw for the first time fear in his eyes. The monster afraid and no longer at ease in his habitat. "What's wrong?" She teased. "Afraid of the big bad wolf blowing your house down?"

"Don't you mock me girl." Theiler glared tightening his grip on his gun. "You respect your daddy!"

"Ha!Ha!Ha!" Tara held her stomach as if to vomit. "What kind of father beds his own children?" She shook her head. "You aim that gun at me with bad intentions." Tara swallowed hard. "You want to end me? Too late. You did that the first time you touched me with your filthy carcass."

Theiler delivered a hard backhand knocking her to the floor. "You shut your mouth bitch! You shut your mouth!" He reached down taking her by the wrist jerking her from the floor. He dragged Tara to a wall, then move a paperweight sideways. A wall panel offered a passage way. Theiler took it. The wall closed behind them. The passage dim lighted. Theiler turned to look at Tara.

"Girl, it ain't over till I say so,"

The sight of men raining from the sky, the sounds of gunfire filled the air helped Pone find dry land. He would have drop to his knees kissing mother earth, but felt he already in touch with her thanks to Theiler half dressing him for his swamp adventure. Pone hid among the trees taking baby steps staying out of the line of fire. Bodies littered the ground with the pedophile's men and law enforcement agents. Pone didn't count though by the looks of things the good guys were winning.

"Hold it right there," A strong female voice commanded. "Don't move a muscle."

Pone smirked raising his arms. The Asian accent distinct.

"You're not dressed for the occasion." Ling remarked. She wore a tight fitting black suit, shoulder strap holster carrying two glocks, clips and assault rifle.

Ling motioned to an officer holding clothes and combat boots. "Hope these are to your liking?"

Pone grabbed the garments nodding. "Better than what I have on." He replied. "How did you find me?"

"Look whose full of himself?" Ling remarked. "Our last rendezvous,"

Pone inhaled. He recur Mai experimenting with his bowler then handed it to him. "A transmitter."

Ling smiled. "Inside the brim."

Pone looked around. "The target?"

"Not yet,"

"He's mine." said Pone.

"If you find him first."

Pone gave a look. "I better get started."

"Hold on." Ling ordered. "You might need this." She gave Pone one of her guns.

"Where the hell is Ludwig?" Theiler muttered trying to call his right-hand man. He placed the cell inside his pants pocket. Then pushed Tara ahead of him.

"Hold up!" said Theiler unzipping his pants. "Today's events don got me stressed. I need to get greased to relieve the tension."

Tara shook her head. "No! No more!"

Theiler aimed his gun. "Don't test me girl. Get your ass over here."

"No!"

Theiler exhaled taking aim. The weapon flew from his hand getting tackled from behind. A flurry of punches to his face drew blood from his nose and mouth. The pedophile bring up his knee to his attacker's groin leveling the playing field.

Theiler delivered a kick to the abdomen leaving his assailant winded. He recovered his gun pointing it at the young man.

"He's your son you bastard!" Tara blurted. Beef came to her rescue and failed clutching to glimpse of hope Tara's words would preserve his life.

Theiler laughed. "Got plenty of them and this one here never showed me no respect ain't that right , boy?"

"Please," Tara pleaded. "I will do what you want."

Theiler raised his gun away from Beef. "Here that boy, I better never see you again or I will shoot you dead I guarantee."

Beef sat up straight watching his and Tara's father approach her.

"Just like Ludwig." said Beef.

Theiler stopped then inhaled. "What the hell you say, boy?"

"He met his match." Beef remarked.

Theiler stumbled then regained his balance. He got a chill something wasn't right since Ludwig always responded when he called. So the black giant bested his man. Ludwig wasn't his biological son, but he felt closer to him than any of his inbred. Theiler pivoted with accuracy putting a bullet in Beef's head.

"No!" Tara screamed running away.

"You come back here, girl." Theiler roared.

Pone considered the gunshot another bread crumb. He made his way through the labyrinth careful to tread where he remembered from his brief visit before getting sent to the marshland. Pone entered Theiler's office grabbing a five inch knife on a display mantle off the desk thinking he might need another weapon in case he ran out of bullets. He exit heading upstairs after hearing a young girl cry for help.

The troubleshooter recognize Tara's voice and pondered why she didn't go outside where Ling and her men would have offered protection. Pone figured that room despite the monster owning the key to enter gave her a safe place though she was never safe from Theiler and perverted men who wanted sex with young girls half their age. His thoughts turned to anger hearing the pedophiles gravel voice threatening Tara. Pone kicked in the door. He aimed his gun at Theiler.

"Tara, let's go.".

Theiler eyed his gun on the bed then raised his arms. "This ain't the end boy, I got money and lots of lawyers to spin this in my favor."

Pone laughed. "You'll have to break the bank in order to that and I don't see that happening."

"As good as advertised ain't you boy, surviving the swamp." Theiler retorted.

Tara looked at Theiler then spat before leaving.

"Toss the gun over here." Pone demanded.

"Sure thing boy," Theiler said flicking the gun at Pone who caught it. "Live to fight another day."

Pone shook his head turning to leave.

"That's right boy, I ain't going no where. You go on and take Tara. I get out and got plenty of more daughters and some my nieces to satisfy me." said Theiler.

Pone stood in the doorway with his back to Theiler. He tossed the gun back to him landing at his feet getting a dubious look from the pedophile. Pone whirled throwing the blade into Theiler's heart. The troubleshooter watched Theiler's eyes roll back, and for a moment he thought of how the man built his crumbled empire; blackmail with incriminating pictures of judges, politicians, sheriff turning a blind eye, child prostitution, and murder. Ling rushed in brushing by Pone.

"The girl told us where you were." She said observing Theiler's body. "What happened?"

"He went for his gun." Pone responded handing Ling back hers exiting.

"We're not done here." Ling replied.

Pone nodded. "I need some fresh air."

Pone made a beeline to Tara who stood among the other young girls getting medical attention.

"You okay?" Pone asked.

"Is he dead?" Tara inquired.

"He won't hurt anyone again." Pone replied.

Tara exhaled. "He killed his own son."

Pone squeezed her shoulder before responding to Ling motioning for him.

"He deserved to die." said Pone.

"No tears from my eyes." Ling retorted. "But my superiors are going have questions."

"You can hold me accountable." said Pone.

"No." Ling shook her head gesturing toward a nerdy man in custody wearing eye-specs. "He gave up as soon as we arrived."

Pone snorted. "Made a deal no doubt?"

"Agreed to sing like a bird." Ling remarked.

"Another man," Pone frowned. He didn't want to give up Ben. "Blond Pony-tail?"

Ling straighten. "One of our own," She whispered.

Pone nodded. An inside man, nice." He turned sideways. "My fingerprints?"

Ling winked. "I did a touch-up before the guys got there."

Pone swallowed. "Too bad you you couldn't fix everything."

Ling frowned. "What do you mean?"

"Some people suffered for associating with me." Pone remarked.

"She's fine," Ling said. "Well... okay."

Pone got moon-eye. "Lola... she's alive?"

"We got to her before things got worse." Ling retorted. "I put her under surveylance the night she intervened."

Pone gave a look. "How bad?"

Ling inhaled. "She's in therapy, but sound minded enough not to ever hear from you again."

Pone nodded. He knew Lola's life got turned upside down because of him. It took weight off his shoulders knowing she alive. Her death would have been a burden he couldn't handle. Pone drifted to his own thoughts; Ben, where was his giant friend? Dead or alive he did not know. An officer came up giving Ling clothes, cell phone and bowler.

"These belong to you." Ling handing the garments to Pone.

He took them then check his phone. Jock sent him a text." Got to take this," said Pone.

Ling saluted him joining the rest of the agents.

Pone breathed a sigh of relief, Jock giving good news Ben broken, but in his care. Pone pondered how Jock got around all the raucous, then didn't care. Two people he cared about alive and a good thing. Jock's text made it clear, Ben would find his own way back to Metro. Pone swallowed hard after seeing what they put his friend through he understood he didn't want to be around him. Pone hoped the big man could forgive and keep their friendship intact. Lola and Ben safe, but wanted nothing to do with him. He nodded realizing there were somethings you had to live with. A text to Jock giving him information about Theiler and his little girl should be in his arms soon. Pone strolled over to Ling.

"This belongs to you." He said handing her the transmitter. "A lifesaver."

Ling put it inside her vest, "Will I see you again?"

"If there's a situation... you know who to call." Pone said looking at Tara. "I need to get us home."

"I guess we have room for two more." said Ling.

The convention center standing room for Thomas Randolph Maxwell to announce his campaign for Mayor of Metro City. Red Brigand, scarlet hair draped over and pass her shoulders, cream dressed gloved her body and pearly whites blending in with the applause of her appearance stepped up to the podium to introduce the District Attorney.

Red smiled at the patrons, who showed up for the gala. She frowned, pondering why the expressions and hand gestures replace smiles, whistling, and clapping to gasp, hands over mouths, and security rushing to the stage. Red felt a pinch inside her left shoulder, she examine it and saw a bloodstain. Behind her, one of the security men held his chest, falling backwards into the crowd. His shirt exploded with plasma. She felt faint losing control of her body. Red found herself in Maxwell's arms. He was taller than her. She no longer standing, his face full of despair and before closing her eyes, she heard him scream.

REVEREND, I WANT YOU TO PRAY

Mercury Slim: Miscellaneous.
by
Wilson Jackson

S hirley Mae Anderson was a devoted church member. The widow of four adult children and grandchildren. You could count on one hand how many times she missed church service. Prosperity baptist her place of worship and the proprietor of the Reverend Woodrow L. Price. He gave inspirational sermons that brought his congregation out of their seats: clapping, dancing in the aisle, and singing with the church choir.

Every Sunday a Jamboree and Shirley Mae had a front row sitting beside her oldest grandchild, Elise who shared her love attending service. Price loomed large, over six feet tall, weighing two-hundred and fifty pounds, with his thunderous voice echoing throughout the building. His smile caught everyone's attention and was no exception when observing the collection plate making its rounds.

After service, Shirley made a beeline to Price's off to praise him for a job well done. Elise went to get the car and hated waiting. She let her grandmother have her moment with the pastor. Every Sunday, she performed her ritual. Shirley's trip this day down the hall toward Price's office. She heard two strong, abrasive voices. She knocked and intervene.

"Reverend Price... everything okay?" Shirley asked.

Price swallowed hard and though he towered over the man with a medium build and height, dressed in a burgundy suit. The man wore glasses giving him an intellect look, a neat haircut, and clean shave face. He gave Shirley an icy glare. Price seemed nervous.

"Sister Anderson... " Price's eyes bulging and wide. "It's all good."

The strange man gave a look at his talk with Price more than church business.

Price stood between Shirley Mae and the man shielding her. "I can't have my usual talk with you, but next Sunday, I'm all yours."

Shirley Mae nodded. "The sun doesn't shine all the time. Make do."

She peeked around Price to dagger eyes. The pastor escorted her out.

Shirley Mae walked down the steps where Elise waited for her arrival sitting inside the blue Toyota Camry. Elise was surprised to see her grandmother earlier than in the past. She'd go to the restroom and still make it back to the car before Shirley Mae.

"That was fast," said Elise. "Everything all right?"

Shirley Mae got comfortable. "He was talking to some man, and it didn't sound friendly and when saw the two of them it look serious."

Elise frowned looking around her grandmother." Why is that man staring at you?"

Shirley whirled." That's him."

"Did you say something to him?" Elise asked. "I don't like the way he's looking at you."

Elise got out of the car. Shirley Mae stopped her.

"Child, let it go. Ain't no time for foolishness." Shirley Mae retorted. "People got demons inside them and hopefully Reverend Price can get it out of him. Let's go home."

Elise shook her head." That still doesn't give him the right to be rude."

"Just pray for him. Pray for him," said Shirley Mae.

276

Corey Singleton rushed up to Price, pressing the bigger man up against the wall.

"Give me her name and address." Singleton demanded.

Price frowned." She's an old woman. What do you want with her?"

Singleton smiled, adjusting his glasses after releasing Price. He stepped back, giving the Pastor space. "She barged in like you were in trouble coming to your rescue."

"I told you not to talk business here," Price replied. "You had a base in your voice."

"So you agree she heard our conversation?"

"I didn't say that... she knew it wasn't pleasant and the way you looked at her made her suspect I may be in trouble."

"You don't answer my calls or texts?' Singleton questioned. "How many people know about your church?"

"You threatening me?" Price asked, giving a stern look.

Singleton got a moon-eye. He considered Price a bloated push over. The rise from him impressed Singleton. "Look at you getting salty."

"She's harmless, and she comes by after service every Sunday to give me praise."

"A groupie? Singleton questioned with a ghoulish grin. "Are you swimming inside that old bag?"

"You watch your mouth!" Price demanded..

Singleton crossed his heart." Forgot that I'm in the house of the lord."

"You worry too much," said Price.

"That's how I keep businesses rolling." Singleton replied." Speaking of rolling, tonight we get back on track."

Price exhaled. "Okay... alright... you get things going again."

"So that cop in your congregation cools it with the questions?"

Price snorted. "Told you he was looking for the restroom."

"Glad you put up the signs," said Singleton. "I hope you ain't ignorant that they don't whisper?"

"Where are you going with this?"

"I own a barber-shop and people talk while they wait."

Price frowned." You ain't all that busy."

"Hold that thought." Singleton pointed. "Church ties?"

"What about it?"

"You got a big lavishing house. A luxury car, SUV... the collection plate doesn't pay for all or none of that." Singleton clarified.

The reverend straightened." We'll be like Butch and Sun-dance jumping off the cliff."

"Well played," said Singleton. "We need each other. We need to be careful. Give me a name and address."

"What are you going to do?" Price asked.

"Things have been going well," Singleton replied.

Price wasn't concerned about his well being. Singleton needed his church for the dividends it produced. The mysterious door leads to an underground complex built during the prohibition era when making moonshine. Singleton though turned the illegal underground distillery into a coke distribution that Price wasn't hip with, but the money was too good to pass up. Singleton hit the bulls-eye, commenting about the collection plate not paying for his fine living.

The clergyman focused his worry on Shirley Mae. He would not put a loyal member of his congregation in harm's way for a hoodlum like Singleton. "She is no threat to us."

Singleton nodded. "The hard way it is,"

2

"Another service," said Shirley Mae with glee.

"Thank you, sister Anderson, thank you," Price replied." It's always fills my heart with joy, having you drop by with your praise. He held her one hand in both of his.

Shirley frowned.

Price gave a look. "Sister Anderson, are you all right? You seem troubled."

Shirley Mae exhaled. "Last week."

Price shrugged, taking a seat on the edge of his desk." What's troubling you?"

"I was worried when heard that man talking aggressive to you."

Price smiles." My guardian angel. What did you hear?"

Shirley Mae shook her head." Nothing but somebody who is not happy."

"You need not be concerned." Price stood aside, putting himself on display." I'm standing in front of you, smiling."

Shirley Mae nodded. "Missing our get together last Sunday made me feel... "

"Naked." said Price.

Shirley Mae got a moon-eye." Reverend!"

"Church humor, Sister Anderson. Church humor."

They both laugh.

"If you say so." She turned toward the door." Well, I best be going. Can't keep my granddaughter waiting and I know you have things to do."

"Always a glee," said Price, escorting her to the door.

"Same time next Sunday." She smiled.

"I look forward to it," Price replied, flashing his pearly whites. He pursed his lips after seeing Singleton stepping out from the shadows with a man name Dreads wearing a dark gray suit. Price stormed toward the two men. Singleton stepped to his pursuer. They looked like two rams about to butt heads. Singleton took Price by the shoulder, then nodded toward the man as if to say follow the woman.

"Why is that man following Sister Anderson?" Price asked.

Singleton smirked." I see a man going on about his business."

"Lets not play games." Price demanded.

"Look," said Singleton. "We got a thing going and I want to make sure we keep our business up and running."

Price frowned." What that got to do with Sister Anderson?"

"A fly in the ointment?" Singleton shrugged.

Price exhaled. He started thinking the worse. "He doesn't look like no diplomat."

"You worry too much."

"The pot calling the kettle black." Price remarked. "She is not a threat."

"The way she barged in doesn't sit well with me."

Price swallowed hard." The woman has always dropped by after service for a chat. Telling me service was enlightening." He shook his head." You raise your voice and thought I was in trouble."

"See... " Singleton pointed." She heard something, and this is businesses."

"I don't like the way you make that sound."

Singleton chuckled. "You want to keep up your fine living?"

"We agreed not by blood," Price replied.

"Our hands are clean." Singleton remarked.

Price shook his head. The conversation kept spiraling into something sinister for Shirley Mae. A good-heart widow who heard nothing but a loud mouth hoodlum scolding her pastor. "No harm bet not come to Sister Anderson."

"At the pulpit, you're in Heaven." Singleton pointed down. "Below is the other place that got you living the high-roller life. You ain't no saint."

"You will not hurt her."

Singleton walked over to the window looking out. "Hope you don't mind the use of your car?"

Price brushed by him." I still have my keys."

Singleton gave a gruesome smile." I'll give you a ride. We can finish our talk while I drive you home."

3

Shirley Mae handed the grocery clerk her debit card, paying for her groceries. They shared a cordial conversation while her replenishment got bagged. The employees of the supermarket knew her since she was a regular. Elise was a familiar face to the employees of the supermarket. The two women discuss meats, fruits, and vegetables walking side by side down the aisle. Shirley Mae used to shop with Mister Anderson, but they'd argue over what foods good and bad for them as they got older. Elise took up the banner after he passed, yet Shirley Mae didn't aspire to be a bother.

She respected her family, had their own lives and didn't need to be around an old woman 24/7, but the company was good. Shirley Mae could still drive and valued her independence. Age was just a number for her. She gathered her two bags without help to say goodbye to the clerk and no need for a cart. Shirley Mae stepped out of the sliding doors, looking both ways before heading to her car. A sunny day made her smile. Her mind focused on what to cook once she got home. People were shouting, their voices drowned out by a rev up engine.

Shirley Mae felt something hitting her. Blinded by the sunlight while off her feet, a childhood memory playing with her siblings in the backyard taking turns on the swing set. She was getting pushed high into the air, hanging onto the chains while seated, laughing and giggling. Shirley Mae fell out of the seat, landing hard on the lawn. Her sisters and brothers came to the rescue getting her up. She landed hard not on grass, but on pavement. People gathered and not her family, since most of them passed on. Shirley Mae felt excruciating pain and breathless. She heard a car speeding off, people leaning over, blocking out the sun. Her eyes felt heavy. She found it hard to breathe, and the pain went away once it got dark.

4

Mercury sat in his office as he shared with the dollar movie house on South Boulevard. He propped his feet on the desk, leaning back, enjoying a cup of coffee. Things were slow, and he counted that as a good thing. Mercury didn't hurt for money, the military took care of him and he considered that one of the perks signing up and being smart with his dividends. He wanted a place away from home to make him want to go home, and he found it. Mercury knew for most people in his line of work that would be a thing not having clients bringing drama through their door, which made the business move, but he was unique.

He wasn't lonely; the mailman took time to shoot the breeze bringing the mail, and the landlord asked from time to time how things were going and if he needed anything. Mercury spotted a young woman pulling up, getting out of her car. Before she got through the door, he could see her puffy red eyes.

"May I help you, Miss?" Mercury asked, "… "

"I hope so," she replied.

"Have a seat and tell me what troubles you?"

The young woman sat down, wiping her eyes. "I am Elise Anderson," the young woman said, wiping her eyes, " and someone murdered my grandmother."

Mercury got up from behind his desk, pulling up one of his stray chairs to sit close to Elise, who park herself on the couch near the far wall." Would like something to drink? Water? Coffee?"

Elise sniffed. "Coffee."

Mercury rose. "Cream? Sugar?"

"Cream, please."

Mercury nodded, heading off to the scullery. He came back in a flash handing Elise a steaming cup and a bottle of Coffee Mate caramel flavor cream.. She places her refreshments on the table, pouring and stirring together with the thin straw that came with the java. Elise sipped, closed her eyes, nodding.

"How did you hear about me?" Mercury asked.

"Louis Lewis." Elise replied. "He goes to my church."

Mercury straightened. His friend when it suited him. He wanted to frown but substitute with a deep inhale. Elise young and Louis have used his youthful condition to have flings with women young enough to be his daughter. Mercury hoped Elise wasn't one of them and Louis wasn't using church as a pickup spot. He made a mental note to interrogate ageless Casanova.

Elise frowned. "Are you okay?"

"We're friends when it suits us."

She smiled. "He's a character, but seems to have a good-heart."

"Nobody's perfect." Mercury remarked. Mercury pointed out, "You mentioned your grandmother was murdered."

"A hit- and -run driver struck her down."

Mercury swallowed hard." Sounds more like an accident."

"The car is black and has no license plates. Witnesses say the car sped up when she started crossing the street." Elise fought back tears. "I picked the wrong day not to go shopping with her. I believe he had her rundown."

"How old was she?"

"Seventy." said Elise.

"You sound like you know who would want to harm her?" Mercury questioned.

"A man who I never saw at church kept glaring at her as if she did something to him. My grandmother was a kind soul." Elise replied.

Mercury found it hard to believe someone would target an elderly woman unless she walked upon something she shouldn't have." I have to make sure everything is solid."

Elise gave a stern look." She was murdered."

Mercury shrugged." Do you know why?"

Elise exhaled. "Two Sundays ago, that strange man looking almost like Farrakhan was eyeing a hole through her outside in the parking lot till she got inside the car. She came back early than usual. My grand always stopped by Reverend Price's office to compliment him on delivering a good service."

"Your grandmother said nothing about the man?" Mercury asked.

"It was the first time we both saw him."

"What did the driver look like if anyone saw him?" Mercury questioned.

"Police told me witnesses said he had dreads."

Mercury exhaled, knowing that narrows it down to a who's who since the hair-style popular.

"I know what you're thinking and I agree, but Louis said he knew the man with the icy stare... " She frowned." Singleton... Cory Singleton and own a barber-shop."

"A preacher and a barber in a heated conversation, according to your grandmother?"

"You think there's something to it?" Elise asked.

"I doubt it was about a haircut and your grandmother wouldn't have anything to do with that, anyway?"

Mercury pondered putting things together inside his head. Did a conversation lead to a death of an old woman and why? Did Singleton and Price utter something that they shouldn't have? "A black sedan, no license plates, and a dread headed driver."

"Not enough to go on?"

"You said he sped up when your grandmother started crossing the street so that alone brings suspicion." said Mercury. "Anything else you can add?"

Elise nodded, sipping her coffee. "She mentioned every time she went to the mailbox that same car would inch by with the window halfway down and she felt angry eyes on her." The driver sometimes parked the car down the street in view of my grandmother to see it out her kitchen window."

Mercury frowned, shaking his head. The thought of an old woman getting harassed and feeling uncomfortable in her own home didn't sit well with him. His nosy neighbor Mrs. Crabtree came to mind feeling the same if someone hounded her.

"This was a hit and run?" Mercury questioned.

Elise nodded. Elise nodded, indicating that it was planned.

"And you said no plates?" Mercury inquired. "How about a model?"

Elise pursed her lips." I think a Lincoln long, black , four-door, rectangle front, and back with a driver wearing dreads."

"And your grandmother said that this Singleton and the Reverend Price sounded like they were arguing." Mercury swallowed hard. "If this caused her death, then it bears looking into."

Elise got a moon-eye. "Does that mean... "

Mercury stood up, offering his hand. "I have a client."

Elise shook his hand." How much do you charge?"

"Louis will foot the bill." Mercury remarked.

5

Mercury arrived at the Louis Lewis estate parking the Cougar inside the circle drive-way.

He killed the engine then got out, making himself to the grand door, pressing the speaker button. Mercury inhaled, expecting the coming storm.

"You know the drill," Louis stated on the intercom.

Mercury exhaled. "Beatles: John Lennon, Paul McCartney, George

Harrison, and Ringo Starr. The Monkees: Peter Tork, Michael Nesmith, Davy Jones, and Micky Dolenz." He paused. "Ninja Turtles: Raphael, Leonardo, Donatello, and Michelangelo. Musketeers: Athos, Porthos, Aramis, and D'Artagnan. Now open the damn door!"

A chuckle and the door open by Louis's handyman, Rochester shaking his head as if to say why does he continue to do this, knowing it's you.

"Rochester." Mercury nodded. "It's his way of getting back at me."

As the mystery man guided Mercury to the study, he separated himself and headed towards the scullery, given that he was Louis's Swiss Army knife. The ageless man sat on his sofa in his traditional satin pajamas like a black Hugh Hefner. Most people who usually wear a button or polo shirt and slacks rarely adhere to a dress code. Louis made sure he'd live a life of luxury without the daily grind. A stock market wizard with a habit of using his curse to lure the affection of young women to Mercury's chagrin.

A curse that got him chased to Mercury's house by shot-gun and not for a wedding. The teen said Louis wasn't the father, but Mercury knew better. Louis kept a picture of the Lass on the Mantel above the fireplace. A picture for each year showed how she has her mother's looks, but Louis's mid-night complexion. Mercury didn't bother to ask the girl's grandfather if he knew about the year-to-year photos. A hunch the old man had no clue. Mercury figured for the best since the man wanted to put a hole through his when it suit him friend. Louis created a love child with a girl that grew up to be a woman.

"I hope you don't wear that to church?" Mercury suggested. "So, Elise Anderson?" The miscellaneous stated giving a look.

"I got plenty of suits and ties every day of the week and man, please," Louis replied, rolling his eyes. "Give that shit a rest."

"You know I got to ask."

"I was tight with her grandmother Shirley Mae and that's how we met," said Louis.

"Wow? That's a switch." Mercury remarked.

"She wanted to know about the stock market so she could set money for her grand-kids." Louis shook his head.

"You gave her any leads?"

Louis nodded. "Stock dividends that pay out monthly. I was watching over them for her and now I doing the same with Elise."

Mercury snorted, realizing that's how his name got mentioned, thinking the two of them struck up a conversation about Shirley Mae and Elise believing she got murdered. "Let me guess, that's how she ended up at my door."

Louis shrugged. "I told her if there was foul play, you're the man who could find out. She's a nice person."

"I noticed." Mercury took a seat across from Louis." Those dividends for her grandchildren?"

"She'd be proud. They will be comfortable," Louis replied.

Mercury smiled." What can you tell me about Shirley Mae?"

"She wouldn't hurt a fly. Loved going to church. Cordial with anybody. You wouldn't be a stranger long once you met her."

"What about Reverend Price?" Mercury asked.

Louis frowned." You don't think he has anything to do with her death?"

Mercury swallowed hard." Got to look at all angles."

"He seems nice, but I know his lifestyle is questionable."

"Mercury straightened. "What do you mean?"

Louis inhaled." People talk. He ain't a TV evangelist, but he can't say he's not used to fine living."

Mercury never questioned how the minister got paid or how much money they made, yet he never heard of them having second jobs. "How much you put on the collection plate?"

"Funny man," Louis replied. "I give more to than the average. The man knows how to get the joint jumping."

Mercury laughed. "You got the holy ghost?"

"You feel fine going home."

"Impressive, even for a sinner like you," Mercury remarked.

Louis grabbed his chest." That's unconscious man... I know I'm your friend when it suits you."

"My apology." Mercury bowed.

"I got baptize." said Louis.

Baptism a soap and hot water to wash away your sins. Mercury knew his friend when it suited him was not a terrible person, yet he used his youthful curse to woo young women. He pondered if Louis had his fingers crossed when getting dunk in the cleansing water. The ageless wonder did a commendable deed, helping a young woman mourning her grandmother. Mercury didn't want to keep stepping on Louis's toes so he'd keep his judgment to himself for now.

"Elise mentioned a barber name Cory Singleton."

"A paranoid brother. Loves burning incense." Louis snorted. "Strange character will stare a hole right through you."

"What do you mean, paranoid?" Mercury questioned.

"I went to his shop five times." Louis shook his head. "Don't know how he stays in business."

"It's that bad?"

Louis shrugged." You want a quick cut, then you go to him without the wait. His shop looks like a garage sale: T-shirts, sweatshirts, over-size pants, ball caps and what not. Twist your way to the barber chair. He might have one customer before you, but most times you walk in and instant service."

Mercury got a moon-eye." Are there any other barbers?"

"From what I could tell, he runs it by himself."

"You mentioned paranoid?"

Louis nodded." Always asking questions, or at least me, about what I do for a living. Not a trusting guy as if something happened to him and he wants to make sure it won't happen again."

"He still cut your hair?"

Louis inhaled. "One day I got out of his chair paying for the cut and as I walked to the door, he was right behind me, spitting."

Mercury frowned. "On you?"

"He would've got back handed," Louis retorted. "I think he was putting a curse on me and it worked since I haven't gone back since."

"Superstitious?" Mercury asked.

"Rude." Louis retorted." You aspire to be that nasty, then you lose a customer."

"So retail his side hustle?"

Louis smirked." I saw the clothes every time I went there."

"What can you tell me about the church?"

Louis pursed his lips." Old... historic... restored... born back in the prohibition era." A smile came across his face.

"What's funny?' Mercury asked.

"You like taking swipes, judging me?" Louis snorted. "He has a Beyonce poster on his wall and an open magazine on the floor of a woman in hot pants squatting for everyone to see."

Beyonce, a legendary crooner back in the day decorating the wall of a barbershop... unusual, but a squatting woman in a magazine on the floor... disturbing. Mercury thought that was something you kept discrete for your lone eyes.

"You saw no other customers?" Mercury asked.

Louis frowned. "He almost finished every time I walked in,"

"Any information you give me may help me solve this murder."

"I guess you can call them associates," said Louis.

"As in business associates?"

Louis smirk." The barber-shop is a more side hustle. I mean, I don't know where or how he lives, but with the lack of customers and he works the shop by himself."

"Describe the men you've seen in his shop?" Mercury asked.

Mercury knew barber-shop owners who work with other hair-cutters, charging them a $100 a month to keep their chair. The importance of having a clientele.

Louis pursed his lips. "Young... street smarts rather than corporate. They drove nice cars, which don't mean they make their living on the wrong side of the law, but being callow and wearing oversize clothing put them on the radar of a bored police officer sitting on the side of the road in a squad car.

Mercury snorted. "Still don't explain why he'd want an old woman dead."

"Paranoid!" Louis blurted. "The times he cut my hair, he gave me the third-degree. Asking me what I did for a living more than once. I didn't tell him my talent for trading stocks and what not, but he grilled me like he was trying to protect something."

Mercury nodded, thinking what Louis said sounded like a man with something to hide. Elise mentioned her grandmother walked in on what she thought was a heated conversation. Singleton stared at the both of them till they drove out of sight. Whatever Shirley heard or thought she heard got her killed. Mercury's special place in his heart for grandmothers would make sure the perpetrator brought to justice.

"I know that look," said Louis.

"He's worth looking into." Mercury replied. "When was the last time you got your haircut?"

"He doesn't cut my hair anymore," said Louis." I tired of feeling like an undercover agent."

Mercury shook his head. "A barber asking questions like that has something he wants to keep off the radar. Arguing with a preacher like their partners means Price might be corrupt."

"Shirley Mae was a fine woman," Louis retorted.

"When is the funeral?" Mercury asked.

"Saturday." said Louis. "Why?"

"I want to meet this reverend Price."

"He's a good man," Louis replied.

Mercury gave a look. He didn't need Einstein to know men of the cloth had their own dark agendas. Young boys getting molested by men bonded by stricter religions. Celibacy, a promise to the church, yet some overwhelmed by lead me not into temptation. The miscellaneous man heard and read about preachers making out with their congregation both sexes while married with children standing behind the pulpit without guilt. Price's life a mystery to Mercury, but what he'd be searching for guilt of Shirley Mae's death on the reverend's face.

6

Mercury got comfortable playing with the keys on his desktop. He Google Singleton barber-shop. The miscellaneous man got moon-eye reading. The scraper had history with the law. A report written by the MPD stated a barber-shop on Monroe road selling non-tax paid liquor to an undercover police officer leading to the arrest of shop owner Corey Singleton. *No wonder he's so paranoid.* Everyone is under suspicion, as if he continues to have something to hide. A dangerous man cutting hair of customers looking for a simple haircut.

He studied the barber-shop location. The note of it, 4203 Monroe Road, 28205. A picture of the area came up on the screen. It sat between a beauty salon and a nightclub. The sign above it displayed simplicity, with a black background board and white bold letters spelling "barbershop" and a phone number. Mercury continued to read. A fire inspector alerted investigators back in September two years ago when he did a walk through, noticing a billiard table and serving style bar with several bottles of alcohol on the counter.

Mercury shrugged about the billiard table, thinking of a way to keep customers waiting for a cut not to get bored, but leaving bottles of alcohol on the counter of a serving bar... dumb. If he knew he didn't have a license to serve and if he knew the fire inspector was coming by, then common sense should have kicked in to straighten up the place. *Can you say, idiot? He* thought, shaking his head. Investigators said the barber-shop didn't have a permit to sell alcohol. According to a search warrant, an undercover officer went into Singleton's shop a month later and ordered 16 ounces of beverage.

The warrant issued stated an unknown black male went to the back of the establishment out of sight of the undercover officer and came back with a water bottle filled with non-tax paid liquor. The officer said he would ask the man about the bottle and the patron said he paid for it cash in front of the owner, Corey Singleton. Mercury exhaled, thinking why the other coiffeur didn't follow suit, but legal. A way to pastime before getting a cut, yet be sober in case a barber makes a mistake. He scrolls down the page and reads where a longtime customer supporting Singleton saying he is a family man. Mercury smirked.

He Google Prosperity Church coming up with information about an ancient church dating back to Prohibition. Black and white photos making the setting periodic with a picture capturing his eye. Mercury saw a truck with jugs he assumed to be holding liquor. The house of the lord must have had a distillery. He noticed the church background on a hill. Such an establishment must contain a cellar or basement and an engineer could draw a layout of an underground business. A moonshine venture makes a good profit for those manipulating the law.

It was shut down, but with influence and deep pocket backing, all you would need is a in between liaison to run things and that would be Cory Singleton. Mercury didn't want to take down the conglomerate... he just wanted the man he believed behind the death of Shirley Mae Anderson.

7

Mercury attended Shirley Mae's funeral. The woman he heard good things about from her granddaughter and his friend when it suited him got a respectful send off. The miscellaneous man commended the reverend for a job well done inside and out at the grave site. Mercury saw Elise sitting with the rest of the brood grieving. He got her attention nodding his respect.

Slim parked the Cougar close to the church hoping to catch Price at the right time. Mercury lean back resting his eyes. He awoke hearing a car drive up. Mercury saw a long black luxury limousine pull up next to his car. Price got out ignoring him making a beeline to the church. Mercury eased out of his heap.

"Reverend." said Mercury. "Reverend Price,"

Price whirled around to see who was calling his name. He studied the long fit athletic man wearing a paper-boy cap. The man offered his hand.

"Mercury Slim."

Price shook it. "What can I do for you?"

"You gave a good sermon.."

Price flinched a smile. "Thank you Mister Slim."

Mercury swallowed hard. "I want talk about the death of Shirley Mae Anderson."

Price frowned. "Are you a cop?"

"I was hired by her granddaughter."

"Follow me to my office." said Price.

Both men got comfortable. Mercury parked himself in front of Price's desk and Price made himself at home behind his desk.

"I heard it was a tragic accident." said Price.

Mercury snorted. "Wish it was that simple."

"I don't understand?"

"Elise believes foul play is at hand." Mercury retorted.

Price gasped putting his hands together as if to pray. "This must be a mistake. Sister Anderson wouldn't be involved in anything sinister."

"That's what I'm looking into."

"You say you're not the police?"

"I call what I do miscellaneous affairs. Murders, harassment, or anything that endangers the innocent. Then I'm the man to call."

"I see." Price nodded, unfolding his hands, making a V-shape covering his mouth, supporting his chin. "Could you give me more clarity?"

Mercury smirked. "Elise said a man was staring a hole through her and Shirley Mae after Shirley heard angry voices inside your office." Mercury exhaled. "Not long after that, Shirley Mae is dead."

Price's neck constricted as if he wore a noose. He cleared his throat, taking a deep breath to relax his nerves. A sign Mercury saw as hitting a nerve. "I'm investigating because the family believes someone murdered her."

The reverend straightened in his chair, looking focused. "The conversation got tense, but nothing Sister Anderson heard or thought she heard should have nothing to do with her death."

Mercury shrugged. "I read the police report; she was crossing the street while carrying her groceries and got... hit by a car."

"Well." said Price, getting a moon-eye. "Sounds like an accident."

"A hit and run makes it a crime." Mercury stated. That bystanders say the car sped up getting my ire." He shook his head. "The car they describe looked much like yours."

Price swallowed hard. "You're not implying?"

Mercury pursed his lips. "Oh no. There are a lot of cars like yours and the driver wore dreads. You have a thinning mini Afro. The car didn't have any plates, and yours does."

Price's body deflated like a balloon." Lord have mercy."

"That you're not a suspect?" Mercury inquired.

"On the soul of the person who has failed to come forth." Price remarked. "You say the driver's hair was dreads?"

Mercury scanned the office." You've done good restoring this cathedral. A lot of history... secrets."

"City council and money from the congregation." Price replied.

"Money from the plate? You're generous."

Price swallowed. "I love my church."

"Serving the lord is profitable."

"Are the police looking for the driver?" Price asked.

"Turn over the right rock… who knows? Elise mentioned her grandmother saying a man kept driving by every time she went to the mailbox and parking his car where she could see him from her kitchen window." said Mercury.

"A lot of things happen outside of this church I'm not aware of."

"What puzzles me?" Mercury frowned. "All this after she came to your rescue."

"She walked in on a disagreement that was handled after she left."

Mercury pointed. "Yet he followed her out of the church and stared till they drove out of sight."

"Maybe he fancied Elise. She's a fetching young woman." Price remarked.

"With an evil-eye glare?" Mercury questioned. "Strange."

"I wasn't there." said Price.

Mercury shrugged. "Going on what Elise said."

"I hope she finds closure."

Mercury rose offering his hand to Price who took it. The miscellaneous man slip a business card in the reverend's hand.

"My card in case you remember anything." Mercury nodded and left.

Price jumped on the phone. "We need to talk."

8

Singleton raced to the church. He stood in front of Price as if a stick wedged up his ass.

Price gritted his teeth. "You used my car for a rundown?" He shook his head. "Lord have mercy."

"I bet she said the same thing, seeing that car barreling down on her." Singleton smirked.

Price glared. "You think murdering an old woman is funny?"

"I'm protecting our business."

"I am not a murderer." Price stated.

Singleton flashed a gruesome grin. "You didn't pull the trigger, but you own the gun."

Price sat down behind his desk, reaching inside his drawer and taking out a bottle of hooch. He took a long drink, then frowned off the effect. "I knew something wasn't right... you harassed Shirley Mae, then run her down like a dog in the street."

Singleton shrugged. "Had to keep you in the loop. You sounded like you were about to stray."

Price took another crack at the bottle. "I don't care how or when... I want out."

Singleton braced himself on Price's desk. "You think the collection plate going to continue your fine living?"

Price face buried inside his hands breathing heavy. He lifted his head giving Singleton a look. The church bottom level used for wine then contraband during the earlier days. Prohibition benefit from the cathedral keeping the law at bay then undercover agents infiltrated shutting it down till Price convince the city the house of the lord would be used for church goers. The reverend met Singleton who sold him on the idea of a profitable side hustle. Murder though not part of the deal.

"You're in too deep now and one day at time will help you forget about the old woman." said Singleton.

Price exhaled. "I told you she didn't hear a thing."

Singleton shrugged. "Got to dot the I's and cross the T's."

A knock on the door and the dread-headed man walk in. Price got moon-eye. He rushed the man clamping his hands around his throat.

Singleton stepped in separating the two men.

"You crazy old man?" said the Dread-headed man reaching behind his back getting stopped by Singleton shaking his head.

Price swallowed hard. "I don't allow firearms in the house of the lord."

Singleton lead the man to a corner whispering in his ear. Dread-head nodded then gave Price an icy glare walking out the door.

"He is to never set foot in my church again." said Price.

"Topside anyway." Singleton remarked.

"My God!" Price gasped." He's the one... you made me an accessory to murder."

"Took you long enough to catch on."

Price grabbed his chest and sat back down. "How do you expect me to drive that car?"

"Sit behind the wheel, turn the ignition, and well you know the rest."

"You are a heartless bastard." said Price.

"I'm a business man." Singleton replied.

Price pursed his lips. "The granddaughter, Elise, hired a man to look into Sister Anderson's death."

Singleton straighten and got moon-eye adjusting his glasses. "You just telling me this now?"

Price smirked. He enjoyed the stress look on Singleton's face. The reverend feared for his future about his side hustle, but his religious side wanted this sinner to feel some heat for his wrongdoing.

"Is that why you asked me to come over?" Singleton questioned. "Is he still here?"

"You look worried?" said Price. The clergyman contemplated why his wicked partner acted paranoid. He didn't know everything about the barber, knew his location on the outskirts of the city where he worked wasn't a magnet attracting customers. He met Singleton after one of his service and being a nature man, he met him in his office. Singleton gave him more information than he already knew about the church's history. He convinces Price the side hustle would be profitable, and he was right. Price is not ignorant knowing the collection plate could do but so much for his cost of living. He didn't want a 9 to 5 part-time job, and he got used to being his own boss.

Price saw no problem using the lower part of the cathedral to make illegal liquor. It would hurt the government's pocket for not paying taxes, and that was fine with him. His gamble paid off, reaping the benefits. It bothered him when Singleton expanded the contraband wine... they drank vino in the bible. Moonshine... he got concerned. A Methlab made him worry. Price became blind as long as no one got hurt... until now. Sweet Sister Anderson died because of a paranoid hoodlum plotted her death using his car, making him a culprit. The guilt burdened him.

"Earth to preacher man," said Singleton. "He ain't the police, so no worries."

Price rose, handing Singleton a card.

"What's this miscellaneous shit? Singleton frowned, looking the card over. "Mercury Slim?"

"The investigator." Price replied. "Police or not, he could still be a problem."

"Does he know who I am?"

Price shook his head. "Your name never came up."

"Right answer." Singleton remarked. "Act naturally and everything will be like Sister Shirley Mae." Dead and buried."

Price shook his head. "He mentioned the car and a dread-head driver." He swallowed hard. "I can't drive that car!"

"You can and you will." said Singleton. "Act natural. You dump the car and he will be on you like a skin tag you can't get rid of."

"It was used for murder."

"Consider it an initiation into the brother-hood." Singleton said giving a stern look. "I go down... you go down."

Price inhaled grabbing his chest.

"Don't die on me now preacher." said Singleton. "Then again if things go south I could spin this all on your good name."

"The good lord ain't ready for me yet." Price replied.

"Glad to hear it." Singleton remarked.

Price shook his head. "I wouldn't feel right driving that car. How can I face my congregation?"

Singleton laughed. "Think of those Catholic Priest, molesting those boys and standing at the pulpit as if no wrongdoings."

Price swallowed hard. A devoted man of God turning the other cheek for greed. Underneath his church, illegal alcohol and Meth produced in the house of worship. The money was good and he couldn't argue that. He felt the need to enjoy the luxuries of life and currency made it possible for him to get accustom to fine living. Now Singleton, this demon brought murder to his door, telling him to keep driving his death machine to keep the miscellaneous man from suspicion.

The clergyman pointed. "You keep that dread-head heathen from setting foot in my church again!"

Singleton nodded. "Consider it done."

"You have to be discreet in case this Mercury Slim keeps snooping around."

Singleton smiled. "Glad we're getting on the same page."

"Lord have mercy on my soul." Price murmured.

9

Mercury sat at his desk in the Queen Park business located on South Boulevard. His office conjoined with a dollar movie fleapit. A benefit he liked for perks of watching movies for free based on an agreement to do light security for the owner. He didn't have a lot a clients which for him was a good thing since either someone needed protection or a love one died at because foul play like his current client. Mercury leaned back taking a deep breath. The bells above his front door jingled.

Elise popped in for an update after getting his text. She exhaled taking a seat. "You said you had something to ask me?"

"How well do you know Reverend Price?" Mercury asked leaning forward on his desk.

Elise shrugged. "He's a good man... like anybody he's not perfect, but who is?"

"What kind of car does he drive?"

Elise snorted. "A black Lincoln Continental."

"Did your grandmother describe what type of car she saw outside her kitchen window and drove by when she walked to the mailbox?" Mercury asked.

"A long black sedan." Elise replied. "It wasn't the reverend since he don't wear dreads."

Lincoln Continental is a long sedan and black is a popular color, thought Mercury. The car though had no plates and Elise has yet to say her grandmother mentioned the actual model. Mercury's gut told him the reverend's car was the one that ran her down.

Elsie inhaled. "She said a man with hair like snakes kept driving up and down the street giving her the evil eye when she came out of the house."

Mercury clenched his fist. He hated hearing the elderly getting harassed and bully. "I need you to be calm and not do anything drastic for what I am about to tell you."

Elise nodded exhaling sitting up straight. "That's why I came to you. If something needs to be done, you have my blessing."

"Good answer." said Mercury. "I believe the car in question belongs to Reverend Price."

Elise got moon-eye and then frowned "I'm confused."

"He didn't authorize it and unaware his car would be used for murder. He and Singleton are involved in something and the incident with your grandmother sealed Price's involvement in what they're doing."

Elise shook her head. "You're making it sound like the reverend's breaking the law?"

"He wouldn't be the first." Mercury replied. "I think he had no idea what Singleton's plans were with his car."

"Then he knows Singleton had something to do with my grandmother's death."

Mercury nodded.

"My grandmother held him in such high standards." She said. "We need to go to the police."

Mercury shrugged. "Tell them what?"

"You said they are breaking the law."

"I don't know what they are doing or who is working with them." said Mercury. "They'd throw a blanket on everything and your grandmother's murder would be an accident or a cold case."

Elise knew cold case meant shelved away for years and she didn't want that. Shirley Mae deserved swift justice. "We can't have that."

Mercury nodded. "I keep digging... bound to come up with something."

Elise exhaled. "I don't think I can go to church anymore. I don't think I can look at him."

"Sit on the front row." Mercury stated.

"Pardon?"

"Keep up appearances." said Mercury. "Let him get a good look at you."

"A close look at the guilt on his face?"

Mercury smirked. "Time to turn up the heat."

"You think he told Singleton about you?" Elise asked.

Mercury leaned back. "Trouble is what I do."

"You told me so much... yet we seem so far away."

Mercury felt he might have said too much to his client. Elise breathed heavy talking about the reverend told him she wanted a confrontation. He hope her emotions wouldn't get the best of her.

"Did I tell you too much?" Mercury asked.

"I will act normal, Mister Slim."

10

Price gave his Sunday speech, but his congregation wasn't entrance to his words as previous Sundays. One person had an inclination what made the preacher seem to lack his pizzazz and she sat in front burning a hole through the clergyman. Price fought hard not to make eye contact with Elise. Church members whispered among themselves about the demeanor of the man who had no problem whipping them into a frenzy. Prosperity baptist was a shouting, dancing in the aisle, jumping for joy cathedral. Not this day and some pondered if this would become the norm.

Reverend Price stuttered, paused, and frowned as if he forgot what he wanted to talk about. He inhaled and exhaled like trying to catch his breath after a morning run. He look around his church like a stranger in a foreign land. One of his deacons walked up to him asking if he was okay. Price nodded and smiled then went back to battle with his words. He felt relief when the choir sang giving him a break to sit down to drink a glass of water. The church got energized for a brief moment. Price returned to the podium struggling to finish service and when he did a sigh of relief swept through Prosperity baptist almost leading to a stampede toward the exit.

Price made it back to his office. He slumped down in his chair wiping a tear from his eye that he knew was for his fallen church member Shirley Mae. He missed seeing her on the front row and now no more visits to compliment him on a well done service. He look at his door feeling a presence. Price rose from his chair, he inhaled and opened the door. Elise stood in the doorway. She gave a stern look, shook her head, and walked away.

11

"You sure that preacher ain't going to crack?" Dreads asked.

"He's got too much to lose." Singleton replied.

Dreads rub his chin. "I'll find us a new location. We don't need that church."

"Stay in your lane." Singleton retorted giving a look. "Thinking don't suit you."

Singleton shook his head. He kept his dread-head goon in the dark and glad he did. Investors help put together the church operation enabling them to expand and to shake things would be serious consequences.

"I'm just saying now that the cloth knows what went down, he might not be able to handle it."

"I'll worry if cops show up and so far the po po has stayed away." said Singleton.

"Alright man, whatever you say, but is everything cool?"

"What do you hear?" Singleton asked.

Dreads shrugged. "They looking for a black sedan and I took the plates off." He ran his hand through his dreads. "I ain't the only one sporting this style. No static this way."

Singleton snorted. "Not from the police."

"What going down?" Dreads asked.

Singleton handed Dreads a card.

Dreads gave a dubious look. "Mercury Slim... miscellaneous?

Singleton shrugged. "I drew a blank on the miscellaneous, but he looking into this shit." He sat down on an empty barber chair. "Thought you should this ain't solid."

Dreads nodded. "This ain't going away like we thought."

"Nothing's ever easy." Singleton replied.

Singleton leaned back in his own thoughts. If Dreads could read his mind he'd know Singleton considered he and the reverend expendable. He was the head on the snake with no intention having it cut off. He heard about snakes surviving with out their tails.

"You want me to look into this cat?" Dreads asked.

Singleton took off his specs fogging them up with his breath wiping the glasses clean with a tissue. "He might mess with our money."

Dreads placed the card in his pants pocket.

"Do your homework before taking the test." said Singleton. "He sounds like he can handle himself."

Dreads waved him off. "It's a damn name and it ain't Superman."

12

Mercury sat at his desk staring at his desktop. He was reading over Singleton's arrest file for serving unlicensed liquor to an undercover officer. The bells above the entrance door jingled. Mercury rubbed his weary eyes wondering who has come a calling. Darryl Pulley dropped by from time to time to shoot the breeze. Bella surprise him with lunch and chat about her new gig as a plus size fashion model. Mercury got up to greet his guest. He got a surprise when he saw twenty-one year old Vanessa. A college student working at the dollar cinema. Her '5 8" 125lb. lean body donned a white blouse, red ribbon neck tie, black vest and skirt above the knee, and black heels. She carried a tray with a box of popcorn, medium cup fountain drink, and kit kat. They connected when Mercury took in a picture show.

"Hey girl." said Mercury. "Things must be slow?" He took the tray placing on the desk waiting for a receptionist to sit behind it.

She smiled. "Things will pick up tonight like they always do."

Mercury nodded. "It is a Friday night and everyone loves the weekend. He picked up a popcorn tossing it in his mouth."

"Can I ask you a question?" Vanessa asked.

Mercury sat on the edge of the desk. "Sure."

"I know on the door it says your name and miscellaneous. Are you an investigator or something?"

"If it's in my skill set then I take it on." said Mercury.

"Is what you do dangerous?"

"It can be." Mercury replied.

Vanessa frowned. "So you might have people out to get you?"

Mercury shrugged. "I been fortunate so far... their love ones know what they do and some don't approve and accept whatever fate brought them."

"Okay," Vanessa snorted.

Mercury gave a dubious look. "What?"

Vanessa inhaled raising her youthful bosom. "When I was bringing you food, a silver car parked up on the hill and man got out, sat on the hood making himself comfortable looking down watching your office."

Mercury got moon-eye. "You don't say." He stepped to his window peering through the crack blinds. "Perfect." He'd hope for sloppiness and got it to pave his way for a chance meeting with Singleton. The Miscellaneous man's intuition told him the goon worked for the barber and maybe the man who ran down Shirley Mae Anderson.

"Mind doing me a favor?" Mercury asked.

The young woman beamed with excitement. Mercury knew she had a mad crush on him. She wore legging staying in the color code of black. Vanessa bend, squat, sat, when Mercury came to cash for a soft drink. She wore them once making him figure too many leering eyes made her uncomfortable. Vanessa's slacks, and skirts showed her figure in a tasteful manner favoring her butt. Mercury handed her the box of goodies she brought.

"He looks hungry." said Mercury.

"Should I be worried?"

Mercury glance out the window. His baby-sitter no longer sat on his hood.

"Place the food on his hood and if he gets out of the car, give him my regards. Then walk back calm and cool."

Vanessa strolled up the hill and did as instructed. Dreads got out of his car wearing a frown.

"He sends his regards." said Vanessa as she pivoted heading back to the office.

Mercury stood out front waving with his back against the wall. Dreads move to the hood and with on swipe he knocked the refreshments off his car. He got inside his vehicle and sped off. Mercury smiled, *thanks for the invite,* he thought.

"Think he got the message?" Vanessa asked.

Mercury took off his paperboy cap rubbing his head. "Time for a haircut."

"Wish I could tag along."

Mercury shook his head. "You'll have plenty of time for excitement."

"Promise?"

Mercury didn't know where Vanessa was going with her comment, but knew he needed an escape. He took out his cell and she grabbed it.

"Hey!" said Mercury. "What are you doing?"

Vanessa punched in her number. "You cool and just in case I need protection." She tested his phone calling her own from his then gave it back to him.

Mercury looked to the parking lot. "Starting to get crowded."

Vanessa nodded. "Yeah, you got work to do." She whirled heading back to the movie house.

13

4203 Monroe Road. Singleton's barber-shop sandwich between a night club, auto-body shop, pawn shop, and hair salon. Mercury drove pass a Ethiopian eatery called the Red Sea. They displayed a menu of meats from beef, chicken, fish, and goat made it authentic. The Cougar found it's place between faded parking lines near a lamp post at the edge of the lot. Mercury surveyed the business village. Louis Lewis was right when he said not a pack house. He opened the glove compartment looking at his glock and it stared back.

Mercury closed it shaking is head. "No fire arms." He muttered. The miscellaneous man assumed like most businesses no weapons allowed. Mercury looked at his hair in the rear-view mirror rubbing his hand over his head then put on the black paperboy cap. "Showtime."

He opened the door and saw the bifocal face man sitting where customers sat watching TV. The seating area surrounded by incense and T-shirts. Singleton a hustler trying to make money any way he could even selling unlicensed liquor. Mercury respected side hustles except for the ones putting lives in danger. He figured the man on the hill belong to Singleton and knew Price reached out to him. Mercury intuition told him Singleton's man had yet to contact him which he gambled leaving his gun in the car. Singleton got up and Mercury couldn't help notice the open magazine page of a woman squatting wearing hot pants. Louis Lewis was right again.

"Can I help you?" Singleton asked.

Mercury took off his hat. "I need a trim."

Singleton act like a matador giving him free passage to take a seat. Mercury developed thoughts whether if this was a cat and mouse game. He pondered if Singleton's man told him what he looked like and thought it was best to get him in the chair where he could use a straight razor to slit his throat. Mercury wanted a haircut and electric razors were used for that so if he picked up a straight razor then the gig would be up. Singleton placed a white sheet over him covering his lap then tapered a strip around his neck. He clicked on the electric razor.

"What can I do you for?" Singleton asked.

"A tight fade." Mercury replied. Either Singleton was a good actor or he didn't hear back from his man telling him what he looked like. So far a basic hair cut.

"Where you from if you don't mind me asking?" Singleton questioned. "I try to start a conversation to make the customers feel comfortable."

"I understand." said Mercury. "Born and raised right here."

"What you do for a living?"

Mercury shrugged. "Anything that pays the bill... no career type jobs to speak of. Security, courier, and bartending."

Singleton snorted. "Hey it tough out there. Do what you got to do."

Mercury shook his head. "Yeah, my resume` is miscellaneous."

The hair cutting came to a halt. Mercury caught a glimpse of Singleton's eyes almost bulging out from his glasses. The front mirror covered with news paper celebrating the football's team going to the Superbowl five years ago. The trim continued with Singleton swallowing hard. Mercury kept an eye on the barber's reflection. He smirked thinking about the old west when a gunslinger with a reputation sat in the barber's chair pressing his gun in the cutter's gut to make sure he kept a steady hand. It kept the barber honest keeping him from slitting his throat.

Time has change since this barber use electric clippers for his handy work. Singleton paused to answer his cell. Mercury bobbed his head playing a tune to himself glancing in the mirror at the barber. Singleton put his cell inside his back pocket then grabbed a can of shave cream, and a straight razor. He gave Mercury a hot towel facial then rub cream around his hair-line. Mercury thought about the old west seeing the razor in Singleton's hand.

"Everything all right?" Mercury asked.

"I get interrupted some times in the middle of work." Singleton responded.

"Family comes first." Mercury remarked keeping an eye on the razor touching the edges of his forehead. So far so good no funny business. The gunfighter alert still in effect, the man ordered the murder of an old woman. Mercury remembered a watching a western and a barber not looking like the typical hair-cutter placing the razor on the gunfighter's neck, but gave him an excellent shave to avoid getting a bullet.

"You think the football team going to be good this year?" Singleton asked.

Mercury pursed his lips. "They kept the core of their key players and some quality through free agency and had a solid draft."

"Damn man," said Singleton. "You know your football."

"Watched a lot of it growing up." Mercury remarked. "Played in high school."

"Oh yeah? What position?"

"Wide-receiver." Mercury smiled. "Made all-state, but hitting the books wasn't my thing so off to the military."

"Don't know what you do for a living, but you seem in good spirits." said Singleton.

"Being your own boss can do that." Mercury replied.

"Get no argument from me."

"Do things by your own set of rules." Mercury snorted. "They call you an outlaw 'cause you don't follow the rules."

Singleton inhaled and nodded. "Like it or not money rules the world."

"Got to do what you got to do." Mercury retorted.

"Yeah." said Singleton. "That's what I'm talking about."

"At any cost, right?"

Singleton shrugged. "You got something going, you can't let nobody stop you."

Mercury nodded. "Got to keep it flowing."

"Sounds like a man after my own heart." Singleton retorted.

Mercury cleared his throat. "If the weak, old, and frail get in your way you squash them."

Singleton snorted. "At the end of the day it's all about you."

Mercury smirked.

"Did I say something funny?" Singleton asked.

"No." Mercury swallowed hard. "What just came to me is not funny at all, rather horrific. Not that long ago an old woman got ran down by a dread-head driver in a black sedan." He shook his head. "Guess she must have gotten in his way."

Singleton exhaled grabbing the straight razor and handed Mercury a mirror. "Want me to touch up your mustache?"

"No I'm good." said Mercury shaking his head glancing at the mirror. "I take care of my own facial hair."

Singleton unravel the sheet around Mercury's neck. A car pulled up in front of the shop. Dreads walked in recognizing the miscellaneous man taking out his glock.

"No fool!" Singleton blurted. "They'll hear the shot."

The parking was sparse, but the auto shop and salon open for business. Dreads tried using the gun like a hammer coming down toward Mercury's head. Mercury used the back of his noggin butting Singleton in the face then tossed up the sheet at Dreads for a distraction. A foot to the gut winded him and Mercury ducked a swiping razor getting out of the chair. The miscellaneous man retaliated with a glancing right cross to Singleton's chin knocking him back. He fell between the sea of T-shirts and incense holding the straight razor. Mercury saw Dreads reflection in the back mirror advancing to him and delivered a backward kick to his abdomen.

Mercury whirled grabbing dreads throwing him at Singleton who cut his own man on the chin trying to slice Mercury. The deep cut made Dreads grimace. Singleton lost his balance knocking over bottles on the counter. Dreads dripping blood rose gritting his teeth. Mercury gave him an open hand knife blow crushing his larynx to a sickening crack. Dreads got moon-eye clutching his throat falling face first to the floor holding his wind-pipe.

"That was for Shirley Mae Anderson." Mercury muttered.

The mirrors in the barber-shop worked as Mercury's ally allowing him to see Singleton rise coming for him. The barber got greeted with a fierce back-heel kick to his chin. He dropped the razor with his chin pointed toward the ceiling. His head came back to normal position staring at Mercury like a deer in head lights. Singleton fell to the floor in slow motion making a thump. The miscellaneous man reached down checking for a pulse... he was relieved Singleton still breathed. He searched the body grabbing his cell. Mercury thumb through the list of names till he found Price. The reverend got text to meet at the church in his office.

Mercury waited until the clergyman's response. He did. Mercury called Bolden telling him to get his boys and an ambulance to 4203 Monroe Road and meet him at Prosperity baptist church with a search warrant. He asked Bolden to make sure Price would be alone in his office and leave the preacher to him.

14

The drive to Prosperity Baptist Church long and slow. The circus in town how Mercury saw the situation with police escorting men out the cathedral from the depths below in handcuffs. He parked on the side of the road killing the engine. No officer bothered to stop him to ask his business, Bolden must have describe him to his men and he was cool with that. Mercury made it to the hallway making a beeline to the pastor's office. He arrived at the door to knock, but instead tried the knob turning it slow after hearing a man blubber on the other side.

Mercury opened the door and saw Price sitting at his desk crying like a child. The miscellaneous man sensed not because his lifestyle coming to an end, but feeling guilt for Shirley Mae Anderson's death. The woman who came by every Sunday to praise him on how he delivered the word of God. Price lifted his head feeling a gentle hand on his shoulder. He look at Mercury through teary bloodshot eyes with peace in them. His face laid on Mercury's hand and the miscellaneous man didn't mind.

"What... do you want?" Price asked.

"Reverend." said Mercury. "I want you to pray."

THE END.

www.ingramcontent.com/pod-product-compliance
Lightning Source LLC
Chambersburg PA
CBHW030148310726
48970CB00005B/1642